Shining City

Shining City

A Novel

Seth Greenland

BLOOMSBURY

Published by Bloomsbury USA, New York
Distributed to the trade by Macmillan

All papers used by Bloomsbury USA are natural, recyclable products
made from wood grown in well-managed forests. The manufacturing processes
conform to the environmental regulations of the country of origin.

Library of Congress Cataloging-in-Publication Data

Greenland, Seth.
Shining city: a novel / Seth Greenland.—1st U.S. ed.
p. cm.
ISBN-13: 978-1-59691-504-6
ISBN-10: 1-59691-504-8
1. Single men—Fiction. 2. Escort services—Fiction.
3. Los Angeles (Calif.)—Fiction. I. Title.

PS3557. R3952S55 2008
813'. 54—dc22
2007038069

First U.S. Edition 2008

1 3 5 7 9 10 8 6 4 2

Typeset by Hewer Text UK Ltd, Edinburgh

Printed in the United States of America
by Quebecor World Fairfield

Once again, to Susan

"For we must consider that we shall be as a city upon a hill. The eyes of all people are upon us."

—John Winthrop

Prologue

Julian Ripps was too fat to be reclining in a hot tub between a pair of naked women, unless he was rich or they were prostitutes. He wasn't, but they were. And they worked for him, so it was an office party, only with group sex. The three revelers had just performed an aquatic Kama Sutra in Julian's hilltop backyard and now were resting underneath a canopy of stars. It was a warm September night, and the San Fernando Valley sprawled in the distance like a corpse strewn with festive lights. Unlike Julian, who was pushing forty with a short stick, his companions were young and lithe. One Brazilian, a product of the world economy, flesh flowing north and south, a corporeal commodity. Long dark hair lay wet against her back, her implants bobbing in the churning water, two bulbous boats with nipples for prows. The other girl from some state in the Midwest he couldn't bother to remember. Illinois? Maybe it was Kansas, but who cared, it was all the same in the waving wheat. A blonde dye job cut spiky, and too much piercing for Julian's taste: ears, nose, labia.

The hot tub was flush with the flagstone deck, and its overflow sluiced through a gap in the masonry and into the adjacent infinity pool that glowed eerily blue from the underwater lights. Julian leaned back and draped his arms over the shoulders of the women in a desultory show of post-coital solidarity, but he was preoccupied, restless. He reached for his lighter and fired up a Montecristo, his dark eyes squinting against the smoke. Despite Julian's fleshy nakedness, there was nothing soft in his expression and the women watched him warily.

1

Julian looked at his house, a glass-and-metal box built in the bright flash of his first success, and wondered if he would have to sell it. He had laundered his money, but it was not clean enough. Now the IRS was sweating him, and he'd been warned by his attorney that a criminal indictment could arrive with his coffee any morning.

"I gotta get going," the pierced girl said. Then: "Do you have any more blow?" Julian liked how she spoke, *do you have*, not *got any* or *you got*. He enjoyed it when someone made an attempt to sound civilized, life being so debased these days.

"On the kitchen counter," Julian told her. "Leave some for me."

When she emerged from the hot tub and began toweling off, the Latina (working name: Tabitha) took it as her cue and got out too.

"You both have to leave?" he asked, loneliness appearing from nowhere.

"You tired me out," the Latina lied, wrapping up in the terry cloth robe Julian provided. Her colleague was walking to the house now, carrying the towel, still naked. The Latina blew him a kiss, and as he turned to watch her go, he noticed the blue glow of the plasma TV in the otherwise dark living room. The local news was broadcasting footage of a high-speed freeway chase. Julian liked the high-speed chases that were a staple on local television news in the Southland. He watched them to relax, the way some people contemplate a fish tank. He was counting the police cars when he noticed a slight tightening in his chest.

Julian settled back into the water, flexing his shoulders, trying to loosen the muscles in his upper back. The chest tweaked again, then nothing. He looked down at his manhandle but couldn't see it, his paunch having reached the point of no return, a level of obesity that augured crash diets or surgery. This was emasculating under any circumstance, but particularly to a man in his line of work. Julian knew he was going to have to get serious about his physical condition. He felt the two cheeseburgers he'd had for dinner bouncing off the walls in his gut, cartwheeling, doing backflips, a couple of acrobats.

2

And how much coke had he done before climbing into the hot tub? Beads of moisture were glistening on his slick forehead. It seemed to him that he was perspiring more than usual. Didn't matter, he'd get out in a minute anyway.

Through the glass walls of the house he could see the girls walking around the living room; one of them on a cell phone, the other drinking a diet soda. He suddenly found himself hoping these two would leave. He needed some time by himself to figure out how he was going to handle this money situation.

He could move dope, certainly. That was something for which the market was bottomless, and he'd done it before. He had some contacts in that area, clients whose needs he had serviced and would perhaps be willing to cut him into a deal. But there was little margin for error in that business, and if anything went wrong, it usually went spectacularly wrong and could reliably be counted on to end in either a hail of bullets or a prison cell.

Julian noticed that he was feeling slightly nauseous. He thought maybe if he drank a beer, it would calm his stomach. The girls were getting dressed now, preparing to leave. He wanted to call out to them but couldn't remember their names. The one with the spiked hair was pulling a stonewashed denim jacket over a tiny white tank top when his recalcitrant brain suddenly fired. "Manna!" he yelled, but she didn't hear him. She was talking to Tabitha now, who had gotten off the phone. Julian tried again. "Manna!" His voice slightly weaker this time. A shortness of breath. The water getting hotter. In the distance a coyote was howling, his plangent cry echoing faintly off the moonlit hillside. Ordinarily Julian would have pulled himself up and walked unclothed into the kitchen, but the spreading of his ample middle played with his ordinarily reliable self-confidence. He didn't want to parade around wondering if these two slim twinkies were thinking he was a fatty-boy, a roly-poly tub of nearly middle-aged lard. *Nearly?* Who was he kidding? He *was* middle-aged.

"Manna!" This time he could barely hear himself as he looked at the glass house, receding before him. He tried to inhale but could only take a shallow breath, the twin pumps in his chest cavity apparently having clocked out for the night. The pain that began to radiate down his left arm was nothing at first except a distraction from suddenly being unable to fill his nicotine-stained and straining lungs. Then it hit him like a hollow-point bullet and he felt his torso exploding, thirty-nine years old, way early for a myocardial infarction, so he barely knew what was happening—although he would have had some indication if he'd been to the doctor recently. Arteriosclerosis wasn't that hard to diagnose, and you could see Julian's from an aerial photograph. He knew if he was to save his life, yes, his life, because it was finally dawning on him that something big was going on, he would have to climb out of the turbulent water, stagger naked, never mind the love handles and retractable cock, to the house and get one of these girls to phone an ambulance and tell the operator Julian Ripps was dying, dying, yes! And would they please get someone up to his place, just off Mulholland on the Valley side, with some nitro and a set of shock paddles.

Julian placed his hands on the side of the bubbling cauldron and, with arms entirely lacking in muscular definition, pushed as hard as he could. Then he entered a realm of pain more extreme than any he'd previously experienced. Realizing the stakes, Julian called forth a degree of will heretofore unknown and, grunting, wheezing, he propelled his bulk to the deck. Lying on his side like a beached sea creature, he contemplated his home. He could see Tabitha drifting out of the chrome-and-marble kitchen. Manna had already gone.

Julian was able to get one leg under him, and finding a trace of strength in the upper reaches of his thigh, pressed his foot to the wet stone. Dripping and racked with pain but buoyed by an enviable survival instinct, he was determined to make it back to the house, the phone, and the licentious life he believed awaited him.

The hot wind continued to blow in from the desert. He could

hear the coyote howling again, closer now. The sky seemed lower, the stars increasingly near as consciousness began to soft-shoe toward the shadows. His mouth hung open, and he once again attempted to call for help, but nothing came except a sledgehammer blow to his chest that sent him twisting to the side and then tumbling back and splashing into the hot tub, where he was found the following morning by a Salvadoran pool man in a tableau that so upset the poor net-wielding illegal that he took the rest of the day off and spent it praying in Our Lady of the Freeways.

Chapter 1

The previous April, Julian's younger brother was attending a bar mitzvah in a ballroom at the Beverly Hills Hotel. Marcus Ripps was an unassuming height, trim, and possessed of such conventionally pleasant looks that you could watch the man commit a crime and not be able to identify him. He had brown, slightly wavy hair that he kept short and dark eyes hooded by a thoughtful brow, knitted lately as the complications of an ordinary life began to add up. His lips were often curled in a sardonic smile, and they were surrounded by smoothly shaven cheeks ready to sprout a beard thick as winter if he didn't shave. Not exactly handsome, Marcus exuded an ineffable goodness and his open expression and easy manner made him a well-liked man.

As he gazed around the capacious room, he noticed an expansive stairwell sweeping down from a magnificent pair of gilded faux doors and marveled that so much attention could be lavished on something with no discernible function. It lent the room the feeling of a stage set, which made sense to Marcus, who was acting the part of someone enjoying himself. Around him, several hundred expensively dressed revelers floated among tables laden with lobster, prime rib, cracked crab, caviar, champagne, and a scale model of the Staples Center built entirely out of sushi. Two chocolate fountains gushed toward the ornate ceiling. Elaborate floral arrangements flown in from Japan sweetened the filtered air. In one corner a famous professional wrestler was signing autographs for the younger guests. In another, a photographer from *Vanity Fair* shot portraits of the attendees, and a video crew roamed freely, taping the event for posterity.

Marcus didn't care much for this kind of bar mitzvah. He believed the intended function had been leached by a combination of a society that stripped most spiritual practices of meaning, and the bar mitzvah boy's craving for lucre and a celebration. It was an empty exercise in his view, an opportunity for the hosts to throw a wedding-sized party for two hundred and fifty of their closest friends. The guests put on their best clothes, ate fine food, and behaved as if they were at a fund-raiser for a trendy disease that just happened to feature klezmer music during the cocktail hour. That Marcus was consuming a succulent hors d'oeuvre lamb chop served from a silver tray by a kohl-eyed aspiring porn star did nothing to mitigate this thought.

His antipathy for these events had not been a lifelong condition. Growing up in a home where no formal religion was practiced, Marcus had envied the Jews their bar mitzvahs, the Catholics their communions, the Mayans their human sacrifices. Anyone who chose to plumb the depths of the universe in a ritualistic manner was all right with him. Marcus was a deontologist, a believer in unbendable rules. Religion had rules, *ergo* it was good. Alas, the requisite belief in God made it more complicated for him. But Marcus wasn't thinking about eschatology right now. What he was thinking about, as he watched an animal trainer in gold lamé harem pants and a bejeweled turban give children rides on a baby elephant, was this: the Mississippi River could be re-routed for what they're spending today.

He looked out over the crowd and self-consciously fingered the lapel of his six-year-old blue suit. A discernible run had developed in the left sleeve.

"I want to ask who their caterer is, not that we could afford them." This was his wife Jan, nibbling on a lamb bone with no remaining traces of animal flesh. She wore a knitted blazer composed of innumerable variations of the color red, over a fitted white blouse. A pleated knee-length black wool skirt showed off shapely calves curving into black pumps. Jan co-owned a local boutique and was a walking advertisement for their clothes: trendy, but not aggressively so, fashion-hipster on a budget. She had wide hazel eyes, delicately shadowed this evening, a creamy complexion slightly tanned in the manner of all southern Californians who don't habitually avoid the sun, a medium-sized nose the contours of which she had never considered altering (nor did she need to), and lips she thought were a little too thin but in actuality worked in concert with the rest of her physiognomy to produce a picture of forthright, if not over-whelming, attractiveness. She kept herself firm at the local branch of an affordable chain health club, and Marcus often thought that if she walked past him on the street, he would turn around for a second look. Despite this, they hadn't had sex in over a month, a source of increasing consternation for him.

Along with the hundreds of celebrants, Marcus and Jan were patiently awaiting the entrance of the bar mitzvah boy, Takeshi Primus. Although Marcus had grown up with Takeshi's father Roon, he was here now because he worked for him, not because Roon had invited old friends. Roon Primus had hit it big in the novelty end of the toy manufacturing business, a success he had parlayed into other, non-toy-related activities, and had ascended to fawning profiles in business journals and a palatial home in Bel Air, far above their scrappy origins. Marcus, who was the production manager at the only one of Roon's factories still in the continental United States, had not. So there were all the mixed feelings that working for an old friend could engender. Marcus was alternately grateful to be the beneficiary of Roon's loyalty and, when he listened to the whispers of darker voices, resentful that his situation required it. Inwardly, although he would never acknowledge it, he was ashamed that he had not gone out on his own and made an entrepreneurial success of himself, as his father, who owned a shoe store in Seal Beach, had wished.

Marcus had been a better student than Roon, who considered school nothing more than a way station on the path to his platinum destiny. Upon graduation from high school Roon had enrolled at Cal State, Fullerton, where he'd earned a business degree of no distinction.

Marcus had majored in philosophy at Berkeley. He worked at the college radio station and for a time thought he might pursue a career as a disc jockey, one of those late-night denizens of the low-frequency world who plays music by bands nobody's heard of and whines about how the "corporatocracy" has taken over the world. This plan lasted until he discovered that those positions generally came without salaries.

When Marcus got out of college (B.A., *cum laude*) he found he had a talent for getting jobs, just not particularly good ones, which is to say anything with a future attached. So while working as an orderly in a hospital and sending fifty letters out, he finally found himself in the glamorous communications industry selling cable television subscriptions door-to-door in East Los Angeles. He dutifully read the want ads in the paper each day, and after four months of traipsing through the barrio hawking premium packages to querulous Mexicans (many of whom thought he was working for the Immigration and Naturalization Service and refused to open the door), managed to land a job in sales at a small AM station that was playing Top 40 hits in the twilight of the format. Marcus had moved home after college, and the commute from San Pedro to their Glendale offices was ninety minutes each way. He didn't like the job, but he had no idea what else to do. Unlike Roon, he lacked a grand plan, a vision. Everything he did was a placeholder for he didn't know what, and while casting about for his next opportunity he made a sales call to a clothing store called Changes on Colorado Boulevard in Pasadena and spoke to the manager, Jan Griesbach. Although the store did not have the budget to advertise on the radio station, Jan was charmed by his self-deprecating sales pitch, and when he asked her out she quickly said yes. Jan's arrival took care of his personal life, but he was still dissatisfied in his job. As he was unhappily thrashing out a solution in between telephone pitches, he received a call from Roon, who needed to replace a production manager at a factory in the northern reaches of the San Fernando Valley. Roon wanted someone he could trust. Now Marcus had been working for his friend nearly fifteen years, and although he would have liked to do something more exciting than make toys, he knew it would be churlish to complain.

Marcus assumed his own anodyne biography was far less impressive than those of the swells swirling around him and Jan at the bar mitzvah. It was a prosperous crowd and their expensive clothes, complexions, and teeth reflected an enviable absence of financial worries. Though he would have been loath to admit it, he was uncomfortable and slightly intimidated.

"Dad, check this out!" Marcus looked down and saw his son Nathan displaying a henna tattoo of a smiling young woman in a bikini on his forearm. The words HELLO, SAILOR were stenciled above her head. Nathan was an eleven-year-old slip of a boy, small for his age, whose most salient feature was his wide mouth, where his blue braces contained enough metal to craft a small suspension bridge.

Jan craned her neck to see the tattoo and began to laugh.

"Can we get the tattoo dude to come to my bar mitzvah?" Nathan said. Although Marcus was not Jewish, his wife was. Like her husband, Jan was not religious, but Nathan had asked to have a bar mitzvah and his parents, after much discussion (mostly about whether they could afford the party), had decided to accommodate his request.

Nathan pointed, and Marcus swung his eyes to a corner of the room. What appeared to be a bearded, three-hundred-pound motorcycle gang member was stenciling a tattoo of a snake curled around an apple next to the spaghetti strap on the bare shoulder of a ten-year-old girl.

"So, can we hire the dude?" Nathan asked. Marcus smiled and shook his head in a way intended to convey amusement at the question, but gave no hint of a real answer. Nathan, his receptors pulsating in anticipation of his own bacchanal, ran off before Marcus had a chance to reply.

Marcus had heard plenty of stories of local bar mitzvahs: the Laker Girls gyrating to "Hava Nagila"; a boy entering his circus-tented reception borne aloft in a fringed carriage by four steroid-engorged, silver-thonged Nubians whose bulging muscles glistened beneath the ten-thousand-dollar lighting design; a proud father, who held the patent to a Velcro-like material, had reconfigured, flooded, then frozen a ballroom at the Four Seasons Hotel, giving everyone ice skates as party favors and presiding over a Winter Extravaganza. This wasn't the circle in which the Ripps family moved—the spare-no-expense world of the grandiose gesture. They had heard about these events and had been thinking Roon Primus would do something equally opulent and frivolous. But Marcus and Jan were surprised, maybe even a little disappointed, when he proved a more tasteful host than anticipated, the half-naked woman on their son's slender forearm and the baby elephant notwithstanding.

Roon was placing a big hand on his shoulder now and kissing Jan on the cheek as he thanked them for coming.

"I liked your speech," Marcus told Roon, who had given a sentimental talk about his son at the service that morning and seemed nearly on the verge of tears in doing so.

"I had one of my corporate communications guys write it. He clarified how I felt." Roon's voice was deep and resonant. Even when he spoke quietly, it seemed to boom. He whispered in Marcus's ear: "Don't think I don't know this whole deal is bullshit. But you gotta give the people what they want, and you try and get some good out of it. You're doing a bar mitzvah, right?"

"You're on the guest list."

Roon magnanimously ignored the social equality implied in Marcus's statement.

"Kyoko looks beautiful," Jan said. Kyoko was Roon's tall, slim, and elegant Japanese-American wife, who at that moment could be seen posing for the *Vanity Fair* photographer beneath a life-sized ice sculpture of her son.

Roon thanked Jan with a distracted nod. He was a big man, over six feet, and weighed nearly two hundred pounds. His real name was Ronald, which he found pompous and old-fashioned. He'd been given the name Roon in high school by a friend who was so stoned that

12

his brain had misfired, and instead of Ron the word *Roon* tripped off his coated tongue. Marcus wasn't surprised at how easily Ron Primus let go of his name, encouraging everyone to call him Roon, even his teachers. Roon knew how to let go of things, move on, as his previous wife would have been happy to attest.

Roon's hand felt heavy on Marcus's shoulder, where he had left it a little longer than Marcus would have liked. Then, suddenly, it was gone. Roon greeted a tall, elegantly dressed man with a smile like a cash register. It took Marcus a moment to realize that it was the governor of California. Marcus listened to their conversation for a moment (reminiscing about a conference in Davos), then, when it became apparent that he was now invisible, turned his attention back to Jan. She shook her head at the politician's rudeness, but before she could say what she was thinking the overhead lights (cued by an unseen and well-paid stage manager) dimmed, and a spotlight hit a DJ who was standing in the middle of the dance floor. He was a youngish, grinning Caucasian, with thick curly hair and a Chiclet grin, in a white suit over a black silk T-shirt and two-toned, black-and-white wingtips. Crackling with nervous energy, he waved his hand like a wand and parted the buoyant revelers.

When the DJ intoned "Let's kick it old school!" barely audible music gave way to the overly familiar thumping bass and drum of the hip-hop nation, now expanded to include seemingly every white child in America, and the recorded voice of a rapper, whose shrewdest career move involved getting shot, began to discourse at great length, and with appropriate sound effects, about his scrotum. The toothy DJ had the guests clapping along to the admittedly infectious song when another spotlight illuminated the faux doors at the head of the stairwell, and they turned out to not be faux at all. The doors, bright lights bouncing off their gold veneer, burst open to reveal a thirteen-year-old, barely five feet tall, Takeshi Primus, grinning maniacally. But Takeshi was not alone. On each arm was a motivational dancer, a professional let's-get-this-party-started girl whose job consisted of dragging funk-impaired guests onto the dance floor, where they endeavored, through a combination of bumping, grinding, and generally exhorting, to ramp the energy of the event up to the desired level of hysteria. Clad in skintight spandex catsuits, these women each held one of the Amerasian bar mitzvah boy's arms and, to the adoring cheers of the assembled guests, together led him down the grand staircase and into the roiling maw of his celebration.

Marcus took in the spectacle with stunned disbelief. He looked at his wife, who didn't return his glance, so amazed was she by the picture of the prepubescent Takeshi strutting between the adult women. As the crowd continued to applaud, the music increased in volume. Takeshi and his escorts reached the floor, and the trio danced together for a moment, the boy doing a slightly spastic amalgamation of the moves he'd seen in videos. The women enthusiastically followed along, then encouraged the surging throng to join them on the dance floor. Meanwhile, the rapper had reached the refrain of his song, so as the happy partygoers moved as one in a celebratory mosh, the incantational words thrusting from the speakers were:

She a ho, she a ho, she a mothafuckin' ho, ho-ohhh . . .

Chapter 2

No one aspired to live in Van Nuys. In a gamy corner of the San Fernando Valley, it was a hardscrabble neighborhood of mini-malls, fast-food joints, and cheap motels with rooms by the hour. The air was thick with skyborne detritus, and in the summer the mercury spiked to a hundred and twenty degrees. The people who resided there were mostly hard-working Hispanics who wanted a better life for their families, preferably somewhere with less gunfire. But on the western reaches was an enclave of several streets where the lawns were wider, the houses larger, and the occupants slightly more prosperous. No one here belonged to a country club, but neither did they fear that the finance company was going to repossess their pickup truck. This is where the Ripps family lived, in a two-story, three-bedroom house at 112 Magdalene Lane.

It was after eleven o'clock that night, and a cool wind was blowing in from the desert. They had arrived home from the party an hour earlier, and Marcus was in the bathroom, preparing himself for bed more elaborately than usual. He ordinarily performed his serious ablutions in the morning, but he intended to seduce his wife tonight and didn't want her to be able to cite his not having taken a shower, or having a stubbly beard, as an excuse. After Nathan was born, they had gone through a period where, like many couples with young children, their sexuality assumed the aspect of a grizzly bear in January, which is to say it went into hibernation. This woeful situation was compounded by Nathan's regular nocturnal visits to their bed. But as their son grew older and better able to make it through the night without coming in to confer with his parents, they began to have sex more regularly. As the years went on, they would reliably consummate once or, if they were feeling particularly relaxed, twice a week. Now, Marcus would have settled for occasional sex, but Jan seemed to have lost interest—money worries, Nathan's learning issues, the uncertain future of the boutique she co-owned—it was all enough to make her behave as if physical intimacy was not only off the agenda, but gone from her consciousness entirely. She had told Marcus it was just for the time being, that the fires would be stoked and they would once again behave as they had in the past. But he had serious doubts. Tonight he intended to force the issue. In a reasonable manner, of course, since Marcus was not the kind of man who would actually force anything.

Fresh from his hot shower, there was a fine sheen of perspiration on his body as he finished shaving. He wiped off a couple of errant wisps of shave cream that flecked his face and examined his reflection in the mirror. Marcus looked relatively good. His cheeks were smooth and the skin on his face was tight. He still had most of his hair, and, unlike many men his age, he didn't have to suck in his stomach when he stood naked in front of his wife. He noticed a lonely nose whisker extruding from his right nostril. Wielding a tweezer, he quickly excised it. Then he grabbed a bottle of Listerine from the medicine chest, took a mouthful of the foul-tasting liquid, swished it around, and spat into the sink.

Marcus self-fluffed in the manner of a peacock displaying his feathers. Having achieved the hoped-for degree of subtle tumescence, the one that said *I don't have a full erection beneath this towel wrapped around my waist, but one could quickly appear should the conditions be propitious*, he stepped into the bedroom, where he was greeted by the sight of his mother-in-law seated on the bed. Dressed in a turquoise track suit, Lenore Griesbach was an elfin woman with short, graying hair. She wore large, heavy-rimmed glasses that made her milky eyes appear as if they were expanding. Jan sat next to her.

"Mom got fired today," she said. Lenore had moved in with them two months ago, having been widowed a year earlier. Wanting to contribute to the household, she had gotten a job at a nearby megastore called JackMart and each day would pack a bag lunch and ride the bus to work. She looked crestfallen.

"I would have qualified for the health plan if I'd worked another two weeks," she informed him. Marcus was feeling ridiculous in his towel, the sight of his mother-in-law having considerably dimmed his ardor. "You two have been so nice. I wanted to show my appreciation, so I was baking peanut butter meringue cookies. Anyway, I came in to ask if someone could come down and help me read the label on the peanut butter. I want to make sure it doesn't have any transfats." Although Lenore had been raised in Brooklyn, she bore no trace of the accent.

"Would you go down with her, Marcus?" A glimmer of sweetness was visible in Jan's end-of-day fatigue. Marcus put a robe on over the towel and dutifully accompanied his mother-in-law downstairs.

The house had been built in the postwar boom of the 1950s, the original kitchen torn out and replaced over thirty years ago in a style that could only be called unfortunate. Awash in olive green, the countertops, oven, stove, and refrigerator had all faded at different rates. The combined effect was that of being inside a large avocado. The cracked linoleum, once a bright, cheery yellow, was now the shade of bad teeth. Cabinets of pressed wood were lined with peeling paper on which chipped dishware reposed. It was all neatly kept, so its threadbare aspect was ignored. They did not have the means to do anything about it anyway. Bertrand Russell, their ten-year-old terrier, was stretched out on his tartan bed chewing a plastic stick when Marcus and Lenore entered. The dog was named for the author of *A History of Western Philosophy* and possessed none of the yip-snap qualities than can make the small breeds so annoying. He dropped his stick and ambled over to Marcus, who reached down and scratched his head.

Marcus glanced at the peanut butter jar and in an even voice that did not belie his irritation told Lenore that it contained no dangerous ingredients. Marcus did not generally resent Lenore's presence. He liked his mother-in-law the way he liked house plants or cumulonimbus clouds, things that didn't require much attention but could be appreciated when you had the time. She intended to stay indefinitely, though, so it was important that he encourage as much self-sufficiency as possible. As he was about to leave, she touched him lightly on the arm, peered through her glasses, and said "I want to pitch in, Marcus, so if you've got a job for me around the house . . ."

He told her she could walk the dog if she'd like. "And you might want to get a stronger prescription for your glasses." Then he hitched up his towel and went back upstairs.

The diaphanous yellow curtains ruffled in the bedroom where Jan was propped up on pillows, reading medical literature she'd downloaded from the Internet.

"I'm not really in the mood," she said.

Marcus lay next to his wife completely naked, having dropped the towel to the floor as he climbed into bed, and was rubbing her breast with the palm of his hand. He loved his wife's breasts and usually began his foreplay there. They were of medium size, not too big or too small, their pleasing symmetry undisturbed by the infinitesimal southerly migration that had begun a year or two earlier. That they were enshrouded in the suburban burka of a fraying flannel nightgown did nothing to curtail his passion this evening. His semi-erection lay against her leg, but the way she was reacting, you would have thought he was rubbing the bed post. "Can you *get* in the mood?" he asked gently. Knowing this was going to be challenging, he had vowed to keep his tone as seductive as possible and not reveal any frustration, no matter how initially recalcitrant she was. When Jan didn't respond, despite the continued circular movements of his palm over her nipple (which refused to react in any measurable way), he sensed that the breast strategy was not working and, ever the optimist, moved his hand between his wife's thighs and attempted to part them. It was like trying to crack a safe that had no combination.

"Marcus, don't," she said, pushing his hand away. He nuzzled her neck, brushed his lips against it lightly.

"Come on, baby . . ." and, once more into the breach, Marcus sent his hand toward her warm pudendum. Despite lack of interest, Jan could not stop generating natural mammalian warmth, and Marcus mistook this heat for desire, so when he began rubbing again, she shoved his hand away with considerably more force.

"I said no! Stop!"

This order was as unmistakable as a rock falling on his head. Marcus rolled onto his back and stifled the urge to leave the room immediately, punctuating his departure with a theatrical door slam that would let her know exactly how he felt. But he just stared at the ceiling and waited a moment before he looked at her and said "Jan, let me ask you something, and, look, I don't want you to be upset . . ."

"What?"

"Are we ever going to make love again?"

"Of course."

"Any idea when?"

"I'm worried about my mother's eyes, Marcus. She thinks she might be going blind."

Now he folded his arms across his chest, exhaled, and resumed his examination of the ceiling. A crack had begun to form there. The house needed a paint job, but that was going to have to wait. How is a normal husband supposed to respond to something like this, he reasonably wondered? What is the strategy of a married man when his sex life has been hijacked by the health of his mother-in-law? It was blurred vision this week, next week it could be a broken hip. Once the body started to go, it was just a farrago of decay, one thing after another in a morbid parade of decomposition that could go on for years.

"She's really upset about getting fired from JackMart." It was as if Jan was consciously trying to tamp down any possibility of a sexual connection between them. She might as well talk about ethnic cleansing.

Marcus contemplated his future and audibly moaned. If his wife intended to create a link between her mother's physical condition and their sex life, he faced the horrifying possibility of their never having sex again. He glanced at Jan who, freed from the discomfort of his advances, was again perusing the medical literature. She didn't look particularly fetching. Her nightclothes swallowed her, and Marcus realized the effect was not uncalculated. Jan hadn't been sleeping well and, with her face free of makeup, the dark circles under her eyes were more vivid.

Marcus was not the type of man who cheated on his wife. It wasn't so much that he didn't desire other women when he found himself in a relationship. He did. Yet the guilt, the double-dealing, the play-acting philandering required were too much of a strain on what was an essentially gentle soul. Just thinking about it made him nervous.

He had slept with fewer than ten women before he met Jan, and six of them were in college (four of them were inebriated at the time, so he wasn't sure if they really counted). He was not a man who kept score. Rather, he was one of those males burdened with a need to feel genuine affection for his sexual partner, or at least be convinced he did, and this limited his encounters when he was single. As for divorce, that was not in his calculations. For one thing, there was Nathan, who Marcus loved in a way that was difficult for him to describe. He did not envision seeing the boy on Wednesdays and alternate weekends. No, Marcus was sticking around. He was not going to allow his libido to dictate the general condition of his life. His thoughts wandered to the Guatemalan woman who worked at the taco stand where he occasionally ate lunch. She was slender, and wore faded jeans over scuffed boots, and fitted white blouses against which her burnished brown skin glowed. Once, when he'd been standing in line, she had needed to get past him and had lightly squeezed his upper arm as she did. He had tried to flex his muscle before she removed her fingertips. As he lay silently next to his brooding wife, his hand had strayed absently to his groin and without realizing it he had begun stroking himself.

"What are you doing?" Jan had looked up from a paragraph on the draining of fluid from the eye, her gaze drawn by the subtle motions taking place next to her.

Marcus quickly removed his offending hand and blurted, perhaps a little defensively, "Nothing!"

"If you're going to play with yourself, go into the bathroom or something. Jeez, Marcus . . . and put something on. What if Nathan walks in . . . or my mother? Is the door even locked?"

Marcus got up from the bed and ambled to the dresser. Opening one of his drawers, he pulled out a pair of cotton pajama bottoms. Marcus never liked stepping into pajamas in front of his wife. He thought he looked silly. But now, his sex life apparently somnolent, if not dead, he didn't care.

"Marcus . . .?" The sudden honey of her tone shot through him like a burst of sweet music. Had she experienced a change of heart? Had she recognized the incipient despair in her husband's voice? Did her witnessing the vulnerability in the act of stepping unclothed into his pajamas, the slight loss of balance he experienced as he stuck one foot through the pajama leg while standing flamingo-like on the other, re-kindle her love in some way about to be made physically manifest? "Can I ask you a question?"

He hitched the pajamas up and turned to face her, smiling now. "Sure. What?"

"Do you think you might be able to get my mother on your health insurance?" That question spelled the end of his evening. He told her he would try. Then he willed himself to go to sleep and was only able to accomplish this when he realized that he should first unclench his fists.

Chapter 3

Marcus had a morning routine. He rose around six thirty, usually a half hour before anyone else, and brewed coffee. Then he would pick up the *Los Angeles Times* from the mottled front lawn, prepare a bowl of high-fiber cereal into which he would slice a banana, and, sitting at the kitchen table, work his way through the paper.

Early Monday, Marcus sat in the kitchen waiting for his coffee to brew. He was in the middle of an article about prostate maintenance when Lenore walked in. She was dressed in a turquoise tracksuit and cross-trainers.

"I'm going to get another job," she said, skipping the small talk.

"Lenore, you don't have to get a job."

She began to do stretches, bending at the waist and touching her toes. Although Marcus knew that Lenore had aspired to a career as a dancer in her early years and remained in reasonably good shape, he nonetheless hoped she wouldn't snap a tendon. "Want me to make you an omelet?" she asked, her nose nearly brushing her knees. Marcus politely declined her offer. He liked that Lenore wanted to pitch in. She insisted on contributing to the grocery bills, so the loss of the JackMart position was particularly onerous to her. "Maybe I'll get Jan to hire me at the boutique," Lenore said, now reaching for the ceiling, first with one hand then the other.

"I don't think she's making enough money at the store to hire anyone." Jan's boutique had become a sore point for him. After two years of operation, it was still in the red. Lenore said good-bye and left for her morning speed walk with Bertrand Russell. Marcus was worried about her eyes but didn't want to say anything. He hoped she didn't fall into a manhole.

Because Jan liked to sleep in, Marcus would usually wake Nathan, give him breakfast, make his lunch, and then drive him to school. They hadn't been in the ten-year-old maroon Honda Civic a minute when Nathan said "Dad, about my bar mitzvah. I know we don't have that much money and all?" This was phrased like a question, almost as if he was hoping Marcus would contradict him and say something like "No, no, we're rich!" When Marcus did not respond but merely lifted an eyebrow inquisitively, Nathan continued "So . . . uh . . . I just want you to know, whatever you want to do? It's fine. I mean, I want a big party and everything, but . . . you know . . . if we can't afford one?"

"Don't worry, Nato. We can afford a party."

Nathan was a sweet boy who worked hard at school and tried to please his parents. When he was eight he had been diagnosed with ADD, and a doctor had put him on a drug to control it. Reluctantly taking the pill each morning, he would eat nothing for the next twelve hours and when, in six months, he hadn't gained any weight, his parents decided to let him try to succeed without it. This he did by summoning forth a supreme effort and willing himself to pay attention. Once he got to middle school, however, he began to back-slide. He stared out the window during class, failed tests he should've passed. The school recommended he see an educational therapist, someone whose job it was to teach a child *how* to learn, and now he was being tutored in every academic subject. Eventually he asked to go back on the meds, a sign of maturity that impressed his parents greatly. Although Nathan had not had an easy time, the boy continued to try as hard as he could to excel, and his father admired him all the more for his efforts.

But now Marcus was thinking: *My sweet nonexistent Lord! Where did the kid get the idea we couldn't pay for a party?* He wondered if he was letting his own financial anxiety show more than he realized.

And if so, what else of his hidden inner life had his son begun to discern?

"We're not poor, okay? I don't want you to think we're poor."

"I know we're not poor. Lenore's poor." Nathan's grandmother insisted he call her by her first name because she thought all the derivatives of Grandmother made her sound superannuated and did not take into consideration the fine shape she was in, if one could ignore her impending blindness.

"Lenore told you she was poor?"

"She wants to get a job as a hostess at Applebee's."

"We can take care of her, Nate. She won't have to work at Applebee's."

Marcus drove through the imposing stone gates of Winthrop Hall and up the road that wound through the tree-lined campus. Oxonian by local standards, the school had been founded in the 1930s. Mock-Tudor buildings evoked millennia passing. Closing your eyes, it was easy to imagine Rupert Brooke, a book of verse cradled under his thin arm, strolling languidly beneath the boughs a short distance from where a sixth-grader was selling his Ritalin to a high school sophomore. The campus was a former country club (restricted, of course) and exuded an old-money flavor the ruling class could taste by paying the annual twenty-five-thousand-dollar tuition fees. This was significantly beyond the financial wherewithal of the Ripps family, so it was no surprise that Nathan was receiving financial aid. This was not an issue for him, as boys were mostly unconcerned with such things, but it made it difficult for his parents when they found themselves in social contact at school events with the parents of his classmates. The parent body of Winthrop Hall, a type-A hothouse of ambition, overachievement, and large investment portfolios was not a demographic into which Marcus and Jan Ripps comfortably fit. But Roon Primus was on the board, and when he suggested to Marcus that he might be able to swing a scholarship package for Nathan, the Ripps family leaped at the chance to extract their son from the dysfunctional miasma of the California public school system and present him with a gold-plated education.

When Nathan got out of the car, Marcus said "Nato, don't worry about your party, okay?"

The love in the boy's smile when he said "Okay" back to his father made Marcus feel for a moment that his struggles were not without purpose. Nathan reached into the car to get his backpack and clarinet case. At that moment Marcus noticed a woman wearing spiked-heel boots, torn fishnet stockings, a miniskirt that stopped an eyelash below her vulva, and a ribbed T-shirt that hugged her high breasts like liquid polymer. When her face broke into a smile, he could see her braces. She was twelve.

Marcus drove away wondering how Nathan managed, at his tender age, to navigate this nexus of treasure and hormones.

The Wazoo Toys factory was in an industrial corner of North Hollywood. Flanked by an auto-salvage lot that broke down old cars and sold their parts to repair shops, and a beer distributorship, the factory occupied an old brick building surrounded by a chain-link fence.

Although Wazoo had manufactured a wide variety of toys over the years, their most consistently successful item was a line of Presidential action figures. Though they were originally called Play Presidents, the always-prescient Roon had seen the future. Now reconfigured and christened Praying Presidents, the dolls were rendered in devotional poses and fitted with a button on the shoulder that, when pushed, made them declaim quotes from the Bible. The Franklin Delano Roosevelt model (with accompanying wheelchair at no extra cost) said in an elegant accent that today would be called elitist: "I know the plans I have for you, declares the Lord, plans to prosper you and not harm you, plans to give you hope and a future." The Abraham Lincoln doll proclaimed: "For they have sown the wind and they shall reap the whirlwind" in a voice that sounded suspiciously like that of a black man. The grits-and-butter intonation of Jimmy Carter (the poorest selling of all the dolls) said: "All things are possible to him that believeth." The John F. Kennedy one, in his unmistakable New England honk, advised: "Be not righteous overmuch." But the model that was outperforming all of the other former presidents combined was the Ronald Reagan doll, which, in a voice redolent of optimism, intoned: "Weeping may endure for a night, but joy cometh in the morning."

Marcus drove onto the factory grounds and pulled into his reserved parking place near the front entrance. It was one of his few perks, and he relished it since more impressive ones did not exist in the environs of the factory. His office was on the second level of the two-story building and overlooked the factory floor where the Central American workforce of forty-two fashioned the Presidential dolls. Settling himself behind his metal desk, Marcus turned on his computer. As the screen hummed to life, he gazed through the interior window and observed the workers industriously engaged in their labors. Each Praying President was handcrafted with the same care the artisans' ancestors displayed in the hazy, pre-syphilis-and-Christianity past when these peoples, who had had no indication their traditional way of life was about to be sucked into the maelstrom of progress, spent long tropical days creating religious objects out of native materials. Marcus was impressed by the care that went into the construction of each polyurethane President, and the irony of these craftspeople using their age-old skills, passed down through the dexterous fingers of countless generations, to manufacture the idols of their oppressors was not lost on him. But Roon paid a working wage and it enabled the employees to look after their families so, unless he was in a bad mood about the world, Marcus had given up bothering himself about the historical/political implications of his job.

Marcus sipped coffee from a green ceramic mug on which the letters D-A-D had been painted in a child's hand and regarded the two framed photographs on his desk. One was of Nathan when he was

27

around five. He was wearing his first baseball uniform and smiling at the camera. Marcus was one of the coaches that year. The players had elected to call the team the Fire Dragons. Several of them, including Nathan, ran to third base when they hit the ball, but it had been a lot of fun for Marcus, who hardly knew where the interceding six years had gone. His son would be out of the house in a blink. Marcus didn't like contemplating how quickly time passed because it had the unfortunate side effect of reminding him of how little he had done with his life.

The other framed picture on his desk was one of Jan, taken on a trip to the Sierra Nevada mountains. They had just come back from a long hike in the high-altitude autumn air, and her face was flushed. A stray lock of chestnut hair fell against her cheek, and her smile was exhausted but glad. There was a familiarity to the pictures, so, like furniture, he usually didn't notice them. But something this morning made him take them in, and in doing so he realized two things: how old Nathan had become, that he was no longer the little boy in the picture, and that he had not seen that expression on his wife's face in a long time, one that suggested something resembling contentment.

As he went back and forth between verifying orders, making sure deliveries were running smoothly, ensuring that the correct amounts of raw materials were being purchased, and checking the status of his negotiations with a maker of corrugated boxes from whom he hoped to extract more favorable terms, he considered how best to approach Roon about getting Lenore on the health plan.

Marcus kept several books in his desk, and he would browse through them occasionally, as a way of both keeping his mind nimble and reminding himself that he had one. There was a copy of Aristotle's *The Nicomachean Ethics, Meditations* by Marcus Aurelius, and Machiavelli's *The Prince*. For particularly dire occasions there was a well-thumbed copy of Friedrich Nietzsche's *Thus Spoke Zarathustra*, a book he'd treasured since his sophomore year in college despite never having had the courage to live by its bold precepts. Occasionally, when dealing with a business quandary, he would dip into one of these texts, not to find answers, but to focus his mind.

Now he reached for the Aristotle and began flipping through the dog-eared pages. He noticed that he had underlined this passage: *The magnanimous man, since he deserves most, must be good in the highest degree; for the better man always deserves more and the best man most. Therefore the truly magnanimous man must be good.* Marcus was wondering whether Roon was either *good* or *magnanimous* when he noticed Clara Ortiz standing in his doorway. A heavyset woman in her fifties, she worked as a supervisor.

"Sorry to bother you, Mr. Ripps. My grandson is sick and my daughter, she can't pick him up at school since she works in Riverside. Is it okay if I go get him?"

This was not a good day for her to leave, since they were training two new workers and Marcus wanted Clara there in case there were any difficulties. But he told her it was all right. His willingness to do things like this made him a popular boss. He checked that everything was running smoothly on the factory floor, then went out to lunch at the taco stand, where he ate two enchiladas and fantasized about the dark-skinned Guatemalan woman who worked behind the counter.

The boutique Jan co-owned was called Ripcord. It sat on the west side of Van Nuys Boulevard, a broad street slicing across the San Fernando Valley. As the road ran north toward the mountains it became increasingly Hispanic, and it was in this neighborhood that Ripcord was located. Given the excitable nature of the Los Angeles real estate market, those of a more optimistic nature hoped the area would become another Silver Lake, a neighborhood where non-chain coffeehouses, music clubs, and other indicators of bohemian rhapsody bloomed and thrived. Right now there was a *pupuserie* on one side of Ripcord, and on the other a place that cashed checks. The pace of gentrification on which Jan and her partner Plum Le Fevre had been banking was agonizingly slow.

The two women had met in the early nineties at the Los Angeles School of Visual Studies, where Plum was enrolled in the fine arts program and Jan was honing her skills as a fashion designer. Plum's career as a painter stalled out after a few group shows in east side storefront galleries, and Jan's designer dreams were eventually crushed like so much tulle beneath the heel of a buttery leather boot. Ripcord was a life raft, a place that would utilize their creative interests in a commercially viable way. The store was meant to be a combination gallery/retail space, and to that end several of Plum's canvases (abstract smudges borrowing heavily from Mark Rothko) were on display. The place had been open two years, and Plum was still the only artist they had showed. When it became clear that no one was buying her work, it was tacitly agreed that the paintings would become part of the permanent décor.

The two women liked being on the west side of the street. Sunlight streamed through the plate glass window for much of the day and filled the place with a warm light that made it easier to be optimistic about their prospects. This sleepy Monday, Jan was changing the window display while Plum sat behind the counter nibbling on a fruit-and-nut bar which would have been healthful were it not her fourth one of the day, and perusing the *Art Forum* Web site on her laptop. Plum had done nude modeling for life drawing classes in art school and had been justifiably proud of her figure, which, while never svelte, had a pleasing suppleness. But now a sweet tooth combined with low-level depression had turned her into a Cézanne pear. None of the fad diets and sporadic workout regimens in which she habitually engaged could coax her body back into shape, because she lacked the will to stick with any of them for more than a few hours. She always told herself (and Jan) she could lose the weight if she had to. I have will power, she'd say, I just don't like to use it.

When Jan worked on the window displays, it allowed her to ignore Plum while doing something she actually liked. Dressing the mannequins and arranging them in aesthetically pleasing ways was the only professional outlet she had left for her considerable creative urges. Today, Jan was arranging two female mannequins, each of which was wearing a sweater and pants of vaguely military aspect, into appropriately war-like poses. The first one stood and aimed a large squirt gun at an unseen target in the Vietnamese nail salon across the street. The second crouched and peered through binoculars at an enemy encampment in a nearby tire store.

"How did that bitch get a show at a major New York gallery?" Plum was looking at a computer image of a life-sized Tyrannosaurus rex a young Welsh artist had crafted from kipper cans. Anyone with a gallery show was a personal bête noire. "Sometimes I think I should just give up. Here's this girl building model dinosaurs out of her recycling bin, and . . ." The thought was too horrible for Plum to finish.

"The art world is like anything else. It's about what people are willing to pay for," Jan said as she adjusted the gun in the mannequin's hand. "Dead sharks and floating basketballs in fish tanks and golden Michael Jacksons—it's all kitsch. It's about money, like everything else."

"That's kind of cynical."

"I'm not cynical. It just is what it is."

"I've been thinking about a video project," Plum said, as she clicked the mouse with greater force than was necessary, closing the Web site.

"Really?" Jan continued to fuss with the angle of the mannequin's gun. Plum's narration of her internal process was usually a signal for Jan to stop paying attention. It was like listening to someone giving a detailed description of their dreams. Unless they were going to pay you three hundred dollars an hour while you sat there and wrote them a prescription, what was the point?

"But I need to have a baby to do it."

31

"What?"

"I think I want to have a baby."

Jan had no idea why Plum would want a child. She was not maternal. She didn't particularly like other people's children. Since her divorce she had dated a series of men, none of whom were prospective fathers in anything but the strictest biological sense. The most recent one was a cosmetic dentist who had offered her free porcelain veneers if she agreed to participate in a threesome. His work was high quality, so Plum nearly went along with it, but she knew the relationship wasn't going anywhere and didn't want to think of Dr. Pradip Singh, D.D.S., every time she caught herself smiling. A child did not seem to be a logical fit in her current life.

"Who would be the father?"

"Why does there have to be a father?"

"Okay, technically you don't need a guy in the room, but, still. You want to have a baby for a piece of video art?"

"Wouldn't it be an amazing subject? I could shoot every moment of the experience and make something incredible."

"Plum, I think that's called 'home movies.'"

"Context is everything," Plum said as she typed *sperm donor* into a search engine and clicked. When Jan returned her attention to the window display, she wondered at the way Plum's mind worked. There was an ongoing creative impulse that Jan admired. No matter how much rejection Plum received from the art world, her desire to make art, however misguided, was undiminished. Jan no longer felt the same way. She had been impelled toward design when she graduated from school, but that feeling had waned with her twenties. Ripcord, with its constant mercantile demands, was not providing the creative outlet she craved. Jan recognized that she was more practical than Plum. Finding a means by which she could fly her freak flag was now less important to her than helping her family pay the bills. Jan had recently purchased a minivan. A new, more practical career would be a logical step. She glanced at Plum, who steamed like a dumpling as she worked her way through lists of prospective fathers for her imaginary child. Traffic floated by on Van Nuys Boulevard. Dust motes swam in the wan morning light. No one came into the store.

Roon had been delayed at the board meeting of a textile company he had recently acquired in Mexico, and his Gulfstream jet had landed only forty-five minutes earlier. He and Marcus were in a small office Roon kept at the factory for his brief *droit du seigneur* visits. Although it was his first real business office, the bareness of its walls and the functional simplicity of its furniture attested to the utterly utilitarian lens through which the increasingly peripatetic magnate regarded the seed of his empire. As they made small talk, Marcus reflected on how their relationship had evolved.

The two men had become friends while playing high school basketball in San Pedro, a South Bay town whose curving, primal coastline formed the western border of the asphalt-paved, smoke-spewing Port of Los Angeles. Roon's father, a liquor distributor who never touched his product, sent his son to a Junior Achievement convention where the speakers, avatars of the new economy, pronounced business an exalted calling. Roon heard the good news. Marcus would listen to his friend's ramblings on weekend nights—if they had nothing else going on, they'd get a six-pack and head for the cliffs overlooking the Pacific Ocean. One evening Roon cracked open a beer and informed Marcus that a speaker at the Junior Achievement convention had given the following piece of advice: If you find yourself in Hell, you have to keep walking. Roon said that was going to be his motto. Marcus was impressed that his friend was the kind of guy who could commit to a motto. He didn't think it was something he'd ever have, since he lacked that kind of certainty. Even in the beery haze, Marcus knew Roon was going to make something large happen, and he imagined a future where the two of them would be in business, thriving and prospering together. That Roon could now play the panjandrum to Marcus's supplicant struck him as a perverse twist.

"That was some event on Saturday," Marcus said, referring to the Caligulan bar mitzvah. He hated to be so overtly ingratiating. Roon nodded, waiting for him to continue. The man's actual presence had drained some of the self-assurance Marcus had been feeling five minutes earlier. "I've got a bit of a situation with Jan's mother, who's living with us now." Here, Roon chuckled sympathetically but otherwise remained silent. His subtly patronizing look said it all: *you poor schmuck.* "Anyway she's got this physical condition something with her eyes so I'm wondering if I can put her on my health insurance." Marcus said this in a rush of words, the speed of his tongue reflecting his desire to get the task over with. Roon smiled and nodded, his manner having shifted from patronization to amused forbearance. Marcus's heart leaped. Perhaps he would get lucky.

"Can she speak Mandarin?"

"Mandarin?" This was certainly incongruous. Was Roon playing with him? "Why do you ask?"

"Because we're closing down the factory here in North Hollywood and moving to China." Roon said these words with the rue he believed his suddenly poleaxed old friend deserved to hear. Marcus reacted to the news with an audible intake of breath, as if Roon had whacked his sternum with a bag of office supplies. Wazoo Toys moving to China? How could this be? For nearly fifteen years Marcus had driven through the gates, parked in his spot, and marched up to his modest office. He had naïvely assumed this would continue as long as it was convenient for him. Now he fought the urge to put his head in his hands and immediately thought of his father, the unlucky Joe Ripps.

Roon continued talking, but Marcus had stopped listening. Unlike the senior Primus, who had so adeptly steered his son, luck had not smiled on Marcus's progenitor. Despite staff cuts, frequent sales, and a name change from Joe's Shoes to the trendier Sole Man, his Seal Beach store slowly bled to death, a victim of the rising bargain leviathans. Joe never saw it coming, clinging to the belief that people cared about tradition. When the store finally went belly-up, the Ripps family had to sell their modest house and move into a rental. Marcus's mother, a high school English teacher, resented her husband for allowing this calamity to occur, and this led to constant low-level friction in their marriage. Now Marcus lamented that he was going to become a victim of the exact same industrial myopia that had turned his father into roadkill on New Economy Highway.

Emerging from this brief fugue, he registered what Roon was wearing. A crew-necked sweater that looked to be made of expensive wool hugged his barrel chest. Trousers, creased and cuffed, were woven from an equally rich material. Then there were the shoes: loafers of an oxblood hue, their tassels dangling gaily. And his socks probably cost fifty dollars.

As Roon's image came back into focus, Marcus began to once more discern words. ". . . a reason the American manufacturing base is disappearing. You have to look at it like the Amazon rain forest or the polar ice caps. Things change. What do you do when there's no more ozone layer? You adapt. Wear sunscreen!"

"This is a little different," Marcus said, feebly.

"No, it's not! China's the future, Marcus. You have any idea what's going on in that place? They got entire towns over there—entire towns!—devoted to sneakers! They got towns devoted to pants! Golf shirts! Underwear! A whole city in China is dedicated to making underwear with a single-minded purpose, and you know what that purpose is? World domination! Guess what, pal? These people are gonna be our masters and they won't need tanks and guns. All they'll need are tube socks. Billions and billions of tube socks." Roon was inexorable, like the weather, and Marcus couldn't do anything about it. He looked out the window toward the parking lot, the chain-link fence, the uncertain sky, an unhealthy gray on this momentous day. "What do you think? You wanna move there? You could enroll in a Berlitz course, get a head start."

Marcus was thinking of Sun Tzu's enduring observation: If you sit on a hill above the river long enough, eventually you will see the body of your enemy float by. Right now he was picturing Roon's bloated carcass drifting lazily along, fish nibbling at the decomposing flesh. Marcus then imagined himself telling Jan they'd be moving six thousand miles away to a country where none of them spoke the language so he could keep his job, a job that had not led to happiness or fulfillment, and which he no longer particularly liked. With Nathan's bar mitzvah coming up. And Lenore's medical condition, a situation that would only decline. That was how those things usually went, wasn't it? They got worse. How were people with glaucoma treated in China, anyway? They probably shot them and then harvested their organs. He knew things had eased up economically over there, but China was still world-class when it came to repressing their population. He had read about Tiananmen Square. The Chinese Army had not been shy about ventilating their comrades with volleys of hot lead produced by their increasingly aggressive mining industry. Admittedly, that was near the end of the previous century, but it nonetheless was not the manifestation of a nurturing culture. And he'd heard from friends who traveled there that the food was inedible, not at all like the Chinese food they ate at Tung Sing Hunan on Ventura Boulevard. Marcus had particularly enjoyed the spring rolls and the Meu Gai crab, never thinking he would have to consider whether he wanted to switch to an all-Chinese diet.

The enchiladas he had eaten at lunch had started to misbehave. He swallowed a belch and had to cover his mouth as the sickly sweet taste of the cheap meat burst forth from his intestine. He felt as if he might throw up, but he didn't want to allow Roon to think this news was having a negative effect on him. He swallowed and took a deep breath.

"Are *you* going to learn Chinese?"

"I won't need to, I'll hire interpreters. But you . . . if you're gonna be my guy in Guodong . . ."

"What's Guodong?"

"It's where the factory's gonna be. You're gonna need to speak the lingo. Do you want to take some time and think about it?" When Roon saw that Marcus was still ruminating on the question, he began to describe his efforts to salve the blow to the workers. "I had T-shirts made and I'm giving 'em to everyone on the line along with two months' pay." Here he reached into a bag at his feet, and suddenly Marcus noticed a piece of cloth flying his way. Reflexively catching it, he held it up and saw it was a T-shirt with large black letters embossed on a white background.

WAZOO THANKS YOU.

Marcus knew this jaunty gesture would not mollify workers who were about to lose their livelihoods, but didn't want to get into a discussion about Roon's pathetic attempt at employee relations. What he said was: "When are you closing the operation down?"

"Today."

"*Today?*" Marcus's distress was conspicious.

"I know this is kind of a shock, so take a couple of days and let me know. 'Cause if you're not gonna do it, I need to find someone who will. I need an American running the show. Tell me you'll think about it."

Marcus felt himself seeping into the floor, beneath the concrete and into the hard earth where he envisioned himself comfortably dematerializing, ceasing to exist in his present form as a man with troubles he believed he would not be able to solve. "I'll think about it," he said.

"It'll be an adventure! I walked into a bar over there in some town I can't even pronounce and I ordered a Diet Coke, and you know what? They had it! I'm telling you, China rocks. In the meantime, you should clean out your desk. I sold the factory, and an equipment broker is coming to liquidate the place on Wednesday." By naming the actual day the factory would cease to exist, Roon had placed an exclamation point at the end of this chapter of Marcus's life. It thudded on the page, the vibrations of its landing resonating through his being which was beginning to seem increasingly insubstantial to him.

When Marcus managed to speak, all that came out was "*Wednesday?*"

"Day after tomorrow," Roon pointed out helpfully.

"Don't I at least get a gold watch?" It was a joke, exemplary under the circumstances.

"A gold watch? I'm giving you a new life."

"In China."

"The town already has an American school your boy could go to. Marcus, we're the last American factory that's *not* there. I'm trying to run a business."

"It's all vanishing, isn't it?" Marcus regretted saying something so trite, but at the moment he couldn't do any better.

"And the bank that's holding your mortgage won't be sentimental when you start missing payments. Don't be afraid to take risks. Your brother Julian . . . you remember that time he gave us a ride to the Dodger game, going like a hundred and twenty miles an hour on the 405?" Marcus nodded. It was not a memory he wanted to relive. "He cut off that guy in the Corvette, the guy followed us to the exit and we thought we were gonna get killed?" Roon smiled now, cherishing the memory, his misspent youth. "Then your brother gets out of the car waving the toy gun. I thought the guy in the Corvette was going to piss his pants! Julian was a risk-taker. How's he doing, anyway?"

"We're not really in touch." Marcus didn't want to talk about his brother.

"That's too bad. Great guy." Roon got up from his chair, indicating the meeting was over. "I want you to understand something, Marcus. The world is made up of masters and slaves. I'm not saying it's bad to be a slave, hell, most people are slaves. I'm not saying it can't be comforting to have someone towering over you with a whip telling you what the hell to do. But it's your choice today. You can be a master or you can be a bootlicker."

Although Marcus had been blindsided by Roon and was feeling slightly disoriented, he had enough mental wherewithal to know that he wanted to retain his options. "What about the health insurance?"

"If you go to China, I'll put your mother-in-law on the policy."

Chapter 4

Marcus withdrew, his mind reeling. A toxic blend of rage and bafflement mixed with a sense of betrayal that he already knew was unjustified. Because where was it written that the status quo must be maintained? To everything, there is a season: A time to expand, a time to downsize, a time to move the entire operation to the Far East. Wrestling to get his emotions under a semblance of control, Marcus opened his desk and, hitting DefCon 4, reached for the Nietzsche volume. It was nearly twenty years old, and he had underlined so many passages that it was hard to find ones he was looking for. After a few minutes of anxious reading, he came upon the following:

A living thing desires above all to vent its strength—life as such is will to power.

In those increasingly rare moments of reflection when he considered what he'd done with his life, Marcus knew that all he had vented was a will to mediocrity. Yes, he'd supported his family. Yes, he'd paid his taxes. And he was buried in the middle class with no hope of upward movement. Philosophy for Marcus had always been academic, to be read, debated, and contemplated, not actually *lived*. If asked to characterize his own belief, he would have said he had become an accidental Stoic, a purveyor of the Gospel of Endurance, one who was glad to simply get by. This was fine in theory, when he was receiving a paycheck every two weeks and living in the *terra cognito* of Van Nuys. But he had an unnerving feeling the *Letters of Seneca* (or any other canonical Stoic text) would be cold comfort were he to find himself trying to function on the other side of the world in Chinese.

At the end of the workday, he appeared on the factory floor and broke the news to the stunned workforce. He informed them they were eligible for unemployment benefits and suggested they apply immediately. Then he thanked them for their years of service to the company and wished them good luck. There was a great deal of consternation among the workers, and Marcus answered a lot of questions after the meeting. He understood the pain they felt and the uncertain future they faced. He was greatly sympathetic. And entirely impotent.

Marcus drove home through the early-spring twilight and tried not to panic. In an attempt to put the situation into perspective, to concretize it and give it actual heft, he stopped at Tung Sing and purchased Chinese takeout for dinner. Now Jan, Nathan, Lenore, and Marcus were sitting in the kitchen eating egg rolls, pork lo mein, orange chicken, and moo goo gai pan. As Marcus maneuvered his chopsticks to pick up a piece of orange chicken, he turned to his son. "What's your favorite kind of food?"

Nathan, chewing a mouthful of lo mein, paused for a moment and said "Focaccia," indicating he hadn't entirely understood the question.

"Focaccia? Really?" Marcus asked, nonplussed. He hadn't heard the word *focaccia* before he was thirty, and here it was dancing off his son's tongue as easily as *lollipop*. "I thought you liked Chinese," he said, holding out hope Nathan's lifelong proclivity for egg rolls would give him an entrée to the subject of moving to their ostensible place of origin.

"I like Chinese," Lenore chirped. Marcus sensed that she thought he needed to be bailed out of something.

"It's actually kind of fatty," Jan said. "I was surprised when you called and told me you were going to pick up Chinese."

"Something happened at work and I got a craving."

"I'm glad you did," Lenore said, squinting at Marcus and nodding.

He appreciated that she was always trying to make him feel good, to assuage the guilt she experienced for availing herself of his hospitality. Marcus hoped Jan would ask what had happened, but she chose not to and a silence of several seconds ensued.

"Can I be excused?" Nathan asked. "I need to practice the clarinet."

Nathan was duly released, and, after deflecting Lenore's offer to help, Marcus and Jan set about cleaning up. When Lenore had gone to her room, Jan said, "The glaucoma's worse. The doctor's thinking she might need surgery."

Wiping food remnants off a plate and into the garbage, Marcus did not want to talk about Lenore's condition right now. "How do you think the store is doing?"

"Great."

He sensed that she didn't even think for a second before answering him. Her response was entirely reflexive. "*Great?*" His voice rose slightly with the strain of not saying what he really wanted to say, which was: When can we stop pretending that that money pit is going to succeed?

"Well, not *great* as in terrific and we're going to be opening another branch, but not bad."

Marcus had finished wiping the plates and rinsing them off. He took a dish towel from a rack above the sink and began drying them. He didn't notice he was using enough force to wipe off the glaze. "Any chance you're going to be able to support the family with what you're making?" It was taking all his effort to make himself not sound as if he was baiting her.

"That wasn't the plan," she said. "We never . . ." He stiffened at her use of the word *we* when discussing the store. It was always *we* and never *I*. He knew she believed that by using *we* she could make him feel complicit and so, in her view, less inclined to question how Ripcord was doing. "We never talked about the store supporting the family. The plan was that it would contribute, right?"

42

"Yes, right." Marcus understood that he had not performed due diligence before endorsing Jan's idea of opening a clothing boutique. Had he encouraged her in a more practical pursuit, they would not be engaged in this exchange. "But there's a slight . . ." Having not yet arrived at a plan for imparting this information, he hesitated.

"A slight what?"

"How would you feel about moving to China?"

"Excuse me?"

From the way she looked at him, Marcus thought he might as well have asked her if she wanted to hold a séance, or go hot-air ballooning. Then he realized, given that the only lead-in he'd managed before posing an unmistakably epic question was a meal of Chinese takeout food, his query *did* have the quality of a non-sequitur. "Roon is transferring the manufacturing of Wazoo Toys there, and he asked me if I wanted to run the operation."

"In *China?*" The planes of her face coalesced into a portrait of stupefaction.

"I told him I'd have to discuss it with you."

He watched and awaited some kind of response, but she said nothing for several moments. Marcus was pleased that Jan was not the type to get hysterical. He remembered the time Nathan had fallen down the stairs as a two-year-old and his incisor had punctured his cheek. They had rushed him to the hospital, where he was placed in what amounted to a tiny straitjacket, then strapped to a gurney and operated on by a solicitous female ER doctor from Poona, India. Jan was with their son for every moment of this, maintained eye contact with him at all times, and comforted him in his distress, but Marcus nearly fainted and was greatly relieved when one of the nurses gave him a sedative and told him to lie down on a nearby bed.

Removing a pitcher of iced tea from the aging refrigerator, Jan poured herself a glass, took a sip, and looked at Marcus levelly. "Do *you* want to move there?"

He took a deep breath and said "I don't know."

She did not immediately respond. Instead, she nodded her head slowly, appearing to process this information. "You don't *know*? Really? So you might want to move to China?"

"Yes. I might. I'm not saying I *do*. I'd like to think I'm someone who could, you know, *do* that. I'm taking the idea out for a test drive." He planed his hand through the air in front of him, miming the movement of a car.

She suddenly exploded. "Are you insane, Marcus? China? What am I supposed to do in China? And Nathan? And my mother? And the dog? What is our family going to do in China?"

"Roon offered to relocate us. There's an American school, *and* he said he'd put your mother on my health insurance." He presented this last bit of information triumphantly, as if to say: *See? I'm not a complete fool.*

"What if you refuse to go?"

"I don't have a job."

"Roon owns lots of companies. He didn't offer you anything else?"

"No."

"After fifteen years, this is how he treats you? That *asshole!* How can he do this to us? You're supposed to be his friend!" Marcus tried to calm her down, but all she could say was "Fuck him." A minute of complete silence followed, during which Jan drained her entire glass of iced tea in one continuous gulp. "I wish we could go into business together."

"You and me?"

"Wouldn't it be great? I'm getting kind of tired of being in business with Plum. She's talking about having a baby."

"With who?"

"A turkey baster. As part of an art project. It's so insane, I can't even talk about it."

To Marcus, the idea of Plum having a child was nearly as absurd as the prospect of their moving to China. He was glad she was not his problem. A clarinet melody drifted downstairs. Nathan was trying to play a song they had heard on the radio while driving to school that morning. Every third note squeaked and it sounded terrible. Marcus listened for a moment. He knew how much he would eventually miss that sound.

"This China thing, Marcus . . . is not going to happen. You can get another job." Then she kissed his cheek and left him alone in the kitchen.

Plum and her ex-husband, Atlas Boot, had lived together in the west San Fernando Valley neighborhood of Reseda until the day she read one of his private e-mails and learned that he was screwing a foot model he'd met in an Internet chat room. Now she lived there by herself. Reseda was a quiet place where neat green lawns surrounded modest homes and children rode bicycles down sun-baked streets. Plum hated it. She wanted to live someplace artier, more combustible, but they'd gotten a good deal on the house and it had been awarded to her in the settlement.

Plum had turned half of the garage into an art studio, and she spent most evenings out there. Just before nine o'clock on Monday night, she ran her hands down her loose black pants and looked around the room. Although Plum had trained as a painter, she now saw that everything vivifying in the art world was taking place off the easel. That this school of thought had had a gray beard fifty years ago did not matter to her. Perception was what mattered, and the art world pooh-bahs who issued these aesthetic fiats (Magritte down! Schwitters up!) had decreed painting over. So Plum set her course: conceptualism or bust. Unfortunately, while Plum was not without talent as a painter, the ability to craft provocative "installations" continued to elude her. It was one thing to create something from a combination of old hubcaps and cell phones; it was another thing entirely for it to have meaning. Now she was surrounded by an accumulation of flotsam gleaned during her travels around town:

several broken clock radios and toasters, a freezer door, a bicycle wheel, a large plastic dollhouse, five dolls, three mannequins, a bird-cage, bottles of various sizes and shapes, a couple of old board games, a tattered sports jacket, a moose head with one antler she had purchased at a garage sale, and two bags of cement. Over the past several months she had desultorily tried to conjure something compelling out of the bric-a-brac she'd accumulated, but what to make? She had toyed with the dollhouse metaphor and had spent a few days encrusting the one she'd salvaged with small appliance parts, intending to populate it with old Barbies. But eventually she saw this as hackneyed and the whole Ibsen-by-way-of-Radio-Shack statement struck her as trite. She had considered gluing feathers to male and female mannequins, then placing them on perches in a custom-built birdcage. That piece had progressed as far as the pasting of the feathers, but, try as she might, Plum was not able to get the feathered mannequins to remain on the perches. Before this engineering dilemma was surmounted, she had been undone by the realization that the birdcage was no more original than the dollhouse. A defining metaphor continued to hover just beyond her grasp. Undaunted, Plum would spend her free time puttering in the studio, drinking English breakfast tea and reflecting on her artistic forebears. Edvard Munch had been miserable, yet he'd managed to wring immortal work from the blackest depths of Scandinavian depression. She considered herself to be at least as unhappy as Munch, if slightly less talented, and she wished she could blame this impasse on her physical surroundings. Plum liked to believe that, turned loose in the land of the fjords rather than stuck in Reseda, she too might conjure up something mysterious and heartbreaking. But down deep she knew that that wasn't it at all. Plum was terrified that she had run dry. Rather than being the ingredients of a great artistic leap forward, the things she gathered remained junk in a garage in the San Fernando Valley.

Looking away from this pile of rubbish, so recently imbued with aesthetic promise, but now forlorn and useless-seeming, Plum noticed her dog-eared copy of the poems of Paul Verlaine on a bookshelf, where it was gathering dust among a pile of old art magazines. Picking it up, she opened it and began to read:

> *The long sobs*
> *Of the violins*
> *Of autumn*
> *Wound my heart*
> *With a monotonous*
> *Languor.*

She immediately closed the book. In her youth, Plum had been drawn to artists who trafficked in emotional pain. Her experience of them as a young person allowed the suffering they elucidated to occur at a romantic distance. When she encountered them a few years later, through a scrim of disappointment and regret, they became too real for her. Sobbing violins of autumn were one thing when you were lying around your college dorm room eating mushrooms and listening to Patti Smith. They were something entirely different when experienced years later in Reseda. Plum thought about whether or not having a baby was really going to make her feel better. She was desperate to try something new. The idea of reinvention held great appeal, and she understood that a baby would shake things up. Right now, though, it was one more idea fighting for space with sundry others, and none of them was adding up to anything. Plum was aware that trying to get any work done in her present state of mind would only make her feel worse, so she went back into the house.

She leaned against the doorjamb that separated the kitchen from the living room, listened to the hum of the dishwasher, and ran her finger along the soft leather belt she was wearing. When she realized what she was doing, it made her remember Dr. Pradip

47

Singh, D.D.S., since he had begged her to whip him with it. Dr. Singh enjoyed having his bare bottom flagellated, and Plum found the act of administering mild corporal punishment curiously titillating. Once, while striking him a little too forcefully, she had been so transported that a hematoma was raised before she realized he was yelling *Costco*, their agreed-upon safe word. Other than their taste in sex play, the two of them didn't share much common ground. She didn't miss the amorous dentist tonight. Plum just wanted to thrash someone.

Marcus sat at the desk in his converted garage, enduring the increasingly challenging task of paying the monthly bills. His sixty-thousand-dollar salary was no longer enough to cover expenses. The mortgage was eighteen hundred a month, he had two car payments, and along with all the other bills there was Nathan's phalanx of tutors, his educational therapist, and his private clarinet teacher (every child in the Winthrop Hall Middle School band was required to take private lessons). They had drawn a fifty-thousand-dollar home-equity loan two years earlier. Servicing that cost five hundred a month, and the principal was nearly gone. Marcus was very conscious of the hole they were in—it was a crater. He looked up from a four-thousand-dollar invoice for the new roof when he heard his wife's voice asking him if he was coming to bed soon. Jan was standing at the office/garage door, dressed in sweat-pants and a voluminous wool sweater, a sympathetic look in her soft hazel eyes. She walked over to him and began rubbing his shoulders. "You're carrying a lot of tension up there. You should get a massage." This was a surprise, coming from Jan. The concept of paying someone to work trained hands over a sore body was out of place in their world. Massages were an indulgence that required disposable income they did not possess.

Marcus glanced at the pile of bills, which seemed to have magically grown since he'd last looked at it, and realized he'd done nothing for nearly an hour. And his neck was stiff. He would love a massage. He turned and looked up at his wife. "Hey, why don't *you* give me a massage?"

"Tomorrow night, I promise." He tried to hide his disappointment. He didn't think she'd actually give him a massage (what had he done to earn one, after all?), but he'd been hoping. "I want to talk to you about something," she said, looking away for a moment. Marcus wondered how bad this was going be, *I want to talk to you* rarely portending anything good. "I'm sorry about the store."

This was a shock. "What do you mean?"

"I think maybe it was a bad idea. There's nothing happening on Van Nuys Boulevard. Right now *we're* the gentrification, Plum and I . . ." She hesitated again. Marcus hoped she wasn't counting on him to provide a silver bullet. "What do you think? We've been doing it two years . . ."

"Can you get her to buy you out?"

"I doubt it."

Marcus was surprised by Jan's revelation. Apparently the China option had spurred her into serious reflection. Although he'd always harbored a sense that she had persuaded herself to embrace retailing, she'd never revealed her doubts about what she'd done until tonight. The family had dropped twenty thousand dollars of the home equity loan into Ripcord, and it was looking like that money had gone the way of the buffalo.

"What do you want to do?"

"I can't just quit."

"No, you can't." He stood up and kissed her on the cheek, pulling her to him. "We don't have to solve this right now."

Marcus did not sleep well that night, turning his impending decision over and over in his mind, holding it up to the light, examining it from every possible angle. If he really wanted to follow his job overseas, he thought he could convince Jan to go. Failing that, he could go alone, like the nineteenth-century New England whalers who left families behind for years at a time, braving typhoons, scurvy, and the blandishments of naked Polynesian women to provide for them. And it would be an adventure. That part of it he liked. How do you say *yes* in Mandarin?

Dawn was breaking over the Woodley Lakes Public Golf Course as Marcus placed his ball on the tee at the first hole. It was a Wednesday morning, two days after he'd spoken to Roon, and he was standing with Atlas Boot. The name Atlas had been bestowed on him by his parents, the more prosaically named John and Mary Boot of Eau Claire, Wisconsin. They had hoped their only son would be inspired by the mythic appellation, but his shambling, essentially soft physical presence suggested otherwise.

Marcus had met Atlas while he and Plum were married, and they remained friends after the divorce. The two men had a monthly game, and they always played nine holes in the early morning, giving them each enough time to complain about what was wrong with their lives and still get to work on time. Now Marcus walked six feet behind the ball and squatted, peering down the fairway as he lined up a shot. Although he was not a good golfer, Marcus appreciated that it allowed him to not think about whatever it was he believed he *should* be thinking about on the days he played. This morning it was Roon, China, and the future of his family. Mercifully, none of these things gained purchase in his head as he tried to envision the ball on a straight 250-yard trajectory. Attempting to achieve a state of complete calm, he rose to a standing position and placed himself to the side of the ball. He stared at it, took a deep breath. There was a water hazard on the left, where a flock of geese was going about its early-morning business, oblivious to the imminent onslaught. Across the course was a glade of trees. Marcus took all this in, then rotated his head toward the ground and looked at the ball again. One more deep breath. He brought the club slowly back, remembering to extend his arms and keep his wrist at the correct angle, then began his downswing. He shifted his hips and swung through the ball, which went skittering to the left, rolling toward the geese, who were not sufficiently intimidated to move, or even to look his way, and then into the pond. Marcus glanced at Atlas, who was standing at a respectful distance watching this debacle.

"Did you like that?" Marcus said, trying to laugh.

"Impressive." Atlas was no better at golf than Marcus, and they had an unspoken pact that whenever one of them misfired, which was often, the offending party should be the first one to make light of it. It kept humiliation at bay. "You sure you don't want to play for five bucks a hole? I'll give you ten strokes."

"No, thanks."

This was a friendly game during which no hard currency changed hands, although Atlas suggested it every time they played. He told Marcus to take a mulligan.

Marcus's do-over, while not particularly impressive in its slow fade to the right, was at least playable. Relieved, he walked to the side of the tee box so he could watch Atlas take his first swing of the day. Like many men who were slightly overweight and out of shape, Atlas wore his clothes a little too large. A faded blue cap sat on the back of his head and his green golf shirt was untucked. These elements combined to create a genially relaxed effect.

Atlas swung and connected squarely with the ball. Rocketing off the tee, it flew up the center of the fairway, bouncing on the short grass then rolling to a stop two hundred and twenty yards from the tee. Marcus complimented him on the shot and then went to fish his first ball out of the shallows of the pond. Atlas politely waited for him, and once Marcus had managed to rescue his errant shot, the two of them marched up the fairway as the sun peeked out from the mountains to the east and the horizon bled pink to blue.

When they finished the first hole, Marcus told his friend about the China opportunity. Atlas blamed the shock of this news when he missed the putt that would have given him a bogey.

"As your attorney, I'd advise you to go," Atlas said, though he was not Marcus's attorney. He'd heard the phrase *as your attorney* in a movie. "I'd go to China tomorrow."

"You would?"

Marcus was surprised at how quickly Atlas had formulated an opinion. In the manner of many lawyers, he was circumspect, and Marcus had expected him to take more time examining the subtleties of the situation.

"I'd be out of here so fast, your head would spin."

They were walking up to the tee box of the second hole, a par four. As Atlas scrutinized two golf balls, trying to decide which one to use, Marcus asked him why he would be in such a rush to go to China.

"The Chinese love card games, did you know that? I'd be in pig heaven. I'm already in Gardena a few nights a week, playing poker in the clubs. You oughtta come with me some time."

"I'm not a gambler."

"No kidding."

"What's that supposed to mean?"

"Marcus, look at you. Married to the same woman, what, fifteen years? Same job almost since you got out of school. Hey, I'm not saying it's wrong . . . but you should think about China."

"I *am* thinking about it."

"You don't want to go. I can tell." How could Atlas tell, Marcus wondered? Was it that painfully obvious? Marcus didn't want to ask. He watched Atlas line up his tee shot. "Would you take your family?"

"Absolutely," Marcus said.

"I'd like to be somewhere Plum couldn't ask me for money." Atlas began his backswing. Reaching the apex, the club glided down and—CRACK!—the ball shot off the tee traveling high and far from where the two men were standing. Marcus turned his attention from the flight of the ball to Atlas, who was smiling enigmatically. Marcus couldn't tell whether his friend was thinking about his golf shot or savoring the prospect of moving five thousand miles away from his ex-wife.

Atlas didn't discuss Plum for the rest of their nine holes, although he did bring up China several times, encouraging Marcus to at least go for a year. Yes, civil liberties were nonexistent, their attitude toward baby girls reprehensible, and what they had done to Tibet unconscionable, but they had the most dynamic economy in the world and what was so great about Van Nuys? Marcus said he would take it under advisement, which was what he usually said after Atlas began a speech with the phrase *as your attorney*. After hitting a rare good tee shot on the sixth hole, Marcus brought up the subject of Ripcord, asking Atlas how long he thought the store could last. Atlas shouldered his bag for the walk up the fairway and audibly sighed. He told Marcus he had no idea, but hoped the end would come soon.

"Last week Plum asked me if I'd be willing to put more money into it. I said hell, no. I'm your *ex*-husband, goddammit, and business is slow." Atlas hiked up his pants. "You know what my biggest case is right now? I'm defending some pissant USC sophomore who killed a fantail goldfish in a campus pond as part of a fraternity initiation. Shishkebabbed the damn thing on a skewer." Atlas shook his head in dismay, not so much at the fate of the fish as at his own situation. He had made his bones as a lawyer in the mid-nineties when he successfully defended a former flight attendant named Cricket Bulger who had married a much older man worth nearly forty million dollars. When the man died, his middle-aged son had paid a visit to Cricket, during which he attempted to dissuade her from claiming an inheritance. She shot him with the gold-handled gun her husband had thoughtfully provided before he died. She hired Atlas, who convinced the jury the stepson intended to rape her. The seamy nature of the crime, combined with the large amount of money involved, created a media feeding frenzy, and when the trigger-happy stewardess hired Atlas his profile skyrocketed. That the dead man had no history of violence or sexual assault made his victory all the more remarkable, and for a brief period Atlas was one of the better-known members of the Los Angeles bar. In his middle thirties at the time, he expected a major career to grow out of the Cricket Bulger trial, but it never materialized. If it had, Marcus sometimes reflected, his friend would have been recreating with the captains of industry at the Bel Air Country Club instead of with a factory manager on a public course in the Valley.

Marcus watched as Atlas lined up a long putt on the ninth hole. He wanted to talk more about the opportunity in China and the fear that he was trying to overcome in taking it. He was scared of Jan's reaction should he decide to push this, and he was scared to relocate his family to an unfamiliar place, much less a different country. But his fear was overcome by his embarrassment: Admitting trepidation about this was simply too emasculating. So he watched as Atlas missed the putt, the ball rolling long by about a foot. Atlas tapped the ball in, and his round was over. Marcus had a fifteen-foot putt to attempt. He took two practice strokes with his putter, remembering to keep his shoulders relaxed and to bend his knees. Then he hit the ball. It rolled toward the hole but lost momentum and came to rest nearly two feet short.

"You gotta *hit* the ball," Atlas said.

They were done playing by nine o'clock. Since there was no point in going to the factory, Marcus drove home, mulling his future in the slow-moving morning traffic.

With Bertrand Russell nestled at his feet in the kitchen, he dialed the number of the main office and asked to be connected to Mr. Primus. Roon picked up the phone.

"*Ni hao.*"

"What?"

"That's *hello* in Mandarin. We move like the wind here, pal. What's up? I'm in a meeting."

"I'm not going."

After an uncomfortable pause, Roon said "Jeez, Marcus, I'm not sure you're making the best decision for your family." Marcus knew the concern he sensed in Roon's voice hid a less altruistic agenda.

Now this titan of commerce would have to find someone else to run the plant in Guodong. "Are you sure? It's a hell of an opportunity."

"I know, I know. It's just that . . ."

"China, Marcus! It's the future!"

"Is there some other kind of situation in Los Angeles you might have . . ." he asked tentatively.

"What? Like another job?" Roon laughed, as if Marcus's question was preposterous.

"You've got a lot of companies, companies I probably don't even know about . . ."

"I need you in China. That's where you fit in the big picture."

"But I can't go. Are you sure there's . . ."

"Before I offer the job to someone else, I'm going to ask you one more time, because I don't want another guy stealing your bacon. I'm trying to do you a favor here."

"I just can't."

"Marcus, when I hang up the phone, the job is *gone*. I'm trying to take the company public and I'm trimming everywhere right now, so, this offer? There's nothing coming after it. You say 'no' and . . . oh, come on! Are you sure?"

Taking the company public? That was the first Marcus had heard of this plan. How much wealthier was that going to make Roon? How much more could he accumulate? Marcus thought about his family's financial situation. He needed to work, clearly, but not in China. Trying to tamp his resentment down to a less mind-bending level, Marcus said "What about severance?"

"I'm willing to give you a thousand dollars for each year because I'm a nice guy and we'll round it up. So that's what . . .?"

"Fourteen thousand dollars."

"It's a lot more than anyone else is getting."

"Are you kidding me? I've known you my whole life!"

"You should reconsider and come to China."

"I should get at least a year's pay for severance."

"It's costing me a lot of money to move the operation overseas. The guys who do these deals go over the financials very closely. I don't want to have to do any explaining to them. If you want a personal loan, maybe we can work something out . . ."

When Marcus hung up, the silence was all-consuming.

Chapter 5

The heat that summer was peeling the bark off trees. The sun pounded the hills and canyons mercilessly. The valley floor was a kiln. The old air conditioners in the house heaved like they were on a death march, so Marcus usually walked around in nothing but gym shorts, putting on a T-shirt if he needed to do an errand. Jan would go to Ripcord most days. Nathan attended a nearby YMCA day camp where the kids took salt pills and looked for shade. Lenore traveled to Boston and New Jersey, visiting Jan's sisters, and was gone for most of the summer. Marcus could only mow the lawn once a week, and after having cleaned out the garage he had very little to do other than wait for the mail to see if anyone had responded to the hundred and fifty résumés he'd sent out.

No one did.

To escape the heat, Marcus would take Bertrand Russell to Leo Carrillo State Beach in Malibu, where he would sit under an umbrella, stare at the sea, and wonder how his life had come to this. There were no dogs allowed, and Marcus lived in fear he would be served a summons. But in his one piece of good luck, this flouting of the rules escaped detection. He kept up his golf game with Atlas, who regaled him with stories of the killing he was making in sports betting. As they trudged up and down the hot fairways, Marcus had to listen to how Atlas had devised a system whereby he could divine how professional tennis players would do in a given match, based on some incomprehensible algorithm no one else had discovered. Marcus wondered whether his friend had become delusional, until the day Atlas arrived in the Woodley Lakes parking lot driving a new Porsche.

As the summer raged on, the Ripps' home-equity loan dwindled to nothing. Credit card debt began to swell. June passed, then July. Days spent surfing business sites on the Internet, reading daily papers and ancient philosophical tracts in coffee shops, and working out at a health club where his membership was about to run out. One blazing afternoon, Marcus pumped away on a stationary bicycle beneath a bank of televisions, heart racing, perspiration running in rivulets off his face, haggard from lack of sleep. The screens were tuned variously to CNN broadcasting pictures of a desert war, a soap opera, and a financial show hosted by a middle-aged bald man who appeared to be in the throes of advanced dementia. Marcus sensed that this man, despite the wildness in his eyes, was like Roon, a ruler, a conquistador, someone to whom the Gods of Unbridled Money had revealed tantalizing truths in a language he, in his penurious condition, could never hope to understand. Even with the sound off, Marcus could not take his eyes off this avatar of wealth and acquisition. Why was this man so obscenely successful? How had he so assiduously avoided the slave model? He preached a non-emotional, even amoral program for teasing money out of the market. He bragged about investing in firearms stocks, pornography, and tobacco—the provenance of the money had no inherent meaning, only the money itself. And why not? His mantra was this: *Someone's going to get rich; it may as well be you!*

Marcus drove home haunted by the television host's sweaty face. He was drinking a glass of tap water in his kitchen—having cancelled the water delivery account the previous month—when he received a phone call from Dal-Tech, a defense contractor in Sun Valley. There was a job opening for a procurement manager. Did Marcus want to come out there and talk about it? He asked what the job paid and, when he was told it could be anywhere between fifty and a hundred thousand dollars, depending on the level of experience, he scheduled an interview.

58

Five months removed from savoring a lamb chop hors d'oeuvre in the ballroom of the Beverly Hills Hotel, Marcus found himself in the decidedly less enchanting precincts of Sun Valley on a blistering, smoggy August day. Jan had suggested that he do affirmations to get into a positive mindset, and though he laughed when she described how they were supposed to work, he was willing to do anything if it would make him appear a more attractive and less desperate candidate. Thus, he spent the ride repeating *I am a fine executive and a good manager and those who work for me like me* and trying not to feel like an idiot. It actually did seem to put him in a sunnier mood, and by the time he was parking in the vast lot at Dal-Tech, a huge complex in the hot shadows of the ragged Verdugo Hills, he felt a rush of confidence.

"How do you feel about working on a technology that kills people?" Les Claymore asked. Les was the head of human resources at Dal-Tech. He wore a short-sleeved white shirt and squeezed a handgrip as he spoke, which made the muscles of his forearm bulge disconcertingly. He appeared to be in his forties. Marcus guessed his striped tie was a clip-on. There were several family pictures on his desk, and the photographs, blonde and smiling, looked like they came with the frames. Marcus had told him about working at Wazoo and the Praying Presidents line of toys. Les liked the sound of the product, and Marcus told him he already felt like he'd been a government contractor. Les did not laugh.

"A factory is a factory," Marcus said, forcing a smile.

"But it's different when you're really working for the government," Les said. "I'm a Christian, belong to Church of the Redeemer over in San Dimas, and as a Christian, I personally wrestle with what we do at Dal-Tech. I don't kid myself. We're building systems that rain shock and awe on our enemy, yeah, but sometimes the innocent die, too. And I have to ask myself—is that what Jesus would want? Is it?" He paused here. Apparently Les was waiting for an actual answer. Marcus thought before he spoke. The job had good benefits.

"I don't know." Marcus would not be caught in this man's trap, because he sensed something was going on, a hidden agenda of Les Claymore's designed to ferret out anyone who didn't pass a particular litmus test. He believed Les was trying to get him to say the wrong thing.

"Jesus would understand, Marcus. He wouldn't *like* it, but he would understand. We've prayed on it here in our Lunchtime Worship Group, and this is what we believe." When Marcus said nothing in response, Les rose and stuck out his hand. "Okay, buddy. Thanks for coming in." Taking the cue, Marcus got out of his chair and was treated to his interviewer's iron grip.

"Are you meeting with a lot of people?" Marcus didn't want to leave just yet. Although he really did not like Les, he truly needed a job and this was the only interview he'd managed to get.

"I don't have to tell you that," Les said, trying to lighten the mood and failing miserably. When he saw that Marcus's expression didn't change, he said "Yes, we're talking to several candidates."

"The job has full benefits?" Marcus knew the answer but was not giving up easily.

"Yes, it does. Okay, Marcus, thanks for coming in."

Marcus wrote a thank-you note to Les after the meeting, enclosing an article about isometric exercise, a gambit he picked up from a book he'd bought called *Reinvent Yourself: A Guide to Finding Work When You're Over Forty*. He never heard from Les again. In the next month, he had interviews at a manufacturer of pressure-sensitive adhesives, a burglar alarm factory, and a concern that made mesh guards for fluorescent lights that were sold to prisons. All of them paid badly, and none of them went any better.

Marcus and Jan were cleaning up the kitchen after dinner. School had resumed several weeks earlier, and Nathan was doing his homework. Lenore was in her bedroom with an eye-pain-induced headache. Marcus had attended a group meeting for potential salespeople that day at Pep-Togs, a purveyor of cheerleading uniforms. When he told Jan he'd left the meeting early, she asked why.

"Because I can't do that on commission, cold-call people . . . I can't make enough money doing it to justify the time."

"Do you have a plan?"

"Do I have a *plan*? Yeah, I have a plan. My plan is to get a job."

"Do you know how much we owe? With the home-equity loan and the credit cards and everything?" Marcus knew the debt had been growing and believed nothing was to be gained by obsessively monitoring its increasingly vertiginous spike.

"How much?"

"Almost eighty thousand dollars."

The deep fear engendered by that figure was bowel-shaking. Not ten or twenty, which were manageable numbers, or even forty, angst-producing but still within the realm of Marcus's comprehension. Eighty thousand rumbled in his gut, slapped his face, broke his nose. The number was on the high side of his worst suspicion. But he did not want to show belly, so he simply said: "Okay."

"*Okay?* All you have to say is *okay*?"

"Why don't *you* get a job?" She looked at him, stricken, and he immediately regretted his words. His suggesting that she get a job broke the unspoken treaty between them, the one that declared he would not do anything to undermine Ripcord. She had poured a great deal of herself into that project and was deeply invested in its success. Her expression told him he had overstepped his bounds. But he felt a hopelessness welling in him that freed his tongue.

"I have a job," she said.

"It isn't working." That was the first salvo. Now the volley: "We need to get real about the situation we're in. You never should have gone into business with Plum, who has no idea what she's doing. The woman is a failed artist, not a retailing expert. We need to cut our losses."

Having managed to control her rising vitriol, Jan regarded him with a dark look. He sensed they were about to have one of those macro-marital conversations that always ended badly, the kind where external pressures threaten the union to a degree where one or both spouses, reacting overemotionally, contemplated calling a lawyer. But Marcus would not back down. He stared at her, equally darkly, and didn't break eye contact. A major conflagration was threatening, one that clearly presaged separate bedrooms later that night. Marcus suddenly realized that he had forgotten to take air into his lungs. When he inhaled, he noticed a familiar scent wafting through the kitchen, something he had not smelled in a long time and was incongruous in the current context: marijuana.

"Do you smell pot?"

"The doctor prescribed it to my mother."

"He prescribed *pot?*"

"For the glaucoma." She said this matter-of-factly, implying that the treatment was so well known it had been on the cover of *Newsweek*, and if Marcus was going to be this egregiously uninformed there was nothing she could do.

"You weren't going to discuss this with me?"

"Discuss what? The woman has a disease. She smokes dope to manage it."

"There's a kid in the house," he said, as if that should settle the matter.

Marcus respected Jan enough not to simply overrule her as a male prerogative. So he crossed his arms and breathed in again, noticing as he did so that the sweet smell of the cannabis had become more pronounced. "Have you thought about what you were going to tell Nate if he asks whether Grandma's a pothead?"

Jan was silent for a moment, musing on this issue. Clearly she hadn't worked that one out yet.

RIIINNGG.

The doorbell?

Who could possibly be ringing their doorbell now?

Marcus opened his eyes a little wider when he saw a cop from the LAPD standing on his doorstep, blue uniform tight over a ramrod-straight physique. The man was of medium height, and his wide brown face was bisected by a trim mustache. A black nameplate on his chest read Vasquez in white lettering.

Marcus instantly tried to remember just exactly how decriminalized pot had become and whether he was about to be hauled off to jail. Then he recalled that Lenore had a prescription. "Officer, I can exp—"

The cop was so intent on delivering his own speech that Marcus never got the word *explain* entirely out of his mouth. "Are you Marcus Ripps?"

"Yes, sir." Marcus believed everyone in a position of authority should be called *sir* as often as possible; it (however infinitesimally) reduced the chances of pain and suffering at their unpredictable whims.

"You're the brother of Julian Ripps?"

This question came as a shock to Marcus. He had written Julian off long ago and, suspecting Julian had done the same, tried to think of his estranged sibling as seldom as possible. He knew the presence of a police officer did not bode well. As this unhappy thought dawned on him, he again noticed the sweet pot fragrance now permeating the house. Marcus answered in the affirmative, hoping to keep the conversation from veering toward his having to explain anything further. Marcus noticed the cop's nostrils seemed to quiver. Did he smell the dope?

"I'm sorry to have to tell you this, Mr. Ripps, but . . . uhh . . . your brother?"

"Yes?"

". . . is deceased."

Julian, only thirty-nine, was dead? It had been several years since Marcus had seen him, and it wasn't as if he imagined a rapprochement could have been effected, but dead? That was a kick in the teeth. He heard an audible intake of breath behind him, Jan weighing in word-lessly. Marcus took a moment to collect himself.

"Why did they send the police to notify me? Was he in trouble?"

"My sergeant told me to come down, Mr. Ripps."

"How did he die?"

"I don't know."

Officer Vasquez mumbled condolences and returned to his patrol car. Marcus closed the door and turned to face Jan. She embraced him, whispering "I'm sorry." He reflexively hugged her, more because he sensed she expected him to than because he was experiencing the need to be comforted. He felt curiously light, as if a burden had been lifted, a weight he had shouldered removed. As his wife held him, he realized this was the closest physical contact he'd had with her in months.

Lenore appeared in the foyer, maraschino-eyed, and said: "I need a ride to the market so I can get some hummus and a box of crackers." Then she began laughing uncontrollably, great golden giggles tumbling forth from her slender frame, liberating her for a moment. After a few seconds, the laughter began to subside and Marcus and Jan waited patiently for conversation to resume. When Lenore noticed them looking at her so attentively, the laughter began to roll forth again and took a full minute to bring back under control.

"Mother, I hate to harsh your mellow, but Marcus's brother just died."

Lenore looked expectantly from Jan to Marcus, awaiting the punch line.

Chapter 6

"Is Lenore going to be arrested?"

Nathan glanced at Marcus with a mouth full of candied toothpaste, from which the tips of his blue braces were peeking. The boy was at the sink in the upstairs hallway bathroom. Marcus was standing in the doorway.

"No . . . no, she's not." Here Marcus gave a rueful laugh. He was still off-balance from the unexpected reek of pot, the arrival of the police, and the shocking news about Julian.

"So why was that guy here?"

"The cop came to tell us that my brother died."

"He died?" Marcus nodded. "I liked him. Didn't he try to give me a minibike?"

Marcus knew that Nathan had only the vaguest recollection of his uncle. Did the boy remember Julian showing up uninvited on his fifth birthday? There was a party taking place in the backyard and his friends from school were there. Julian arrived with a blowsy-looking woman and a gleaming red minibike, one of those gizmos with a gasoline motor which, given the right conditions, could burst into flames and maim the child riding it. Marcus had no idea how Julian had known it was Nathan's birthday, but, miraculously, he did. Nathan could barely ride a two-wheeler. Giving him a minibike was a ludicrous idea. He and Julian had argued and Julian had left, leaving his gift behind, like a grenade waiting to detonate. Marcus told Nathan he was donating it to charity since he wouldn't have anything that belonged to his brother in their home. Nathan hadn't understood at the time, and Marcus suspected he still didn't.

Given the news about Julian, Marcus appreciated that Jan put aside her grievances with him. Normally, an exchange like the one they'd had would have required at least twenty-four uncomfortable hours before a truce was declared. But death changed the equation.

Marcus assured Jan that he was all right, that he could handle whatever emotions were roiling him. When she went to bed, he filled a glass with ice and poured three fingers of whiskey. Then he fell into a chair in the living room. They had bought the furniture—a love seat, two club chairs, a sofa, and an oblong oak coffee table—when they were first married. But now its longevity suggested incipient decrepitude rather than comfort, and its tired aspect intensified the unforeseen sadness he was feeling.

Marcus remembered Julian as someone who took the noble out of savage. Sixth grade blowing up mailboxes with M–80s, high school dealing quaaludes. Then: a boosted car, a joyride with two cheerleaders, a month in Juvenile Hall. Julian was the total entertainment package, constantly butting heads with the parents who would periodically take a break from sniping at each other to try and rein in their increasingly unmanageable son.

Unwilling to accept the constraints of an after-school job at his father's store, the ever-cunning Julian started scalping concert tickets and could be seen weekend nights outside popular Los Angeles venues, moving merchandise under the watchful eyes of undercover cops. Enlisting Marcus and Roon in the sales force, Julian drove to places like the Forum, Santa Monica Civic Auditorium, and the Hollywood Palladium where they would work shows by aging rock dinosaurs, hair metal acts, and punk bands (when Julian eventually fired his brother for not being an aggressive enough salesman, Roon quit in protest. Marcus subsequently reflected that it had been the last time Roon would do anything on principle).

He recalled his parents' reaction when Julian beat his wings and fled home at sixteen. While they ached on one level, on another they were palpably relieved. His mere presence had become a harbinger of bad tidings. Julian crashed at the homes of friends, moving from place to place every few weeks. Marcus would occasionally run into him in the neighborhood and they would exchange uneasy pleasantries, as people who had known each other once will do.

A spring afternoon and Marcus is fifteen. He sees Julian walking out of Flaco's Diner in San Pedro with Patty DeWitt, all pale skin and green eyes, a river of wavy red hair running down her back. She's wearing gold hoop earrings that tickle her soft neck. In faded jeans and a tight black T-shirt that says THE MISFITS in red letters across her full breasts, she is Venus on the high school half shell. Marcus lusts after Patty, but Julian has his arm around her, the fingers of his hand dipping lightly into the pocket of her jeans. Marcus is amazed at the ease with which his brother can slip his fingers into someone else's pants. Now Patty laughs at something Julian says, and on a whim Marcus decides to shadow them.

They walk to Averill Park, an urban oasis of meandering streams and shady groves that evoke weddings, family picnics, and teenage groping. It's curiously empty today. Marcus keeps a safe distance back. Julian's been gone several months and Marcus has no idea what he's doing, although he's certain it's illegal. He wants a window into his brother's life since, in a strange way, he misses him. Julian and Patty walk around a pond and disappear in a copse of pine trees. Marcus has never done this before, follow someone like a spy, and he feels a churning in his stomach. Something is making him hesitate. The late-afternoon light slants through the trees and hits the surface of the pond, where it shatters into a million diamonds, sparkling on the water. He knows this is something he shouldn't be doing, but the treachery excites him. He is invading Julian's privacy, betraying him. But hadn't Julian fired him from the ticket-scalping business? Marcus doesn't owe him anything. Besides, he is curious. When he comes upon them in the darkening glade, Patty is on her knees in front of Julian, and he is in her mouth. Marcus has never had a blow job, so along with shock he feels jealousy, doubly so since Julian was getting one from Patty DeWitt, whose thick red hair is lustrous against Julian's black jeans. Oh, for a blow job, Marcus thinks. How is it that Julian, who ignores every boundary, is the one moving in and out of Patty DeWitt's mouth? Doesn't being good count for something? What is wrong with the world? Marcus wants to back up, step away, leave the park, allay the shame he is feeling for watching his brother and this girl, for rending their intimacy with his presence, but he is held there by a force he does not understand and he keeps looking until Julian arches his back. Marcus can't tell what happens next, whether Patty does something, or says something, or maybe it is nothing at all, but it causes Julian to smash her face with his open palm so hard that she falls to the ground. Marcus doesn't know some people like getting slapped. He is shocked by the sudden spasm of violence and, without thinking, he emerges from his hiding place and walks toward them. He is not a hero, does not want to be Superman, has no idea what he is doing other than maybe this will be a welcome opportunity to kick the shit out of his brother. Julian looks up. He is zipping his fly as Patty, her lip bleeding, struggles to her feet.

"Julian!" Marcus says. Julian's grin is lopsided, too cool. Patty looks at Marcus, startled.

"Get outta here!" she shouts, her voice like broken glass. He is confused. Is she yelling at his brother? Marcus asks her if she is okay. "Get the fuck outta here!" she says. She is addressing Marcus. Julian does not say anything. He looks vaguely amused as if they are playing a game and now he is bored. Marcus feels the air going out of him.

Patty says nothing, but her eyes are untamed. Marcus does not know what else to do, so he turns and runs through the trees, around the pond, to the road and out of the park, and keeps running until he arrives at the cliffs overlooking the Pacific Ocean where, gasping for breath, he sits down. It is early evening and the sun has dipped below the horizon, leaving the sky a purple bruise. Marcus knows Julian lives in a dark place. He didn't know he would hit a girl, but it does not surprise him. What freaks Marcus out is the way Patty reacts. It's like she is mad at *him* for intruding, and at fifteen that is entirely too difficult for him to get a handle on. Julian's mojo works on her, and Patty DeWitt isn't the only one. Marcus sees it when his brother is doing business with strangers at concerts, how he handles them, how he sells them. Julian gets what he wants.

Marcus finished his drink and poured another. The house was muffled in sleep. Images of Julian kept coming. As Marcus matured, he tried to see his brother as a wild child, refusing to be constrained by the dictates of bourgeois society—someone who merely wanted to roam free. But he knew in his heart that this was a fancy excuse. Julian was a criminal, and though Marcus could tie this up in theoretical ribbons and bows, there was no avoiding it. He drained the remains of the second whiskey, put fresh water in Bertrand Russell's dish and went to bed.

Marcus glanced at the digital clock on the night table and saw that he'd been lying there for nearly an hour. Propping himself on his elbow, he gazed at his soundly sleeping wife and found himself experiencing, along with deep fatigue, a sense of great comfort at her presence. He watched Jan for a moment, her chest rising and falling rhythmically, a few strands of hair in her face. He felt the urge to reach over and caress her cheek but didn't want to wake her up.

The next day, Marcus drove down a dicey stretch of Beverly Boulevard looking for an address. Half an hour after Officer Vasquez had left, a lawyer had called, summoning Marcus to his office to discuss Julian's will. What could Julian possibly have bequeathed him? When their parents had died—his mother seven years before, of a bad heart, and his father four years later, from cancer—Julian hadn't come to the funerals, hadn't sent flowers, couldn't be bothered. Family meant nothing to him, so what did this meeting portend? Marcus would have preferred not to think about it, but a combination of his brutal financial situation and his innate curiosity left him anticipating the meeting with something bordering on eagerness.

"So, Dominic, how did my brother die?"

Dominic Festa, Esq., had an aversion to giving people painful news, particularly when it involved death, and it was this weakness that had brought Officer Vasquez to the doorstep of the Ripps family the previous evening. Dominic had diverted moneys from another client's estate to the Policeman's Teddy Bear Fund in return for their services as a bad-tidings delivery system. So he paused before saying: "Bum ticker."

As Julian's attorney and the executor of his will, Dominic needed to see Marcus. Normally, the lawyer for an estate simply sends a letter explaining what was to be done on the deceased client's behalf but, since Julian's state of affairs was slightly unusual, Dominic thought a face-to-face meeting would be beneficial. This was how Marcus came to be sitting in the office Dominic shared with a usurious lender above the Primo World Laundromat on Beverly Boulevard, just east of La Brea (a large sign in their window read: BAD CREDIT? NO PROBLEM! WE'LL LEND TO YOU!!).

Overweight and balding, Dominic wore a green polo shirt under a brown blazer, cream slacks, and brown shoes, one of which rested languidly on a knee as he leaned back in his imitation-leather desk chair. His earth-toned wardrobe lent him the mien of a large, benevolent woodland creature, and he chortled as he recalled his dealings with Julian, whom he referred to fondly as "Your fuckin' brother." Marcus wasn't sure he'd heard right when Dominic described Julian as a *pip*, but he wanted to seem casual, to appear successful—to project anything other than desperation—so he said "Definitely. A pip." He nearly cringed as the words came out of his mouth. A *pip*? Julian had been a braggart and a bully. Frankly, he had been a

70

sociopath. But Marcus didn't need to get into any of that with Dominic Festa, Esq.

"Me and him flew to Bangkok one time, Thailand?" Dominic continued, as if Marcus was not aware of where it was. "Julian knew that fuckin' town, right? All the bars and shows? Two of us spent the whole time in Patpong, saw girls do shit with their pussies the Ringling Brothers couldna thought of." He smiled warmly at the recollection. "I'm telling you . . . it was always a party when he was around." Here his voice trailed off, having gone soft at the recollection of his deceased client and the Garden of Earthly Delights, to which Julian admitted anyone with a major credit card. Then, regaining a soupçon of the probity he felt was professionally necessary, Dominic said, "You're his brother, so you know, right?"

"Sure, right."

"Here's basically what we're looking at. Julian lived better than he earned, which wouldn't surprise anybody who ever saw his house . . . some place, right?" Marcus nodded, although he had never seen the house in question. "Fact is, the IRS is gonna seize it. What I'm saying is, forget the house. He had some jewelry, which I'm having valued—believe me, it won't be worth much . . ." Marcus knew that when someone like Dominic Festa said *believe me*, it was the last thing he should do. But he also quickly realized that pursuing the imagined bounty of Julian's estate would be fruitless. ". . . and some clothes, and about the clothes let me say that unless you have a forty-two-inch waistline, and looking at you I can pretty much see you don't, you might as well forget those, too." Marcus shifted uncomfortably in his seat, recalibrating his already low expectations.

"I'll tell you right now, the IRS is dunning him and I think they're gonna take the cash reserve in the estate—but don't worry, it's minuscule anyway. He held the lease on an apartment Beverly Hills-adjacent, you might want to look at it if you're in the market for a sugar shack." Dominic winked at Marcus, who was too crestfallen to notice.

Would there be nothing positive to emerge from Julian's untimely demise? "*However*"—the lawyer said this word with such emphasis that Marcus resumed paying attention—"He did own a business, a dry cleaning operation on Melrose in West Hollywood." Marcus's visage sparked, almost as if the electrical current running in his body had suddenly shifted course. This reaction caused Dominic to instantly adjust his message. "Now don't get your hopes up, he doesn't own the building, but he's been running the business out of there for more than five years and, according to the will, it belongs to you, my friend."

"A dry cleaner?" Marcus said this with a degree of hopefulness not generally associated with those two words. To him they represented nothing less than deliverance from his predicament. "How many people does he employ?"

"I have no idea. I'm his lawyer, not his accountant."

"Is there anyone I can talk to?"

Festa removed a small, slightly soiled envelope from his desk drawer and handed it to Marcus. "Here's the key. And you might want this, too." He gave Marcus a cell phone and told him it was Julian's. Marcus was puzzled, but realized perhaps the lawyer thought he might want a keepsake, something personal of his brother's. So he thanked him and slid the phone, a thin silver item with a camera lens, into his pocket. Dominic Festa gave Marcus his card, told him to call if he had any questions, and wished him good luck.

Marcus left the office supremely thankful his run of bad luck had abated. Some men were meant to cure diseases, others to explore new planets. The world needed dry cleaners, and if that was Marcus's fate, at this point he saw no alternative to pursuing it. Potentially freed from the horror show of his family's financial implosion, he was slightly giddy. The complexities of running a business didn't matter, the health hazards of a carcinogen-intensive industry were irrelevant, and the hours he would be forced to work—as a sole proprietor, since he realized no one could be trusted to not skim the proceeds—didn't strike him as onerous. Marcus pictured himself smiling rakishly on the cover of *American Drycleaner,* clad in an expensive bespoke suit, freshly dry-cleaned.

Chapter 7

Jan sat behind the cash register of Ripcord, saying good-bye to Marcus, who had called to inform her of this encouraging turn of events. Although she was pleased by the excitement in his voice, she wondered at the strangeness of his news and what it actually boded for their family. What if this new business turned out to be a reliable source of income? The novelty of running a boutique had worn off after the first few months, and the ongoing struggle to keep it afloat was a source of constant low-level tension. Jan eyed a young woman, with cropped, zebra-striped hair and a lip ring, fingering a rack of Lycra bustiers, and reflected that it was unlikely this person would purchase anything. She hated worrying about it. The idea of dry cleaning may not have quickened her heartbeat, but at least it was popular. The doors opened, the customers arrived. You could get accustomed to that.

Plum was standing at the front of the store, contemplating the window display, devouring another fruit and nut bar. After a moment she stepped into the window and made a slight adjustment to a mannequin's head. Satisfied, she swallowed the remainder of her snack and sauntered toward the cash register. Jan told her the news.

"He's going to be a *dry cleaner?*" she said. Her tone was slightly patronizing.

"What's wrong with that?"

"Nothing, nothing. It's just kind of, I don't know, incredibly boring?" Jan let the remark just hang there. Plum gave a little laugh. "Who would have thought I'd marry a lawyer and you'd hook up with a dry cleaner? Weren't you hoping things would be a little jazzier?"

"If the choice is between having a husband who's unemployed and one who's a dry cleaner . . ." Jan didn't bother to finish the point. She was annoyed by Plum's attitude and was about to tell her that if this new venture succeeded, she intended to bail out of Ripcord. But before she could, Plum said "I sent an e-mail to Crystal last night, and she answered me this morning."

"Crystal?"

"My egg donor, remember?" Jan had only been half-listening, as had become her habit, during that monologue. "I had to get in line to meet with this girl—she probably does this a lot. Anyway, before I get started . . ." here she offered a little half-smile meant to suggest an impish insouciance ". . . I need to ask you one thing. The procedure costs nearly nine thousand dollars, and that's just for one cycle, closer to sixteen for three." She paused for a breath, as if she was exhausted by the effort of imparting the previous information. Taking advantage of the halt in Plum's spiel, Jan jumped in.

"I wish I could lend you the money, but we're broke."

"I wasn't going to ask you to lend me money," Plum said. Jan wondered if she had actually planned on doing exactly that. "But I'd like your eggs."

"*My* eggs?" This request was alarmingly personal, and Jan's hand reflexively flew to her abdomen. "Really? Plum! Oooo, this is weird . . ."

"I know, I know . . . but mine are all messed up and we're close and . . . you know . . . it's a good cause. This project is going to be *amazing*."

"Whose sperm are you going to use? Because I thought you said . . ."

"I found some on eBay."

Jan ran her fingers along the countertop, the touch of something solid allowing her to believe she was still in the known world. She began to shake her head.

"Online sperm? Really? What do you know about the donor?"

"He's a college graduate."

Jan pointed out that he could just as easily be an ex-con with a family history of mental illness and a symphony of STDs as yet undiscovered.

This was Plum's response: "I won't videotape the part where I get the eggs implanted if you don't want. I'm taping everything else for the piece. I told you that. Didn't I? Of course I did. You said it was a *home movie*. At least think about it."

Jan was not a confrontational person under normal circumstances and knew the quickest way to change the subject was to agree to consider the request.

Plum was too overjoyed to divine the timbre of Jan's answer. Had she done so, she would have understood that what her friend had meant to say was please don't ask me such a bizarre thing again. But having heard what she wanted to hear, Plum said good-bye, telling Jan she was going on a lunch break. Jan wondered how she was going to inform Plum that under no circumstances would she willingly pry a single egg from her precious ovary, given the stated purpose of the request.

Shining City Dry Cleaner was at the corner of Melrose and Gehenna, near several overpriced purveyors of trendy fashion and grooming ephemera favored by the young and feckless. Marcus parked his Honda Civic on a side street, and, as he emerged on Melrose, walked past a small theater emblazoned with a banner for its current show, *The Boys of Northanger Abbey*, a musical adaptation of the Jane Austen novel.

Everyone on this West Hollywood sidewalk was slim, youthful, and attractive. The women obviously paid a great deal of attention to their physical presentation, and the men were either gay or undeclared.

There was nary a stroller in sight, only disposable income as far as the eye could see. The locals wore the kind of two-hundred-dollar ripped jeans that required dry cleaning. Marcus was nearly salivating at his prospects as he opened the glass door and walked into a new life.

Velour curtains obscured the windows and rendered the interior more shadowy than the usual Melrose establishment. Several cheap oil paintings done in lurid colors lined the walls, all with religious themes. There was a robed St. Augustine chockablock with Moses holding a staff above his head, adjacent to a multi-armed Vishnu, looking at a reclining Buddha resting on the opposite wall. What was this religious iconography doing here? Marcus surmised that it belonged to whoever had owned the business before Julian.

Behind the Formica counter hovered a motorized rack on which a profusion of plastic-encased garments hung like swollen fruit waiting to be picked. Along with the religious art were framed and autographed glossies of entertainment personalities Marcus had never heard of who, he assumed, had brought their clothes to be freshened on the premises. Perhaps Julian gave these people discounts in the hope that the presence of their signed likenesses would impress the hoi polloi and thus increase business. Marcus made a mental note to learn about marketing in the dry cleaning world. But why was the place not open? Where were the customers? He looked into the shadowy depths and saw a door.

Flipping on the light, Marcus found himself gazing upon a room furnished with two chairs and a desk with a telephone and a laptop computer. Everything appeared utterly ordinary, and this baffled him. What had Julian meant in leaving Shining City to Marcus? Was it a gesture of goodwill from the depths of a life marked by its total absence? An apology for the thoughtless manner he had treated his mother, father, and brother? Was it a plaintive plea for forgiveness from beyond the grave? Marcus couldn't divine Julian's intention, but he felt grateful for what his brother had done. Ultimately, the reason didn't matter, and he had given up trying to fathom Julian years earlier anyway.

So Marcus made plans. A coffeemaker would allow him to spend the days well caffeinated and present an upbeat face to his new customers, whose loyalty he would earn with the crackerjack service he intended to provide. Perhaps he would offer favored customers free coffee. He would have cups made with SHINING CITY emblazoned on the side so they would see the name of his business when they took their coffee on the road and be reminded of his friendliness and generosity. He would purchase a sound system and have music playing, nothing too jangly and off-putting, but nothing that implied New Age soft-headedness either. Maybe Chet Baker.

Marcus was navigating his way through the files on the laptop (mostly pornography and gambling) when a someone walked in and said "Who are you?" in a European accent whose exact geographical origins he couldn't place but sensed was an area of whimsical castles, bad food, and a tortured relationship with Russia. Looking up from a card-counting program, Marcus saw a tall, slender woman with shoulder-length platinum blonde hair just beginning to go dark at the roots. She wore tight jeans, a ribbed forest-green sweater, and blue cowboy boots. A red purse hung from her shoulder, and she was holding a large cup of coffee with a lipstick smudge on the rim. Her skin was pale, and as she removed her sunglasses, Marcus guessed she was around thirty. He sensed that she hadn't slept much the previous night.

He got up from the desk and introduced himself. Then he extended his hand, which she shook perfunctorily. Her skin felt cool, and he wondered if she was one of those people with below-normal body temperatures.

"Where is Juice?" *Juice?* Was that Julian's nickname?

"You haven't heard?" Marcus was suddenly dreading the remainder of this exchange. She could be someone to whom Julian was close—a girlfriend perhaps, or, worse, an ex-wife. "He's dead—heart attack."

Looking away from Marcus for a moment to absorb this information, she nodded her head, conveying that it was not entirely unexpected. Greatly relieved that no histrionics had ensued, Marcus asked the woman her name.

"Amstel." She told him she was sorry for his loss. Then she said "Are you taking over business?"

"Yes."

"So this is for you." She removed an envelope from her purse and handed it to him. The envelope was unsealed and, looking in it, Marcus saw a wad of cash. He was nonplussed for a moment. He took out the money and quickly counted eighteen hundred dollars, in twenties, fifties, and hundreds. Was she a delivery person for Shining City? It occurred to him that collecting payment at the time of delivery was not the most efficient way to run a dry cleaning business. "How many people does Julian have working for him?"

"About twenty, maybe," Amstel said.

Now Marcus was genuinely confused. Unless there was a volume of business that the relatively modest-seeming operation did not seem able to support, he had no idea how it could sustain a workforce that size.

He found himself involuntarily nodding his head, as if to say Twenty! Of course! But what he said was "Really?" which didn't do much to hide his surprise.

"It varies. Girls take time off . . . go . . . come back. Okay I smoke?"

"Sure." Marcus hated cigarette smoke, couldn't be around it. But, too intrigued to care, he gestured to the Naugahyde chair opposite the desk. Had she just described the workforce as entirely female? The *girls* take time off? The delivery drivers, the cashiers, the people who did the actual cleaning—all women? Perhaps that was Julian's gimmick, although Marcus couldn't imagine it was much of a selling point in the dry cleaning industry. He dimly recalled hearing about a topless gas station out in the desert a few years earlier, but Shining City did not appear to be that kind of operation.

Amstel seemed happy to take the weight off her feet as she settled into the chair. She rummaged in her purse, pulled out a pack of clove cigarettes and a lighter, placed one to her lips, and lit it. Drawing deeply, she exhaled the smoke and said "You seem kind of normal for someone related to a guy like Juice."

"How so?"

"He was a freak." Marcus liked her accent, which reminded him of a cheesy sixties spy movie. He imagined it emanating in sultry tones from a trenchcoat-clad lady Communist who secretly wanted to tumble with the American hero. She crossed her slender legs, one thigh over another. "So, Marcus . . ." Amstel continued in her spy movie accent. "Anything for me tonight?" This was what he was dreading: having to reveal the extent of his ignorance. He knew enough about running a company to recognize that workforce motivation depended on making workers believe in management's essential grasp of how the business functioned. That meant a familiarity with each worker's job, and an understanding of the essential role played by that employee within the larger organization. What then, he wondered, was Amstel's responsibility?

"Any . . .?" He said this in hopes of getting her to provide the information he lacked. But either she did not pick up on his total absence of expertise or chose to ignore it, because she took this moment to examine the fingernails of her right hand, which were covered with metallic blue polish. Marcus's own hands, which had been resting on his lap, moved away from his body. His elbows remained slightly bent, and his palms turned up as if to say help me out, please.

Amstel noticed this gesture and, turning her attention from her manicure, she said "Dates, Marcus. I have SUV to pay off. Some guy who likes Greek would be good. Juice told you that costs double, right? Triple if he's Arab."

At that moment, Marcus realized that he had misheard Dominic Festa when he'd said Julian was a *pip*.

Chapter 8

It was a disorientating sensation, as if he'd been exploring a Pacific atoll and had come upon a production of *Porgy and Bess* being performed by a cast of house cats. Several seconds passed before Marcus realized that his jaw had dropped open. Amstel was blowing smoke rings. He hoped she hadn't noticed. Marcus could have asked her to leave, then departed himself, locking the door behind him permanently. Could have gone home to Van Nuys and resumed his search for a more conventional way to salvage his professional life and so continue to bear the burden of his responsibilities. He could have tried to help Jan turn Ripcord into a sustainable business. He could have packed his family up and moved them to a new, less expensive place to live, undergone retraining in another field and remained in mainstream society. But he did none of these things. Instead, he remained in his chair and looked at Amstel. She had an oval face with a pert nose and large blue eyes he wanted to luxuriate in. Her mouth curled upward in a look of bemusement, her delicately glossed lips full. She seemed in no hurry.

Marcus was not certain whether he had ever been in such close proximity to a prostitute before. Certainly, he had seen them on the street, on the eastern reaches of Sunset Boulevard and in the shabbier parts of Hollywood, wearing impossibly short skirts, tight jackets, and fuck-me shoes. But those were streetwalkers, something the woman in front of him was not. Occasionally, he glanced at the ads in the back of the local alternative weekly. These contained a constantly regenerating fantasia of women and men who, for a fee, were available to perform acts unimaginable to him. In the rare instances Marcus looked at them, it was only to marvel at the army of people operating in this below-the-radar world and wonder what they told their families they did for a living. He noticed a paperback book peeking out of Amstel's purse. "What are you reading?" he asked, unable to think of anything else to say.

"Short stories," she said, and mentioned a female writer with a foreign-sounding name Marcus had never heard. "So far I'm not liking them much. Too minimalist." (When she said it, it came out "meena-malist".) Marcus's eyebrows lifted. *Too minimalist?* Clearly Amstel was not what he had in mind when he thought about women in her line of work. "So, Marcus . . ."—she let a jet of smoke stream out of her mouth—"What's going on later?" *Later* was "lay-toor," a sound he found strangely alluring.

He thought for a moment, or at least he pretended to be thinking (the realization of her sexual availability was causing his brain to momentarily function like a third world power grid). Then he said: "I'm not sure." He had to say something. It wasn't as if he could just keep sitting across from her, attempting to appear enigmatic. The room, which was not well ventilated, was starting to fill with the cancerous effluvia of Amstel's lungs. He didn't want to alienate the woman by requesting that she extinguish her cigarette, so he was greatly relieved when she took another drag and then, removing the top of her coffee cup, sent the butt to a wet Colombian death. Marcus usually found that disgusting, but today he was too distracted to mind.

So what he said was this: "Amstel, as you can imagine, I'm still pretty upset about Julian."

"Me too."

That was encouraging. Heartened, he pressed on. "See, he was my only sibling and I haven't really processed his, uhh . . . you know . . . umm . . . *death*. So . . ." Then he searched his mind for a plan because he had none, other than somehow finding a new and reliable revenue stream with which he could support his family and attend to their needs. "Can this wait until tomorrow?"

As he uttered these words, another young woman came into the office. After greeting Amstel and learning Marcus's identity, she introduced herself as Cortina and handed him an envelope stuffed with cash. Then the two women gave him their beeper numbers and left.

Marcus retrieved Dominic Festa's card from his wallet and immediately dialed his cell phone number. The lawyer picked up on the third ring.

"Does the dry cleaner actually do business as a dry cleaner?" Marcus asked, not bothering to say hello.

"It's a dry cleaner."

"So it does *business* as a dry cleaner."

"That, my friend, is not what I said. What I *said* was 'it's a dry cleaner.' "

"I know what you *said*, but that's not what I'm *asking*."

"Is it a dry cleaner, per se? That would depend."

"On what?"

"On what the owner of the business wanted to do with it."

"Did my brother run it as a dry cleaner?"

"Let me just say this: As far as I know, his tax return said that yes he *was* in the dry cleaning business. As far as whether or not any individual actually got their clothes dry cleaned on those premises, I can't speak to that."

During the conversation with Festa, Marcus had the sensation that he'd tumbled off a promontory, one from which he'd been happily surveying the abundant land below. Now he was falling through blackness and picking up speed. When Marcus hung up after thanking the lawyer for clarifying the situation, he remembered that he had Julian's cell phone in his pocket, and it took on new significance now that his brother's life was coming into sharper focus. Marcus had read enough accounts of crime in the popular press to know that cell phones of various criminals contained information that those who worked in law enforcement found extremely helpful. They often contained a record not only of outgoing calls but of incoming ones as well. Marcus realized that he could begin to ascertain the salient details of Julian's world if he could unlock the labyrinthine secrets therein.

If he wanted to.

Which he didn't.

Marcus was in shock. He left moments after the women, and found himself back at his car having no idea how he'd gotten there, because he'd been thinking about his grandfather.

When Marcus was ten years old, his paternal grandmother died and his grandfather Mickey moved in with the family. He had been a stevedore on the Dublin waterfront and made it to America on a freighter, sailing halfway around the world before landing in Long Beach. He found his way to San Pedro, which, with its rolling topography and adjacent harbor, bore a certain resemblance to a more sun-baked County Cork, a quality that attracted more than a few Irish, many of whom worked unloading cargo from around the world. Mickey's convivial nature and his beer barrel build got him work on the docks, and, by being willing to break a few rules, he was able to provide for his family in a way he could not have imagined in Ireland.

The docks of San Pedro were an El Dorado to their immigrant workforce, a treasure trove of waterborne goods arriving in such volume that they could be easily plundered. And Mickey, performing backbreaking labor over long shifts, was never one to miss an opportunity. As a result, there was a room in his bungalow always stuffed with appliances, radios, crates of canned food: anything that moved through the Port of Los Angeles and could be transported without a forklift. These items were sold at a discount to local consumers and eventually allowed Mickey to buy a big-finned Cadillac in which he glided along hilly roads like a seaside king, arm out the side, face to the New World sun.

Only vaguely aware of Mickey's activities, Marcus was devastated when his grandfather was busted after an FBI investigation of the Long-shoreman's Union and wound up doing two years for racketeering. Traveling to Terminal Island to visit him was a great disincentive to a life of crime. When Mickey was released, he moved in with Marcus's family. The time in the stir had diminished him, dimmed his bright immigrant eyes, and though he was only in his early sixties he looked a decade older. He would often play checkers with Marcus and Julian and regale them with tales of his Dublin boyhood and his realization at a young age that the world was fixed. With a voice that sounded like broken rocks in a bag, he'd tell his grandsons: *The lad who don't do it gets done himself.* Shy boy Marcus listened to the stories with a degree of diffidence, drawn to the edge of the fire, then stepping back from the heat to imagined safety. But to audacious Julian, Mickey was a Celtic Sheherazade, a raffish spinner of tales so seductive that they could provide the map of a life. Mickey met his maker in the hold of a freighter when he was crushed by a five-hundred-pound crate of mayonnaise he was trying to steal. His devilish spirit skipped a generation, took a look at Marcus, said no, thank you, and landed squarely in Julian's breast.

With this slide show flashing in his head, Marcus managed to navigate through West Hollywood to the Cahuenga Pass, where he picked up the 101 freeway. Merging into the light afternoon traffic, he drove west, again attempting to divine the true nature of Julian's bequest. That they hadn't been speaking when Julian died made parsing the situation particularly difficult. It wasn't like they had ever really talked anyway, ever expressed anything resembling their actual feelings for each other beyond the subtle contempt that is the lingua franca of so many sibling relationships. What was Julian trying to convey with this ludicrous last will and testament?

Berkeley. Sophomore year: Marcus is in his dorm room one evening, writing a paper on John Locke's theory of knowledge, when Julian appears like an apparition. His clothes are dirty and he smells like a bong. Julian tells him he's in trouble: There's a business deal with some Mexicans and he owes them five thousand dollars. What kind of deal? Never mind. They aren't playing, Julian says, and if I don't get the money and hand it over, they're going to carve me up. Marcus listens to this story, his soft palm on the open copy of Locke's *Essay Concerning Human Understanding* he's highlighted with yellow magic marker, his heart rate increasing with each detail. He doesn't have five thousand dollars. What do you want me to do? Come to Mexico with me, Julian says. I can buy enough dope down there to make a ten-thousand-dollar profit. But I thought you don't have any money, Marcus says. How are you going to buy it? On credit! Marcus can't believe what he's hearing. You're going to buy pot on credit? So you can pay off these guys who want to kill you? I need you to drive my car north across the border, Julian says. I don't want to do it alone and I need you to help me. Can't you get someone else, Marcus says. Julian's pupils are dilated and his foot jiggles madly. You're my brother. I'm asking you. Marcus wants Julian to leave. His roommate is due back from the library soon, and he doesn't want him to walk in on this. I'll pick you up tomorrow morning at ten, Julian says, and we'll be in Tijuana by dinner time. Okay, Marcus tells him. I'll see you then. Marcus leaves his dormitory that night and stays with a friend in Oakland. He remains there for three days, figuring Julian won't hang around. He never mentions the encounter to anyone. A year later, Marcus's parents tell him they've heard from Julian. That is when he finds out the Mexicans haven't killed his brother.

The smell of marijuana smacked him in the face the second he opened the front door of his house. It's almost as if Julian is breathing on me from beyond the grave, Marcus thought. He had discussed this indiscriminate dope smoking with Lenore, asked her to confine it to her room, and then only after placing a rolled-up towel against the door frame. But before Marcus could locate her and unload the requisite opprobrium, he heard voices and then laughter in the kitchen. Lenore's high-pitched giggle was easy to discern, but the other voice was lower, male, the accent an unfamiliar blend of foreign places.

When Marcus walked into the kitchen, he saw a large young man with his feet planted firmly on the floor, knees bent—his hand raised as if to strike. The man looked as if he was getting ready to decapitate Lenore, who was calmly smoking a spliff the size of a plantain.

"Smash elbow like this," the guy said. "Crush windpipe." Then he looked at Marcus and with a tilt of his head performed an instantaneous how-long-will-it-take-me-to-destroy-you? evaluation. Answer: two seconds.

"This is Kostya," Lenore said, exhaling a cloud of smoke. "He worked for your brother." She coughed and immediately took another hit.

Marcus figured Kostya was somewhere in his twenties. A pile of dark dreadlocks bloomed from his head, tips dipped in gold. He wore a maroon tracksuit with parallel black stripes running up the pants and sleeves, Nike hightops on his large feet. And he was big, maybe 6′4″ with a broad chest. A sweeping side kick from this person would crush someone's head like a cantaloupe.

"You look like him, only he outweigh you by hundred pounds, maybe," Kostya said, leaning against the counter.

"Lenore . . ." Marcus said, indicating the spliff. "I asked you not to . . ."

"Chill, Daddy," Kostya said, implying that if Marcus didn't relax, he would be forced to. Lenore informed him she had been smoking—"For *medical* reasons!"—when Kostya showed up. Upon learning of her affinity for pot, he offered her some of his own, she said, "like a gentleman."

Marcus was already so unsettled by what he'd recently learned that he immediately reassessed his inclination to get into house rules with

Lenore. "Do you work at the dry cleaner?" Marcus's voice came out evenly. He was pleased he had reasserted control over his recalcitrant nervous system. It helped immensely that Kostya, at least for the moment, did not seem intent on causing grievous bodily harm.

"Juice my nigga," he said. While Kostya paused, Marcus noted the use of *my nigga* to describe the relationship, since Kostya appeared to be white.

"So you know he's dead?"

"I told the fat mo'fucka cut down on chee'boorgers." The accent was Moscow homeboy, some strange linguistic hybrid, borne on the epic wave of hip-hop that had encircled the globe in the years since Marcus had stopped paying attention to pop culture and had taken root in the unlikeliest of places. "For his own good, you know . . . showing man some love."

"I'm going to make pancakes," Lenore said, removing a box from the cupboard. "Anybody want some?"

"That's brownie mix," Marcus told her. Then, turning his attention to Kostya: "I'm taking over the business." Taking over the business? Why had he said this? When it was a simple dry cleaner, maybe. But now his plans needed to be reassessed, re-imagined. Retrofitted. He looked at Lenore, who was staring at the box trying to get her dull eyes to focus.

"Juice owe me five hundred dollar when he die. I got plans, Gangstaboy."

Marcus didn't need this guy in his kitchen. He just wanted to go upstairs and cogitate on the cosmic seltzer bottle Julian was spraying in his face. He could have given Kostya the money Amstel and Cortina had paid him, but why should he? *Am I my brother's bookkeeper?* "I'll write you a check," Marcus said. He knew he could stop a check.

"Personal checks shit to me."

"I don't have cash on me right now."

"Then we go ATM."

"Whoa, whoa . . . I'm not responsible for his debts . . ."

89

"You take over bid'ness!"

"I know, but . . ."

"*But,* shit, yo! We go ATM. I drive."

Marcus had already lied about not having the money on him and could have saved himself the trip, but he didn't know how Kostya would react to being lied to. He felt as if he was being kidnapped, but his mother-in-law was rummaging in the cabinet for maple syrup when the two men left.

The Shining City van had been parked down the street from his house when Marcus had arrived home, but he had been too distracted to notice. It had three rows of passenger seats and no clothing racks. A residue of incense hung in the air, its particles microscopically pulsing to the beat emanating from the car stereo Kostya had installed "to create pleasing environment for ladies." Marcus slumped in the passenger seat and Kostya drove, rattling on about what it was like working for Julian (not good) and how glad he was to be leaving the business.

"How long you been working for my brother?" Marcus wanted to know, dropping the word *have* from the question in an unacknowledged attempt to emulate Kostya's international street patois.

"Almost three year," Kostya said. "Three long year."

"And you did what?"

"This and that."

"This and that . . . what? Did you do his taxes?" It pleased Marcus that he was now relaxed enough to joke.

"His *texes*?" Kostya snorted. "You funny, Gangstaboy." Marcus was pleased—the kid actually seemed to mean it. "Mo'fucka was pimp! Was not paying mo'fucking texes!" which, when Kostya said it, sounded like *Texas.* Marcus managed to learn that Kostya served as a driver, personal assistant, and general factotum for Julian and seemed to know a fair amount about how the business worked. Upon the realization that he possessed information that could be beneficial, Marcus changed his mind about trying to avoid paying the debt.

The two men were standing in the parking lot of the Ralphs Supermarket on Saticoy Street. Marcus was staring at the cash machine, which, having done a quick computer check of his status as a bank customer, had eaten his card and was refusing to return it. He felt Kostya's eyes on him. Marcus knew that if he gave Kostya the money in his pocket, he might never see him again. Ten minutes ago, that would have been a welcome thought, but now he wasn't so sure. Who knew what hidden knowledge the man possessed? Marcus needed time to think about the choice facing him. If he wanted to ask questions, Kostya was the Rosetta Stone.

"I don't know what's going on with the card, but I'll get it for you by tomorrow." Kostya stared at him suspiciously. "Look, it's not like you don't know where I live."

Marcus was thankful when Kostya scribbled his phone number on a piece of paper instead of beating him to death in the parking lot.

Chapter 9

Rain rarely came to southern California in early October, but it had started to drizzle and the water was running down the windshield of the car as Marcus pulled off the verdant Winthrop Hall campus. Nathan sat in the front seat while his classmates Josh Flicker and Lyric Melchior slouched in back. Marcus thought Nathan had a crush on Lyric, a cute girl with braces and a sprinkling of freckles, and would have preferred sitting next to her. He also knew seventh grade etiquette required that he take the coveted passenger seat, which, to the average twelve-year-old, crooned of the adult pleasures that waited if only they could navigate the pimply shoals of adolescence. Marcus was half-listening as the kids yammered about a recent contretemps—a girl in the eighth grade at Winthrop Hall had taken nude self-portraits and forwarded them to her boyfriend online. He sent them to his friends, who sent them to their friends, and that day the girl's family had been called in for a chat with the headmaster. Ordinarily this would have interested Marcus, but today the children's words hung in a cloud about his head, failing to penetrate his consciousness.

Marcus gripped the wheel a little tighter than usual, reflecting on the highly unusual situation in which he found himself as they cruised through the dirty rain down Laurel Canyon Boulevard toward Temple B'nai Jesherun. What would it be like, he wondered, to step into Julian's business? To make that kind of money? To have that kind of life? It was difficult for him to even take the questions seriously, but still he asked them. Marcus knew, no matter how much of a swash-buckler he might be in his dreams, no matter how many mountains he'd climbed, seas and deserts he'd crossed, no matter how many extraordinary, exhilarating, shoot-the-moon adventures he'd had in the confines of his own head, whenever he'd been given an opportunity to do something out of the ordinary in his real life, he had balked; punted the chance; rolled over and died a little. Even when he and Roon went to Europe in 1989 following the fall of the Berlin Wall. Young and free and still in the thrall of his undergraduate preoccupations, it had been the perfect time to make a pilgrimage to the birthplaces of Kant, Hegel, Nietzsche, and Schopenhauer, to journey further east and see the ravages of Communism up close, meet newly liberated, young blonde women whose evil leaders had been vanquished and wanted to show their gratitude by having sex with Americans, something of which Roon was only too happy to take advantage.

In Hamburg, Roon led them to an S&M club. Marcus lasted until a leather-clad Rumanian dominatrix inquired in a bats-and-vampires accent *Do you want to have some fun?* Roon stayed and, when he returned to their hotel the next day, told Marcus about the impossibly limber Bavarian girl who liked to dress up as von Bismarck and would only let him fuck her if he wore a short skirt with an angora sweater and a pair of slingbacks. Marcus was appalled, but Roon was the one who'd gotten laid, and he laughed when he told the story.

Marcus knew this would be no different. Julian had been a miscreant his entire life, and this attitude led him ineluctably to becoming a procurer of human flesh. Marcus, on the other hand, was a maker of toys, a manufacturer of mirth and merriment. The chasm separating their worlds was too vast.

He would somehow get hold of the women who worked for Julian and tell them Shining City "dry cleaner" was going out of business. Once he had that settled in his mind, he looked forward to telling Jan the entire story.

Every time Marcus dropped the kids at Hebrew school, he said good-bye and then watched them walk into the building, a modest two-story white stucco structure whose utter lack of pretension appealed to the Ripps family. That day, he forgot to say anything and drove off the moment they climbed out of the car.

Marcus headed for the Paradise Room, an old-school Italian restaurant on Ventura with a dark bar decorated in early hired killer—red leather banquettes, impasto renderings of "Sunny Italy" on the walls, and on every table a white candle jammed into an empty Chianti bottle. Other than an old souse in a plaid shirt who sat at the end of the long oak bar reading the *Racing Form* through smudged pince-nez, Marcus was the only customer. He looked at the bartender, a sixty-something woman with hair dyed jet black and a smear of red lipstick looped across her mouth, and ordered a whiskey.

Marcus contemplated his life as he sipped the whiskey. He saw a glittery stage, on which there were three shiny curtains, a different prize behind each one. He opened the first and found a family. The second parted to reveal a man seated behind a desk going over endless ledgers beneath a frozen wall clock and a large sign that said, simply, WAZOO THANKS YOU! Behind the third curtain, as yet unopened, Marcus knew there was mystery, hope, the presumed happiness of dreams fulfilled. He longed to pull it aside, see what it concealed, yearned for an image that would provide the clue to a metamorphosis the nature of which he could not yet conceive. What would he change? Not his family, certainly, for he loved them and, other than his recent lack of physical intimacy with his wife, had little else to complain about. His livelihood? That was changing anyway, whether or not he liked it, but he thought, given his history, he would continue to labor in a traditional field.

What, then?

This: how he looked at the world and himself, how he viewed his life and the inner tape that played in his head and from which he took his cues. The one that said *stop, don't, I shouldn't.*

No longer even tasting the whiskey, Marcus parted the third curtain and saw a bare stage lit in a harsh white light, illuminating nothing but emptiness. It was devoid of anything. A repository of NOTHING.

"Refill, honey?"

Marcus glanced up from his stygian gloom and saw the lipstick-smeared face of the bartender looking at him. Her fake eyelashes reminded Marcus of the little hairs you could see on flies through a microscope. He tapped the rim of the glass with his forefinger.

The second whiskey unleashed the howling dogs, and he found himself starting to wrestle with this stasis, to bang against it, to see if he could jar something loose besides one of his teeth. Recently he had become cognizant of his gums for the first time in his life, after having eaten a piece of steak Jan had bought on sale. Soreness had developed along the gum line on the lower right side of his mouth. What was *that* about? Aging? Disintegration? What had he wanted to do when he was younger, before he had become a slave to his quotidian life? Surely that would provide some indication of the areas he should be considering now, the fields of endeavor that would benefit from his new enthusiasm. But he couldn't think of anything.

What opportunities were there for someone his age with a degree in philosophy and a singularly unimpressive list of contacts? His months of unemployment had provided a vivid answer. He gazed down at the bartender sipping gin and watching a bloviating television psychologist on the wall-mounted screen. What would this well-lit mental health professional tell him if he was seated onstage in the bright studio? This: With all the reading he'd done, with all the time and energy he'd spent examining esoteric belief systems, he should have chosen one by now.

Perhaps he could finally bring his collegiate philosophical rigor to bear on his own life. Marcus knew he didn't want to be a dry cleaner; knew that he'd leapt at the idea because it had taken form in the vacuum of depression, because at least it represented something real. But could he be Julian?

Nursing his drink, feeling its sting against his tongue, he thought:

Why *can't* I be a pimp? It's lucrative, it doesn't seem to involve much work, and the tax bite is nil. Here's *why*, his superego said: It's illegal, for starters. Highly illegal. If you're busted, jail looms, and all that implies for a soft fishbelly like you. You'd be processed in the morning, then gutted and boned, devoured by dinnertime, hard men picking your bits from between their bad teeth. The ignominy attached, impossible to underestimate, would make it necessary for you to conceal this activity from everyone you know, not to mention the IRS, who like to send people to a federal address for nonpayment of society's dues. When someone turns your way at a neighborhood party and asks, innocently enough, "what do you do?" you'll have to lie, which is what your whole life will become—a huge, fetid lie.

Then why not the dry cleaner? The dry cleaner was a lifeline.

That thought was quickly swamped by further ruminations. There was the question of ethics. But they were bendable and widely open to interpretation. Marcus began to consider Immanuel Kant and the categorical imperative. If faced with this situation, one must choose to . . . Then, suddenly, his mind swerved and he thought *Oh, forget Kant and his categorical imperative although I have to admit it's not entirely irrelevant to this but thinking about Kant is one more excuse not to do anything. And blow off Hegel and Nietzsche while we're at it, and the Stoics, and let's cut to the chase, draw some conclusions. What does this situation boil down to? What's the essence here? No, the* quintessence! *What is this about? Do I have a moral code? Should I? Is that even a relevant question? Do I care if I'm breaking the law? What kind of example will I be setting for Nathan? What happens if I get caught? Is anything more moral than taking care of my family? Can I get hurt, beaten, bloodied, shot? Shot! What would* that *be like? Could I wind up dead? Of course I could. You can get killed crossing Wilshire Boulevard. This has to be more dangerous than that. And if I'm dead, what happens then? Do I take that risk? Do I have enough insurance? Did my life insurance lapse? Shit! Did it? Am I tough enough to do this? Can I corral a bunch of prostitutes and make them listen? What would I say? How do you talk to that kind of group? Will they see right through me, or can I fake it? What if they laugh? Prostitutes laughing at me! Could anything be more humiliating? I could think of a few things, but that's right up there. Could I ever get over that, being laughed at by a roomful of prostitutes? Is prostitution a bad thing? I know everyone says it is, but is it? Could I have sex with the women? My wife has no interest, so that sounds pretty good, actually. I wouldn't mind having more sex. More sex would definitely be a good thing. Amstel was hot. I'd like to have sex with her. I wonder if she's gay? I've heard a lot of prostitutes are lesbians and hate men. She didn't seem to hate me, but maybe she was faking. I'm not a saint, although I try to pretend I'm one. I wouldn't even think about sex with Amstel if Jan would stop acting like sex was one more thing on her to-do list. Prostitution has always existed, hasn't it? There's obviously a reason for that. Why can't you give the people what they want? That's what free markets are for. Isn't that the whole idea America is built on? Isn't that why we're fighting wars? To keep markets open? For McDonald's? For Coke? What's the difference between Coke and pussy, anyway? At least pussy doesn't rot your teeth. Why do some people find the word pussy offensive? Cunt—now that's a bad word. I would never say cunt. It's disrespectful. I'm a feminist. I believe in equal pay for equal work, and access to abortion, but I still hold doors open. Would I be exploiting women? Aren't the prostitutes in Los Angeles doing it voluntarily? I know it's a whole other story in the third world, I've seen documentaries, the horrible lives, fifty cents for sex, and AIDS, and early death, but I'm talking about women who are making hundreds of dollars an hour in fancy hotels having sex with customers who probably put it on their expense accounts. Is what they're doing inherently bad? Who says it's bad? That's some Judeo-Christian nonsense that takes Eros and makes it a sin and these Puritans have gotten it wrong for two millennia and it's the reason people stay married and masturbate into their golden years because instead of everyone running around and humping everyone which people would do if they were true to their natures they stay in artificial relationships and pretend that's normal when their deepest, innermost biological nature, their very DNA is telling them to fuck who they want to fuck when they want to fuck them but they're not allowed to because the holy books say it's bad, God says it's bad, it's on the record, look it up, and this causes so much tension to build that prostitutes have been around forever to relieve it so actually it's a kind of social work only everyone is too hypocritical to see it that way. I need to calm down. Take a deep breath. Relax. Should I have gone to China?*

Removing Julian's cell phone from his pocket, Marcus placed it on the bar. He hadn't turned it on since Dominic Festa had given it to him earlier in the day. Now he looked at it lying harmlessly next to a cocktail napkin on the bar, the dim lights softly reflected on its brushed silver surface. He opened the phone and placed the tip of his index finger against the ON button. But he didn't exert any pressure. He was suddenly exhausted.

I'm not Julian.

That evening, Marcus talked about his day, which, in his telling, consisted of the uneventful meeting with Julian's attorney and his inspection of the Shining City premises. He sensibly left out his encounter with Amstel. All during dinner, he longed to pull Julian's cell phone out of his pocket and with a little deft button-pushing begin to divine its contents. It wasn't as if he intended to do anything with this knowledge. He was simply curious. Marcus had never gone to a hooker, nor was he one of those men fascinated by them and the twilight world in which they plied their trade. They played no role in his dark dreams, and he didn't believe that would change. But their mysterious pageant had been rudely thrust upon him, and he found his interest piqued. When Lenore retired to her lair to smoke her third joint of the day, Nathan was in his room grappling with the concept of the dangling participle, and Jan was making calls for a Winthrop Hall canned-food drive, he slipped out to the home office.

The rain had been gaining in intensity over the last couple of hours, and now it was lashing the roof of the garage, a sound that comforted Marcus, creating a sonic buffer against the riot in his head. He had been seated at his desk overlooking the gloomy backyard for half an hour, randomly pressing buttons on the phone. Although he had managed to accidentally photograph every object on his desk with the tiny built-in camera, he was unable to figure out how to play back any of the seventeen messages or access the telephone numbers of the people who had called. This was a source of some frustration to Marcus, for without these numbers he could not learn the names of either Julian's customers or employees. He wasn't sure what he'd do with them once he found them, assuming he did. Perhaps he'd call and tell them Julian had passed away, and in lieu of flowers they might consider contributing to his nephew's bar mitzvah fund.

"Do you know how to work one of these things?"

Nathan glanced up from his desk, where he was reading a homework assignment, to see his father standing in the doorway of his bedroom, brandishing a cell phone. Although he was tired after his day at school and then his afternoon at the temple, he was always keen to help on those rare occasions when Marcus required his assistance.

"I need to figure out who called the phone and what numbers the phone was used to call."

"Isn't it your phone?"

"It's your uncle's."

"What are you doing with it?"

"He left it to me. Would you have a look, please?" Marcus handed Nathan the phone and glanced around the room. The walls were decorated with posters of science fiction and fantasy movies. These were accompanied by several certificates attesting to participation in various sports leagues. A shelf was stuffed with books for young readers that had been given to Nathan in the so-far vain hope that he would read on his own. A beloved stuffed monkey occupied the foot of the bed, where Bertrand Russell was curled up sleeping peacefully. Nathan examined the phone for a moment, pressed a button twice, and held it up to his father.

"Just scroll down. That's who called in. It probably stores, like, fifty numbers," he said with the insouciance of someone who had grown up in a techno-intensive world. Then he pointed to a button and said "See the arrow thingy? Press that and you'll see the list of the numbers called from the phone, okay?"

"Nato, you're a genius."

The boy beamed as his father kissed him on his head, a hasty blessing. The dog awoke and jumped off the bed. He sniffed Marcus's leg before shuffling out of the room. Marcus wanted to go to his office immediately, but he caught himself.

"What are you reading?"

"*Prometheus Bound*. It's about some guy who gets tied to a rock and birds come and peck at his liver all day."

"*Prometheus Bound?*"

"Yeah. Zeus keeps him there. What's up with that?"

"Zeus wanted to punish Prometheus for giving people fire, right? But if Prometheus hadn't done that, humankind would have died out. So here's this guy, he either has to go against the gods or against man. Whatever decision he makes is tricky."

Nathan seemed to understand. It pleased Marcus to be able to discourse on Greek mythology. He believed it was important that Nathan view him as a role model. Perhaps his breadth of arcane knowledge would inspire his son. But he had done enough inspiring for tonight. This brief foray into the classical world felt a little too close to 112 Magdalene Lane.

Marcus returned to his office and furtively transcribed every telephone number banked in Julian's cell phone onto a yellow legal pad, all the while rehearsing what he would say to Jan should she walk in on him ("These are Julian's customers and suppliers at the dry cleaners. They all need to be told what happened, since his business was about personal service"). He looked at the pad when he was finished—it had nearly a hundred phone numbers on it—and felt he had begun to establish a modicum of control. Then he remembered that the disembodied digits on the cell phone represented hookers and johns and wondered over what, exactly, he was hoping to assert control. Certainly not his libido, because in the charged hours since he had discerned the true nature of his brother's life and had been granted putative access to its shadowy hallways, he had not once had a specific sexual urge involving Julian's employees, if that's even what they were. *Were* they employees? Associates? Subcontractors? What exactly was the worker/management relationship? He was curious to know. Alas, there was no trade journal, no *American Pimp* in whose pages he could immerse himself to glean the whys and wherefores. Although he had allowed himself a stray sexual thought about Amstel, he was not viewing these women as a carnal cornucopia. Rather, he was pondering their nature as cogs in an enterprise currently engaged in what appeared to be a lucrative trade in the Greater Los Angeles area, and that was far more than could be said for China-bound Wazoo Toys.

The rains had ceased, and the moon loomed in the sky above the backyard, an all-seeing eye, lidded by gray clouds. He turned off the lights in his office and regarded the pale shadows. The question of why Julian had named him in the will remained unanswered. His business had no inherent value save for the clothes hanging from the racks, which were clearly there as window dressing. They probably weren't sellable and would at best represent a tax deduction should Marcus donate them to charity. The property was rented, there was no office equipment save for the clothing rack, and the human resources, such as they were, looked to be highly unpredictable. Marcus concluded that the entire episode was a postmortem tribute to his brother's malicious sense of humor, a final tweak from the next dimension—a cosmic raspberry.

The deep notes of a bass guitar playing a sinuous hip-hop beat boomed through the office, startling him out of his reverie. Marcus looked around, trying to determine where this unsettling tune was coming from. His eyes veered to a radio on a bookshelf, but that hadn't been on in months. He looked at his laptop, expecting the AOL home page to have morphed into the haunting visage of some dead rapper, but the speaker wasn't on. The ominous rise and fall of the dark melody was playing for the third time when Marcus realized it was the ring tone from Julian's cell phone. He stared at it a moment, uncertain what to do.

"Is this Juice?" The voice on the other end of the line was male. It had a mellifluous quality, as if it liked its own sound.

"This is his brother."

"Are you working with him?"

"Who is this?"

"Gary in Studio City. Is Mariah available tomorrow at eight o'clock?"

"I'll find out." *I'll find out?*

"Call and let me know, okay?"

Beset with a trembling he had not expected as a result of his conversation with Gary from Studio City, Marcus calmed himself and set about calling the numbers he had transcribed, telling people his name was Roon (a dig he could not resist) and he was working for Julian. He left out the part about Julian having died, not wanting to get into dealing with reactions to the news. He found "Mariah" (who had a slight Spanish accent) eventually and told her about Gary, then he told her he was taking over for Julian, and that she should bring him his share of the bill at Shining City. When he hung up, he assured himself this was a one-time thing he was doing only for the sheer perverse thrill, and no one would ever know.

He suddenly realized that eyes were watching him now, causing his adrenal glands to surge in panic. The coyote was standing less than ten feet from his window and staring at him, its snout dipped slightly, looking up at Marcus, casually feral. Although he quickly realized the eyes were not human, the tension remained for several moments after he banged on the window and the creature ran off. Then panic shot through him. Where was Bertrand Russell? Marcus had seen the dog when he walked through the kitchen on his way to the office. Had he let him out? He couldn't remember. Marcus ran out of his office and into the kitchen then heaved a sigh of relief when he saw the dog curled up on his bed, oblivious to the danger lurking just beyond the door.

Chapter 10

It was raining again when Marcus climbed into bed next to his wife, hoping she was asleep. He had not settled anything in his mind and he expected to examine the ceiling for a while before he was able to drift off. This was something he wanted to do in silence.

"Marcus?"

"Hmm?" Marcus hoped a sleepily murmured monosyllabic response would send an unmistakable message.

"You didn't really tell me . . . what happened at the dry cleaner."

What happened at the dry cleaner? Ordinarily an innocuous question, but now fraught with peril. To Marcus's vexation, Jan seemed entirely awake. Not only awake, but chatty. Retaining the sleepy quality in his voice, he said "Nothing happened. What could happen at a dry cleaner?" He paused a moment, hoping this would slow her down, that the very dullness of the word combination *dry cleaner* would lull her into quiescence. "Can we go to sleep now? I'm really tired."

"Were there employees?" Marcus's mind immediately leapt to: *Employees? Does she know something? Is this just an oblique way of getting me to admit that my last response didn't contain the entire truth?* Then he realized that she had asked a logical question, that it could not possibly bespeak any ill-gotten knowledge of the actual situation. He knew his paranoid reaction did not bode well if he had information he did not intend to disclose. And why was he feeling paranoid anyway? It wasn't as if he intended to do anything other than . . . he actually had no idea what he intended to do. Even if he wanted to close the operation down—how is that done? By putting an announcement in the company newsletter? "Marcus? Did you hear me? I asked if anyone worked for your brother."

"Rashid. I think he's from Pakistan." *Rashid from Pakistan?* Where did *that* come from? Marcus could feel his heart race and knew he would have to immediately come up with a brief, convincing story, then plead exhaustion before dropping into a sleep that would have to be feigned at this point. "He lives in El Monte. There's a whole Pakistani community there." *El Monte? Excellent detail!*

"You're not telling the truth, are you?" *WHAT?!* Was he busted already? He had barely done anything. "Who was that guy who was here today?"

"What guy?"

"The one my mother told me about."

"Ohhh." His relief was palpable. "He's a delivery person."

"Is that all he does?"

Had Kostya said anything to Lenore? They were stoned when Marcus saw them. Who knows what they talked about? Perhaps they traded recipes. Perhaps he told her he'd killed someone in the Ukraine. What had Lenore told Jan? Marcus's stomach tightened again. He wanted to get her off the subject of the business as quickly as possible. "What's going on at Ripcord?"

"Plum did something today that kind of weirded me out. She asked if I would donate eggs to her."

"So, what, she would take donated sperm and your eggs . . ."

Marcus felt an almost physical revulsion at this prospect, as he envisioned the ever-expanding Plum being ministered to by a team of doctors depositing his wife's eggs into her alien womb.

"You don't have to worry, I'm not doing it." She leaned over and kissed him on the mouth then lay back on the pillow. "Thank you."

"For what?"

"For being normal."

Jan closed her eyes, seemingly satisfied with this exchange. Marcus fervently hoped she would drift off to sleep and, when five minutes had passed and nothing was forthcoming from her side of the bed, gave silent thanks that his tribulations were over at least until morning.

Unfortunately, they were not.

Marcus woke up with an erection and what felt like an irregular heartbeat. Rain beat against the windows. Sheets of water ran off the roof and down the side of the house. It was still the middle of the night, so he went downstairs and made tea. His hand trembled as he spooned honey into the ceramic mug Nathan had made for him. Sipping it slowly, he searched for the sports page and read it until he calmed down.

When Marcus awoke at six-thirty the next morning and made his way downstairs, he was greeted by the sight of his mother-in-law standing in the middle of the kitchen, smoking a joint as she made oatmeal.

"I couldn't sleep because of the eye pain. You want a hit?"

"Lenore, it's not even seven o'clock yet," he said, waving off the joint. "And you're only supposed to smoke that in your room." They had discussed this the night of the cop's visit, and Lenore had agreed to confine her "treatment" to her own territory, away from Nathan.

"I know, I know. It's just I feel like a junkie in there, getting high all alone. You think Kostya will come back? I liked him." Marcus felt great sympathy for her, standing at the stove in her acrylic jogging outfit with her large glasses that did not appear to be doing any good at all. She turned her attention back to the oatmeal, stirring it with a large spoon. "You sure you don't want some of this?"

"Lenore, put out the joint. Nate's coming down for breakfast soon . . ."

"Nate knows what's going on."

"I know he knows. I just don't think he needs to see his grandmother constantly getting high. It's not good modeling." There was a strain in his voice that he did not like. But circumstances being what they were he was unable to do anything about it. "Did Kostya say anything about my brother's business?"

"We talked about Krav Maga. It's a martial art. I might take a class."

"You're going to study martial arts?"

"That or pole dancing. I'm not sure which one is safer. I saw a story on the local news about this girl who was teaching a pole dancing class. She did an upside down move and landed on her head. Cracked two vertebrae."

"That's all you and Kostya talked about?" He was not going to follow Lenore into the pole dancing cul-de-sac.

"You should loosen up, Marcus. Not that I can see your face, but I bet that vein in your forehead is sticking out." She turned the stove off and spooned some oatmeal into a bowl. Then she took a last toke, licked her fingers, and touched them to the end of the joint, extinguishing its modest flame.

On the ride to school that morning Nathan rattled on about a new online video game his friends were playing. It involved Huns, Visigoths, and other ancient barbarians wreaking brain-deadening havoc on each other in the most sadistic ways. Marcus could barely pay attention. After describing a particularly gory moment, Nathan asked half-seriously if Marcus would buy him an arcade game. These games, far more elaborate, expensive, and coveted than the ones found in boys' bedrooms around the world, were the holy grail for Nathan's peer group. Far superior to ordinary video games, they conferred exalted status on any kid who managed to get his parents to buy one. Marcus locked into the conversation long enough to offer his usual

"We can't afford it." He was relieved when the boy climbed out of the car. No longer would he have to pretend to be anything other than utterly preoccupied with the dilemma tormenting him. The moment his Honda Civic rolled off the leafy Winthrop Hall campus, Marcus pulled out his cell phone and dialed.

An hour later he was seated across from Kostya in a booth at Sal's Diner, a slick memory of a benign 1950s, bereft of racism, polio, and the threat of nuclear annihilation. Kostya was counting the money when the waitress approached. Marcus ordered a tuna sandwich on wheat toast, and Kostya requested macaroni and cheese and a chocolate milkshake. When the waitress left, Marcus asked how much he knew about the business.

After giving his interlocutor a cagey glance, Kostya told him: "Everything."

Impressed but not sure how much to believe, Marcus said "What does 'everything' entail?"

Kostya started ticking information off on his fingers. "Who is girls, how much they make, what they like, don't like, who regoolars are, how much they pay and for what, who like to work when, where from girls come, recruitment. I know *all* that shit, yo. I know they call Juice when they get to where they going, and calls him when they done—safety. Like ho buddy system. Juice hardass mo'fucka, but he look out for ladies. I tell you what also . . ."

"What's that?" Marcus asked, genuinely curious what other intelligence this font might spout.

"Is tough keeping drivers."

"This is L.A. Doesn't everyone have a car?"

"Sure they got the rides, but sometime they like to know mack with gat sitting in car. Client get too freaky, someone bust cap in ass."

Marcus surmised that Kostya had spent a good part of his youth in a wretched Eastern European apartment, watching bootleg DVDs of American blaxploitation movies.

The food arrived, and after they had each taken a few bites, chewing quietly, Kostya took a sip of his milkshake, licked the chalky residue off his upper lip, and said "What business for you?"

"I ran a factory. It moved to China."

Kostya shoved another spoonful of the mac and cheese into his mouth, chewed, and swallowed. "Why you want to be hustla? The business . . ." He made a sour face.

"The whole economy's bad."

"No doubt," Kostya said, sprinkling some pepper on his macaroni and cheese, then mixing it in with his fork. "But supply/demand, yo. Mo'fuckas *always* wanting pussy." As Kostya continued to eat his food, pontificating about the sex business and how Julian ran his little corner, it dawned on Marcus that if he was going to use this as a means to pay his bills, crawl out of debt, and spring for his son's bar mitzvah, it would not be a bad idea to have a more experienced hand at his side until such time as he could run things himself with some degree of confidence.

"How much did Julian pay you?" He quickly corrected himself. "Juice, I mean. I'm curious because I'm going to need to hire someone."

"Not enough, Gangstaboy."

Marcus had done some calculations in his head as they were sitting in the diner and had worked out how much on average Julian must have been earning.

"How's four hundred dollars a week?"

"I'm laughing," Kostya said, not laughing at all.

Marcus quickly changed tactics. "What do you want to do? Professionally, I mean. You said you had plans?"

Kostya smiled. This was a topic to which he warmed. "Niggas and Koreans be loving barbecue. But since L.A. riots, niggas and Koreans hating mo'fucking guts of each other. Most niggas Christian. I know Allah-worshipping mo'fuckas trying to get niggas to Islam but you take from me, Gangstaboy, most niggas with Jesus." Marcus nodded his head, dumbly. As a philosopher manqué adrift in the world of toy manufacturing for nearly fifteen years, Marcus was painfully aware of how a person could be judged solely by his external circumstances, and he made a point of not doing it himself. He was impressed by the beginning of Kostya's sociological exegesis, the way this son of Mother Russia free-styled like he was born in Detroit. "Most Koreans Christian, too, right? At least ones in L.A. My homeboy Jesus say you gots to love enemy like sibling. I will open Jesus-Loves-2-Barbecue on Crenshaw Boulevard halfway between Koreatown and South Central, put big-ass cross made of two giant ribs on roof. 2 Barbecue, okay?" He drew the number two with his finger in the air to make his meaning clear. "T-O, okay? Then I get peoples from both communities eating barbecue side by side, yo. Dr. King not only one with mo'fucking dream, Gangstaboy. I got dream, too. I see Koreans eating cornbread sitting next to niggas eating kimchi, everybody eating ribs. Is my dream."

It took Marcus a moment to recover from this image of a cross made out of two huge ribs. When he did the first thought he had was: If I ever said anything like that, I'd be called a racist, but coming from this guy it sounds nearly legitimate. "Where are you going to get the money?"

"I'm saving my dollars, yo. Peoples going to *looovve* concept."

"You're probably right . . . I'm not saying they won't." Marcus nodded thoughtfully here, paying homage to Kostya's vision. "But in case they don't? How about working for me?"

"On salary? Fuck that shit." Marcus asked him what it would take to make a deal. Kostya drained his milkshake, then took a sip of water from the glass in front of him. He placed the paper napkin to his lips and daubed at the remains of his drink. Then he looked at Marcus and said "A piece of business."

"You know the whole shebang. You could take it over yourself, outmaneuver me . . . I know how this shit goes down." *Shit goes down?* Marcus was tentatively gangsterizing his tone, although he wished he hadn't said *shebang*. "Why don't you want to take it over yourself?"

"Because if we get busted, yo. It's your black ass doing time."

And so before the check arrived (which Marcus graciously picked up) he had a partner, who was in for twenty percent of whatever turned out to be Marcus's share. They agreed to contact all of the girls and ask them to come to the dry cleaner for a meeting where Marcus would explain his plans. It was very important this be done quickly—they were far from the only game in town and, as in the African bush, the danger of poaching was great. Marcus didn't want to move to the recruitment phase of the plan until he had to. He was hoping he could induce enough of the girls to stay until he had time to acclimate himself to the business.

As they walked to their cars, parked in a lot behind the diner, Marcus asked "What kind of operation was my brother running? The girls . . . what are they like?"

"Juice was trying to keep it classy, best he could. You know, these girls, they not brain surgeons. But Juice liking them to have intelligent conversation. Thinking he get more money johns that way, less likely to beat up girls. Bad for girls, bad for you. It maybe surprise you what some guys ask girl. One night, she in bathtub, making piss on guy—the next night some mo'fucka want to take her to movie, talk about where should invest money, and no fucking. Is weird business, meet all kinds peoples. But for me is not career."

"Me neither," Marcus said, trying to maintain his positive attitude.

Kostya ran down the list of girls, told Marcus about their quirks and foibles (this one was always late, that one didn't tip the drivers, another refused to do bondage) and most important, which of them might be using drugs. "Permit me to be telling you about hoes and dope," Kostya said. He waited a moment while a young mother clad in a magenta catsuit strapped her three-year-old into a car seat. When she climbed behind the wheel of her Volvo station wagon, he continued "Many of these services liking ladies doing the coke because then they go all night with sex. And if they get hooked, less likely to leave business because one thing junkie needs? Mo'

111

money. About the coke, Juice was sometimes easy. You want to not be so easy. Some of johns high but you always wanting girl in control. Lots of variables in business. Whole idea is control variables." Marcus was more impressed with his new colleague every minute. His logic was right out of an M.B.A. program. "And wear tomorrow a decent suit. You want confidence from girls."

"What's wrong with what I'm wearing?" Marcus said, gesturing to his chino/golf shirt ensemble.

"You look like square biscuit, yo. Plus you need new name. Don't want girls calling you by real name. Less they knowing, more okay for you." Then he made a fist and attempted to engage Marcus in the latest street handshake.

As per Dominic Festa's report, Julian kept an apartment for assignations that didn't take place in either hotels or private homes, nestled on a side street just north of Burton Way in a modern five-story building. It was a generically furnished studio with a living room set and a freshly made double bed. Taped to the refrigerator was a note from the maid asking to be paid. Helpfully, she'd written her phone number on the note, and when Marcus called, he both apprised her of Julian's passing and retained her services.

By the early afternoon, Marcus was driving home. His life was going in a new direction and he tried his best to put a good face on it. This time would be short, lucrative, and secret. There was an optimistic grain deep in Marcus's core, a quality that allowed him to believe in the future no matter the current circumstances, and now he found himself excited about the possibilities of his new business. Roon had been rapacious in his approach to the workforce at Wazoo—low wages, minimum benefits, mediocre working conditions. Marcus would be benevolent. Roon viewed his employees as fungible units in an economic machine. Marcus would regard them as individuals and treat them with dignity. Roon's management style was high-handed, un-empathic. Marcus would be caring. He'd try to understand his labor force and work *with* them. He vowed to be an enlightened potentate, running the business according to the highest standards of American management practice, not like Roon, who ran Wazoo like a pimp.

Chapter 11

Marcus was not an easy liar, so it was with some misgiving that he returned to what was now a distinctly separate life in Van Nuys. As he drove home beneath a threatening autumn sky, Marcus calculated that, if he was able to maintain the level of Julian's workforce, his financial situation could be ameliorated in approximately six months, and in a year, roughly the time of Nathan's bar mitzvah, he would be significantly in the black. With an additional couple of years he could pay off the mortgage on his house. But he didn't want to get ahead of himself. He figured he would dive into the demimonde and start swimming. When he arrived at the far shore he would climb out, towel off, and act like nothing had happened.

At dinner that night Lenore was twirling spaghetti on her fork. She paused before placing it in her mouth. "It combines dance, sensual movement, and traditional stripper moves."

"Stripper moves?" Nathan said.

"The flying body spiral, the fire fly, the descending angel . . . it's like ballet."

"In a G-string," Jan said.

"Why should I be afraid of my body? I'm not *that* old. Jan, you should come with me. You'd really like the teacher. She's a former exotic dancer." Lenore said this in the same tone she would have used had the words been *formerly with Twyla Tharp*.

"Maybe I'll take a class with you," Jan said.

"Mom, eww . . ." Nathan was mortified at the mental image of his barely clad mother slinging herself around a pole with incongruous abandon.

While his family continued the dinner conversation, Marcus was reflecting on his secret and experiencing the disorienting sensation that accompanied it. No longer was he the anonymous factory manager of Wazoo Toys, late of North Hollywood, now of Guodong, and of supreme unimportance to anyone, save to those who coveted toy replicas of praying American presidents. Now he was a man whose cover as a mild-mannered small business owner obscured a transgressor of the social norm, a citizen of the night. Indeed, a criminal.

"More brussels sprouts?" Jan said, holding a serving bowl for Marcus. She was smiling and he smiled back at her, as he ladled the globular vegetables on to his plate. He knew his wife looked at him and saw her husband, a family man who, through a well-deserved stroke of luck, was going to be operating a successful dry cleaning establishment. He sensed that she felt far more secure than she had recently, the crumbling edifice on which she had been standing now patched and reinforced. Steady Marcus, easy Marcus, good provider, good father, exceedingly good husband. He knew her look was one of affection, certainly, but also of relief, because he had delivered her from the edge of an abyss.

Marcus returned her smile, her love, calmly. There was a serene quality in his look achieved through a subtle breathing technique he had learned watching a martial arts movie on cable one of the many nights he couldn't sleep. Behind his eyes, an entire dance company was performing a Las Vegas confection of glitz and sleaze. Leggy, high-heeled chorines were pirouetting down curving silver staircases in silk stockings and clinging gold spandex, holding signs lettered with words like Whoremonger and Flesh Peddler. They were wheeling, kicking, bumping, grinding, executing the most complicated chore-ography to the raucous blare of a horn section only Marcus could hear as he ate his dinner and tried to listen while the members of his family talked about their days. He was now a clandestine agent in his own home, a man whose innermost thoughts could not be shared with those closest to him. He was surprised at the frisson he was experiencing.

"You watch me," Lenore was saying. "I'll get a job as a stripper!"

After dinner, Nathan took Bertrand Russell for a walk and Lenore smoked a postprandial joint in her room. When they were alone, Marcus asked Jan what she'd told Plum regarding her request for an egg donation.

"I told her to forget it," Jan said, wiping the table with a dishrag. "Can you imagine Plum walking around with *my* eggs in her so she can make some wacky video? I don't need the drama. We need *less* drama around here, right?" Then she kissed his guilty lips. He noticed it was a chaste kiss, with a residue of anxiety, and it caused him to realize that she had still not internalized their change in fortune.

Marcus did not try to make love to Jan that night. Instead, he lay in bed next to her as she slept and ran through what he would say to the Shining City workforce the next day. Although he had run the factory at Wazoo Toys for over a decade, the management skill required to do the job was rudimentary. The workers arrived at the factory at nine, lunch was at twelve-thirty, and the day ended at five o'clock. Payday was Friday every other week. Employees were given two weeks of paid vacation per year and up to a week of sick days. Occasionally, Marcus would have to hire a new worker, but usually someone on the line had a relative who needed a job, so replacing those who left was generally effortless. It had been a very simple arrangement, running Wazoo, and none of it prepared Marcus for the endeavor in which he was now engaged. Nor had he anticipated having a partner, albeit one who, so far, was only in for twenty percent of the business. Kostya seemed like he knew what he was doing, but what if he was a living Russian nested doll, with innumerable other Kostyas inside waiting to reveal themselves. Would they be merry and bright, or murderous and low? Marcus felt a rumbling in his gut.

There was tension in his neck. He took two Tylenol and chased them with a shot of Pepto-Bismol.

He didn't think he should wear a tie to the meeting—that was too formal. Not wanting to appear aloof, he selected a navy blue merino wool sweater and khakis, an ensemble he thought sent exactly the right message of casual confidence. He was feeling anything but casual and confident as he drove toward West Hollywood, but that was beside the point. He knew it was incumbent upon him to fake both of these qualities, which would be a problem if he couldn't get his pulse to slow down. He regretted the coffee he'd had at breakfast.

The gathering had been called for one o'clock in the afternoon because Kostya had informed Marcus that people in this line of employment tended to be late sleepers. There were twelve women in the room ranging in age from what he dearly hoped was at least eighteen all the way up to what looked like forty. They were milling around in an open area behind the clothing rack, talking in small groups, catching up on gossip, exchanging work stories. Occasionally one of them would furtively examine Marcus, but he was careful not to make eye contact. He wasn't ready for that yet. As he stole sidelong glances, he was struck by the ordinariness of the women. Far from ravenous sex monsters, oozing carnality and appetite, they all appeared normal, particularly to someone who lived in Los Angeles. They could have been shoppers randomly gleaned from a mall, or a group of women gathered for a seminar on how to sell vitamin supplements. Julian clearly operated a fairly rigorous screening process when it came to the physical qualities of the girls he chose to employ. All of them were attractive and in what appeared to be good physical shape. Those who had visible body piercings and tattoos didn't look like sideshow freaks. Hair was well-cut and appeared in the same shades of blonde, brunette, and red one would see on prosperous pedestrians strolling along the upscale boulevards of any American city. Several of the girls wore short skirts but, again, nothing that would have been out of place at Winthrop Hall. Ethnically, they were a rainbow coalition:

whites of varying complexions ranging from Nordic to Mediterranean, Latinas, Asians, and two light-skinned black women. A Crayola box of prostitutes.

Kostya, who had been standing nearby talking to a short Asian woman in jeans and a leather jacket, approached Marcus and said "You better get started."

"Is everyone here?"

"Enough so you do your thing." Then he leaned in and whispered "Make 'em believe you care, Marcus. Everyone is needing love." Kostya turned away, then remembered something. "What is your name?"

"My name?"

"You are supposed to have new name for girls today."

Marcus had forgotten to come up with a new identity, preoccupied as he was with other aspects of the radical shift taking place. He racked his already overtaxed brain for a moment and said "Cool Breeze." It was the name he had given himself six years ago at an Indian Guides campfire in the backyard of an investment banker in a gated community north of Mulholland. He and Nathan had sat in a circle and each father and son, in turn, chose an Indian handle. Nathan had been Great Salmon, which Marcus had thought had the perfect ring (although his friends quickly changed it to Nate Salmon). At the time, he was pleased with Cool Breeze as well, and he hoped it would suit the current situation.

"Cool breeze?" Kostya asked, stifling a laugh. "Maybe just Breeze."

Marcus nodded, slightly embarrassed by his tin ear. "You like my sweater?" he asked sotto voce, trying to lighten what was clearly a stressful moment for him.

Kostya reached over, pulled a thread from where the weave had begun unraveling, and whispered "I take you shopping after this." Then he turned to the assembled labor force and said "Everybody, I know this is confuckulated and we are having shock about Juice . . ." He paused here, allowing the women to nod in sympathetic agreement, something two of them actually did. "But you got bills and life is going on. Now, I am asking you to give it up for Juice's man, Breeze." Kostya stepped aside with a flourish and was met with dead silence.

Marcus grimaced tightly and faced his audience. They stared back at him, a few of them smiling reflexively, but from the rest—nothing. He might as well have been a sport fish mounted on a wall. He watched them holding back, waiting. He assumed they were wondering if this was someone upon whom they could rely, imagined many of them were considering jumping ship. Marcus felt his forehead prickle and beads of sweat begin to form. He wished he hadn't worn the merino wool sweater. It was warmer than he'd remembered.

"My name is Breeze," he began. They looked at him phlegmatically. At least they weren't laughing. His formal bearing suddenly struck him as absurd, given that he was addressing a roomful of hookers, but he did not have an alternative demeanor upon which to draw at that moment. "Juice was my brother, although we weren't very close," he added completely unnecessarily and in a way that suggested trepidation. As he considered what to say next he looked at the faces of his audience and began the breathing technique he practiced in moments of stress. He hoped this would suggest it was *he* who was sizing *them* up, as opposed to the other way around.

What he noticed first was that many of the women had intelligent faces. Dimly, he recalled Kostya telling him that Julian liked to employ women capable of carrying on a conversation. He noticed Amstel standing in the back and remembered that she had been reading the short stories of an obscure European author. He imagined her accepting payment from a UCLA-funded deconstructionist who had chosen to spend his grant money to further pursue an interest in sodomy. Marcus knew his pause had gotten longer than dramatic and was heading for soporific, so he continued "I want to thank you all for coming," groaning inwardly as he said it. He admonished himself to get to the point. Which was what? To get these workers to agree to run their business under his aegis. Then do it now, he told himself, now!

"I am not a pimp," he said. This declaration sounded jarring to his ears, but he noticed it got their attention. Temporarily buoyed, he continued "What I am is a *businessman*. I ran a toy business for a long time in the Valley, and I think I can say with some accuracy that I was a popular boss." A few of them nodded, pleased at this revelation. "I'm not equating selling toys with selling what we're going to be selling here . . ." he paused for the expected laugh and actually received a few appreciative giggles. "But business is business and what I'm about is people. I can tell you categorically that I am a people person." Marcus found the words *people person* singularly idiotic, yet knew it was a phrase to which, for some reason, many individuals seemed to respond. If millions of American idiots can choose a president based on whom they would want to have a beer with, it was probably not a bad yardstick by which a prostitute can choose a pimp, even if it's a pimp who does not embrace the designation. "The fact is, I love people. Black people, white people, Asian people." As he said *Asian people*, he made eye contact with the Asian woman Kostya had been talking to before the meeting started. She grinned at him, showing a perfect row of large bleached teeth. Marcus briefly wondered if they were real, and if, with their Cuisinart aspect, they would frighten a client who hoped for a blow job. "I want to meet with each one of you individually to see if we can work together. I want to get to *know* you. Now you're probably thinking we've been working for Juice, we trusted Juice. Who is this guy from the toy business, and why should we believe him? I'll tell you why. Because I'm fair, I'm honest, and I will help set up a 401(k) for anyone who wants it." There were murmurs of assent, and as Marcus leaned back on his heels for a moment he asked himself where the idea for the retirement plans had arrived from. Truly, he had no answer, nor did he have any idea how to set up a 401(k) account, but he was on a roll now. "There's going to be health insurance, and, for those who log a certain number of hours—paid vacation. I want to make one last point. Things don't always go the way we want them to, and a situation might arise where someone needs a lawyer. My closest friend is one of the finest criminal lawyers in Los Angeles. Anything happens to someone working for me . . . just know you will have the finest legal representation available." It hadn't occurred to him until that moment to invoke Atlas, but he was pleased with himself for having thought to cite their relationship. Conversely, he would not be mentioning any of this to Atlas. Marcus concluded his remarks with a public-service announcement about the necessity of condoms.

The moment Amstel began to applaud and was followed by a second woman and then a third, Marcus vowed to himself that he would figure out how all this would work as soon as possible. For an encore, he told them he would be accessible, that he intended to listen to whatever grievances they might have and their proposed solutions to those grievances, should they have any to suggest. To this end, he circulated a sheet of paper on which he asked everyone to write their e-mail addresses. Marcus thanked them for coming and assured the group he was looking forward to working with each and every one. Marcus understood the value of being liked. You would have thought he was running for office.

His general bonhomie appeared to affect the women, who seemed willing to—for the time being at least—place their livelihoods in his care. Thus the meeting ended on a positive note, with many of the workers appearing confident they were in the capable hands of someone who knew what he was doing.

Two women approached, one of whom spoke in the flat tones of the Midwest, the other in a musical Brazilian accent. They informed him they'd been with Julian in the hot tub prior to his having expired and seemed genuinely distressed by what had happened. Marcus assumed they were led to this spontaneous display of condolence by the sincerity with which he had addressed the group. It would have been a perfect encounter had the Brazilian woman not ended it this way: "We think Juice dying is a sign for us, and we came today to show respect. So you're cool and everything, Breeze, but we're getting out of the business."

After the women left, Kostya told him not to worry. "In Los Angeles a hundred girls a day are signing up." They ran an ad in the local alternative weekly, and days later they had four new recruits. When Marcus wondered how to keep potential dry cleaning customers at bay, Kostya informed him that the CLOSED sign was a permanent feature in the Shining City window.

Chapter 12

If everyone in the business was presumed to be at least a little dishonest, then discreet supervision was common sense. So Marcus decided that he would serve as a driver and rotate between the various members of his organization. He believed it would give him a chance to bond with the women and render them less likely to explore their larcenous impulses. He explained his nocturnal absences to Jan by telling her he was personally delivering the dry cleaning so he could get to know his customers and learn the business from the ground up. Since people were likelier to be home in the evenings, that was when he would work. Jan was so relieved that money was coming in that she didn't think to question the plan.

More women could fit in the minivan than the Honda, so Marcus asked Jan if she would mind temporarily trading cars. He told her he needed it for deliveries, and she was only too happy to help out. This is how he found himself early one cool autumn evening behind the wheel of the Ripps family minivan stuck in traffic on the 405 freeway with three prostitutes—one in the passenger seat and two in the back. They had gathered at Shining City so Marcus could chauffeur them to their appointments. Kostya was driving three women in the dry cleaning van, and two other women would be working in shifts at the Beverly Hills-adjacent apartment that night.

One of the women with Marcus, a Nicaraguan named Xiomara, was new to the business. She sat in the back seat with Amstel. Mink was in the passenger seat. As the women chatted amiably, Marcus thought about the conversation he'd had with Kostya after the meeting.

They had gone around the corner to an organic restaurant for lunch. Marcus wanted to talk about expanding the workforce. He needed to know how the hiring process worked.

"You ask them what can do, can't do," Kostya said.

"Like what?" Marcus was speaking in such low tones you would have thought he suspected someone had bugged the salt shaker.

"What?" Kostya said, unable to hear him.

"I said *what*," Marcus said, barely louder. He hadn't touched his bran muffin.

"Like *what*?" Kostya said as he sipped iced green tea through a straw. "Like will they fuck? Some girls so stupid, they don't know what is job."

Marcus glanced around the restaurant to make sure no one was listening. A couple of high school boys in skate shirts and cargo shorts were seated at a nearby table, but they appeared deep in conversation. The young Mexican counterman was taking a businessman's order. Marcus relaxed slightly. He was never comfortable discussing sex, even with friends, and to have conversations of an intimate nature with a series of strange women was clearly anathema to him. Just talking about talking about it was difficult enough. "What else?"

Kostya rolled his eyes. He couldn't believe someone could get to Marcus's age and not know something so rudimentary. Putting his tuna on seven-grain bread down, he said "You ask them with what they are comfortable doing. Will they fuck, will they suck, will they fuck black guy? Some girls don't like black cock . . . ethnic groups sometime bad . . . we had Armenian girl would not fuck Turk . . . bad history, so her pussy is closed for business . . . since 9/11 some girls refuse to fuck Arabs . . . will they do multiple hours, overnight, traveling? Will they allow kissing?" Marcus again looked around to make sure no one was listening. The counterman handed the businessman his order. The high school boys were laughing at a private joke.

"Some girls all right with sodomy, but no kissing her . . . crazy

124

shit . . . couples, group sex, bukkake, rusty trombone, dirty sanchez, woman-on-woman love act, whipping, spanking, tying up, having toes sucked, golden showers, hitting, spitting . . . do they have equipment? Handcuffs, whips, dildos . . . what drink they like, some guys want to know bring vodka or bring white wine for romantic evening. Then Aunt Flo comes to visit, girls on rag. Personal shit, but you got to know. Some girls want to work then, but what if client freak out? Do they have tattoos, body piercing? Some guys into serious weird shit. One guy dress like Tarzan, want to fuck in tree house. Girl scared of heights, bad night for everyone. Guys want to know they will get what they are paying for, so you gots to know, Breeze. You gots to *know*."

Marcus had the radio in the van tuned to a classical station on the theory that the music would be calming, but the DJ had chosen that moment to play *Night on Bald Mountain*, which led Mink to say "Could you turn this shit off and put on some rap?" Mink was a Korean-American from Irvine; long black hair and a rockstar pout. She was the pretty woman with large teeth he had noticed during his I'm-a-people-person meeting. Now she smiled at Marcus, lightly drumming her fingers on his thigh. This gave him an instant erection. *That* is a problem, he thought, and vowed to do something about it, even if it necessitated a visit to his internist and prescribed medication. He told Mink to put on whatever station she preferred. When she leaned forward to touch the radio, Marcus smelled her perfume, subtle and lemony. Her makeup was lightly applied, and as she started to bob her head to the easy roll of a song she found on one of the hip-hop stations, he had to fight the urge to run his hand up her fishnet-encased leg. Taking a deep breath, he focused on the traffic as Mink closed her eyes and settled back into the seat.

Sex outside the confines of his marriage had never particularly interested Marcus, so it came as something of a surprise when he found himself fantasizing about his new colleagues. The absence of sex in his own life had created a buildup of desire that was more profound than he had been willing to acknowledge. With monumental self-control he forced himself to think about golf, or pizza, or death—anything other than the inner trips to empyrean realms of perfect sexuality that existed in distant unmapped corners of his consciousness. He vowed not to think about the women; the white ones, the Latinas, the Asians, the African-Americans, the tall ones, the short ones, the thin ones and the plus-sized, their hair, their lips, their legs, their breasts, anything and everything about them.

But it was difficult to stop.

Marcus realized this could create difficulties.

So he vowed there would be no sampling of the goods, no fraternizing with the workforce, no office romance. He would not extract so much as a single sexual favor from even *one* of the women in his charge. Why would he not avail himself of this Dionysian smorgasbord now a mere speed-dial away? Because of Jan. She may have withheld sex from him, but he perceived that to be because of tension, worry, fatigue—all of the bugaboos that subtly undermine otherwise healthy marriages. He *loved* her. Yes, it was simple, even banal. Yet there it was. He knew Jan would be upset if she found out—no, not upset, *apoplectic*—and that was reason enough to endure this self-torture.

Marcus looked at Xiomara in the rearview mirror. She wanted to work under the name Jenna since no American she'd met could pronounce Xiomara (*Zho-mah-ra*). Tight white jeans, a loose jersey, and violet pumps made her look like she'd been in Los Angeles a while. Black hair fell loosely below her shoulders. She had large dark eyes and an unlined, delicately made-up face.

"Nicaragua," Xiomara/Jenna was saying, "is much nicer with the Sandinistas gone. Any political system that tells you to love everyone . . . watch out for those guys."

"Why don't you stay, you like it so much?" Amstel said.

"I have a daughter, so I need to make money. In Managua I was a secretary, but the pay is not so good." Xiomara/Jenna took out a box of Tic Tacs and popped one in her mouth. She offered one to Amstel, who accepted it.

Rolling the Tic Tac on her tongue, Amstel said "I am from Latvia and I tell you, is complete dump, okay? Was dump under Communists and is dump now." This was intoned with the certainty of a guest on a Sunday morning talk show. No one was going to argue. They rode in silence for a few moments, listening to the hip-hop pounding from the speakers. "Latvian peoples all want big-screen TV and shiny car, same as here, but they have no money. In Riga I was actress. Successful, too. I was cast member in Latvian National Theater all-female production *Twelve Angry Men*. Drama critic of *Latvietis Latvija* writes 'She shows great promise in demanding role of holdout.' Here, look." Amstel removed a laminated clipping from her black suede purse and handed it to Xiomara/Jenna, who glanced at it, more impressed now (although she could not read the Cyrillic in which the review was written). "I had small part in *Skroderdienas Silmacos* at State Theatre. Is by Rüdolfs Blaumanis. You know him?"

"Who?" She handed the clipping back to Amstel.

"He is Latvian Chekhov. You know Chekhov?"

"I didn't bring any condoms," Mink said over her shoulder. "Could I borrow a few?" Amstel reached into her purse and handed her a pack. "I owe you," Mink said, stuffing them in her red leather purse.

"Did you go to university?" Xiomara/Jenna asked Amstel. When Amstel shook her head, Xiomara/Jenna made a clicking sound with her tongue intended to convey disapproval of her colleague's cavalier attitude toward higher education. "You should. It's not too late. You can't do this forever."

"I will be actress in America," Amstel said.

"I'll get another job when I have a green card," Xiomara/Jenna said.

"I have two years of college and I'm doing this," Mink chimed in.

Marcus had been listening so intently, he didn't notice when the car in front of him pulled ahead in the slow-moving traffic, leaving a fifty-foot gap. Two other cars, believing his lane was now moving, cut in front of him before he realized what was going on. He stepped on the gas pedal too quickly, causing the van to jerk forward.

"Breeze, you ever drive van before?" Amstel said. "Or do you need learner's permit?" Everyone laughed, relaxing the slight tension in the van.

Marcus dropped Mink off at a business hotel near LAX and made plans to pick her up in two hours. She would see a salesman in town from Toronto. He then drove to a modern house in Venice, a futuristic two-story glass-and-steel structure, where Xiomara/Jenna had a date with a member of the Los Angeles Opera who wanted oral sex and a back rub. Amstel had a date at a condo in Marina del Rey, where the middle-aged owner of a hamburger chain watched hungrily as she stripped down to her (pre-requested) nylons, garters, and stiletto pumps, then strapped on a dildo and repeatedly penetrated his wife, who slipped Amstel an extra hundred when her husband turned his back.

Because of the way the drop-offs and pick-ups were scheduled, Marcus had nothing to do other than drive, which was fine with him. Eventually he collected them all, received his share of their earnings, then ferried them back to Shining City. Marcus told them about the health plan he'd selected. There was a wellness program (with discounted health club membership), a prescription drug plan, a vision/eyewear plan, and dental insurance. The women were pleased and he reveled in their volubly appreciative reactions. The time for reflection had ended. He was starting to feel good again.

Jan offered a sleepy hello when Marcus lay down beside her later that night. He had thought she was asleep. Marcus placed his hand on her hip and felt the long flannel nightgown. He wanted to burn it. She asked him how his day had gone, and he told her everything was fine. Then he kissed her on the lips and was pleasantly surprised when she kissed him back. Hers was not a sensual kiss, exactly, but it intimated more than she had recently offered and, still keyed up from the effects of the evening, Marcus kissed her again. She groaned pleasurably and he moved toward her neck, kissing her there and on her earlobe and her eyelids.

"Mmmm, Marcus, I think the dry cleaning business agrees with you." He continued kissing her as he reached down, hiked up the flannel and slipped her panties off. He was thrilled when she didn't object. As they rocked back and forth, Marcus found it difficult not to think about the women with whom he'd spent the evening, their skin, scents, contours. For years now his sex life had been prosaic, familiar and predictable, loving and boring. Marcus pined for the early days, the frenzied, peppered excitement of the new and unexpected. He didn't want to be with other women, he only wanted to be with Jan, but in a special, more fulfilling way. It wasn't something he intended to discuss, not at the moment. Tonight he wanted to try something different, tonight he *would* try something different, and as Marcus felt the force gathering in his sacrum he realized now was the time, right now, and he withdrew. Before Jan apprehended the plan, she felt a warm wetness on her chest.

"Marcus . . . what did you do?" Her tone was accusatory.

"Nothing!"

"I'm all . . . ughh . . . I can't believe you just did that! What is *wrong* with you?"

He was surprised at her reaction, mistakenly believing twin orgasms had lulled her to quiescence.

"It's not like it was molten lava," he said.

She was already out of the bed and walking toward the bathroom. He could hear the waves of displeasure emanating from her, vibrating, banging around the room. She turned the light on in the bathroom and it shined in his eyes for the second before she closed the door behind her. A moment later, she returned, wiping her chest with a hand towel.

"Have you been watching porn or something?"

"No."

She pulled her nightgown down over her shoulders and settled back into bed, shaking her head. He had been hoping for an entirely different response. He wasn't sure what exactly, just not *this*. "Where did that come from?"

"Jeez, I'm sorry." He lay on his back with his eyes closed and tried to be less annoyed. "Is it such a big deal?"

"No, but you've never done it before and if you're going to do something like that, I'd like it if you warned me . . ."

Now he opened his eyes and looked at her: "*Warn* you?"

"So I could have a few drinks to get ready." He laughed, relieved her voice was missing some of the edge it had a moment ago. The tone still wasn't one you'd hear on a meditation tape, but the overt hostility had ebbed. "It's not that I won't let you do it, if that's what you want, but we've barely been having sex and then I'm half asleep and I get jumped in my bed by Porn Guy. I was just surprised." Marcus apologized again, and squeezed her hand. She told him she wasn't mad. They nestled into the spoon position and Jan drifted off to sleep. Marcus disengaged when his back began to hurt.

The first bottle of sake barely lasted ten minutes. Marcus threw back the last of it and ordered another one from the pretty Japanese waitress whose left arm was entirely covered by a series of elaborate anime-inspired tattoos. It was early on a Tuesday evening, and he and Amstel were seated in a small sushi restaurant in West Hollywood. Colored lights had been strung above the sushi bar, and a small silver Christmas tree was doing time near the entrance, small Eastern acknowledgments of the dominant seasonal myth. Amstel was perusing the piece of paper Marcus had placed in front of her. He had given extensive thought to legal liability, and with that in mind had downloaded a document from the Internet. It stated: I (fill in the blank) AGREE THAT MARCUS RIPPS WILL BE SETTING APPOINTMENTS

BY PHONE FOR ME. WE HAVE DISCUSSED AND AGREED THAT HE DOES NOT EXPECT ME TO PERFORM ANY ILLEGAL ACTS FOR MONEY. IF I DECIDE TO PERFORM OR PARTICIPATE IN ANYTHING ILLEGAL DURING THE APPOINTMENTS HE HAS SET UP FOR ME, I AM 100% COMPLETELY RESPONSIBLE FOR MY OWN ACTIONS. Marcus, exhibiting a touching belief in the sanctity of contracts, intended to get everyone to sign. He was certain this would take care of whatever problems might arise.

Amstel signed it with the pen Marcus gave her and slid it back across the table.

"You look tired, Breeze."

"I haven't been sleeping well."

"You are married?" They had never discussed anything personal before (not counting the variety of sex acts Amstel was willing to perform for money), and Marcus was taken aback. He told her he was.

"You are good guy, Breeze, not looking for free samples at work. Let me tell you secret. Next time you are in bed with wife, listen to her breathe, then match your breath with hers, in and out, in and out, you are breathing together. She will not understand what you are doing, but she will sense you are . . . what? Congenial. Okay?"

Marcus thought about that for a moment. Given how Jan had reacted to his sex play the last time, perhaps just breathing together would have a salutary effect. He told Amstel he'd try it.

"If breathing does not work, I will tell you about the egg."

"The egg?"

"It vibrates. I give them for Easter."

He tossed back some more sake, taking pleasure in the warmth as it coursed down his throat. Amstel was wearing tight black pants and a loose red sweater. Her face had only the slightest trace of makeup, and her blonde hair was held back by a pale yellow silk band. She leaned back in her seat, relaxed. Taking a sip of sake, she said "I like you, Breeze, so I want to be honest." Marcus was sharp enough to know that the phrase *I want to be honest* was generally the prelude to a lie, but now his head was slightly hazy from the sake. He leaned forward and looked into her eyes. They were blue and he could see flecks of brown in the iris. "I don't know how long I will do this." Marcus nodded and told her she could stop whenever she wanted. "Juice would not have told me that."

"What would he have said?" Marcus asked, genuinely curious.

"He would tell me keep working." Amstel took another sip of her drink. "You guys were . . .?" Marcus saw she was searching her database for the correct English word.

"Close? No." He told Amstel about his relationship with Julian, how he barely knew him as an adult, how they weren't even speaking when he died.

Amstel said she thought that was sad. "I didn't like him, he was kind of prick . . . I'm being honest, okay? But he watched out for girls." The waitress came with another round.

Marcus asked about her personal life, and she told him she wasn't involved with anyone right now, that it was difficult given what she did for a living. He wondered if she'd been married but didn't want to ask. Amstel told him about emigrating from Latvia, how she tried to get work as an actress in America but it had been impossible. He told her how he got into the business and that he had almost moved to China. She laughed a few times and touched his arm when she wanted to emphasize a point. Marcus was starting to feel as if he was on a date. He wanted to lean across the table and kiss her, but he knew that was a bad idea.

The plan was for Amstel to drive herself to an assignation in Huntington Beach. It was too far for Marcus to take her with the other women in the van, and he trusted her not to cheat him. He paid the check and walked her to her SUV. She had parked on a side street, and when she clicked the door open a light came on in the interior that cast a soft glow in the darkness. The second sake had gone to his head, so Marcus didn't resist when Amstel said good night and kissed him gently on the lips, lingering a little longer than he would have expected. She reached behind his neck with her fingertips and pulled him forward until their foreheads touched for just a moment. Then she released him and smiled, her head tilted down slightly, a wry expression on her pretty face. He could tell she was a little drunk.

"I like you, Breeze . . . you are okay. If I can do for you, ask me."

Despite the alcohol he'd ingested, Marcus resisted the temptation. He told Amstel he'd enjoyed talking to her and walked back to his own car wondering how he could possibly maintain the vow he had made to himself.

"What are you doing, Marcus?"

"I'm breathing."

It was one in the morning, and he had been lying next to Jan for twenty minutes. She had been sleeping when he arrived, having spent the evening chauffeuring his workforce all over the Los Angeles area. He climbed into bed naked, snuggling next to her. She faced away from him, and now his erection pressed against her thigh. When she rolled onto her back, Marcus caressed her breast, his breath in rhythm with hers. This went on until he had counted twelve breaths in and twelve breaths out, all of them synchronized.

"You're imitating me."

"No, no. I'm just breathing."

"I'm too tired to make love right now."

"I just want to breathe."

"Okay."

He continued to mirror her breaths, his chest rising and falling. This went on for another few minutes, and Marcus was overjoyed when Jan reached down and began to stroke him. He knew he should not push his luck and try to introduce any new dishes to the menu tonight. As they sleepily made love, Marcus thought about how closely their sex life was tied to the balance in their checking account. He found himself wondering if this was a particularly middle-class affliction. Great swaths of the world were peopled by those with little money who had a great deal of sex, at least if the numbers of their offspring were any indication. But this was a fleeting thought. More than anything, he was pleased that Jan was relaxed enough to get physical.

Marcus was stunned to find that by Christmas he was grossing around twenty-five thousand dollars a week, most of which was in cash (he was informed by Kostya that regular clients were allowed to write checks; credit cards were never accepted). He got to keep twenty-five percent of what his workers earned, which meant his take was in the area of six thousand five hundred a week, out of which he had to give Kostya twenty percent or, roughly, twelve hundred and change. After accounting for a few hundred dollars in business costs, Marcus found himself making forty-five hundred tax-free dollars a week. This projected to eighteen thousand dollars a month, or two hundred and sixteen thousand a year, almost quadruple what he had been making while working for Wazoo Toys. If things continued to go smoothly, the Ripps family debt, so recently overwhelming, was going to be retired far sooner than expected. Marcus didn't have a family health plan, but now he could afford one, along with whatever prize he desired should he want to conjure an external symbol of his change in fortune. Lenore's eyes could be properly looked after, and if she needed to ease the pressure on her ocular nerves, she would be able to smoke more pot than a village of Rastafarians. Nathan's educational therapist, tutors, clarinet teacher, and orthodonist could be paid. Marcus could even float Ripcord, should he choose. It was a brilliant setup. He did the math and made a silent pact with himself—he would operate the business for two years. In that time, he would get out of debt, build a nest egg, and find a new line of work.

Despite his philosophical search for an overarching justification, a vestigial, difficult-to-eradicate sense of doing something wrong lingered on the edge of his consciousness. However much he tried to banish these thoughts, the nature of the work continued to trouble him, and he worried about the women in his employ. Who were these people? It was impossible to generalize, other than to say they were relatively young, in good physical shape, and not unskilled in the traditional sense of the word. Along with Amstel, Xiomara/Jenna, and Mink there was a Chinese-American and an African-American. There was a white girl from Redondo Beach, and a Latina from Boyle Heights. There were two students at local colleges, and, this being Los Angeles, there was an actress. There was a woman going through a divorce whose soon-to-be-ex-husband was recalcitrant about paying alimony, and there was a single mother whose daughter was on a partial scholarship at a Catholic school and was doing this to make up the difference. There was a little model who, at 5′4″, was finding her height to be more of an impediment than she was previously willing to consider. There was a former funeral-home cosmetologist who could no longer bear the nearness of death, and so was drawn to the opposite primordial experience. They were women who didn't want to test their work skills on a market that would have them be a waitress at Bennigan's, or a sales associate at the Gap, or a *barista* at Starbucks, when they could earn more in an afternoon than someone laboring at one of those places could make in a week and so what if they did it by selling sex. If America was having an epic party in its pants, why shouldn't they make a buck out of it? As for Marcus, it was like the man on the financial TV show said: *Someone's going to get rich; it may as well be you!*

He purchased a copy of *Tax Preparation for Dummies* at a local Staples store and taught himself how to set up 401(k) retirement accounts. He sent a group e-mail in which he reiterated his offer to the workers, and many of them availed themselves of the proffered financial services, making weekly contributions into the accounts he set up for them.

Rising every morning, Marcus would discharge his familial duties and then go to the dry cleaner, where he would field calls and book appointments. He joined an upscale gym where he would ride a stationary bike, play pickup basketball, and then relax in the sauna. Twice a week he would play golf at the Woodley Lakes course. They hired several drivers, so in the evenings he would go home, his cell phone and BlackBerry on vibrate, and deal with calls and messages as they came in until ten o'clock, always making an excuse to go to his home office, where he would contact the provider and arrange the "date." To allay whatever suspicions Jan might have, he told her he was dealing with a group of investors he had found with whom he intended to expand the dry cleaning business into a chain. Jan was able to bring her mother to a Beverly Hills eye surgeon, who attended to her condition with optimal results. Lenore expressed deep gratitude, and Marcus drew great satisfaction from being able to help her.

Although everything was going smoothly, his new existence brought on an inchoate sense of dread that waxed and waned but would not abate. Marcus had a preternatural early warning system in his lower back. Often, during moments of great stress, he would experience excruciating back spasms, which were preceded by a heightened sensitivity in his lumbar region. He had felt some twinges down there, which gave him pause, but he would do stretches a chiropractor had prescribed for him years earlier, and he was able to stave off an attack.

Marcus leased a Mercedes sedan, thinking the leather seats, superb climate control, and easy ride might help him relax. He explained the indulgence to Jan by telling her that business was going exceedingly well.

But the secrecy began to exact a toll. Marcus attended one of Nathan's basketball games on a weekday afternoon. His cell phone rang as he slid into the seat beside Jan. The phone rang three more times in the next fifteen minutes, and when he excused himself to return the calls at halftime, she said "You *are* a popular dry cleaner." He wasn't sure how to interpret the remark, but the fifteen points Nathan scored in his team's victory seemed to interest Jan more than whatever Marcus was doing.

Early in the afternoon on a clear winter day, he was at Shining City going over the accounts with Kostya. They'd been running the business for several months, and it had been going smoothly. The radio was playing a Van Halen song Marcus had liked in high school, but his mind was on the sixteenth hole at Woodley Lakes.

"Mink only worked three nights last week," Kostya said.

"Is that significant?"

"I think she's maybe making dates independent-like."

"Should I talk to her?"

"*Talk* to her? For why?"

"To get her to stop."

"You want her to stop . . . other ways to make her stop." Kostya looked at him in a manner intended to convey that even if this was not the kind of business Marcus was accustomed to, it was now the one he was in.

This was more than Marcus had bargained for, and he had to set boundaries. Smacking the girls around was not something he would condone.

"I'm not comfortable . . ."

"Other girls hear what's going on, they do same thing. Business kaput. You hit with open hand, she will understand."

Marcus gave Kostya a pained look. "I can't hit anyone."

"You know what your problem is, Breeze? You want everyone to like you. Does not matter if *anyone* likes you. What matters is you have gas in car, food on table. Don't forget—you are helping with 401(k)s. You want me do it for you?" Marcus sipped his coffee. This was certainly a more palatable option. After all, his business was at risk, according to Kostya, who knew a lot more about it than Marcus did. What was he being so squeamish for? Kostya looked at him, awaiting a response. "Breeze, you want me to do it?"

"Yes . . . no! I want you to talk to her, but no hitting. We're not running that kind of operation." Like a carnivore who could not abide the abattoir, Marcus was happy to pass the responsibility to someone less uncomfortable than he. "Kostya, I'm not kidding. Look at me."

"I'm looking, okay?"

"No violence."

Kostya shook his head and gave him a patronizing glance. Marcus didn't care. There were things he wouldn't do.

"Anybody back there? Hello!"

It was Jan. Marcus briefly considered running out the back, but the thought flitted away as soon as it arrived.

"That's my wife," he whispered. "Be cool—she has no idea what's going on." As Kostya looked at him incredulously, Marcus called out, "We're in the office!" Jan stuck her head in the door a moment later.

"Nice place," she said.

Marcus introduced Jan to Kostya and they nodded to each other.

"Where is everyone? I thought there would be more bustle."

"Slow time of day. What are you doing here?"

"I just dropped my mother off at her pole-dancing class and I have some time before I have to pick her up. I thought you might want to get lunch."

Marcus heard the front door open, and another voice rang out: "Breeze, I gotta tell you what happened with that guy at the Peninsula last night." It was Cassie, a girl they had hired the previous week. The place was starting to feel like Union Station. When Jan looked in the direction of the sound, Marcus and Kostya exchanged a glance.

"Right here, yo!" Kostya called out. He bounded from the chair, squeezed past Jan, and loped in Cassie's direction.

"Let's eat," Marcus said. When they left, Kostya and Cassie were nowhere in sight.

"Who was that?" Jan asked as they walked toward his car. Marcus told her it was Kostya's girlfriend.

They went out for Indian food and ordered a bottle of wine with lunch, something that would never have happened at any other time in their lives together. Jan did not ask any questions about the business. Freed from the money woes that had dogged them for so long, they took slow pleasure in each other's company. They even talked about where they might go for a getaway. Jan liked the idea of Ojai. She chased the last piece of saag paneer with a sip of Chardonnay and smiled at Marcus. She was wearing jeans and a white sweater with horizontal blue stripes. Her chestnut hair was swept back and her face was clear and open.

"Let's go to a hotel," he said.

"Now?"

"I have a light afternoon."

"My mother needs to be picked up."

"She can take a cab. Nate has basketball practice until six. That gives us nearly . . ."—he checked his watch—"four hours."

"Marcus . . ." She said his name in a voice that indicated that the unexpected lunch had unlocked a hidden chamber, dimly lit, richly upholstered. She was drunk, but in an agreeable way. He paid the bill, and they headed for the Mondrian Hotel on Sunset Boulevard because he knew they gave a discount to AAA members.

In their room on the tenth floor overlooking the Hollywood Hills, a nearly empty bottle of pinot grigio rested in a silver bucket. The blinds were only partially closed, so while half the room was lit with the afternoon klieg of the sun, the two of them lay beneath the covers, luxuriating in the shadows. The wine had tucked in their inhibitions, kissing them good night, and Marcus sensed the timing was propitious. He produced a gleaming silver egg. Jan regarded it curiously.

"What's this?"

"It's an egg."

"I can see that it's an egg, Marcus. What does it do?"

"You're supposed to put it . . . you know."

"Excuse me?"

"Down there."

"No!"

"Um-hmm."

"And then . . .?"

"It vibrates."

"Really?"

"That's what the instructions say."

"Where'd you get it?"

"I bought it on the Internet." Amstel had given it to him a week earlier, but he didn't think one small lie mattered, given the major ones he'd been telling lately. Jan held the object in her fingertips, examining it in the light. She eyed it with drunken concentration. Before Marcus had to launch into a sales pitch, it vanished into her nether region like a magic trick.

"What happens now?" she said brightly, game. Thrilled by her willingness to play, Marcus showed her what looked like a television remote control. "What's that?"

He pressed a button on the device. Jan nearly swooned.

"Oh, god . . . Marcus . . . Oh . . ." She breathed evenly as the hidden egg pulsed, sending powerful vibrations coursing through her body. "This is . . . oohh."

"It's got ten settings," he said helpfully.

"Which one is it on?" Her voice was shaky, a passenger on a heaving ship.

"The first."

"You're . . . oh . . . kidding." Marcus pressed the button again. "Oh, Marcus . . . oh, God!"

"That's three." Her orgasm approached like a drunk trying to beat last call, barreling, arms waving. Her eyes were closed, her head thrown back, the dam breaking, a torrent gushing. Then it passed, but the electronic pulsations that conjured the wild river did not cease.

"Put it on two!" she ordered. "*Put it on two!*" Marcus obliged and punched #2 in. Jan settled down slightly. Her eyes were half open, her head to the side.

"It does more stuff," he said, but Jan didn't appear to be listening. She was lazing in the swirls and eddies now, savoring the slow ride. Marcus kissed her, and she flicked her tongue along his lips and teeth, then toward his throat, something she had not done in a long time. After she came again, she took him in her mouth, sucking and stroking, as he played with the remote control, alternating between #1 and #2. He thought about the tension he carried and the tightness in his lumbar region. He worried about the long-term health effects of leading a double life. Shifting his weight to relieve the pressure on his back, he watched his wife as she concentrated on pleasing him. She was unburdened now, relaxed enough to have hotel sex on a weekday afternoon with her loving husband and a vibrating egg. Emboldened, Marcus again pressed the remote control and suddenly there was another human sound in the room, soft and feminine. Jan stopped what she was doing and looked at Marcus.

"What is that?"

"The egg has a chip in it."

The smoky croon of a well-known pop diva was emanating from Jan's interior. The expression on her face, wonder entwined with delight, all coated in a gossamer membrane of the purest sensuality, was one with which Marcus was unfamiliar. It was good she was drunk, he reflected, given that her vagina had started to sing.

As Marcus gazed at his wife, he forgot the passage of the years, how they had gone by in a wash of pregnancy, diapers, sleep deprivation, weekly carpools, shopping, cooking, cleaning, endless ever-regenerating bills, the ongoing responsibilities of adulthood. All that faded away in the soft afternoon light of the hotel room.

They listened to the singer's breathy voice for a moment and then both began to laugh, freely, without inhibition or anxiety, the most innocent, happiest sound either of them had made in years. When she kissed him, he knew he had witnessed the dawning of the second phase of their marriage.

Jan had not discovered what was going on that day, but Marcus believed it would be impossible to keep news of his activities from her forever. Although their hotel encounter temporarily relaxed him, the close call at the dry cleaner exacerbated the general level of tension he was feeling. He needed to talk, to unburden himself to someone he knew would not pass judgment. Atlas would be willing to listen and could be relied upon to be discreet. The two of them were scheduled to play nine holes at noon the next day. He was waiting at the starter's window at Woodley Lakes when his phone rang. It was Kostya.

He did not bother with a greeting: "Mink will not be causing more troubles."

"You didn't . . ." Marcus said.

"You tell me not to," Kostya said, "so I don't." Marcus did not want to know what had transpired. What mattered was that the issue would no longer be a problem.

Atlas appeared as the conversation ended, and he greeted Marcus desultorily, not looking him in the eye when they shook hands. Marcus said there was something he wanted to talk about, but he'd get into it later. Atlas didn't seem to be listening.

It was a warm day and Marcus started to perspire after his third practice swing. He played the first couple of holes well, relieved that he would finally be able to tell someone what his life had become and discuss a means of coping.

Atlas was four shots over par by the time they were on the third hole, and his mood seemed to have gotten worse. After a bad tee shot on the second hole, followed by an equally ugly mulligan, he threw his club, something Marcus had never seen him do. He tried to laugh about it a moment later, but Marcus could tell he was upset. Still, there was the need to talk, to describe what was happening in his life to someone who knew him well, if only to concretize it, make it slightly less hallucinatory. While Atlas lined up his tee shot on the fifth hole, Marcus made a pact with himself. He would tell him by the end of the round. Atlas swung, and the shot faded to the right. Marcus squinted as he followed the flight of the ball.

"I'm not going to be able to play for the next month," Atlas said as the ball dribbled into a grove of old-growth trees.

"Going somewhere?"

"Rehab."

Marcus wasn't sure if this was a joke. "For what?"

"I lost ninety thou at the sports book in Vegas over the last month, and it's gotta stop. My life's gone completely to shit."

Marcus was stunned. "Oh, man, I'm sorry."

"I was ordering a double cappuccino this morning and I wanted to know the over/under on the guy making my drink in thirty seconds. Can you believe that? I wanted to bet on the fucking coffee guy."

"That's pretty bad." Marcus tried to be sympathetic, but it was a strain. *He* was the one who needed peace, love, and understanding.

"Anyway, I'm checking in tomorrow. Would you mind looking in on my house once a week? I already suspended the mail delivery."

Marcus told him he'd be happy to, hiding the annoyance he felt. His problem was indisputably greater, but far less socially acceptable. At least Atlas could stand in a circle with a bunch of other out-of-control gamblers and talk about his situation. What was Marcus supposed to do? Now he didn't even want to finish the round of golf.

Chapter 13

Jan sipped her lemonade, hoping Plum wouldn't begin to cry at the table. It was just after one in the afternoon, and they were seated in the dining room of the Sportsman's Lodge, a popular venue on Ventura Boulevard that was both a restaurant and a hotel. Since the expansion of Marcus's earning capacity, Jan had gotten Plum to agree to work on alternate days. Today was Jan's day to not work. They were having lunch because Plum had insisted.

After the waitress took their order, Plum told Jan about a date she had gone on the previous evening with someone she'd met on the Internet.

"He had a great voice on the phone, but I think the picture he posted was, like, ten years old and he had about a week's worth of stubble on his face which is fine if you're twenty-three but this guy looked like Charles Bukowski, and not in a good way, you know, like he's written some great poems and books. He looked more like he was sleeping in his car. I actually thought about having sex, but I didn't see the point. Then I felt so lousy about the whole thing this morning, I went to get a manicure and pedicure at the Vietnamese place in the mini-mall near my house where I always think they're talking about me." Jan knew that Plum desperately felt the desire for someone to touch her fingers, and, more intimately, her toes, even if it was only a Vietnamese woman wielding an emery board as if she was in a Hong Kong chopsocky film. Now Plum examined the results on her right hand, stretching it in front of her.

"Did we sell anything today?" Jan asked.

"Nearly five hundred dollars' worth of stuff," Plum informed her. It had actually been a rare good morning at the store, which pleased Jan, since it would allow her to encourage Plum to buy her out with a slightly clearer conscience. "A woman came in and bought three pair of those French jeans with the rips and the piping." The conversation had been proceeding in fits and starts for five minutes now, and Jan was trying to figure out how to touch upon the subject of selling out in a way that would not make her soon-to-be erstwhile partner overly emotional.

This is when Plum said: "I have to get my hands on fifteen thousand dollars."

Jan was not going to give her an opening, having told herself on the ride over that she would not let Plum rope her into any more craziness. So she waited, pretending to read the menu. Jan had been thinking about asking what Plum was going to have for lunch, but now she was angry—Plum dropped that conversational bomb and then held back, as if Jan would just jump in and begin helping her figure out how to get the money. The truth was, Jan had reached her limit. If Plum wanted to talk about another ridiculous idea, treating time as a renewable resource, let her do the work. "Would you like to know why?" Plum asked.

Since she had phrased it as a direct question, Jan could no longer ignore the gambit without appearing as self-involved as Plum. So she finally gave in, audibly sighing, hoping this would let Plum know where things stood. "Sure. Why?" She said the words with no emotion, since she didn't want Plum to think she was actually interested.

"I started spotting this morning, and because I went to a cut-rate clinic, they only give you one shot and that was my . . ."

"You were pregnant? How?"

"I told you I found an egg donor on the Internet. You don't listen." Jan stared in disbelief. The word *egg* had a new association for her now, and she had to fight to maintain her concentration on Plum. There was a stirring in her loins but she willed it away. "I've

145

already shot five hours of footage for the video piece, and if I can't get pregnant . . ." and here Plum's words dissolved into guttural sounds accompanied by barely muffled sobbing. Jan's eyes darted around the dining room, looking for a way to escape, some tear in the San Fernando Valley time-space continuum she could slip through. Plum foraged in her purse and produced a packet of tissues from which she removed one and blew her nose. Taking another, she daubed her eyes. "I won't get a dime out of Atlas any time soon."

"Maybe you should talk to someone."

"What, a therapist? All they do is confirm every bad thing you already know about yourself. That's not what I need right now."

Jan waited to see if Plum would continue down this road, but it appeared that she had run out of gas.

"There's something else we kind of need to deal with," Jan said. "I want to get out of the business." Plum opened her mouth, but no sound emerged. She looked like a fish being gutted while it was still alive. Jan continued: "I didn't want to do this for a living, run a store."

"I went to art school!" Plum interjected, as if implying that *her* life was meant to be a round of gallery openings and museum retrospectives.

"Yeah, I did, too, okay? Remember? With you? I hadn't planned on sitting in a little boutique on Van Nuys Boulevard praying for customers to walk in." Jan noticed that Plum was clearly taken aback by her tone, which was more assertive than usual. "We have to stop pretending it's working, because it's just not. I have to be honest with you. Ripcord is over." She paused a moment and said "I'm sorry you're spotting," even though she wasn't sorry at all.

Plum daubed her nose with a fresh tissue, sniffled, and said "Isn't that Marcus?"

Jan turned her head looking for her husband, greatly relieved. She knew Plum was not likely to continue in a weepy vein as long as Marcus was around. But the feeling of reprieve soon turned to something queasier when she gazed across the room and saw him sitting at a table for two opposite an attractive woman in a tight blouse, short skirt, and ankle-high, spike-heeled leather boots.

"Who's he having lunch with?" Plum asked.

Fighting a rising nervousness, Jan threaded her way between the other diners to arrive at her husband's table. Marcus appeared so engrossed with the woman to whom he was speaking that it was a moment before he realized someone was standing next to them, and still another moment before he registered that it was Jan. She watched him glance quickly at his companion, then back to her, a squirrel trying to determine the best path across a treacherous road.

"Hi, honey. Who's your friend?" Jan said. Grateful that she was able to control the timbre of her voice, she turned and presented a steel smile to the woman who greeted her in an accent that struck Jan as Eastern European. Where could Marcus possibly have met a woman like this?

"Amstel, this is Jan," Marcus said.

"His wife," Jan responded, cogitating on the name *Amstel*. Had he made it up? What was Marcus doing with an attractive European woman named Amstel? "We're married."

"We sure are," Marcus said, in a neutral tone.

Amstel nodded in approval. "Congratulations."

Marcus and Jan stood nearly nose to nose in the corner of the Sportsman's Lodge lobby, their backs to whoever might be looking at them. Today it was a blonde family from Utah and three Japanese businessmen. No one was paying attention to the drama in the corner. Jan asked who the woman was and what was the nature of her relationship with Marcus?

"She's a business associate." The notion that someone who looked like Amstel had anything to do with dry cleaning was so implausible, Jan didn't quite know how to respond.

"A *dry cleaner?*"

"Yes," he said, his confidence wilting like a camellia in a microwave.

"So if I march back in there she's going to tell me, what, she presses pants for a living? Marcus, if you're having an affair, I want you to admit it. It'll be easier."

"Listen, sweetheart . . ."

"Don't call me sweetheart!"

"Fine. *Jan.* I can't get into it right now, but I swear to you on our son, I have *never* cheated on you!"

"Then tell me what's going on."

"I'm an agent."

"An *agent*? Is that woman an actress?"

"Not exactly. But I represent her."

"Marcus, this isn't making sense."

"I swear I'll tell you everything tonight."

Marcus waited as Jan decided whether this was an acceptable offer. It was hard for her to believe that this was the man with whom she had so recently spent several erotic hours at the Mondrian Hotel. She thought they had broken through to a new level of their marriage, and now everything was suddenly at risk.

"I'll wait up," Jan said, and returned to the dining room.

Chapter 14

The Mercedes was parked outside the Beverly Hills Hotel in the cool evening. Marcus sat in the front seat, saying good night to Nathan on his cell phone. It was just after nine thirty. He'd been so upset by his surprise encounter with Jan, he had spent the afternoon trying to track down an arcade game called Soul Stealer, which he intended to give to Nathan as a surprise. Several hours of investigation had led him to a warehouse east of downtown, where he located one being sold for two thousand dollars. The bulky machine was now wedged in the trunk. Showing his love for their son was a way of deflecting the opprobrium he expected was headed his way. He wondered if he should have bought a diamond bracelet instead. There was no way to tell how Jan was going to react when she discovered what was going on.

"Can you come to my baseball game next week?"

"I'll be there," Marcus said, relieved for the opportunity to do something familial. He couldn't hear Nathan's response and had to cover his other ear with his palm to drown out the chatter from the women seated behind him. When Jan got on the phone, he told her he was taking care of some business and would talk to her later tonight. She hung up without saying good-bye. Feeling deeply unappreciated, Marcus sighed and looked toward the hotel, where a new girl was working. Xiomara/Jenna was in the car with Cindy, a transplant from Dallas where until recently she had been studying anthropology in graduate school. Cindy was telling Xiomara/Jenna about the mating habits of the Hmong people of Laos when his cell phone rang. He checked the caller ID: Amstel.

"Breeze, we have predicament."

"What kind of predicament?"

"*Big* one."

Marcus felt the muscles in his lower back contract.

For someone looking at a dead body on a bed, Amstel was relatively calm. It was half an hour later, and Marcus was standing in the Beverly Hills-adjacent apartment, his back hurtling toward a full-throttle spasm. He'd put the women in cabs and arrived as fast as he was able. Now, feet planted on the imitation Persian rug in the center of the room, eyes fixed on the rumpled sheets, he tried to formulate a plan. The dead man was slightly overweight, swarthy, and naked. Probably in his middle fifties.

And he was handcuffed to the bed frame.

Amstel had gotten dressed after calling Marcus. Sitting in a chair holding a clove cigarette, she appeared outwardly composed, but the manner in which she was smoking—a sharp inhale followed by a long exhalation, during which a river of smoke coursed from her, then repeated immediately—gave the lie to her cool. "I am riding his face, you know, for maybe two minutes he is eating me out. He makes weird noise and his eyes bug. So I climb off, get glass of water. I am at sink, I look over, face is red, eyes are wide open—he is dead. I call you."

"You think he had a heart attack?"

"Breeze, do I look like doctor?"

"You did the right thing, calling me."

"I go now."

"What do you mean you go now?"

"Is what I mean. *I. Go. Now.* Good-bye. I quit this life. You are nice guy, Breeze. You quit, too."

"Whoa, whoa, whoa, Amstel, first of all, you can't just leave. This guy is handcuffed to the bed. Where's the key?"

"I don't know where is key."

A brief tour of the dead man's clothes did not reveal the answer to this mystery, although it did yield a wallet with several credit cards, nearly seven hundred dollars in cash, and a California driver's license that identified him as Mahmoud Ghorbanifar of 1563 Summit Drive, Beverly Hills. He was local. That wasn't good. If anyone was expecting him home, they'd be looking by the next day.

"I can't move the body myself, Amstel. My back . . . it's like someone's chewing on the nerve."

"Listen to me, please," she said, her tone beseeching him to understand her compromised position. "I am not citizen. I get caught with dead body, after jail I am back in Latvia."

He was a lot less charmed by her accent now. "If you leave, you're not working for the service any more."

"I already tell you I quit! Are you fucking idiot?"

"You can't go!"

"Bad idea to threaten, Breeze." *Threaten?* He didn't think he had threatened her. "One phone call, I put you out of business. Anon . . . anon . . . Shit! How do you say?"

"Anonymous." When he fed her the word, it felt like he was wrapping a rope around his own neck.

"Anonymous phone call, okay? To police, and you are cooked like sausage. Don't drag me into mess of yours." It *was* his mess, ultimately. He couldn't deny that. But Amstel's total abdication of responsibility was even more of a rough surprise than the black cats her eyes were throwing him. "Do we understand?"

Marcus nodded. He thought they had bonded, but obviously he'd been mistaken. She closed the door silently as she left, discreet to the last. His first thought was to call Kostya and let him deal with the situation. But when Kostya had agreed to work with him, he had made it abundantly clear that Marcus was to assume all risk in the running of the business, so that plan was immediately scotched. The maid was due to arrive the next morning and she had a key to the apartment.

She was always hard to reach, and Marcus didn't want to have to remain here only to tell her she couldn't come in and clean the place. He wished he'd had the foresight to hide a bottle of whiskey in the apartment. A drink might calm him down; allow him to focus his thoughts. He needed to get rid of the body tonight, but his back was in so much pain he couldn't stand up straight.

Julian would have known what to do in these circumstances. He wouldn't panic. Years earlier, Marcus could have called him in a situation like this. Or Roon. Those two knew how to get away with things. He thought about calling Atlas, but he was not scheduled to get out of rehab for another several days.

The muscles running across his lower back suddenly jerked angrily inward, yanking his left hip out of alignment and causing his upper torso to tip in that direction. He grunted in pain. His body was beginning to assume the contour of a question mark. He tried to recall if he had any painkillers at home.

"Jan, it's me."

"Marcus?" He voice was groggy, far away. "I waited up for you. I thought we were going to talk, but I fell asleep. What's going on?"

Seated on the sofa across from the dead man with a pillow propped against his lower back to relieve the discomfort, cell phone pressed to his ear, he was temporarily pain-free. But he knew that if he moved a centimeter in any direction, his nerve endings would detonate. "We *are* going to talk. Just not this second. There's an emergency."

Now she was awake. "Oh, god, Marcus, are you all right? Is everything okay?"

"No. It's not. It's *really* not. I'm in kind of a bad situation." He told her where he was and asked how soon she could be there. His tone let her know that staying home was not an option.

"What's going on?"

"I can't tell you on the phone."

"You have to, or I'm not coming."

"I can't, please believe me." He couldn't take the risk of telling her, then have her freak out to the degree she might not be willing to help. "I really need you right now. *Please*. There's an all-night Home Depot on Ventura. Go there and buy a hacksaw and some duct tape."

"*What?*"

"Would you just do it? And then go to a drugstore and get me some painkillers."

Marcus sat completely still. No sound drifted up from the street. He was conscious of his pounding heart, the pulse in his neck, the dryness of his mouth. What is marriage supposed to be about?

"Give me forty-five minutes."

A dead body any other place than a funeral home is the worst kind of surprise. Strolling back to their car in Chinatown one evening, Marcus and Jan had found themselves taking a shortcut through an alley. In the shadow of a building, next to a mound of packing crates had been a corpse. It was that of a young man lying on his back, legs splayed, his neck at an unnatural angle. Jan nearly jumped out of her skin. Marcus said they needed to report it and wanted to notify the police. Jan told him he could just as easily call from the car, which is what he ended up doing. Remembering her reaction that evening, he pulled a sheet over the body so she wouldn't have a meltdown immediately upon walking into the apartment.

It was after midnight. Marcus was attempting to alleviate the pain by lying on his back in the middle of the room with his knees pulled up to his chest when he heard Jan knock.

"I'll be right there," he said. Then he rolled over to his side, placed both hands on the floor and pushed himself into a position from which he could get his legs under him without causing undue stress on his lower back. It was a move he'd had to perform many times. Marcus thanked her for coming as soon as he opened the door, and asked if she'd brought the painkillers.

She handed him a small bottle of Advil and walked quickly past, looking around. He was relieved to see the Home Depot bag. When

153

she noticed the large lump under the sheets from which a cuffed hand was protruding, she shot Marcus a surprised look. "Is someone here?" she asked, whispering, unnerved. It was a rhetorical question.

"That's Mr. Ghorbi-something."

"Who is he?"

"I don't know exactly, but he's dead."

Her audible gasp involved most of the oxygen in the room. "Oh, god . . . he's . . . who . . .?"

"He's some guy. It's not important who he is. He's dead, is the point."

"What's the hacksaw for, Marcus?" Jan seemed to lose her balance for a moment. Marcus gently touched her arm as shock coursed through her, momentarily impeding brain function. "He's dead? Oh god, he's dead, oh god, god . . . no! Marcus, ohhh! How did you . . . no, no, no!"

"You have to stay cool."

Marcus's neck felt stiff. He filled a glass with water and swallowed four Advils.

Jan collapsed into an upholstered chair and stared at him. The shock was giving way to vulnerability, and tenderness. Truly, this was far worse than she'd imagined.

"I think you better come clean right now."

Marcus completed a lightning-quick cost-benefit analysis, then told her everything: Julian's real occupation, Dominic Festa, the cell phone, the Shining City reality, Kostya, the women, the signing of the releases, the arranging of the assignations. It all ran together in a torrent of revelation that Marcus hoped would, in its clean-breasted completeness, both expiate his sins and cause her to understand why he had committed them in the first place. He pleaded with her to understand that this was a strictly a business venture, not a salacious fantasy that had attacked him in early middle age, leaving him bereft of his standards and senses. Marcus wished she would interrupt, ask a question. But she just sat there, flabbergasted. He sensed she would not be much help right now. Marcus concluded by swearing he had never touched any of the women.

Jan waited a long moment before she said "So this explains the vibrating egg."

"Yes," he agreed. "It does."

Prying the Home Depot bag from Jan's nervous grip, he removed the hacksaw. Then he pulled the sheet back, crouched next to the corpse, and began to slash at the chain holding the wrist to the bed. The dissonant grinding of metal on metal further set his nerves on edge. The lifeless hand cuffed to the bed jiggled in mad pantomime as Marcus sawed away, trying not to come into contact with the cool flesh. Light from the bedside lamp caught a blue stone in a pinky ring on the dead man's pale finger.

Jan sank deeper into the chair and watched in despair, having still not entirely digested what Marcus had revealed to her about his working life.

"Shouldn't you call the police?"

"I can't call the police," he said, not looking at her as he continued to saw the chain. "What am I going to tell them?"

She thought a moment and realized he had a point. "Where are we?" she asked. "Whose apartment is this?"

"It's mine, and the women who work for me use it to entertain."

"*Entertain?*"

"For chrissakes, could you please not bust my balls right now?" Shifting his legs, Marcus tried to find a position that would lessen the pressure on his inflamed lower back. He wondered if he'd slipped a disc this time. Howling messages of pain pulsed through his nervous system and into his perfervid brain. He continued to manipulate the hacksaw, adjusting the angle slightly in hopes of increasing his efficiency. "I'm sorry I had to call you. Someone was here who could have helped me, but they left. My back is killing me. I can't move the body myself." His breath quickened as a result of his exertions.

"Why do we have to move the body? Why can't you just tell the

155

police he had a . . . what? What happened? Heart attack, stroke?" She said this as if diagnosing the physiological goings-on would somehow allow her to better comprehend the underlying meaning of the event.

"It doesn't matter," Marcus said. He had found a position where the pain was bearable if he didn't move his hips. "I don't know who he is, beyond his name which I can't even pronounce. And I can't risk having to answer all the questions they're going to ask when they find a dead guy."

"Why did you need *me*?"

"You have to help move the body."

"Marcus . . . how am I supposed to . . .?"

"We've got to get him in the van."

She looked at him as if he'd lost his mind. "Oh, no. No, no, no, no, no, no, no. You're not going to put a dead body in the van we drive our son to school in."

Marcus thought about the argument she was making and found it to be so utterly unconsidered, he allowed himself a hint of sarcasm.

"Oh, okay. I guess I'll call a cab."

"You think this is *funny*?"

"Listen, Jan, I'd still be working at Wazoo if things were okay, but they're not, so if you want me in jail you can go home."

"What's wrong with your car?"

"There's an arcade game in the trunk and it's too heavy to move."

"Why is there an arcade game in the trunk?"

"I'm giving it to Nathan."

"You bought him an arcade game without discussing it with me?"

"Can we not talk about that right now?"

"Fine."

Marcus wanted to maintain some shred of dignity but understood supplication was in order. "Please help me tonight and I'll never . . ."

"Where are you planning to take . . .?"

"About an hour north of here."

"Do you have any lime?"

"Why do I need lime?"

"It's what they put on dead bodies to make them decompose."

"We don't need lime."

"You get it at a gardening store. Maybe you should pick some up."

"*I SAID WE DON'T NEED LIME!*" Marcus's face was red. Sweat had begun to trickle down his brow. He saw the way she looked at him and realized he needed to ratchet down the tension level. Silently, he vowed to say as little as possible for the remainder of the evening. Jan was the one who brought up lime. That was complicity. For better or for worse. Marriage was wonderful.

It took Marcus fifteen minutes to hack his way through the slender chain. Then, hunched like Quasimodo and craving morphine, he maneuvered the dead man onto the imitation Persian rug and rolled him in it. Under Jan's nervous gaze, he took the duct tape and sealed both ends of the rug. After a few false starts, during which the pain was so severe that Marcus felt like a dagger had been thrust into his lower back, the two of them were able to lift the rug and its contents off the ground and into the hallway.

Since the apartment was on the fifth floor, the next question was whether to head for the stairs or the elevator. Although the chances of running into someone were far greater in the elevator, Marcus knew trying to get the cargo down five flights of stairs would probably result in a period of prolonged hospitalization. They dragged the rug down the hall, pressed the elevator button, and waited.

The hall was eerily quiet in the half light cast by the dim sconces. It was around one in the morning now, and if anyone appeared, Marcus would simply tell them they were moving late at night to avoid the crush of people during the day. As excuses went, this was not a good one, and he was hugely relieved when the elevator arrived before an interloper did. They were able to maneuver the body through the deserted lobby and out the front door. Marcus and Jan were panting from the effort, and the chill of the night air was welcome. Marcus told her he was going to get the van.

"You're not leaving me on the sidewalk with a dead body," Jan hissed, her look daring him to take even one step away.

Marcus gazed around. The apartment building they had come from loomed behind them, and there was another one across the street. Several lights were on in both buildings, units containing who knew how many sets of prying eyes. Someone in a station wagon was pulling out of a parking space across the street and driving toward them. They watched as the car drove past, but the driver was looking straight ahead. Jan told Marcus she would get the van and left him standing on the sidewalk next to the rolled-up rug.

Half an hour earlier, while he was lying on the floor waiting for Jan to arrive, Marcus had considered where he might dispose of Amstel's deceased client. He recalled a voluminous "Best of L.A." feature done by a local magazine where the editors variously held forth on where to find the Best Vintage Autos, the Best Dim Sum, the Best Teeth Whitening, the Best Whatever-The-Bourgeoisie-Requires. He dimly remembered a sub-category in the "Best Of" compendia called "The Best Place to Dump a Body." The winner: Angeles National Forest.

Jan drove up the 405 freeway staring through the windshield like a zombie and gripping the wheel so tightly, her fingers were becoming numb. Because the seats in the van could not be moved, Marcus was lying on top of the rug that contained the corpse. Jan had turned the heater on so it was warm in the rear of the van, and Marcus began to notice the too-sweet smell of the dead man's cologne. He would have preferred to be driving himself, but getting the body out of the apartment and into the van had further aggravated his injury, necessitating his prone position. Trying to forget that he was lying on a cadaver, Marcus adjusted his sore neck so he could see Jan in the driver's seat. He was happy she was here—no, ecstatic. No longer did he feel like he was writhing on the end of a fishhook. He thought she might never forgive him, but at least she was going to help get rid of the body. If that wasn't love, he reflected, he didn't know what love was.

After forty-five minutes during which the only sound was the humming of the engine, Jan asked Marcus to tell her about the business. Her interest revived his spirits, and in confidential tones he told her about how the operation worked, who was on the payroll, and, most important, how little contact he had with the women. He did, however, emphasize that he had helped several of them set up 401(k)s, and when Jan evinced amusement at this incongruity, Marcus believed whatever he was doing at that moment was working. Then he delivered the coup de grace: "I'm going to stop eventually, but let's remember that we have health insurance now and it paid for your mother's eye surgery."

Jan absorbed this information silently.

They drove past Magic Mountain, where Marcus had ridden the roller coasters with Nathan the year before, and out of the San Fernando Valley. Past Castaic, where he'd gone on family picnics when he was a boy, before things had soured with Julian. Past Santa Clarita, where Marcus and Jan had gone to a birthday party Plum threw for Atlas at an art deco bowling alley in a happier time that was receding behind them at warp speed.

The van was surrounded by a herd of groaning semis as it climbed the steep northerly incline. Pushing himself off the floor, Marcus rose to his feet and lurched to the passenger seat. He told Jan to take the exit for Solitario Canyon, a remote place where he remembered camping with Roon the summer after they'd graduated from high school. A dirt road there ran deep into the mountains. Jan eased the van off the freeway, then headed west on the overpass before dipping into the canyon.

Marcus directed her to an access road that led into the backwoods. After a couple of minutes he told her to turn off the headlights and pull over. She did as she was directed.

"Stop the van and get out."

"Why?"

"I don't want you driving, okay? So if anything bad happens, it's my fault." Marcus believed the least he could do in this situation was be chivalrous.

Jan got and walked around to the passenger side as Marcus slid into the driver's seat, his back throbbing. They turned off the main road and onto a dirt road that led directly into the woods. He cracked the window slightly, and the scent of pine blew in as they bumped along, climbing into the hills, dense chaparral rising on both sides. They rode in silence, their path illuminated by moonlight. Marcus stared straight ahead. Never in his fifteen years of marriage could he have imagined the two of them dumping a corpse together. He was impressed she had come and amazed she had stayed. It was a high-water mark in their relationship, a life-or-death test Jan had passed admirably. That she wanted to throttle him—which he could discern from the severe expression on her face—was immaterial. She was here. That was the important thing. Moreover, he knew how she felt. Had their positions been reversed, he believed he would have acted similarly, and wanted to throttle her, too, for having created such a regrettable situation. He suffered greatly for putting her in this position. Not quite as much as he was suffering from the back pain—which had become transcendentally agonizing—but close. After ascending for nearly ten minutes, during which he prayed for a giant Vicodin lick to magically appear, Marcus pulled the van to the side of the road.

"Where are we?"

"I have no idea."

"You have *no idea*? Then why are we here, Marcus?"

"Shhhh. Be quiet for a second." He spoke with an authority to which she was not accustomed. "Do you see anything? Do you hear anything?" She had to admit that she didn't. "*That's* why we're here." He pulled the emergency brake and got out. They were over four thousand feet above sea level and the night was cold. His breath was visible, but he didn't feel the chill. He walked to the side of the van and pulled the door open. "Would you give me a hand? I can barely move." She got out and stood next to him. "I need you to rub right . . . there." He indicated a spot just above his right hip.

"You want a massage?" Jan had zipped her jacket up to her chin and was rubbing her hands together for warmth.

"Please?" He sensed she would have liked to reach through his skin, remove the closest organ, and feed it to the owl that was hooting in the distance. Instead, she surprised him by digging her fingertips into his lower back and kneading the taut muscle. He exhaled gratefully.

In a moment, they had maneuvered the rug and its contents out of the van. Jan climbed back into the passenger seat. Marcus asked her what she was doing.

"Getting ready to go."

"We can't leave the body here," he said. Once again, she got out of the van and the two of them dragged the wrapped corpse fifty feet off the road. A coyote barked and was quickly answered by another. They sounded very near. Across the canyon the headlights of a car could be seen navigating a fire road. It was miles away.

"I think we're deep enough in the woods," she said. "What do you want to do about the rug?"

"Let's leave it." She nodded and tried to catch her breath. "I love you," he said.

Jan did not respond to this cheap-sounding stumble toward connection. That it was not cheap, that it was the opposite, as sincere, earnest, and forthright as Marcus had ever been, meant nothing to her at this moment. Marcus was reeling from the pain—it was radiating down his legs now—and walking back to the van, gingerly shuffling through the woods so as not to further exacerbate it. Ten minutes later they were on the paved road, and five minutes

161

after that, fleeing south on the freeway. Jan drove and Marcus lay in the rear.

They had been riding quietly for fifteen minutes when Jan said "Should we call that guy's family?"

"Why?"

"If you died and someone knew where your body was, I'd want them to tell me."

Marcus thought about it for a moment. "I don't think we need to do that. I mean, what would we say? That he died in flagrante with a prostitute? It's probably better they don't know that."

"I would want closure."

"*Closure* is a pathetic word. There is no such thing as closure. It implies things can be put in a box and filed away. Nothing can be filed away. Everything is always present."

"I'm just saying."

"We're not calling anyone."

"It's wrong not to call."

"Right and wrong doesn't enter into it."

Jan didn't answer. Marcus thought about what he'd said for a moment, reflecting on whether he actually thought it was true. His back still ached, and he watched the lights flash by the windows of the van through eyes chalky from lack of sleep. Had he completely jettisoned the moral belief system he had subscribed to for his entire life, or had his standards simply become more elastic? A year earlier, he would have recoiled at the thought of what he'd done this evening. But recoiling was not a realistic option any longer. Leaving a dead body in the forest was something that now went with the territory. Why should he tell anyone where it was? So he could feel good about himself?

"I'm worried about you, Marcus. I'm worried about what could happen to you."

"Well, that's two of us."

"The pressure could kill you."

162

"What do you propose we do about it?"

"I want to be your partner."

Marcus was astonished by her offer. He thought about it for a moment and was struck by the unexpected nature of what he'd concluded. Jan was smart and hardworking. Temptation would be held at bay. All things considered, this was a splendid idea.

Chapter 15

When Jan woke up the next morning her first thought was not What have I done? It was this: How could Marcus have kept his life as a pimp hidden from me? Normally slow to ease from the arms of sleep, her mind was already sprinting. As Marcus quietly snored on the other side of the bed, Jan quickly reviewed his behavior over the past several months, scrutinizing random moments for clues that had eluded her. Other than the newfound confidence he'd been exuding, something she had naïvely ascribed to his success as a dry cleaner, she could recall nothing unusual. Then she remembered—the sex! After years of married copulation he had suddenly, and with no prior warning, ejaculated on her breasts. Shouldn't it have been obvious that *something* unusual was going on? She upbraided herself for not picking up on the hint, then quickly realized, behavior of that nature did not necessarily mean someone was engaged in the sex trade—he could have gotten the idea from the Internet, or a cable movie, the kind that comes on after midnight and stars actors no one's heard of. But Jan's momentary sanguinity vanished the second she remembered the toy Marcus had introduced during their hotel room tryst. How could she have ignored the significance of a vibrating egg? Alone, the egg could have been attributed to media influences, or a momentary flash of wanton lunacy, but in tandem with his unprecedented bedroom acrobatics—there was an obvious pattern and she had missed it. How she yearned for yesterday, life before the phone call and the trip to the forest.

The trip to the forest!

The memory struck like a meteor, bursting to the center of her consciousness where it fractured into pulsing particles of angst and dread. She had helped dispose of a dead body! She, Jan Ripps. A small business owner. A working mom. A loving mom. A woman who had baked cookies when Nathan's Indian Guides tribe had met in her well-tended, suburban home. It seemed incomprehensible.

As Marcus continued to snore, temporarily blissful in a drugged sleep, Jan was overcome with a sense of shame. How could she have taken part in last night's macabre escapade? But what else could she have done? Her husband had found himself in extremis and *someone* had to help. In sickness, and in health and, apparently, in crime. And if she hadn't pitched in, then what? He could have gone to jail! If you were a famous person in Los Angeles, you were immune to the vicissitudes of the judicial system. You could kill your girlfriend or your wife and still get a book deal and a good tee time, provided you played on public courses. But Marcus wasn't famous, laid no claim on celebrity and the ethical pass it bought. So, yes, they could have done the "right thing" and called the police and maybe they could have come up with some kind of explanation about why there just happened to be a corpse in the apartment. But what if the story didn't fly? And what if Marcus had to answer some uncomfortable questions? And what if . . .

It didn't matter now. The deed was done.

On the bright side: she had gotten her wish. They were in business together.

The hot stream of the shower felt good on her aching muscles. As she applied shampoo, she wondered how a decision like this could have been arrived at with such alacrity. Had some atavistic survival instinct kicked in? A circle-the-wagons, stand-by-your-man gene she had forgotten she possessed? She had suffered twin shocks. Either of them alone—the realization of what Marcus actually did for a living or the dark farce of the dead body—would have knocked her off the beam. Together, their power increased exponentially. Had she been taken so far out of her comfort zone that rational deliberation was no longer possible? In the clear light of morning, she didn't think so.

By the time Jan stepped out of the shower and was toweling off, she had reached a conclusion. She was a practical woman. Her dreams of a career had foundered. Ripcord had failed, and she felt guilty about her part in burning through the family finances. She needed to contribute. She could get a job of some kind, but having watched Marcus go through that, the thought of repeating his experience made her want to curl up in a ball and beat her fists. As for the criminal nature of the enterprise, Jan didn't see how a crime that didn't involve a victim was really a crime. And it was legal in Nevada, only one state away. Why should something Nevadans view as a legitimate source of tax revenue trouble her if it allowed the Ripps family to not lose their house?

Marcus had downed four Tylenol PMs when they got home and had slept late. Jan didn't mention her second thoughts to him, since by the time he was drinking his morning coffee she had convinced herself that she could live with them. The disturbance in his lower back had not abated, so she took him to the doctor, who prescribed a muscle relaxant chased with a strong painkiller and advised several days of bed rest. When the drugs kicked in and Marcus drifted off to sleep, Jan opened her underwear drawer and removed the contents. Then she placed them in a plastic trash bag and deposited the bag in the garbage. That afternoon, after dropping Nathan off for a session with his educational therapist, she drove to *Something Blue*, an erotic boutique in Sherman Oaks. Feeling empowered in her new purple thong bikini underwear and matching lace-trimmed push-up bra, Jan went grocery shopping. They ate chicken pot pies for dinner, and while Nathan was doing his homework and Marcus was enjoying the effects of the narcotics, Jan and Lenore settled in to watch a police show. At least Jan settled in. Lenore stood to the side of the sofa, doing curls with the five-pound weights she had recently purchased.

"I like how you're taking care of yourself," Jan told her. "You're inspiring me."

"You should come to my class," Lenore said, resting her right arm at her side and beginning another set of curls with her left. Jan nodded, staring at the television, where a triple murder was being dissected by a cast of chiseled actors. While Jan contemplated how to tell her mother that a criminal enterprise was unfolding under their roof, Lenore leaned forward to touch her toes. A thin piece of magenta satin peeked from the top of her sweatpants.

"What's that you're wearing?"

"A tracksuit," Lenore said simply, as if that was all Jan wanted to know.

"Underneath it."

"Oh! This thing," Lenore said, fingering the material and grinning. "I got my level 2 thong in class today."

"Level 2?"

"It's got my initials on it," Lenore said proudly.

"Congratulations," Jan said. She felt a twinge of sympathy for her mother, so pleased right now, and still unaware of Jan's news, which hovered like a swarm of quiet bees. For a moment she thought of not telling her, but didn't want to lie. "Mom, there's something I need to talk to you about."

"I am *not* quitting this class, so you can forget that."

"No, no. I'm all for you pole dancing. It's about Marcus and me."

"Is everything all right?"

Jan proceeded to inform her mother about the recent series of events. Lenore listened with increasing surprise, an occasional intake of breath, and three ohmigods. But when Jan finished, she said "I'm actually kind of relieved. I was worried you were going to tell me you were splitting up."

"We're fine."

"Well," Lenore said, pondering the matter further. "This is not what I expected when I moved in here."

Jan nodded as she took this in. The situation was not what she had been expecting either. "I understand that. And if you're uncomfortable with it, I get that too. You could probably move in with Jessica or Amanda," Jan said, naming her younger and older sisters.

"I did the books for Dad," Lenore said. "I can do them for you."

Jan was not certain she had heard her mother correctly. "You want to work for us?"

"I want to install a stripper pole in my room. They cost over three hundred dollars, even with the senior discount. I don't want to have to ask you for the money."

"Are you sure?" She looked at her mother, not believing she could be so sanguine about the prospect.

"What? Do you think I'm going to say something about morals? While we're being moral, they'll cut off the electricity."

Lenore was nothing if not a survivor. The family had moved from New Jersey to Arizona when Jan's father, Shel Griesbach, bought a share in a business that sold "authentic" Indian blankets to Native Americans who would then sell them to tourists. He went broke when his biggest clients abandoned souvenirs to go into the casino business. Shel Griesbach died in a Carl's Jr. where he was drinking soda and circling the want ads with a red pen. When Lenore buried him, she vowed to carry on. She was not a widow looking to throw herself on a flaming pyre. Life was to be lived, their family had to eat, she needed a stripper pole. Who couldn't understand that?

Jan was astounded by her mother's reaction, but said she would discuss her offer with Marcus later that evening. Jan brought it up when they were getting ready for bed, and Marcus told her it was all right with him. So it was decided that Lenore would be allowed to participate in the business, within certain parameters. They agreed that no one would tell her about the dead body. If this was going to work, they would have to compartmentalize.

*   *   *

168

It was Jan's belief, since they had agreed this would not go on indefinitely, that it was their responsibility to maximize earnings in the brief window available. To this end, she asked if Marcus had a Web site and was surprised when he answered in the negative. Was he not aware that the two biggest businesses on the Internet were sex and financial services? That night, at Jan's behest, Marcus sent an e-mail blast to the workforce, announcing that the operation was going online and requesting that they each come to Shining City to have pictures taken for the Web site.

Jan spent the following day doing Internet reconnaissance, exploring the slippery byways of the cybersex world. Sitting at the kitchen table with her laptop open, she began her journey by doing a search for the word "sex." The number of sites that popped up was 393,000,000—more than one for every American citizen. Though hardly puritanical, Jan was nonetheless amazed by the sheer size and unimaginable variety of the international sex bazaar readily accessible to anyone with a computer. She traveled through webcam sites, where for a small fee a person on the other end would engage in an infinite variety of auto-erotic acts, sex club sites where lovers of cunnilingus could get together to share their interest with strangers, fetish sites where those who enjoyed collecting the "shaved body hair of horny housewives" could find a sense of warmth and community. As Jan navigated through the flotsam and jetsam of this phantasmagorical universe, it dawned on her: Prostitution was refreshingly low on the scale of deviance, almost innocent, in comparison to so much else. Narrowing her research, she returned to the main page of the search engine and typed in "Escort Services Los Angeles," both to absorb the aesthetic of the sites themselves and to see what she could borrow from the competition. This time, the figure that came up was an eyebrow-raising 2,780,000. Jan was savvy enough to realize that that wasn't the actual number of services with which they would be competing, but it was nonetheless a trumpet blast in her ear. As an experiment, she typed in "Shoe Repair Los Angeles" and was amused when the number

2,050,000 popped up on the screen. What had made her think of shoes in a business context? Was it a fleeting memory of Joe Ripps, her unlucky father-in-law, proprietor of Sole Man? Not everyone was able to be an entrepreneur. Marcus apparently possessed the gene. She still couldn't believe it.

Jan began to consider how Shining City could distinguish itself, stand out somehow in this riotous garden, a sunflower among posies. *Sunflower!* There was a good name, and something they needed— Shining City, in her estimation, did not exude the correct level of je ne sais quoi. She realized, though, that Sunflower was a trifle hippie, suggesting love beads and the scent of patchouli oil. The hippie image hadn't been marketable since the heyday of Haight-Ashbury, and Jan instinctively knew this was not the context in which it should be revived. Even if she *were* to call it Sunflower; Sunflower what? Escorts? She found the word *escort* risible in this context. She knew a euphemism was necessary in this delicate business, but *escort?* Jan was determined to come up with a clever name that would serve to re-brand the operation.

She had loved the word Ripcord. The verb *rip* was an active one that implied a tear in the fabric of the ordinary, and *cord* suggested strength, versatility, and perhaps a hint of bondage for those whose thoughts leaned that way (she was intrigued by where her mind was now leaping). The two discrete words when combined formed some- thing even more powerful. So what that it had triggered a resounding thud in the retailing sector? She briefly considered borrowing the appellation, but decided a clean break with the past was best. Jan took out a pad and made a list of names.

Elite . . . Discreet . . . Tout Suite . . .

They all had a certain predictability about them, a generic aspect indicating to her that they must already exist. It was important that Jan's new business be perceived by those who knew about it as high- end. It wasn't that she was a snob, exactly; it was hard for someone who lived in Van Nuys to be a snob. Even the most minimally refined sensibility kept bumping against the Del Taco reality of the neighborhood. Whatever Jan was involved in, however questionable, had to satisfy her personal aesthetic. Perhaps she didn't live in a fancy house or drive an expensive car, but she could still control the smaller details, and that mattered to her.

Jan stared at her computer screen, where a pop-up window advertising *Conversations With She-Males!* was vying for her attention. Jan opened her computer dictionary, typed the word "prostitute," and clicked Synonyms. She read: harlot, strumpet, whore. None of them was better than *escort*.

The next day, Jan was at Ripcord going through a rack of jackets, marking down the prices with a Sharpie.

"I can't buy you out," Plum said. She was seated behind the cash register, sipping a protein shake, the cornerstone of her new diet, which consisted of nothing else. "I wanted to talk it over with Atlas, but when I tried to track him down, I found out he'd checked into rehab."

"Marcus told me."

"You knew?"

"I assumed *you* knew."

"Well, I didn't. Do you ever wonder what your husband isn't telling you?"

Behind Jan's quiet eyes, an ancient tribe exalted terrifying gods on the tip of a fiery volcano while a brass band played speed metal, but all she did was smile calmly and say: "Sometimes."

"Anyway, I tried to figure the money out from every angle, but I can't get it together."

"Then let's mark down the merchandise and have a going-out-of-business sale."

Plum didn't respond immediately, giving Jan a chance to take in the beginning of what was becoming a noticeable physical transformation. The portly Plum was losing a significant amount of weight and, while still more zaftig than svelte, was looking increasingly like her old self. Now Jan waited. Ordinarily, she would have let the conversation trickle toward a vague conclusion, but today would be different. Jan knew the Ripcord dream had a toe tag. The store no longer figured in her calculations. And now there was a new career. She wished she could tell Plum about it.

The rest of the conversation had a melancholic tone. They took turns reminiscing about their venture, taking pains not to cast it as the folly it had so clearly been, and made plans for a going-out-of-business sale. Then Plum said "So, who was that woman Marcus was with yesterday?"

Jan wondered if her soon-to-be-erstwhile partner was baiting her, but Plum's expression revealed nothing. "I thought I told you. She's a business associate."

"She was pretty hot for someone in dry cleaning."

Jan was not going to allow herself to be drawn into yet another personal conversation with Plum. She summoned all the equanimity available to someone who had recently dumped a corpse in the Angeles National Forest and said "No kidding."

"And you believe him?"

"Yes."

Later that day, as Jan waited in the carpool line at Winthrop Hall, her mind ranged over what had recently transpired. She had gone from wretched shock and distress, through rigorous critical analysis, to some kind of acceptance—if not an embracing—of her new and unexpected fate. The next few months would be critical ones in the life of her family, and it was very important that she remain circumspect. What would she call the business? And when would her new thong stop chafing?

Jan was startled from her reverie by the rapping of delicate knuckles on her car window. She looked over and saw a well-manicured hand striking the glass. The woman was about Jan's age, but a daily routine of professional pore cleansing, massage, and aromatherapy worked in concert with a four-hundred-dollar haircut to take ten years off. She was pretty, but not breathtakingly so, and keen. You could tell she wanted to be liked. Jan rolled down her window.

"Hi, I'm Corinne Vandeveer. We're having an auction to raise money for the victims of the Guatemala earthquake." Corinne talked as if ten cups of coffee whirred though her system, but her breath was fragrant with mint. "I thought you might be able to donate some items from Ripcord." How did Corinne even know that Jan owned Ripcord? None of her three kids was in Nathan's year, and the two women had never spoken. But Corinne was a Turbo Mom, and these women possessed a kind of subtle acuity when it came to school-related endeavors that awed Jan. "Can you help us out? You could just drop the stuff at my house."

Corinne's timing could not have been more propitious, and Jan readily acceded to her request, although she had been so preoccupied with the events of her life that the earthquake, which had claimed nearly twenty thousand victims, had escaped her notice. Jan was already working her way down the carpool line and away from Corinne when Nathan threw his backpack into the back of the car and climbed into the passenger seat. He grunted a greeting and began to eat a pastry.

When the car in front of her began to move, Jan stepped on the gas and they pulled off the school grounds. She looked at Nathan.

"What are you eating?"

"Apple tart. They sell them in the vending machines."

Then it hit her.

Tart! An excellent word! It says *whore,* but cheekily, in a saucy, naughty Victorian way. As she drove home, Jan conjured with this newfound philological bauble her son had unknowingly dropped in her lap. It was good, certainly, but somehow incomplete.

Chapter 16

Rabbi Rachel appeared to be around forty. Slightly overweight, with a masculine haircut that framed a kind face, accented by quiet brown eyes that opened up to the Ripps family and invited them in. Wearing jeans, a work shirt, and no makeup, she projected the aspect of an earnest graduate student. On her head perched the kind of cap Lenin wore to the Revolution. It had not occurred to Marcus that the rabbi who would be officiating at Nathan's bar mitzvah would be a lesbian. It didn't particularly bother him, it didn't bother him at all, really, but it *was* something he noticed. He was ambivalent enough about the whole bar mitzvah concept to welcome anything that would bring it out of the realm of the ordinary and make the experience a more memorable one. This was a good start. Marcus shifted in his seat, trying to find a position that was comfortable for his back, as he listened.

"Too many families get caught up in the frou-frou of the bar mitzvah," Rabbi Rachel was saying. "It's easy to forget what the experience is supposed to be about."

They were in Rabbi Rachel's modest office just off the sanctuary. The rabbi was seated behind her desk, and Nathan sat across from her, flanked by his parents. Jan's hands were folded on her lap as she listened. Nathan was nodding at the rabbi's words. Marcus noticed a beat-up acoustic guitar on a stand in the corner. Was she a folkie? He was too young to have experienced the sixties, but the multifarious manifestations of pop culture circa 1966 appealed to him, and an acoustic guitar was an unavoidable one. Its presence in Rabbi Rachel's office made him like her more than he would have had she displayed, say, a banjo.

"Between dealing with the caterer and the DJ and the people coming in from out of town, it can turn into something you have to get through, as opposed to something you're supposed to revel in. So I would say to you now . . . enjoy this. Nathan's going to do great, he'll chant his Torah portion, which we've been discussing . . ." Here she winked at Nathan and smiled at Marcus and Jan. Marcus liked the way she implicitly allied herself with his son. Perhaps the experience would actually have some resonance for the boy. He had thought Nathan's main interest was in having a big party, so this was a new wrinkle. Marcus had never felt a connection to anyone in the religion racket in his life. Perhaps Rabbi Rachel would lead Nathan down a godly path that would actually serve him as he grew older, something Marcus had never experienced. The agnostic-leaning-toward-atheist in him was pricked by the nascent religiosity of his son, a boy still a step removed from the chaotic, often overwhelming reality that necessitated religion in the first place. Marcus was of two minds about this. He welcomed Nathan's exploration of this half of his ancestral background, hoped that perhaps it could provide a concrete moral framework by which to live. But it also reminded him of the wind-blasted place where *he* dwelt, pondering his own flexible ethics, uncertain where he was heading. May Nathan be spared the darkness of doubt, Marcus thought.

"Nathan is learning the prayers, he's working on his haftarah, and he's going to be writing a sermon," Rabbi Rachel said.

"I'm writing about Abraham," Nathan informed his parents.

"Not Moses, or Noah?" Marcus said, in a tone he hoped conveyed jocularity, and did not reveal that his biblical frame of reference was limited. If pressed, he could come up with Adam and Eve, Cain and Abel, and perhaps Moses. But that was about as far as it went.

"The subject of Nate's speech is determined by the time of year it is and where we are in the Torah," Rabbi Rachel informed Nathan's infidel father.

"I like Abraham. He's cool," Nathan said. He *liked* him? This biblical patriarch, this Father of the Jews, this willing participant in human sacrifice? Of his son, no less! Abraham was, in the estimation of Nathan Ripps, *cool?* Surely that was good. If Nathan believed Abraham to be cool, then perhaps he was buying into the deistic view.

Marcus relaxed a little.

"Nate and I are going to meet every few weeks to check on his progress, but it's important that *he* do this. It's his speech, and I like to ask parents to take a step back from the process. This is about your son becoming a man," Rabbi Rachel said with a wry smile, indicating that she appreciated the unspoken irony of such a statement, given that Nathan barely looked twelve. The definition of *man* was malleable.

Nathan appeared eager at that moment, his face exuding an openness and energy that Marcus never would have associated with the present circumstances. Although the boy possessed his father's physical DNA, the spiritual clay of which he was made seemed something else altogether.

When the meeting ended, Rabbi Rachel asked Marcus to stay behind for a moment. She asked him if he was Jewish, and he said he was not. He told her he was more interested in philosophy than religion, but he appreciated what religion could do for some people and was supportive of Nathan's exploration.

"It doesn't have to be about worshipping a traditional god, Marcus. It's really more about doing the right thing."

He was going to tell her he knew this, but then something took hold of him. "But who's to say what the right thing is? Just because most people think something is right, does that make it so? Maybe it's just a collective delusion that people decide to agree on. Maybe the whole idea of God is a delusion." Marcus regretted getting caught up in this kind of undergraduate discussion but he could not stop himself.

"God can be what you want it to be."

"Like an imaginary friend?" He smiled to show he was kidding.

She looked at him inquisitively. This was not the kind of exchange she generally had with the father of a bar mitzvah student. "I don't know if God exists. Does that surprise you?"

"Everyone has to make a living."

"But I think it's important that we act like he does exist. If you want to talk some more about this, my door is open."

Marcus thanked her and left the office. He didn't know what had come over him, but vowed to keep whatever theological differences he may have had with the rabbi, or anyone else for that matter, to himself. No one needed to know what he thought about *anything*.

As he walked to the car, he noticed that his back was no longer hurting.

Upon their return home, they were greeted by the discordant whine of a power tool. Following the noise to Lenore's room, Marcus looked in and saw her standing on a chair, drilling a hole in the ceiling. She was wearing sweatpants and a T-shirt that read GOT POLE?

"What are you doing?"

Lenore stopped drilling and regarded her son-in-law with unmitigated pleasure. "I'm installing my pole." With a toss of her head, she indicated the cylindrical piece of stainless steel resting on her bed. "I could use a hand."

For the next twenty minutes, Marcus and Lenore fiddled with the floor pad and the ceiling mount until they were confident it could bear her small frame. They summoned Nathan and Jan, and when the entire family was assembled Lenore hit a button on her boom box, lately the exclusive haunt of folk rock artists of a certain age. The hip-hop thump that now emerged heralded a changing of the guard. In front of three sets of disbelieving eyes, Lenore leapt onto the pole and executed a routine involving scissor kicks, spins, and hanging upside down, legs akimbo. With great panache, she finally hauled herself upright and dropped to the floor with a lightness that belied her years. Her face was aglow.

For a moment, all anyone could do was exchange speechless glances. Then Nathan began to applaud, followed quickly by his parents. It was agreed that pole dancing was empowering for seniors.

Later that evening, Marcus and Jan were lying in bed, having just turned the lights off. Since deciding to take an active role in the operation, Jan had been examining it from various angles. Marcus had the personnel situation under control, and the money was flowing, so Jan decided, in the interest of increasing revenues and remaining below the radar, to reposition the business, aiming for an exclusive clientele, the theory being that by upgrading the trade, they could decrease the actual number of customers, thereby lowering the risk exponentially. Jan guessed that the market was willing to pay a premium for perceived distinctiveness, and this would make up for the anticipated decline in clients.

Jan wanted to re-launch the business with a name befitting the new identity, but so far had been unable to come up with one that conveyed the right degree of sangfroid.

"What are the qualities a guy looks for when he's at a hotel and he wants to hire a date?" She preferred the euphemisms, as they made it easier for her to process the entirety of the situation.

"The ability to perform the service requested."

"That's not what I mean. What *qualities*, you know—personal things? Sense of humor, stuff like that."

"I think they're into hair color and body type, nice butt, breast size . . ." He began to caress her thigh. She was wearing a fresh thong and a silk T-shirt several sizes too small. Marcus wondered what had happened to the usual bedtime burka.

"What do you think about geishas?"

"Who doesn't like a geisha?" Marcus ran his fingertips along her hip and across the top of her thigh.

"Or the courtesans in France?"

"I like them too," he said, locating her clitoris as he wondered if his wife had spent the afternoon in the library.

"They were trained in the conversational arts."

"Did you get that from a brochure?"

"No . . ." she said, now moaning slightly. "It was on a Web site. I was thinking maybe guys liked the idea of a human being coming to see them, instead of just a sex machine."

"Maybe." Marcus was kissing her neck.

"The geishas were exclusive, which I like for what we're doing, because the more upscale you are, the less likely it is that the police are going to care about you." He took her hand and placed it between his legs. She began to caress him absentmindedly. "Some of these geishas were really impressive. They were educated, well-traveled . . . they knew how to get guys to pay for them."

"They were smart."

Smart?

She climbed on him now, grinding her pelvis down, and proceeded to ride him in an undulating rhythm. Marcus moved his hips up and down, thrusting, his hands playing on her thighs, his breathing shallow and warm. As he ran his fingertips along her soft shoulders and closed his eyes, she said: "SMART TARTS!" Then she fell forward, pressing her breasts to his chest, and kissed him long and hard, her tongue probing his mouth, their breath intermingling.

The next morning, Jan drove down to the now-shuttered Ripcord and liberated several of the boxes she and Plum had recently packed. Loading them in the minivan, she drove to Corinne Vandeveer's house in Coldwater Canyon. The place was gated, and Jan followed the instructions on a sign next to a keypad mounted on a pillar of glazed bricks. She pressed the code and waited. After a moment, the wide gate swung open. The Vandeveers' house was a sprawling Italianate mansion that looked as if it had been airlifted intact from a

Tuscan hillside. In the center of the circular driveway was an impressive three-tiered fountain crowned by the nearly life-sized copper figure of a Tibetan monk. Water gushed from a spout in his forehead and filled a waist-high begging bowl in which a blue jay was currently bathing, before cascading to the orchid-strewn koi pool below. The walkways radiating from the house were inlaid with Travertine tiles of varying hue that glowed in the morning sun. A maroon Bentley was parked nearby.

Jan rang the bell, and a moment later a young Hispanic woman in a black maid's uniform opened the large oak door.

"I'm meeting Mrs. Vandeveer," Jan said. But before the woman could answer, Corinne floated into view and beckoned Jan in. A Bluetooth headset was wrapped around her ear. The maid silently withdrew. She was wearing black leggings and a loose men's white shirt.

"If we take the jet to Montana," Corinne said to the person at the other end of the line, "I don't see why we can't just keep it there for a few days before we go to Spain. I understand that we're sharing it . . ." Jan looked around. The dining room table reminded her of one she'd seen on a long-ago visit to the Metropolitan Museum in New York. The vast living room at the opposite side of the foyer featured several large canvases she recognized as the work of Ed Ruscha and Cy Twombly. They were standing on a rug from Istanbul which, in its exquisite and complex beauty, silently requested that she take her scuffed sandals and go somewhere else. "But I still don't see . . . fine. Okay. Someone's here. I'll call you later." Now Corinne was addressing Jan. "Planning vacations has gotten to be such a hassle, I don't know why we bother to go anywhere."

"Oh, I know," Jan said. Her empathy was convincing. "The clothes are in the car. Should we unload them?"

Corinne adjusted her wireless device and said "Araceli, would you and Ramon . . . excuse me." Corinne never broke eye contact, so

Jan had the unsettling sensation of not being certain to whom she was speaking. Then, to Jan: "Are they in boxes?"

"Yes."

"Would you and Ramon unload the boxes from Mrs. Ripps's car and put them in the garage with the others, please?"

Five minutes later, Jan and Corinne were seated on stools at an island in the vast kitchen. The room was an orgy of marble countertops and large-scale stainless steel appliances that looked as if they'd never been used. The women were nibbling crab canapés as they sipped iced tea from cut-glass goblets.

"I hope you don't mind leftovers," Corinne said. "But we had this fund-raiser for Instant Karma last night. They're this organization that sends Buddhist monks into the jails to work with the inmate population."

"That's a good cause." Jan wasn't sure what else to say to Corinne, so she went with the obvious. People like Corinne generally didn't care what Jan thought anyway. At least she better understood the water-spouting copper monk in front of the house.

"I'll put you on the list for the next one."

Jan gazed toward the backyard, titillated by Corinne's perception of her as a member of the donor class. She noticed a swimming pool that looked as if it had been hewn from rock, surrounded by an acre of blindingly green lawn ornamented with life-sized topiary elephants.

"I like the elephants," Jan offered.

"They're modeled on the ones we saw on a trip to India. I'm getting kind of tired of them," Corinne said. "We were in France last summer at this chateau, and they had a maze, you know, like a labyrinth? I'm thinking about putting one of those in."

Jan nodded. The air was thin at Corinne's elevation. They chatted about their children, the math program at Winthrop Hall, and the annual giving campaign. Then Corinne said "So . . . what does your husband do?"

"Investments." Jan had no idea why she lied. Or, rather, why she told that specific lie. She could have told Corinne he was in the dry cleaning business. Perhaps she had been thrown off by the dense reek of money, or by Corinne's friendliness, which she had not expected. But her answer appeared to please the hostess. "What about yours?"

"He's an arbitrageur, which means he buys in one market and sells in another, but for a lot more money. Sorry, I know *you* know that, but some people don't so I always say it anyway. We'll have the two of you over."

"That would be delightful," Jan said. *Delightful?* From what cobwebbed Victorian recess had she extracted that bon mot? Had she ever used the word in her life? Jan felt a tiny heart palpitation. How many glasses of iced tea had she consumed? She had forgotten there was caffeine in it. Now she looked at her watch. "I would love to stay and chat . . ."

"Don't apologize," Corinne said. "My Reiki person gets here in five minutes. I was going to kick you out anyway."

Jan drove toward West Hollywood, ruminating on her encounter. Corinne ruled Winthrop Hall: queen of committees, hostess of the parent potlucks, organizer of the annual book fair. She was a lioness and, as such, not the kind of woman to whom Jan ordinarily gravitated. But she was affable and treated Jan as if they might be members of the same club, one that used linen tablecloths, high-quality silver, and social assassination as a means of protocol enforcement. The advantage of a friend like that could not be underestimated.

The rest of the day was spent setting up a makeshift photography studio in the back of the dry cleaner. Jan hung a white backdrop from two coat racks and covered a chaise longue (purchased for the purpose at a furniture store on La Brea) with gold satin sheets, turning the farthest reaches of the space into an approximation of a boudoir. Later that week, she used the digital camera that six months ago had been Nathan's twelfth birthday present, and photographed the newly-christened Smart Tarts workforce in various states of dishabille. She designed the Web site, registered the domain, arranged for a Web host and suddenly the 9.0 version of the business was available on the Internet. As Jan scrolled through the site in the home office (her new world headquarters), she was infused with an energy unseen since the halcyon days of Ripcord when its success seemed a foregone conclusion and her future on Van Nuys Boulevard a medley of ripe possibilities. Then she took out the Yellow Pages and turned to the Bs in search of Brazilian bikini wax.

Discreet ads were placed in local publications announcing the business which, along with their presence on the Web, caused a slight increase in bookings. The real surge arrived when she decided to invest in the wider market. Los Angeles was a global financial hub, so Jan persuaded Marcus to purchase ad space in glossy business magazines in New York, London, and Tokyo. She wrote the copy herself, and since the more august publications would not accept advertising from a business called Smart Tarts, Jan decided the organization would have another identity for these markets—International Friendship Guides. These ads were accepted with a wink, and bookings jumped again.

Several weeks into her new role, Jan called Corinne Vandeveer and asked if she was still collecting money for the victims of the Guatemalan earthquake. When Corinne answered in the affirmative, Jan informed her she and Marcus were donating five thousand dollars to the fund. After Corinne thanked her, an invitation was extended to a dinner party Saturday night. Jan accepted. When she told Marcus they were going, he was informed that their hosts believed him to be an "investor." Marcus, now accustomed to dissembling, took this in stride.

Marcus bought a Hugo Boss jacket and Jan an Armani sheath, so they were slightly overdressed for what turned out to be a backyard barbecue. Still, they were happy to be included. Six couples sat around a long table on the capacious patio overlooking the vast lawn and gardens bursting with pink, white, and yellow roses. A sad-eyed Mexican woman wearing a chef's toque manned the grill, and a white-jacketed young waiter with red hair and freckles hovered obsequiously nearby. Corinne's husband Dewey sat at the head of the table. He was a handsome man in his early forties with graying, slightly unkempt hair and a heedless manner. In faded Levis and an untucked white button-front shirt, he radiated money. The other guests included a snack tycoon and his overweight wife, a parking lot magnate and spouse number three (she had formerly been his masseuse), and the owner of a large vineyard in Napa and his wife, who had been a movie star in the eighties and now devoted herself to animal rescue and drinking. Finally, there was an exquisitely beautiful young woman who claimed to be an interior designer. Her husband, at least thirty years her senior, and with a noticeable face-lift, was a partner of Dewey's. The pinot noir flowed, the conversation was convivial, and Marcus and Jan learned that, by bending the truth in a barely perceptible way, they were able to present themselves as just another well-heeled Los Angeles couple who gave to charity and worried about the world they were leaving to the next generation.

Jan ate the pecan pie served for dessert with great enjoyment, slipping her foot out of the black calfskin pump she had purchased that afternoon at a Galleria store she had wanted to shop in for years, and rubbed Marcus's ankle. The woman with the much older husband told a long story about a problem with the renovation of their house on Ibiza, one of five they owned. She was granted the indulgence of beauty and no one interrupted. When she finally found herself at the end of the numbing tale, there was a momentary lull in the conversation.

"So, Marcus," Dewey said, pivoting the spotlight. "Corinne tells me you're in investments. What kind?"

"Oh . . ." Marcus said, stalling for a moment. He'd been staring at the elephant topiary standing sentinel nearby. "You know. The usual. Gold, some timber . . ." Jan glanced at him, and held her breath.

Was he about to tumble from the tightrope? *Gold? Timber?* "And, of course, dry cleaning."

"Certificates? Gold bars?" Dewey wanted to know.

"I like to hold gold, feel that weight," Marcus said. He was slightly buzzed from the wine and feeling expansive. "Sometimes I go to the bank and I fondle a brick . . ."

The other guests laughed. Jan tried not to stare in disbelief. Marcus awaited a follow-up question but was saved when the parking lot magnate said "You can never go wrong with gold" and proceeded to tell a long story involving the conquistadores and their search for the precious metal, before veering off into an exegesis about how gold could be recovered from sea water. Jan struggled to pay attention. A return invitation required that she be a good guest.

Marcus was whistling a movement from a Bach cantata as he pulled out of the Vandeveers' driveway and turned right onto Coldwater. Jan had enjoyed herself and hoped the music Marcus was making reflected his own take on the experience.

"Did you have a good time?"

"I know you like socializing with these people," he said. "So I'm happy to go along."

"Is it all right if I ask you a question?"

"Sure."

"*Sometimes I like to fondle a brick?* Why did you say that?"

"What was I supposed to say?"

"You could have just been vague."

"Did you listen to that woman talk about the problems she was having with the house in Ibiza? Are you sure you want to be friends with these people?"

"I like them."

When they crested the hill, neither of them had spoken for over a minute. Marcus eased the car into a curve as the Valley lights winked below. "What do you think of buying a new house?"

"You want to move?"

"It's not like I want a fancy place, but, it's just, you know . . . now that we might be able to afford something a little better . . ."

"I think this might be a bubble market," she told him, the gentle haze of the wine crystallizing into something harder, as she calculated how to rein him in before he began to apply this logic in a more systemic fashion. Jan may have been attracted to the world of the Vandeveers, but she wasn't going to get carried away. "It's crazy to trade up. And besides, if we move and take on a big mortgage, then we're locked into making this kind of money."

Now that the initial rush of business success had dissipated, Jan nursed more reservations than she would have liked. The illegality of the operation still troubled her, and she had not entirely made her peace with the moral ambiguity. The palaver Marcus had been selling at the dinner party, though amusing to the other guests, made her question what they were doing all over again and her own part in it. After all, *she* was the one who said he was an investor. Now, along with the lingering guilt for which she was looking to do penance, Jan was concerned with how to retain a Van Nuys sensibility in their marriage when Smart Tarts was gushing Bel Air coin. "I have a confession to make," she said. He looked at her quizzically. Then she told him about her donation to the earthquake victims. He smiled and squeezed her hand.

"I'm thrilled we can do that," he said. "We're going to make a chunk of money and invest it. Then we'll take *that* money and spend it however we want. We can have a foundation and give it away if that's what we decide." This seemed to placate her, indicating, as it did, that his behavior would remain reasonable.

They glided off the hill toward Ventura Boulevard. Jan was pleased with how the evening had gone. Marcus had handled himself well, justifying her faith. Since the financial pressures had been relieved, Jan had been thinking of the myriad ways to enrich their lives. She considered getting a subscription to a series of plays, or planning a trip to Europe, but it was difficult to make that kind of time commitment given the unpredictability of their schedules. Now she had a solution.

"I want to start a book club," Jan said.

Marcus turned onto Ventura and headed west. "Who are you going to get to be in it, some moms from school?"

"The Smart Tarts."

"Really?"

"I have this idea. I thought we could read women's books, classics that are hard to read on your own, like *Anna Karenina*. Did you ever read that?"

Marcus admitted he hadn't. Jan told him he was welcome to be in the book club too.

They made love later that night, and Jan was pleased when Marcus noticed she had an entirely waxed undercarriage.

Chapter 17

Jan was vacuuming the living room on a May afternoon when Plum called. It had been a month since they'd spoken. There was no lingering animosity, but neither wanted to be reminded of their mutual failure at Ripcord and communion with the other would only reinforce it. Hence the subsequent radio silence. After a few minutes of idle chat, Plum let it drop that she was starting to stress about money. Atlas was behind in his alimony payments. Jan expressed supportive outrage and, in a spasm of guilt, offered to treat Plum to a day at Gentle, the female-only spa that had recently opened in Studio City.

A considerably thinner Plum greeted Jan there the next day. She had lost twenty pounds, as a result of ingesting nothing but Altoids and vitamin water for the previous month. She appeared tired.

"You look great," Jan said.

"The misery diet," Plum replied, trying to smile.

They were standing in the softly lit reception area. Silent attendants moved solicitously through the artful shadows. The stereo played an abstract tone poem by a pianist who sounded as if he had OD'd on Nembutal five minutes before the recording session. Jan hoped the environment would have a calming effect on Plum, who seemed on edge.

Jan had booked detox wraps, herbal spa baths, and something called a "tranquil mud experience" for them. Half an hour later, the two women, clad in white terry cloth robes, were seated side by side in large distressed-leather chairs in the Quiet Room, waiting for attendants to take them to their respective treatments. They were surrounded by similarly attired women sipping herb tea made with fresh mint or iced water with slices of lemon floating in tall glasses. In deference to spa protocol, they spoke in hushed whispers. Jan listened as Plum tried to convey the positive aspects of Ripcord's closing, but the mixed emotions it had engendered were such that she was having trouble modulating her voice. She drew a hard look from the crisply attired blonde attendant charged with enforcing spa protocol.

After an hour of detox wrap, they were seated side by side, stark naked and completely enveloped in mud. A sprite sporting a name tag that said BEACON had smeared an earthen pudding from their hairlines to the soles of their feet, and now the two women looked like jungle-dwelling creatures from some obscure island off the coast of Borneo, glimpsed in the pages of *National Geographic*. Having not seen Plum's body recently, Jan had been amazed when her former partner undressed, confidently stepping out of her robe before having the muck applied.

The room they were in had terra-cotta tiles and a row of sparkling showers against one wall. Beacon had given them toothpick-like implements to clean the mud from beneath their fingernails and then excused herself, gliding out on cat feet.

Jan smeared a bare patch of elbow with mud. Satisfied that every inch of her was caked, she asked Plum what her plans were now that Ripcord had dematerialized.

"At least I didn't get pregnant." This response surprised Jan. Had Plum not been intent on exactly that? "I wanted a kid for all the wrong reasons anyway. It was like I was insane or something."

"We all go through stuff."

"I'll still make art. I just want to find some way for it to pay." Plum ran her hands through her hair and straightened her back. Then she said she well understood the things people did when faced with dire circumstances and no perceived means to ameliorate them. "Look at strippers," she said. "But who *wants* to do that if they don't have to?"

"What's wrong with it? My mother's taking a pole dancing class."

"Where's the artistic component? When I did nude modeling in art school, it had an aesthetic angle, so I could justify it to myself. And, to be honest, there was something about it . . . I kind of liked it, actually. You had power because no one could touch you. It was almost like worship."

"It was a religious experience?"

"Ha-hah. No. But you're on a pedestal. I like that. People can't give you shit when you're on a pedestal."

"You could model again. I know it doesn't pay a lot, but it might be a good way to meet some interesting people." When Plum didn't respond, Jan noticed that she was suddenly not looking well. "Are you all right?"

"I feel kind of . . ."

"What?"

Plum slid off the stool, and her head struck the tile floor with the sharp crack of a coconut smacking a cinderblock. Naked and mud-smeared, Jan rose and walked quickly to the hallway. She summoned Beacon, who arrived a moment later radiating concern. Beacon propped Plum's head up on a pile of jasmine-scented towels while Jan slipped into a bathrobe. Poor Plum can't even get through a tranquil mud experience without drama, Jan thought, covering her friend in a towel as Beacon took her pulse. Plum was still unconscious, although she appeared to be breathing. Satisfied that she had not expired, Beacon went to call an ambulance. Jan knelt next to the recumbent Plum, her knees uncomfortable on the wet tile. What had happened? Jan guessed it was a fainting spell. But had Plum compounded the problem with the blunt trauma to the head? The sound Plum's skull made when it struck the floor had been sickening. How seriously was she injured? Right now she looked like she was sleeping. But wasn't that what dead people looked like? Jan softly tapped Plum's cheek.

"Plum . . . Plum . . . wake up," she said quietly.

Plum's jaw began to move and her eyelids fluttered. She slowly regained consciousness and said "I think I have mud in my twat." That was a good sign. Jan laughed. Beacon returned with a tall glass of iced water with a lemon slice. Plum sipped it gratefully. But when she tried to get to her feet, she lay back down and complained of head pain.

"I'm really sorry," she said to Jan. "You try and do something nice and I . . . did I faint?"

Beacon suggested that Plum try not to talk.

"Shut up," Plum said. "I'm apologizing to my friend."

By way of explanation, Jan told Beacon: "She hasn't had anything but Altoids and vitamin water for a month."

"You really need to eat something," Beacon said, undaunted.

"I'm sorry," Plum said. "I apologize to both of you."

The ambulance arrived quickly, and Plum was wrapped in towels, placed on a stretcher, and carried through the serene, neutrally toned lobby. The women waiting there barely looked up from the glossy magazines they were reading. As the ambulance sped toward the Valley Medical Center, Plum lay on the gurney still covered with the tranquil mud treatment. Jan was seated next to her in street clothes, fresh from the shower with the four different types of hair conditioner. She silently congratulated herself for having had the foresight to get cleaned off before the ambulance arrived. Plum now looked like a vanilla ice cream bar whose chocolate coating had been licked by a wolf.

She was taken into the emergency room, where Jan filled out the requisite forms. Returning the clipboard to the nurse behind the desk, Jan went in search of Plum. She found her ensconced behind a curtain in the ER, hooked up to an IV through which she was being hydrated. The section of her arm where the needle was inserted had been cleaned off. They had taken her towel, and she was wearing a hospital gown. She smiled at Jan, eyes and teeth gleaming in her dark face.

"I think the mud is a good look for me."

Jan couldn't believe Plum was making light of the situation. Jan asked how she was feeling. Plum said the nurse who admitted her had mentioned she might have a concussion and ordered a scan. She had not seen the doctor yet. Jan sat in the chair next to the bed and took Plum's hand.

"I never know what to say to someone in a hospital bed."

"I'm sorry you didn't get your herbal bath," Plum said, closing her eyes.

She reminded Jan of a Polynesian mask, a Gauguin figure as drawn by Modigliani. How does a person eat nothing but Altoids for a month? Plum had long said she could slim down, and had finally achieved her objective. Yes, it had resulted in her being prostrate and out cold on the floor of a day spa with a potentially serious head injury, but she was extreme. The woman could have survived the Donner Party.

Jan looked around the ER and wondered who else was there. Everyone was behind a curtain. You couldn't see them, but you could hear them murmuring. It was quiet now, just people talking to friends and relatives. No howling, no cries of pain. Jan hoped they would do the scan soon. Nathan had to be picked up after school, but Plum needed her and she was already feeling guilty. Wasn't that why she had invited her to Gentle in the first place? Jan noticed that Plum appeared to have drifted off to sleep. Was that a good idea? Weren't people with head trauma supposed to stay awake? Couldn't a person fade out and die as a result of some as-yet-undiagnosed brain injury? That was all Jan needed. A dead Plum would haunt her forever. Just as she was about to get up from her chair and find a nurse, Plum opened her eyes.

"So, tell me about this new business."

"What new business?"

"The one Marcus is running."

This was not a conversation Jan wanted to have. She was not as deft a liar as her husband. For her, a fib was an ethical compromise—it left a splinter in the soul that could only be excised by confession.

It pained her to have to relate the litany of canards about the nonexistent dry cleaning business, to pretend that everything was normal at the Ripps home. Plum mentioned that she had taken a drive past the dry cleaner, and it didn't appear to be open for business. Suddenly, Jan asked "Do you have insurance?"

"No."

"I want to pay your hospital bill."

"Forget it." Plum shifted her head on the pillow and looked away. "I kind of regret how I behaved with you . . . asking for the eggs . . . I shouldn't have put you in that position. So thanks but no thanks."

"You have bills, Plum, so maybe it's a mistake to think something is below you."

"What, like dry cleaning?"

Jan didn't like the implicit superiority of Plum's tone. So she leaned in and quietly said "Marcus isn't a dry cleaner."

"He's not?"

The two women had shared any number of confidences over the years, and it had been difficult for Jan not to tell Plum about Smart Tarts. But a mixture of guilt, pique, and the vulnerability engendered by being in an emergency room loosened her tongue. When Plum looked at her, suddenly more interested, Jan said "He's got these women working for him."

"What do they do?"

"You know. They're . . . working women. They . . . you know . . . *work*." Jan's expression, at once wry and culpable, suggested that no more questions need be asked.

"They work?"

Plum didn't know what she meant. Was her mind was less agile than usual because of the blow to her head? Jan looked around to make sure no one was within earshot. Then, lowering her voice as if she was passing nuclear secrets, whispered: "He's a pimp."

"Figuratively?"

"Literally."

"He's not!"

"I know it's hard to believe."

"Get out!"

"But a family-values one. The girls have health coverage and retirement plans and everything."

"Get *out!*" Plum's voice sounded like the ringing of a slot machine. She suddenly remembered where they were and looked abashed. "You have to be kidding," she said, far more quietly.

Jan told her everything, leaving out the story about dumping the dead body. Plum listened to the account in a stunned silence that only deepened when Jan began to detail her own complicity. The nurse, a pert, green-eyed blonde whose short hair evoked the crown of a baby bird, came in and said the scan would take place in a few minutes and was Plum comfortable? They didn't hear her. She repeated her question at a louder volume, causing Jan to look up and say Plum was feeling much better. The nurse left to attend to another patient.

"When I found out, I totally flipped. And I mean *totally*. But then I started thinking about it. Remember in art history, the nineteenth-century French guys? Like Manet and Toulouse-Lautrec, Ingres and Delacroix . . ."

"Would *you* ever have sex for money?" Plum whispered.

"They painted tons of prostitutes," Jan said, not certain whether she had heard Plum's question correctly. "So there's this tradition . . ." Jan was losing her train of thought.

"Would you?" Plum repeated.

"Would *I* . . .?"

"*Olympia* by Manet was always one of my favorite paintings," Plum said.

"Toulouse-Lautrec loved prostitutes," Jan said, trying to regain her footing.

"Would you have slept with Toulouse-Lautrec? What if you knew he'd paint you and that the painting would hang in some major museum?"

"Would you?"

"What if your marriage broke up because your husband was fucking a foot model, your store went out of business, you were in debt, and you didn't want to work at Red Lobster? How about then?" It was as if this was something Plum had already considered. Before Jan could answer, a doctor appeared, wielding a clipboard. He was in late middle age, someone who had seen everything. When he beheld the mud-caked Plum, he pushed his tortoiseshell glasses up on the bridge of his nose.

"Oh, my," he said. He took out a pen flashlight and told Plum to look at him while he beamed the light into her eyes. Then he played a Chopin nocturne on the back of her head. He asked Plum if they had ordered a scan and when she told him yes, he excused himself and said he would check on her later.

"Would you?" Plum said, picking up the conversation where they'd left off.

"Why, are you . . . would *you*?"

Plum thought about it a moment, rubbed her hands over her face. When she pulled them away, Jan noticed that her palms were flecked with mud. Then she nodded.

"You would *not*," Jan exclaimed.

"Maybe I should talk to Marcus."

"About *what*?"

"What do you think?"

"Oh, Plum. That is *not* a good idea."

Jan wished she hadn't said anything about Marcus. She accurately attributed the momentary indiscretion to her own over-stimulated emotional state, but this insight did not make her any less angry with herself. Yes, she thought Plum might have been dying. Who, after all, could predict what a blunt trauma head injury might lead to? Internal bleeding, seizures, yes, even death. Yes. It happens. It wasn't

195

as if Jan had been entirely off base. But that was hardly an excuse. There are things a person must keep quiet about.

That night she did not mention Plum's suggestion, nor did she say anything to Marcus the following morning before he left to play an early round of golf. But it was still rattling Jan's cage as she drove Nathan to school. Telling a friend your alleged dry cleaner husband was a pimp—the ensuing inner cacophony was defeaning. But for the friend to then say she wanted to be a prostitute—the synaptic explosions *that* set off were of a significantly higher order.

Nathan was in the passenger seat reviewing vocabulary words for a Latin quiz and did not look up when Jan's phone rang. A sense of frustration and woe overcame her as she listened to Plum's incongruously cheerful voice inquiring whether Marcus had been informed of her request.

"Are you really sure you want to do this?"

"I think I have a good way to approach it," Plum said. Jan could not begin to imagine what that might be, but she promised to talk to Marcus about it later that day.

Tool Box was the Los Angeles nightclub of the moment, and it was the location-to-be of Nathan's bar mitzvah. Marcus and Jan were standing in the unadorned main room.

"The raw space is five thousand dollars. Then you have tables and chairs, linens and centerpieces . . . have you thought about whether you want a band or a DJ?" The speaker was Alison Clive and she appeared to be around thirty. Hipster-nerd eyewear raked across an oval face that was distinguished by a gold nose ring in her left nostril. Her hair appeared to have been cut with a garden tool and was streaked with a shade of green that belonged on a tropical fish. She was a party planner, someone to whom people turned when the fear of faux pas had loosened their billfolds. Alison held a clipboard to her flat chest as she talked to Marcus and Jan. "We've done a bunch of bar mitzvahs here and they've all gone gangbusters," Alison said. "But

I should tell you, I've been talking to another family about the date you want."

"Is it still available?" Jan asked.

"They're hemming and hawing, so if you want to put down a deposit, you could lock it up."

Marcus took in the room, a large black box with little warrens off to the sides and a bar at one end. The exorbitant rental fees were apparently a result of the club's evanescent cachet. Now they would have to pay a significant amount of money for something of no particular value. But it was the venue of the moment, decreed so in Jan's conversations with several of the other mothers whose boys' bar mitzvahs were imminent, and she was intent on having Nathan's party there. Marcus asked Alison how large a deposit was required. A deal was struck, a check written.

Anyone who saw Marcus and Jan in the parking lot outside Tool Box would have thought they looked like any other married couple. Marcus took out his car keys and pressed the clicker. There was the familiar chirp, followed by the unlocking of doors.

"Plum wants to work for us," Jan said. Marcus stared at her, incredulous.

"You told her what we were doing?"

"She was lying in a hospital bed with a head injury."

"I wish you hadn't done that."

"I told her I thought it was a bad idea."

"We already have more girls than we need." Word had gotten around about Smart Tarts, and there had been a spate of defections from other agencies. Women had heard about the health care and the retirement plans, so Marcus and Jan had their pick of the field. "And the idea is ridiculous anyway."

"How many guys do you think she's slept with?" Jan asked. It was a rhetorical question, so he just shrugged as he leaned against the car. "Almost thirty. Three since she got divorced."

"It would be too bizarre." The information had thrown him. The marrying of the personal and professional was discomfiting. "Look at how it was with the store. You didn't want to be in business with her."

"I'm not advocating it. I just told her I'd talk to you. I felt so sorry for her lying in that hospital bed all covered in therapeutic mud."

"We could just lend her money."

Jan told Marcus that Plum had refused her offer of a loan. He said he'd think about it.

It was April now, and Marcus had been in the business since autumn. But the ensuing months had not inured him to the unease he felt while having a frank sexual discussion with anyone other than his wife. So it was with no little discomfort that he asked Plum whether she minded being urinated on. They were seated in the Smart Tarts office, a week after the injury. She was dressed in jeans and a clingy blue V-neck sweater that showed off her newly trim figure. Legs crossed tightly left over right, arms folded in her lap, she looked him directly in the eye.

"Do I *mind?*"

"Are you willing?" Marcus went on to explain to her that clients paid more for increasingly colorful varieties of sexual experience, and golden showers were a lucrative sideline if a person could transcend the taboo. As he awaited her response, he recalled a birthday party of Nathan's that Plum had attended in the Ripps backyard. Nathan had turned six and was dressed as a dinosaur for the occasion. Marcus had a picture of him, taken on that day, stuck in a drawer somewhere. Plum had stayed after the party to help clean up. She had looked radiant in a lime-green blouse and pale yellow pants. Marcus had found her easier to talk to back then.

"Are *you?*"

"To be honest, it's not my thing. But I need to know, because there are clients who pay a premium for it." Ordinarily, Marcus would never have engaged in this kind of revelatory badinage in an employment interview, but this meeting was a bizarre fusion of the personal and the professional, so he was doing what he could to make Plum comfortable. "So?"

"I don't think I want to go there at this point."

If it had been up to him, this get-together would not have been taking place, but Plum had been insistent. He was not unsympathetic to her recent run of bad luck, and if she was willing, of her own volition (this was supremely important to Marcus), to engage in this kind of work, he believed it would be hypocritical to deny her the opportunity. She had already agreed to various other fetishes including woman-on-woman shows, toe sucking, handcuffs, whips, dildos, and sex with people of differing political persuasions, so he was slightly surprised by her squeamishness at the prospect of being urinated on. However, he did not judge, and instead simply made a note on the legal pad in his lap. Then he said "You don't have to do this."

"I know."

"You could get a job doing something else."

Plum appeared uncertain how to respond for a moment. She uncrossed her legs, re-crossed them right over left, and leaned forward. "Marcus, when you were unemployed and looking for work, were there a lot of jobs available? Ones you wanted, I mean. Ones you'd actually be happy to do?"

Marcus pretended to think about this for a moment, although he knew the answer immediately. "Plum . . ."

"I *want* to do this. It's not like I'm enjoying dating." She punctuated her words with a harsh laugh. "I have expenses . . . I need money, and at this point . . ." She didn't complete the thought. "You'll make sure nothing happens to me, right?" Marcus nodded in as reassuring a way as he could manage. "I mean, you screen the . . . what do you call them . . . clients?" Marcus nodded again. "I'll do it once and if it doesn't work out, I can always kill myself." Plum affected a smile as she said this, and Marcus tried to laugh, although it sounded more like he was clearing his throat.

In a conversational turn that caught Marcus unawares, Plum asked him if Atlas knew what he was doing.

"No one knows." This seemed to satisfy her. "Does he know what *you're* doing?"

"You must be kidding."

Plum's howl-at-the-devil attitude reminded Marcus of his own when he had veered onto this road. So, too, did the cape of tight-lipped joviality she hung over it. The whole presentation was familiar, and it made Plum more simpatico than she'd been as Jan's business partner.

"Anything else you want to ask me?" she said.

Marcus wondered how long Plum would maintain her composure. The circumstances that had led her to this juncture were not remotely amusing, but he knew she was not a woman devoid of humor, and this situation felt ridiculous. Marcus, after all, was someone she had known as a workaday householder in Van Nuys, a man whose most immoderate behavior involved occasionally driving solo in the carpool lane. He sensed that she was beset with worry. He observed her as she looked at him, trying to be officious and conduct a business meeting. A small laugh escaped her lips.

"All right. So, what about providing one?" Marcus asked, tapping his pen on the pad.

"One what?"

"What we were just discussing. You know . . ." He didn't even like to use the jargon that went with this line of work, unless it was absolutely necessary. "The peeing thing . . ."

"I don't think so," she said. Marcus made another note on his pad. The two of them were doing their best to pretend that this conversation was not awkward.

"You've got to do what works," he said. Marcus reached into a desk drawer and pulled out a piece of paper, which he handed to her. "Read this and sign it. It says that whatever you do of a sexual nature is voluntary."

Plum signed the document. It was decided that she would begin work in the next few days.

"Did Jan tell you about the book club?"

"No." Ripples of nervous tension floated up Plum's neck to her jaw and cheeks. She bit her lip.

"Our philosophy is to create an environment that's supportive and, you know, human . . . so she thought a book club would be a good idea. They're reading *Anna Karenina*."

"I'll pick up a copy."

"Oh, and one more thing," he told her. "If you actually follow through, and you don't have to, but if you do . . ."

"I'm going to."

"Okay. If you're going to mention me in front of any of your co-workers, my name is Breeze."

At this, the dam broke and Plum started to laugh. At first Marcus was disconcerted, but he quickly surmised that her laughter arose from her discomfort at the situation. He appreciated that she had kept it at bay for the nearly half hour she had been seated in the office, but the strain had become too much for her to bear. Talking in gray tones about the unimaginably diverse permutations of human sexuality as if they were companies on the stock exchange had been stressful. Yet the two had negotiated the conversation with aplomb, despite his being the husband of her former business partner and someone with whom she had played Scrabble. But declaring he was to be referred to as "Breeze" apparently pushed her over the line, and the laughter was now pouring out of her in great, oxygen-depleting torrents, leaving her breathless and gasping.

Marcus watched her, his smile pallid. However effectively he was able to operate in this incarnation, a sense of its essential incongruity never left him. He could fully understand Plum's reaction. He found it slightly excessive, and not a little patronizing, but he sat there and patiently waited for the laughter to subside, which, a full minute later, it did.

"I'm sorry," she said, drawing breath before discharging a final ripple of anxious giggles. "It's just . . ."

"I know." He tried to reassure her, aligning his features into a pattern intended to suggest probity. Plum did not seem to be capable of eye contact. Marcus felt like an actor who had lost focus in a scene. He told her she would need to be photographed for the Smart Tarts Web site, so patrons would have some idea of what they were paying for. Hearing the nuts-and-bolts details calmed her nervous system, which had become hyperkinetic. She considered Internet images, a searchable, eternal, and compromising configuration of pixels and bytes. It felt at one moment abstract, then as lasting as a tattoo, something she could not take back. Plum was less than thrilled at this prospect, but Marcus was able to mollify her with the news that her face would not have to be visible. Many of the workers, he said, chose to highlight what they considered to be their best physical features in the pictures and leave the rest to the consumer's imagination. She told him that would be fine with her.

"Plum . . . really . . ." Marcus said. "Are you sure . . ."

Holding up her hand, as if to stop traffic, she told him not to ask her that again. Her eyes narrowed like caskets closing. "I *want* to do this."

Marcus gave her some money to purchase new lingerie and told her to choose an alias by which she'd like to be known. Kostya took some pictures of her later that afternoon. The images were on the Internet that night next to the name Verlaine, which Plum had selected in homage to the poet.

That night, while Marcus sat on the couch in the den watching a baseball game, Nathan wandered in after having taken a shower. He was wearing plaid pajama bottoms and a T-shirt from Sea World. He settled next to his father, and Marcus ran his fingers over Nathan's still-wet hair, smoothing it down. He asked him if his homework was done, and the boy told him it was. Marcus looked at his watch. It was a little before nine. Nathan's bedtime wasn't until nine thirty, and he was pleased that they would be able to spend some time together.

They watched the game for a few moments, and then Nathan, who did not like silence unless he was concentrating on a video game, turned to his father. "So, how was your day?"

The day had consisted of arranging twenty-seven assignations for his workforce and hiring his wife's former business partner to work as a prostitute.

"Terrific," he said.

"Do you remember the speech you gave at your bar mitzvah?"

"I never had one. I'm not Jewish, remember?"

"Oh, yeah. I forgot." Nathan already knew this information, but he was tired and his brain was in the place where the forces trying to shut it down for the night were tangling with the rowdier elements attempting to extend the day just a little longer. Marcus asked Nathan how his speech was coming and was told that he hadn't started it yet. He didn't want to write it quickly, because it was the one time he could tell a gathering of adults what he thought about an important subject. "You're giving a speech, too, right?"

Marcus assured Nathan that he was, although it was something he had completely forgotten about. Both Jan and he were going to stand in front of the congregation with their son and download whatever parental wisdom they could articulate into Nathan's hard drive. Whereas the child's speech at this event was usually a commentary on a biblical passage, each parent's was meant to be a benediction to a son or daughter, sage counsel to ignite the rockets of their young souls, launching them in a deistic direction, one presumed to lead them toward a happy, fulfilling existence. Marcus blanched at this aspect of the proceedings right now, as he looked at Nathan's clear complexion, unmarked by the garden of acne currently blooming on the faces of several of his friends, and thought about the absurdity of his standing up there and telling his son how to live his life.

"I want to talk to you two about motivational dancers."

They looked up and saw Lenore standing in the doorway in a pink sweatsuit, perspiring from a workout. She took a sip from a sports drink.

"What about them?" Marcus asked.

"Nathan needs them at the bar mitzvah, right, kiddo?"

"I dunno," he said. "I guess. Dad, do I?"

"Who do you have in mind?" Marcus asked.

"Some girls from the studio. They could use the work, and if you're going to hire dancers anyway . . ."

"Are they strippers?" Nathan wanted to know.

"I think two of them are," Lenore said. "But they're really nice girls."

"Strippers at my bar mitzvah?" Nathan again looked at Marcus. His nearly thirteen-year-old mind did not quite know what to make of this opportunity.

"I'll talk about it with Mom," Marcus said.

"They won't be stripping *at* the bar mitzvah," Lenore assured the two of them. "And you of all people shouldn't be worried about this," she said to Marcus. Marcus picked up his son's look, the one that said what did she mean by *that?*

"Thanks for the input, Lenore." Marcus said this in an even tone, but one that he hoped would shut her up. Lenore smiled tightly. Marcus sensed that she realized she had gone too far. When she left the room, Marcus and Nathan returned their attention to the television. After several moments of silence, they began to talk about the ball game.

Chapter 18

Plum approached her initial foray into this new life as Verlaine like a performance artist preparing for a show. She chose a new lipstick and an eye shadow she would not ordinarily wear, and she tousled her hair in a way meant to subtly hint at abandon. Standing in front of the full-length mirror on the back of the closet door in her bedroom, she examined various wardrobe choices. It took nearly an hour to select the costume.

Marcus had not wanted to send Plum to meet a client who was using the service for the first time, and had told her the man she would be seeing was an Italian businessman in town to sell huge quantities of dried fruits to an American supermarket chain. He liked to experiment, so a neophyte was fine with him. Marcus had told Plum that as far as he knew, the client had no unusual proclivities and so would ease her into this new phase as uneventfully as possible. Settling on a pair of designer jeans and a white silk blouse over a chemise, she stepped into a pair of heels and surveyed the result. Not bad. Then she took a Valium.

Marcus had recently hired several new drivers, and one of them, Jerry Cakes, a retired mailman with an avuncular manner, was on duty that night. The van was parked near Shining City, and three Smart Tarts were chatting amiably in the back when Plum eased into the passenger seat. Two others were reading *Anna Karenina*, and a third was reading the Cliff Notes. She introduced herself as Verlaine, and Cadee, Mariah, and Xiomara/Jenna said genial hellos before returning to their conversation, which was about the difficulty

Xiomara/Jenna was having in keeping her boyfriend from discovering that she was not really a paramedic. Plum listened to the exchange, observing the women as Jerry Cakes piloted the minivan toward the freeway. She appreciated that he didn't try to make conversation. It surprised her that none of the others was instantly identifiable as a prostitute. Instead, these women could have been on their way to work at an auto show. Their mode of presentation was sexy, but not overly so, and Plum observed that by current decline-of-the-West standards, her new colleagues were relatively tasteful in their presentation. They were all headed to various hotels on the west side of Los Angeles, where they would do their part to grease the wheels of the world economy.

The days had gotten longer and the early evening sky was the bluish purple of a black eye as the minivan rolled south through the Sepulveda pass toward LAX. Plum was nervous, which surprised her, given the Valium she had dosed herself with an hour earlier. She realized how difficult it would have been had she not taken anything at all. Her palms were perspiring, so she rubbed them on her jeans and hoped no one would notice. Her mouth was dry, but she'd had the foresight to pack a water bottle in her purse, along with the condoms Marcus had reminded her to bring (although clients would offer to pay more were they not required to use them, Marcus insisted that his workforce practice safe sex).

Plum's mind wandered to other times she'd traveled toward the airport. There were the trips to visit her in-laws in Wisconsin, the times she and Atlas had flown down to Mexico. They'd been to Cabo, and Puerto Vallarta, and once to a Club Med in Ixtapa. It seemed to her as if she was recalling someone else's life. There was a lot of traffic on the freeway at this hour, and for a change she didn't mind. Plum was in no hurry to get to where she was going.

As the other women continued to prattle in the background, she stared out the window watching the exit signs: Olympic, Jefferson, and then Century, where the van pulled off the freeway and Plum felt her heart rising in her chest. A few moments later, Jerry Cakes stopped in front of a ten-story monolith of a hotel. He gave her a room number and told her he would be back in about two hours.

Plum walked through the lobby and headed for the elevator bank toward the back. The space struck her as unusually bright and she stared resolutely ahead, fearing that if she made eye contact with anyone, her purpose would be immediately unmasked. At the check-in line, tired travelers stood next to their luggage, waiting to be processed and filed. A light-skinned young black man in a stylish gray suit smiled at her as he passed. She wanted to return his smile, but was too conscious of maintaining a normal demeanor to do anything that was actually normal. She wondered what the man she was meeting looked like.

Plum stood in front of the elevator bank. By herself for a moment, she fervently hoped she would be riding solo, alone with her thoughts, her life, flying above it. Other people tied her to reality, something she believed she could use a little less of. Plum willed one of the doors to open, but all her exertions seemed to produce was a pair of men who could be heard talking behind her. She cursed silently to herself, her solitude shattered. They were discussing a meeting they'd just had and whether it had gone well. She tried to ignore them. The elevators were slow. Someone was touching her on the shoulder. She turned and saw a man's smiling face.

"Excuse me," he said. "Do you know any good restaurants around here?"

The one who had spoken to her was a white guy, medium build, with a trim mustache. His companion was taller, heavyset, and white too. They appeared to be around her age, and both were wearing business suits. She told him she didn't know the restaurant situation. The elevator doors opened and she got in, the men right behind her. She wondered if they realized what she was doing in the hotel. She pressed the button for the ninth floor, stepped back, and stared straight ahead as the larger man pressed another button.

"Where you from?" said the one who wanted to know about the restaurants. It took Plum a moment to realize he was talking to her.

"San Francisco," she said, which was true.

"What are you doing in town?"

"Business." Why wouldn't this guy shut up? Her stomach was fluttering.

"How'd you like to join us for dinner?" She thought he winked at his friend as he said this.

"Thanks, but I have to work." Mercifully the doors opened and the men got out, wishing her good luck. What did they mean by that? She heard their laughter echoing in the hallway when the doors closed, leaving her alone again. Plum shut her eyes for a moment and exhaled through her nostrils. Good luck? Then she looked at her reflection in the elevator mirror mounted next to the door. She didn't like the lighting in the elevator and hoped her client wouldn't mind if what was going to transpire took place in shadows.

The doors opened at the ninth floor and Plum got out. To her relief, there was no one in the hallway. She was looking for Room 916, and a sign on the wall pointed her toward Rooms 900–920. For a moment, she thought about getting back in the elevator, going down to the lobby, and calling a cab. But instead she followed the arrow.

Beppo Molinari was from Rome and traveled to America three times a year. He told this to Plum while refilling her champagne flute with an inexpensive brand she hoped wouldn't leave her with a headache in the morning. His steel-gray hair was cut short, and he had a fleshy face with a prominent nose on which a pair of wire-rimmed glasses perched. She guessed he was in his fifties and thought he would have been almost handsome had it not been for a pronounced overbite that, from Plum's perspective, cancelled out the Italian accent (which she liked). Beppo sat on the king-sized bed. He was wearing black trousers and a pale pink button-front shirt with mother-of-pearl cufflinks. Plum smiled to hide her nervousness. They had been seated side by side for ten minutes, and she had learned about his wife, with whom he had conventional relations once a month, and his two sons, who were in their twenties and still lived at home, a situation he was paradoxically delighted with and disappointed by. Plum appreciated his humanity.

"Sit here," Beppo said, patting his thighs. His voice was friendly. She got off the bed and slid onto Beppo's lap. But Plum's movement was not what he had in mind. Beppo placed his champagne flute on the bedside table. He took Plum's and put it beside his. Then he lifted her leg over his head and to the side so she nearly fell over backward, the awkwardness causing them both to laugh (his playful, hers mortified). When he was done rearranging her limbs, she was straddling his thighs, facing him, heart pounding. He unfastened the top button of her blouse, then ran his fingertips horizontally along her breastbone, barely touching her skin. Plum shivered. She thought about whether there was anything in her refrigerator, glad to know that money would be less tight soon.

Plum didn't like this position, so she pushed off Beppo's lap and told him she'd be right back. She didn't want to walk too quickly to the bathroom, and remembered to smile at him over her shoulder. Alone, she splashed cold water on her face, not caring what happened to her makeup. She needed to calm down.

Beppo called out: "Everything okay?"

"Fabulous!"

Plum pressed a hand towel against her moist face and looked at her reflection. The tension she felt was not evident. She could just tell Beppo she didn't feel well, give him his three hundred dollars back (he'd paid her as soon as she'd arrived), and leave. To do what? Plum didn't want an ordinary job. Then she'd have to admit to the one thing that was death to an artist: that she was ordinary herself. The unflagging desire to be seen as a creative force had come from an unwillingness to live a conventional life, and it was to her great regret that not only had she failed in her chosen career, but she hadn't even managed to be unconventional. She hated herself for marrying Atlas, for living in Reseda, for having fallen so short of her youthful aspirations. Artists pushed limits, smashed taboos, courted disaster. This one was a junkie, that one stabbed his wife, another put rum on his corn flakes, had a thousand lovers, betrayed his country. Everything was fodder for the creative life. *Everything*. She went back into the room.

Beppo smiled when he saw her, his overbite becoming more pronounced. Plum knew those teeth wouldn't stand a chance in the purview of the Los Angeles orthodontic community. Her ruminations on the subject of Beppo's teeth ceased when she realized he had removed his pants and was stroking an impressive uncircumcised erection. She felt a surge of distress, of outrage that decorum had been breached, that the rhythm of the seduction had been thrown so completely off; but then quickly remembered that the rhythm was whatever the client wanted it to be. He was perfectly entitled to do what he was doing. It was the purpose of her visit.

"Please, Verlaine," he said. "Get undressed."

Plum hesitated a moment, thinking about the slight bulge that remained around her middle and the traces of cellulite on the backs of her thighs. How does someone who is in her late thirties, simply take off her clothes while standing in the middle of a room with a complete stranger, even one as friendly as Beppo Molinari? Plum thought about the life-drawing classes she had posed for, how her form had been reduced to a series of linked shapes rendered in charcoal, modular abstractions that held no inherent meaning. She remembered the Manet painting she'd discussed with Jan—a courtesan reclining on her side, languidly regarding the viewer, at once haughty and lubricious. That woman was hardly lithe, and her image had delighted art lovers for over a century. Plum wished she were a painting, admired, inspiring, discussed by scholars.

Turning her back to Beppo, she unbuttoned her blouse and let it slip to the floor. Then she slid out of the camisole. She unbuttoned her jeans, relieved at the release of their tightness but suddenly concerned that she hadn't lost enough weight to be wearing them. She glanced over her shoulder and saw Beppo running his knuckles against the shaft of his penis, grinning. Whatever imperfections of hers he may have noticed apparently did not bother him. He seemed to like her violet panties and matching bra. She made sure her gut was sucked in and hoped he wouldn't see the dimples on her thighs. Like a swimmer facing a cold ocean and wanting to attack the ordeal head-on, she quickly stepped out of the panties and unhooked her bra. Now she was standing naked in the middle of the room. She turned to face him. Beppo's smile had subsided into an expression of calm concentration. Were it not for his pronounced erection, he could have been preparing to give a piano recital. She knew what was supposed to come next but was uncertain how, exactly, to bring it about. Beppo removed a condom packet from his shirt pocket. He held it out to her, and said "Please." Plum opened the condom, willing her hands not to shake. Then she placed it on Beppo and rolled it down, a nurse administering treatment. Beppo indicated that he was ready. His eyelids fluttered as she slid onto him, and his head rolled back. Plum closed her eyes and began to compose a grocery list. She had only gotten as far as whole-wheat bread, yogurt, and mini-carrots when she felt something clamp down on her right breast. Opening her eyes, she saw Beppo ecstatically sucking her nipple. Three seconds later, she felt him quiver. With serpentine quickness, he placed his hands on her hips and lifted her off.

"I'm a premature ejaculator," he said.

Thank god, Plum thought. They hadn't been going for thirty seconds. "You're done?" In her mind she was already in the elevator.

"No, no, no, Verlaine. We stopped in time." Beppo bent forward at the waist, attempting to pacify his mutinous hormones. Her disappointment was massive. When Beppo settled down, he reached for the remote control and found a news channel where a correspondent in a metal helmet and flak jacket was standing on a windswept military base filing a war report. Then he got down on all fours. After a moment he glanced over his shoulder.

"Spank me, Verlaine."

Her heart leapt. Finally someone was playing her tune. Plum kept up a steady rhythm on his bottom for the next twenty minutes while Beppo alternately masturbated and channel-surfed until he finally exploded during the title sequence of a popular medical drama.

Plum didn't like having sex with a stranger, even one as well-meaning as Beppo. But getting paid to inflict mild corporal punishment? That was something to which she could grow accustomed. *There* was a profession. By the time she got to the elevator, Plum knew she had found her calling.

She would be a dominatrix.

Smart Tarts did not yet offer this service, and Marcus and Jan were pleased to include Plum's new specialty on the Web site, where from now on she would be known as *Mistress* Verlaine. Marcus was concerned that Plum's business would not be as brisk, serving only a particular subgroup, but if she was willing to take the risk, he was willing to provide the aegis. Plum acquired a new credit card from one of the many slap-happy lending institutions willing to serve the credit-drunk and drove to an erotic boutique on Sunset Boulevard, where she went on a shopping spree. She filled her cart with studded bustiers, chains, whips, ball-gags, dog collars, all things Lycra and latex, and a pair of black vinyl boots with heels that looked like murder weapons. Then she called Jan, and the two of them worked on the redesign of her Web page on the Smart Tarts site. Plum posed in her new uniform and gazed at the camera with an expression that could turn a grape into a raisin. Next to this image of fierce sexuality, the copy read "Mistress Verlaine wants to know—are you a bad boy? You cannot resist what you crave most. I have what you want. I know what you need . . . no escort sessions available." Bookings were instantaneous, if not extensive. But Plum was attending to a rarefied taste, so her business was not based on volume. She took to her new line of work like a Golden Retriever who has spotted a squirrel. If giving orders provided an erotic charge, having them obeyed was sublime. Years of frustration washed away. Her aggression had finally found an outlet both appropriate and remunerative. Plum had never been happier. Her services were expensive, and there was enough work that within a month she was earning more money than she'd made in her entire life.

Chapter 19

The summer was an inferno, hotter than the last. Traffic choked the freeways, great fingers of hot metal burning oceans of gasoline. Toxic clouds of fumes floated toward the brown sky. Fires raged across forests north of the San Fernando Valley and meadows to the west, leaving great swaths of burnt blackness in their wake. But the Ripps home was cooled by the four new air conditioners Marcus had purchased, and all was comfortable within. Without the financial worries of the previous year, Nathan was able to attend sleepaway camp. Lenore was put in charge of the operation with Kostya while Marcus and Jan travelled to Ojai, where they attended a theater festival, went to a classical music concert, and rusticated comfortably for a week.

By the middle of the summer, Plum was averaging between four and six assignations a week at private homes and hotels. She realized that in order to build her business, she would need her own space, but she didn't want to deal with intrusive neighbors, which ruled out converting her garage/studio. After some investigation, Plum was able to locate Mistress Anita, a Latina dominatrix with a dungeon above a Jamba Juice in Culver City that she was looking to sublet. Marcus agreed to cover the rent in exchange for a slightly higher percentage of the profits. The dungeon was standard-issue medieval with a rack, shackles, and a comfortable cell for lounging. Mistress Anita had even taken the trouble to install wallpaper that looked like the dank interior of a castle wall. A throne sat on a platform above a table laden with clamps, dildos, and various restraints. The first thing Plum did was to install a hidden camera. She had been working on an idea for a video installation, and this would be a fecund source of material. A Tokyo gallery with which she had been corresponding had expressed interest in seeing the finished work.

Late one August night, Marcus found himself unable to sleep. While he was in the kitchen making herbal tea, he noticed he'd left his Black-Berry on the table. He'd forgotten to turn it off, and it was vibrating. He scrolled through his messages and stopped when he saw one from MannishBoy24. Who was that? He opened it and read: *Breeze, U need 2 get out of the business B 4 something happens 2 U.*

There had been a time when receiving an anonymous e-mail threat in the middle of the night might have upset him. But money can breed a sense of invincibility. Who could this be? A disgruntled former employee? It hadn't occurred to him that there could be one. He disdainfully deleted the message. Then he sipped tea and scanned the business section of the day-old newspaper. This headline caught his eye:

PRIMUS TO RECEIVE L.A. BUSINESSMAN OF THE YEAR AWARD.

Roon Primus, CEO of Ameri-Can Industries, has been selected to receive the prestigious award in honor of his philanthropic activities. Primus serves on the boards of City of Hope Hospital, the American Cancer Society, the Southern California Architectural Preservation Association, and the ASPCA. The governor of California will be presenting the award.

Marcus didn't read any further. Rather than getting him agitated, the article had a calming effect. Roon was basking in the adulation of a credulous public, but Marcus was doing fine. Marcus didn't need a dinner. He was happy enough that he, too, could afford to make charitable contributions. He might have liked to be honored for his good works, but it was not something his ego required. And he understood it would never happen.

*   *   *

215

The planning for Nathan's bar mitzvah moved forward. It was going to be lavish but tasteful. He had learned the prayers, and he worked on his speech with the rabbi, going through several drafts under her exacting tutelage. Marcus and Jan had never seen him apply himself to anything like this, and he seemed to have made a great leap forward as he engaged with the challenge of his preparation. They were curious about what the boy intended to say to the congregation, had asked for an advance look at his speech, but Nathan preferred it to be a surprise. It was late on a Tuesday evening in October, and Marcus was in the kitchen loading the new dishwasher, when he heard the first few notes of a clarinet playing "Misty." He walked upstairs and stood in the hallway listening. He could see Nathan seated in a chair with his back to the door, staring at the music on a stand in front of him. His playing was not technically polished, but the melody glided out of the instrument with enough feeling to make Marcus think his son might actually have talent. When the song finished, he couldn't resist applauding. Nathan turned and gave a weary smile. His blue braces had been removed two days earlier, and their absence erased the slightly comical cast his face had assumed and replaced it with something bordering on handsome.

"That was really good."

Nathan nodded thanks and resumed practicing. Marcus liked going to bed knowing his son was in his room, safe, living the kind of life he was able to provide for him; secure, warm, predictable in the finest sense. Sometimes he would find himself counting the years he had left with the boy, before his departure for college and life outside the family. A feeling of profound melancholia would overtake him and he would have to consciously focus his mind on something else to make it dissipate. As Marcus looked at the curly dark hair on Nathan's head, he observed his thoughts turning in that direction, so he quickly said good night and went to his own room, where Jan lay in bed going over the RSVPs. Although there was mild consternation as she struggled with who would sit where, Jan was satisfied that everything was going well. Marcus reflected on this as he climbed between the mauve sheets. *Mauve sheets?* Where had they come from? Marcus nestled next to his wife.

"New sheets?"

"Egyptian cotton. Don't worry, they were on sale."

When Marcus arrived at Shining City after dropping Nathan off at school, he knew something was wrong immediately. The light in the room was odd. He immediately looked toward the back. Did he hear breathing, or a soft footstep? Was someone waiting for him?

"Kostya?"

Silence. Marcus walked past the clothes rack and looked into the office. No one was there. Probably nothing, he thought. He sat at his desk and turned his computer on, doing some shoulder lifts to ease the muscles in his upper back as he waited for the machine to boot up. Marcus clicked on his e-mail icon and checked his inbox. There were fifteen new e-mails. He quickly scanned the list and was not at all pleased to see that MannishBoy24 had written him again. Marcus highlighted the re: line and clicked the mouse.

Breeze, I told U something U would not like was going 2 happen. The next time I do this I will be aiming at U. Close down your business and go 2 China. Learn 2 use chopsticks. If U stay in LA U will not B happy.

He sat up in his chair. This person, whoever he was, had ramped up the threat level exponentially. And what had occurred that Mannish-Boy24 was referring to? What had MannishBoy24 done? His eyes shot around the room. Everything appeared normal. Then it struck him. Jan! He reached for his phone, nearly fumbling it in his nervousness. She answered on the third ring.

"Where are you?" he nearly barked.

"I'm at the plumbing supply store on Van Ness." If she heard his sigh of relief, she did not comment on it. "Why?"

"What are you doing?" he said, trying not to convey the dread he had been feeling until five seconds ago.

217

"Choosing spigots. Is everything okay?"

"It's fine, it's fine."

"We agreed we were going to renovate the downstairs bathroom before the bar mitzvah, didn't we? You signed off on it."

"I know, I know. I was just calling to say hi."

Marcus hung up the phone and attempted to quiet his rampaging nervous system. Not only was Jan still alive, she was selecting spigots. That was a relief. He walked toward the front of the dry cleaner where the sun refracted crazily through the windowpane, throwing jagged shadows against the side wall. Marcus hadn't noticed shadows like that earlier, serrated, gray on white. He looked from the wall to the ceiling to the window, where he saw three bullet holes. Somehow he had missed them before. The image of Jesus was untouched. Moses, too. Ditto Buddha. But on the wall behind the counter he saw the painting of Vishnu, whose contemplative expression remained unchanged despite the bullet lodged near his third eye.

Marcus fought the impulse to throw himself on the floor. He knew it was irrational, since the shooting had already occurred. Instead, he walked back to his office, pulled up MannishBoy24's e-mail and reread it. Then he called Kostya, who was driving to a restaurant supply store in Anaheim. Marcus apprised him of the situation and asked his advice. It was simple:

"Get out of business before you get killed."

"I'm not ready to do that."

"Then buy a gun, Gangstaboy."

Marcus sank back into his chair.

I don't know if I can play the game at this level. But we need the money. It's not like I can just get a job. I can't get a gun. I've never held a gun. What if I have to use it? I don't even know if I could wave it around. What if it went off? What if I accidentally shot myself? Can I shoot anyone? What would that be like? Pointing a gun at someone and pulling the trigger, bang. And what if I killed them? Could I live with myself, or would I be tormented by it for the rest of my life? What would a reasonable man do? Am I even a reasonable man any more? These people aren't reasonable, but they're serious. I'm serious too. I'm running a business here. This is how I make my living, and I can't let myself be intimidated. I have to do something, show strength. They sense weakness, these kinds of people. It's a scent. They smell it. Am I perspiring? Don't perspire. Stop! You can handle this. Calm down calm down calm down. Breathe breathe breathe. There, that's better. All right. You don't have to get a gun. Not yet, anyway. Should I tell Jan what happened? I can't tell Jan. Am I betraying her if I don't tell her? No! I can't tell her. I'll deal with it.

Marcus reflected on what he'd done since he took over the business, the employment benefits he'd enacted, the money he'd brought in. A surge of confidence shot through him, a sense of authority commensurate with his level of achievement.

Turning his attention back to the computer, he moved the cursor to the REPLY icon and typed *I'm not going out of business right now. Let's meet and talk this over. I'll bring the bill for the new window.*

When Marcus was pricing chicken at the supermarket later that day, his BlackBerry started vibrating. He immediately opened the message when he saw it was from MannishBoy24. The text read: *Come 2 my house at 9:00 this evening. 2438 San Mateo Drive, north of Sunset.* This did not strike Marcus as a good idea, for the simple reason that it left him wide open to being stuffed in a car trunk, driven to the desert, and killed. Whatever was going to happen, he would not allow MannishBoy24 to get the drop on him. Common sense said this meeting needed to take place at a neutral site. He didn't want to go to a bar or a restaurant, in the event he was too tense to eat or drink. An open place like a park or plaza would allow MannishBoy24 to slip away quickly in the wake of any mayhem. Marcus racked his brain for an alternative location for their sit-down, someplace he could feel safe. He began tapping on the small keyboard with his thumbs as he moved to let a fat woman in a leopard-print blouse push her shopping cart past him. *Your house does not work. Meet me at 4:00 tomorrow afternoon . . .* He gave the location, hesitated a moment, then punched in *Remember—I know where you live.* For all Marcus knew, the address his correspondent had provided was a false one and the whole thing was meant as a setup. But that did not matter; what mattered was that Marcus be perceived as a man with *cojones.*

After he clicked SEND, he cogitated again on the matter of a gun. MannishBoy24 would be packing. Still, Marcus did not like the idea of being armed. The possibilities for disaster were epic. And what was the point of having a sit-down if he needed to come heavy? He solved the conundrum by asking Kostya to accompany him.

That night, Marcus reaffirmed his decision to not inform Jan that the dry cleaner had been shot up as a warning. Nor did he tell her he was going to meet the perpetrator, since she might consider it a less-than-sterling example of strategic planning. So he was caught unaware in the kitchen the following morning when she looked up from her egg whites and told him that they had a parent-teacher conference after school that day, at the same time he was supposed to be meeting MannishBoy24.

"I can't be there."

When Jan asked him why not, Marcus said he had a pressing piece of business to attend to. His back was to her as he removed two pieces of wheat bread from the toaster and began to apply vegan butter to them. Nathan hadn't come down for breakfast yet, and Lenore had smoked a particularly potent strain of weed the previous evening and was currently lying in bed, her brain waves barely measurable.

"What's so pressing that you have to miss a parent-teacher conference?" Her query was met with silence. Marcus placed the slices of toast on a plate and poured himself a glass of orange juice. "Marcus . . .?"

"I've been getting these e-mails . . ."

"What kind of e-mails?"

He told her someone wanted Smart Tarts to cease operations, and he was going to meet with this person face to face. She looked at him askance.

"What if it's a cop?"

"I don't think the police send e-mail to people they're thinking about busting."

"Maybe it's a sting."

"I'm going to a meeting. It's not a sting. You don't have to worry."

"About what?" Nathan said as he entered the kitchen.

"Nothing," Marcus said. Nathan went to the cabinet, removed the Cheerios, and poured himself a bowl which he drowned in milk. "Why is it whenever you guys are having a conversation and I ask you what it's about, the answer is always 'nothing'?"

"You don't have to worry about it. That's all," Marcus said. Jan was partially mollified by the news that Kostya would accompany him, but she was still not comfortable when he left.

Color Me Mine was a do-it-yourself pottery studio in Brentwood. It was located in a three-tiered mini-mall, and Marcus had attended a birthday party there for one of Nathan's friends several years earlier. It was patronized mostly by families and couples who came in, selected bare cups, plates, pots, vases, or bowls, and painted colorful designs on them. It was where Nathan had made the ceramic cup that said DAD. Marcus knew the place would be crowded after school let out. He and his adversary would be left alone, as long as they were seated at a table with art supplies.

Marcus and Kostya arrived a little before four. Kostya looked the place over and told Marcus to sit alone. He would observe the meeting from a discreet distance and remain as inconspicuous as a 6′4″ Russian with dreadlocks could manage. There was a children's birthday party going on with a dozen eight-year-old girls, and after Marcus selected the vase he was going to paint for Jan, he sat two tables away. Four mothers of the party attendees and two Hispanic caregivers had elected to stay for the party, and a few of them eyed Marcus suspiciously. Who was this middle-aged man decorating a vase by himself at Color Me Mine? But Marcus was wearing soft-leather loafers, khakis, and a navy blue sweater. He looked like a local father whose therapist had told him arts and crafts might distract him from his worries and after a few minutes they lost interest in him. The ever-resourceful Kostya had noticed a Help Wanted ad in the window and was seated at a nearby table filling out a job application. No one gave him a second glance. Marcus arranged several small paper cups filled with paint in a semicircle in front of him. He had all the primary colors. Dipping his brush in the green, he began to daub paint on the side of the vase.

"Breeze?"

He glanced up and saw a woman in a loose flower print dress that stopped modestly just above her knees. She was somewhere near thirty. Her thick honey-blonde hair hung down to the middle of her back and framed a pretty face with a light tan. She had blue eyes, and her lips were lightly glossed with a shade of coral lipstick. The expensive-looking black boots she was wearing added an inch to her modest height. She held an unpainted plate between her hands and smiled. Marcus wondered if this was one of the mothers from the birthday party. But hadn't she just called him Breeze?

"Have we met?"

"I'm Malvina Biggs." He regarded her quizzically. "Mannish-Boy24?" Marcus nearly dropped his paintbrush. "All right if I sit down?" She had a non-regional English accent, devoid of class significance. Sitting opposite him, Malvina picked up a paintbrush, dipped it in the little container of red, and went to work on her plate. Marcus stared at her. Attractive in a Los Angeles bohemian-with-ten-credit-cards way, she had the confident air that accrues to those who simultaneously ooze sex and money.

"What should I call you?"

"Malvina's fine."

"Biggs . . . Biggs . . ." Marcus said, staring at her face. There was something vaguely recognizable about it, but he couldn't possibly have met her before. "That's a familiar name."

"I'm Terry Biggs's daughter."

"No kidding?"

Malvina smiled. She was always happy when someone in America had heard of her father. Terry Biggs was the British actor famous for a series of knockabout comedies he made in the 1950s and 60s known as the *Right You Are* films. Shot in black and white, and featuring titles like *Right You Are, Constable; Right You Are, Prime Minister;* and the immortal *Right You Are, Nurse,* they had been a sensation in the Commonwealth countries and utterly unknown everywhere else. There had been a *Right You Are* festival at Berkeley, and Marcus had enjoyed several of the films, which were broad and silly.

Marcus shook his head slightly, as if to reorient himself. The funny man with the gap-toothed grin and little mustache had a daughter who was shooting bullets through his window? It didn't compute. He had no idea what to say, so he blurted out: "How's your dad?"

"He's dead."

"I'm sorry."

"Yes, well. My inheritance was his cinematic legacy, and now . . . here we are."

"How did you get my e-mail address?"

"So, Breeze," Malvina Biggs said, ignoring his question. "What *are* we going to do?" She was painting calligraphy, her delicate wrist hovering over the sinuous black lines.

"I don't even know what this is about."

"The business you're running has become a problem. The health care, the retirement . . . I don't provide those. I hear you have a book club. I mean, fucking hell!"

223

"You're a . . .?"

"That's why we're here."

"Terry Biggs's daughter . . ."

"Yes, and he wanted to be doing *King Lear* with the Royal Shakespeare Company. We all make accommodations," she said, looking him in the eye. "I had staked out an exclusive piece of real estate in this business, and then you come along. Several of my girls have gone to work for you in the past few months."

Marcus had no idea who these former subcontractors of Malvina's could be. He didn't ask about employment history during the interview process.

"That's the free market," he said.

"You are stepping on my toes. That is not acceptable." Marcus felt her stare and tried to concentrate on the flower he was painting. It had a curved green stem and fat blue petals. He was detailing the third petal with a daub of yellow when a shadow suddenly washed over the table where they were sitting. Marcus looked up and beheld the largest human being he had ever seen. He was well over six feet tall and weighed at least four hundred pounds. His dark, curly hair was pulled into a loose pony tail, and his round nut-colored face had Asian features. The black nylon jersey he was wearing fought a losing battle with his immense bulk, which strained against it insistently. His arms hung off his shoulders at odd angles to his huge torso. The fluorescent light glinted off a piece of gold dangling from his ear. Was that a Star of David?

"I need quarters for the meter," he said to Malvina Biggs.

"Breeze, this is Tommy the Samoan."

Marcus nodded, but the man paid no attention. While Malvina dug into her purse, Marcus glanced over at Kostya, who looked up from his employment application and shrugged as if to say What do you want me to do? Malvina handed several coins to the giant, who departed wordlessly.

"I hate valet parking," she said. Marcus was glad Kostya had a gun.

The girls at the birthday party two tables away were singing a song about rabbits and apples.

"I'm going to keep doing what I've been doing," he said evenly.

"This is a dodgy business. The people are shits. You seem like a nice guy, so I can talk to you like a human being. I probably *won't* have you killed because, really, why would I risk that? The bullets were only for show." She finished the Chinese character she had painted, picked up the plate, and held it away from her so she could examine it. Not entirely satisfied, she dipped the brush back into the black paint and extended one of the lines slightly.

"What does that mean, that thing you just painted?" Marcus asked.

"Long life. Cool, yeah? It was taught to me by this artist in Hong Kong. You should have moved to China when you had the chance."

"How do you know about that?"

"People talk. I like this place," she said, looking around. "You can have a little time to wrap your operation up, all right? I don't want to be unreasonable. But please don't let Smart Tarts—brilliant name, by the way—don't let Smart Tarts be in business in . . . oh, what shall we say? . . . in two weeks?" Malvina got up from the table. Marcus followed suit.

"It's been a pleasure to meet you," he said, "and as much as I'd like to say *yes, fine*—what I'm going to say is kiss my black ass."

"Is that a joke?"

"Only the black part."

Malvina was not pleased to hear this. She nodded, pushed her chair under the table, turned, and walked out, her hips swishing under the sheer material of her dress. Marcus was so pleased with himself, he forgot to give her the bill for the window.

He was still on a high from the meeting, so Kostya's announcement came as an unwelcome surprise.

"You're quitting?"

The two of them were seated outside a frozen yogurt shop three storefronts down from Color Me Mine. Kostya licked his vanilla cone

225

and nodded. His dreadlocks bounced lightly with the movement of his head. It wasn't as if Marcus couldn't run the business, particularly now that Jan was aboard. But Kostya's presence, with its implicit ties to the ancien regime, was comforting and Marcus was loath to let it go.

"Why now? Because of Malvina?"

"I said I would work to make money to open ribs place. Now I got money. You think about getting out too, Gangstaboy. Why you want to mess around with peoples bring big-ass Samoans to meets? You know what that mo'fucka do to you?" Kostya made a series of hand motions intended to convey the idea of limbs being separated from torsos.

"That's why I had you there."

"I ain't no bodyguard, Breeze. I'm a lover."

Marcus licked his cone pensively. He knew Kostya was right, that he should probably think about wrapping things up. But, Malvina aside, everything was going so well right now that if he remained in business a little longer, he could take care of Nathan's college tuition.

"You're sure you won't stay?"

"I give you two weeks' notice."

Marcus still had not informed Jan about the gunshots at Shining City and this contributed to the sanguinity with which she received his report about how he had handled Malvina Biggs at their meeting. But she did not take the news about Kostya's imminent departure as well. They were in their bedroom getting dressed to go out to dinner when Marcus told her he had quit. She stopped applying eyeliner and looked at him.

"It's a disaster."

"No, it isn't. We've been running things."

"He's a real pimp."

"What are we?"

"Not that."

"Neither is he, really. Kostya sees himself as a guy with adaptable business skills."

"Well, he's more of a pimp than you or I."

"Look, this is semantic. I'm not saying he doesn't contribute, but come on, we can do it without him." Marcus buttoned his shirt, a new linen one. He had never worn linen before and liked the way it felt.

"It makes me uncomfortable."

"I tried to talk him into staying." He was debating whether to tell her what had happened at the office, and about the sit-down with Malvina, but decided this was not the best time.

"I like having him around," Jan said. She was brushing her hair now. "I trust him, and he'll know what to do if anything bad happens. Should I talk to him?"

"I don't think that'll do any good."

"It's not like you and I are cut out for this business. Why's he quitting?"

"He's opening a rib place."

"We should be doing that."

"Opening a rib restaurant?"

"No, but we have to get into *something* legitimate. I don't know how much longer I can take this."

Marcus nodded but did not respond.

That night they had dinner at a new Provençal restaurant in Beverly Hills with Corinne and Dewey Vandeveer. Jan had been trying to arrange it for months, but the Vandeveers both had busy schedules and had cancelled several times, once only an hour before their date. Marcus had no desire to go out to dinner this evening, but he knew Jan had been looking forward to it and didn't want to disappoint her. The couples talked about Winthrop Hall, and real estate, and Corinne's latest attempts to bring Buddhism into the California prison system. Corinne was transported by her vision of incarcerated Crips and Bloods chanting sutras with orange-robed monks and went on about it for half an hour. The woman loved to talk about her life, and Marcus was relieved at not having to carry any of the conversational weight. He ate his bouillabaisse and stole glances at

227

Dewey, who reflexively eyed his BlackBerry every few minutes to check on the progress of a deal in Dubai. Marcus could have been checking his BlackBerry, too, but Jan had specifically asked him not to. It must be nice, he thought, to wear jeans, and loafers with no socks, earn unimaginable amounts of money, and never have to worry about someone shooting your windows out. He wished he could live that kind of life, desperately wanted to provide it for Jan, but didn't see how it was possible.

Jan appeared to be enjoying herself, at ease in Corinne's company. She had been working out four times a week for the last several months (she had purchased a gym membership after joining Smart Tarts) and had hired a trainer. Now, luminous with good health, she looked better than she had in years.

"We need people on the decorations committee," Corinne was saying to Jan. Abandoning his ruminations, Marcus quickly surmised that they were talking about a school function.

"I'd love to do it," Jan said.

"We always have a great time," Corinne said. "Marcus, maybe you want to get involved. We love to have the dads!"

Marcus smiled and begged off. "I'm pretty busy," he said.

"What's new in the gold market?" Dewey asked. Marcus couldn't believe he remembered their dinner-party conversation.

"The usual, you know. Up, then down," Marcus said, faking beautifully. "But I like it for the long term."

"You can't beat gold," Dewey said, checking his BlackBerry again.

Marcus and Jan were driving north on Benedict Canyon later that night when Jan said "You're awful quiet."

"Something kind of weird has been going on," he said, looking straight ahead. After the dinner with the Vandeveers, Marcus thought Jan needed to be reminded that they were leading an entirely different life. Recent events were weighing on him, and he had decided it was best to come clean. So he informed her about the gunshots. Jan listened, horrified. Marcus tried to reassure her. The situation was under control, he said, and they couldn't allow themselves to be driven out of business by what he believed were empty threats.

"The only reason they're empty is because the bullets didn't hit you," she said, her voice tight with fresh anxiety.

"This person is a business woman. She doesn't want to kill anyone."

"Why didn't you tell me this sooner?"

"Because I knew this was how you'd react."

"Marcus, we're partners. You have to tell me these things."

The lights of Los Angeles were behind them now as they reached the apex of the canyon and began their descent toward the Valley.

"We just have to ride it out," he said, taking his foot off the brake and letting the car glide down the curving road, picking up speed.

"You're driving too fast. I don't want to get pulled over." Marcus tapped the brake pedal. "Is this why Kostya quit?"

"He was going to quit anyway."

As they got ready to go to sleep, Jan said they needed to begin to think about a schedule for closing down the business. He told her they would talk about it soon.

"Marcus, I'm not kidding," she said, settling into bed next to him.

"I know. We have to get out. But we have to do it the right way."

"Which is . . .?"

"Maximal profit, minimal risk."

"But what does that mean?"

"You have to trust me, okay?"

Affecting confidence and brio, he kissed her on the mouth. He hoped she couldn't sense his nervousness. He was wearing the silk pajamas he had purchased on impulse the previous weekend. Was that perspiration he felt in his armpits? Marcus nestled into his pillow and tried to fall asleep.

*   *   *

Nate, You're a special boy. You are very even-keeled. You play basketball and the clarinet. I wouldn't know how to work my computer or my cell phone if it were not for you. I remember the time at the beach when you were around five. A big wave knocked you over, but you got right up. You were laughing. You are a great son. We're very proud of you today. We love you.

Marcus placed his pen on the kitchen table and looked at the legal pad on which he'd been writing. It was after midnight and he couldn't sleep. He read the speech out loud, timing himself. Bertrand Russell looked up from his bed in the corner of the kitchen, wondering if Marcus was addressing him. It took thirty seconds to read, which made it too short. Nathan had worked hard, and if Marcus wanted to honor his son's accomplishment, he would need something that would take longer to declaim than directions to the post office. He shifted his gaze from the notes he'd made to the new Sub-Zero refrigerator. After laboring on the speech for over an hour, it was time for a break.

He opened the silver behemoth and surveyed the contents through tired eyes: vegetables, lowfat cheese, five-day-old sliced turkey, condiments, whole-wheat bread, green grapes. None of it looked terribly inviting, but sitting at the table and staring into space was not producing anything worthwhile. Perhaps he needed to raise his blood sugar. Grabbing a handful of the grapes, Marcus returned to the pad and reread his notes. While everything he'd written was true, he reflected that it did not constitute a speech. Marcus chewed on the end of the pencil and considered this. How does someone put his most private thoughts and memories down on paper, deeply personal ideas intended to be shared between a parent and child, and then read it in front of an audience? Roon had engaged a professional to draft his remarks at his son's bar mitzvah. Even though Marcus could now afford to do the same, he knew it missed the point by a wide margin. So he continued to struggle with the unwieldly process of refining what he would say.

Marcus had been nibbling grapes and doodling for ten minutes when he heard footsteps on the stairs. Jan entered, sleepy-eyed.

"Couldn't sleep?"

"I was thinking about the bar mitzvah," she said. He told her he was too, smiling at her as if everything was normal. "How many people should we invite to the out-of-towner brunch on Sunday morning? Besides relatives, I mean." The out-of-towner Sunday brunch was a bar mitzvah tradition that, while appearing nowhere in the Torah, had become very popular in southern California. It was a way of thanking those who had traveled to attend the ceremony in the currency of lox, bagels, and whitefish. Occasionally, particularly good friends were invited as well. Right now, the guest list was limited to Jan's sisters and some cousins of Marcus's, who were coming in from Seattle.

Marcus said to invite whomever she liked. Turning his attention back to the speech, he tapped the pad with the sharpened point of the pencil. "Have you written your speech yet?" he asked.

"Did you hear that?"

"What?"

"I thought I heard a sound outside." She moved toward the kitchen window and peered into the darkness.

"There's nothing there."

"Would you look?"

"For what?"

"I *told* you. I heard something." She opened a drawer and took out a foot-long kitchen knife, holding it out to him.

"Am I going out there to carve a turkey?"

"Just take it, please."

Displaying a cool he did not feel, he took the knife and stepped outside. The backyard was empty. The silver moon lit a cloudless sky, illuminating the small yard. He listened. Nothing. Then suddenly he heard someone behind him and, gripping the knife, he wheeled around with a jagged intake of breath. The kitchen light

231

caught his face and there was Jan watching him with an unsettled look. He knew he had heard something. At least he thought he had. So he strained to listen, blood pulsing through his veins. But all he could hear was the quiet hum of the freeway, a rumor in the faint distance. Feeling a strange amalgam of primal and ridiculous, he returned to the house.

"There's no one there," he said.

"Thanks for checking." He nodded, the calm protector. "Are you coming back to bed soon?" Marcus told her he'd be up in a few minutes and returned to his pen and pad.

Thirty minutes later, Marcus was lying in bed, trying to remember amusing anecdotes about Nathan, when he heard a noise downstairs. He thought he might have imagined it, but Jan had unsettled him earlier, so he got out of bed, careful not to wake her. He checked Nathan's room and found him sleeping soundly. It must be Lenore who was banging around. But when he looked in her room, she was on the bed passed out, Laura Nyro playing quietly on her CD player. Marcus cocked his ear. Barely audible beneath the singer's mournful tone was the sound of footsteps. His heart began to thud in his chest, pounding against his ribcage as if it was about to leap from his body and bounce off a wall. He padded warily down the steps, carrying Nathan's baseball bat. Why hadn't he taken the carving knife upstairs with him? He peeked into the living room, where he saw Tommy the Samoan parked on the love seat with Bertrand Russell in his lap. He was stroking the dog's neck, pinching the skin between fingers the size of bratwursts. Bertrand Russell seemed to be enjoying it.

"Don't go crazy, brah."

Marcus stared at the colossal Polynesian and calculated his options. Obviously, he couldn't take him physically. The baseball bat in his hand, a lethal weapon to a garden-variety human, would be like a toothpick wielded against this massive form. He could cry out to Jan, alerting her to the alien presence, but Marcus hoped to get Tommy to leave as quietly as he'd come.

"I'm going to call the cops." Given how terrified Marcus was, he was thrilled that words actually came out of his mouth. He reached for the phone on an end table and picked it up.

"And tell them what? You a criminal. Put the phone down." Marcus hesitated a moment. The man did not seem like he was going to cause imminent harm. He placed the phone back on the cradle.

"What do you want?"

"What Malvina say about not killing you? She lying. Told me if you not gone in two weeks, man, that's it. *Hasta la vista* and shit."

"Why are you telling me?"

"I Googled you, brah. I see you got a bar mitzvah coming up." Marcus shook his head in amazement. "I ain't gonna help her kill no *lantzman*."

Marcus recognized the Yiddish. "You're not Jewish . . .?"

"My girlfriend, she is. I'm taking conversion classes with Rabbi Dunleavy. He a convert too. You hearda him?"

"No."

"Tough-ass ex-Marine can es'plain the *mishnah* like a motherfucker."

Marcus did not think it was a good time to mention that in fact he was *not* Jewish, since this seemed, ironically, to be what was saving his skin at the moment.

"I love this girl, okay? Guy I work with, his name Memo. He with Malvina, too. Memo come to my girl last week, say he give her money, diamonds, all she gotta do is sleep with him one time. But she no listen."

"That's love," Marcus offered.

"You damn right. She make me better person. So, I'm gonna tell you one more time—Malvina serious. You cutting a slice outta her cake and she ready to cap you. Move to Fresno or something before they say *kaddish* for you, brah."

That Bertrand Russell was licking Tommy the Samoan's huge face did not mitigate this thought: A man who could kill him a hundred different ways had crept undetected into his house and was now planted in his living room like a tree trunk. It occurred to Marcus that perhaps things had gone too far. Still, he didn't want to just shut down and walk away tomorrow.

"Would Malvina be willing to negotiate? I do financial planning for the women and maybe . . ."

Tommy interrupted him: "You not understand what I'm telling you. She ready to wax you, see?"

Marcus did a quick calculation. It was October. The approaching holiday season was a national pageant of familial dysfunction and loneliness and thus a potential bonanza for Smart Tarts. Surely, Malvina could live with his being in business a little longer. "Tell her I'll shut down after New Year's."

Tommy the Samoan's watermelon-sized head slowly shook in rueful disappointment. "Might not be Happy Hannukah, brah." Then he gently placed Bertrand Russell on the floor and rose from the chair. It was like watching the Goodyear blimp leave the launch pad. He lumbered to the front door and hesitated for a moment, as if deciding whether to say anything else. Marcus watched him intently. Then he opened the door, filled the frame for a brief instant, and was gone.

Marcus poured himself a whiskey and sat at the kitchen table. He still thought Malvina was bluffing. And even if that analysis proved wrong, he had recently purchased a two-million-dollar life insurance policy. If she had him taken out, his family would be handsomely provided for. His intimate familiarity with the great philosophical texts left him with what he believed to be scant fear of death. He wouldn't seek it, but he'd be ready when it came. In the meantime, precautions could be taken.

Marcus was disconcerted by Tommy the Samoan's midnight ramble and did not sleep well. When he awoke in the morning, he stood in the hallway and listened keenly before going downstairs. He looked in the kitchen, where Bertrand Russell was resting peacefully. *Useless*, he thought, shaking his head. He looked through the kitchen window into the backyard—nothing unusual there. Then he opened the front door and hesitated a moment, peering around. It wasn't quite seven yet and the neighborhood was quiet. Seeing no one in the street, he retrieved the morning paper. When Jan came down for breakfast, Marcus said nothing about the home invasion—why ramp up the domestic anxiety level even further?—but casually mentioned that he wanted to install a burglar alarm. She agreed it was probably a good idea.

That day, Marcus looked in his rearview mirror far more often than usual when he drove, and glanced up at every noise in the office. Even when he had lunch at an Italian place he liked on La Cienega, he made sure to sit facing the door.

The Smart Tarts book group met for the first time at six o'clock that night, early enough to accommodate people's work schedules. It turned out that *Anna Karenina* had not been a judicious choice of reading material. The meeting had already been postponed several times due to the novel's length, five-hundred-plus pages, which stretched before the ambitious readers like the Russian steppe, draining their initial enthusiasm. It was too dense, people said, had too many big words, and what was that chapter from the dog's perspective? Jan had listened to these and other complaints about her choice over the past months, but reiterated the claim that it would be good to start with a book none of them would try on their own. If everyone wanted to read something by John Grisham next, that was fine, but she requested that they all make at least one attempt to be high-toned. Was that not, after all, the purpose of their entire endeavor? Were they not *Smart* Tarts? Finally, Jan had decreed that the book club either meet or disband.

Eight working girls plus Marcus, Jan, and Lenore attended the session at the Ripps home. The unseasonably warm weather was congruent with the Tex-Mex culinary theme (no one wanted Russian food), and everyone brought a covered dish. The assembled literati settled into their seats around the patio table, and the sangria-fueled conversation was lively. But it turned out that the only ones who had actually read the entire book were Plum and Marcus. Jan had only made it two thirds of the way through. No one else had even finished the Cliff Notes. What was all that stuff about Levin, everyone wanted to know. Why was he in the story? Anna and Vronksy, there was meat, the soap opera, the stuff! They liked that, all the lust and the drama. But the women were outraged when Plum told them that Anna threw herself under a train.

"For a guy?" Mink asked, as she bit into an empanada. "What a loser!"

"The options for a woman back then were limited," Marcus explained. "It was a feudal society, and you were either a serf or a noble, or . . ."

"Surf's up," Alicia said. She was a former tennis teacher from Santa Barbara, beloved by Japanese businessmen. She smiled, pleased at her joke.

"It's spelled S-E-R-F," Plum said, with a hint of condescension.

"Excuse me," Alicia said, draining her sangria and refilling her glass.

"Or you were a tradesman," Marcus continued. "If you were a woman like Anna and you left your home, the only option . . ."

"I can't relate to victims," Xiomara/Jenna said as she garnished a chimichanga with salsa before placing it in her mouth.

"Me neither," Lenore said. "I want to read about women characters with balls."

"Madame Bovary killed herself, too," Jan said.

"Who's Madame Bovary?" Madison asked. She was new to the business, having arrived recently from Denver to study acupuncture. Her curly black hair fell into her eyes as she looked at Plum.

"Didn't you go to college?" Mink said.

"I was a science major," Madison explained.

"She was this French housewife," Plum said, "in a really boring marriage. She had an affair with this guy . . ."

"And let me guess," Mink said. "The ho kills herself?"

"That makes it a classic," Lenore said. She was being sarcastic. "What's with these women?"

Although everyone had liked the food, it was decided that if the book group was to continue, they would have to be more astute in their selection of reading material next time.

As they were clearing the table, Lenore said "Maybe we should read Erica Jong. She was a big deal back in the seventies. Anyone know her?"

"I wasn't born in the seventies," Alicia said as she ferried a large tray of uneaten burritos to the kitchen.

"I wasn't born in the nineteenth century, but I tried to read that Tolstoy book," Lenore said, walking inside with a tray of glasses.

"Are there Cliff Notes for Erica Jong?" Mink asked. She was standing in the kitchen, scraping the remains off plates into a plastic garbage bag. Lenore offered to check. Jan mentioned a book about a woman who worked for the British Foreign Service in the Middle East in the early twentieth century. She climbed mountains, translated Persian poetry, and was instrumental in the drawing of national boundaries after the collapse of the Ottoman Empire. Although only three of the eleven people in attendance had heard of the Ottoman Empire, it was agreed that the next book would be *Desert Queen*, a biography of Gertrude Bell.

"Does she kill herself?" Mink asked.

"I'll check," Jan said.

"Even if she does," Lenore said, "at least it's not because of a bad relationship."

The book club was a welcome distraction for Marcus. He enjoyed the discussion, despite its limited scope, and he went to bed with a mild sangria buzz. When he got up to urinate in the middle of the night, he remembered to take two aspirins to avoid a potential hangover.

The next morning Marcus woke up feeling fine. Still in pajamas, he put on a bathrobe and went downstairs, hoping the temperature would be cooler. Autumn in Los Angeles could be indistinguishable from summer. It had been in the high eighties for the previous week, and they had run the air conditioners every night. He immediately felt a blast of warm air when he opened the front door. The plastic-encased copy of the *Los Angeles Times* was not in its typical place near the house. A quick scan revealed it lying near the curb. Must be a substitute paper boy, Marcus thought. The regular guy unfailingly placed it near the front door. He picked up the paper and flipped to the weather page as he walked back toward the house. It was going to be in the nineties today, but he forgot about the heat the second he felt the barrel of the gun in his back.

"Don't make a sound, brah."

Marcus did not have to look over his shoulder to see Tommy the Samoan. The man was like a solar eclipse. Briefly, he wondered how someone that size could possibly hide. Marcus knew he shouldn't have counted on Bertrand Russell to warn him. He *liked* the fucker.

"Walk toward the truck slow."

A black Yukon was parked across the street from the house. It was moving now, making a U-turn and pulling in front of them. The windows were tinted and he couldn't see who was driving. He had the wild thought that Kostya was nearby and would leap from behind a tree and save the day. But this illusion was abandoned the moment Marcus climbed into the backseat of the SUV. The Samoan got in beside him.

The driver was a white guy in his twenties, with a highlighted and gelled haircut, a good-looking kid who probably wanted to be a model. He wore aviator dark glasses, and a silver skull the size of a dime dangled from his right ear.

"We should have jacked his Benz," the kid said to Tommy.

"It's my show, Memo," Tommy the Samoan said. Marcus perked up at the name. *Memo.* Wasn't that the guy Tommy said tried to seduce his fiancée? Unfortunately, the two thugs appeared to have smoked the peace pipe. Memo slammed the car in gear and jammed the accelerator. The G-force threw Marcus against the seat. He wondered where the kid got a name like Memo. This guy looked like his name should have been Brandon.

"Where are we going?" Marcus asked as they sped away from Magdalene Lane.

"Malvina want to talk to you."

"We talked already."

"Don't make it worse, brah."

Marcus settled into the seat. He knew it was hopeless to try to escape. Tommy the Samoan had a large gun pointed at him. What was Malvina's game? If she wanted him smacked around, she could have just ordered Tommy to take care of it. He wished he hadn't told her to kiss his black ass. Arrogance never got you anywhere. Marcus was surprised when the Yukon eased onto the 405 heading north. He thought she lived in the basin. He worried about how he would feel standing in front of her in his bathrobe and pajamas. It was daunting to negotiate with someone while dressed in pajamas. But as the car began the long climb through the pass at the north end of the Valley, he had an entirely different concern. The fear had started slowly at first. Then it began to metastasize until it suffused him. It dried his lips, made his breath shallow. For a moment he felt lightheaded.

"We're not going to Malvina's, are we?" Marcus tried to keep the escalating terror out of his voice, but his vocal cords were strung as tight as the rest of him and it was a losing proposition. Tommy the Samoan didn't answer. He just swung his great head slowly from side to side as if to say *you idiot*. The movement shook the little Star of David hanging from his ear. Marcus wished he could conjure some Yiddish words to throw Tommy's way, as if they would magically defuse the situation, but he was coming up blank. Right now the only one he could think of was *putz*.

They drove past Castaic and Santa Clarita and into the mountains, the Yukon straining as it labored up the long incline. Marcus knew how it went. Malvina was going to have him killed. Today was the day he would die, and he had done nothing to prepare. How do you handle death once you realize it's imminent? Do you go with dignity, or break down and beg? No one who begs gets what they're asking for. All they do is increase their own suffering. No, Marcus would not do that. If philosophy had taught him anything, it was to not fear death. He inhaled deeply, filling his lungs, and tried to calm himself. This made him think of Amstel, who had given him the breathing tip he had used to such great effect with his wife, his beloved, who he would never see again. What did Hegel say? Death is pure being, and in death an isolated individual is raised to universal individuality. Suddenly universal individuality was a lot less attractive than it had seemed when he had encountered it as a college student between the clean pages of a book.

"You ever read any philosophy?" he asked Tommy the Samoan, by way of making conversation. If he could engage the man, perhaps the story would end differently.

"Don't talk, brah. Not now."

Marcus considered Nietzsche's concept of eternal recurring. He wondered if, when *he* next recurred, he might use better judgment. He hoped so. He would hate to have to eternally recur through this again. Schopenhauer believed that to live is to suffer but death is unreal. Marcus wished that pain was unreal. None of the great minds wanted to address *that*. It was one thing to pontificate about an abstraction, something where there could never be a definitive answer. But where was the essay on what it felt like to be kidnapped and shot? As far as Marcus knew, no one had ever weighed in on the subject. He longed for a copy of *A History of Western Philosophy*. It was 895 pages long and could definitely stop a bullet.

Memo pulled the SUV off the freeway and continued north on an access road for a few miles before heading west into a canyon. It was the Angeles National Forest. Marcus flashed on the last time he'd been here. At least they weren't going to where he'd left the body; they had passed that exit several miles back. He thought about whether this was retribution for what he'd done, but knew that was ridiculous. There was no retribution. Things just happened. Then other things happened. All you could do was try to stay out of the way for as long as possible. It all caught up to you eventually.

They were climbing again now, past rock outcroppings and through pine trees. His ears popped from the altitude. Memo had the air conditioning on, so Marcus couldn't tell how hot it was in the mountains this morning. He wondered if Jan would know he was gone yet.

Now they were bouncing along a dirt road surrounded by chaparral. Tommy was holding the gun in his left hand, absently scratching his face with the barrel. One pothole and the big Samoan could blow his own head off, ending everything right there. Marcus thought about grabbing the gun but knew that even if he tried, a single thump from Tommy's paw would immobilize him.

"What are we waiting for?" Memo said.

"Just drive," Tommy said. "I tell you when we stop."

"I got an audition later."

"Oh, yeah? For a job?"

"An industrial."

"Say what?"

"Like a movie, but for a company. These guys make outboard motors."

"So you're like a dancing spark plug?"

"Fuck you."

The conversation was jocular, but Marcus sensed a strain of genuine hostility in Tommy's ball-busting. He wondered whether Memo knew that Tommy's girlfriend had reported the attempted seduction.

"You should come with me," Memo said. "I hear they're looking for an elephant."

Tommy did not reply. Marcus tried to make eye contact, to re-establish the relationship they'd had during their late-night chat. But Tommy was giving him nothing. They rode along in silence for another five minutes until Tommy told Memo to pull over. They slowed to a stop at the side of the road. Memo opened the door and got out. Tommy stared at Marcus.

"Don't say I didn't warn you, brah." Marcus sensed that the man seemed troubled at having to kill him. But it didn't make him feel any better. When would the insurance policy kick in? Did they need to find a body to collect? Tommy told him to get out of the car.

Marcus felt the warm sun on his face. The altitude made the temperature cooler. He could smell the pine, the earth. It was a beautiful day. He was sorry he wouldn't make it to the bar mitzvah, but at least it would be paid for.

"Start walking," Tommy said.

Marcus headed into the woods. He thought about running, knew he should zig-zag if he ran, but there was no way he could escape. He regretted being barefoot and in pajamas. He wished he wasn't going to die in pajamas. And he didn't want to be eaten by little animals. Lifeless on the forest floor; picked clean by chipmunks. That would be horribly undignified. Suddenly, Marcus was feeling less accepting of his fate. He stumbled on a root, twisting his ankle.

"Shit," he said, and stopped walking.

"Keep moving." Memo was right behind him.

Marcus tried to put weight on his leg. His ankle was tender. He could walk, but he wasn't sure if he wanted to. They hadn't reached wherever it was they were going. Perhaps if he could stall, something might intervene, an earthquake, a party of hikers—any distraction that would give him a chance at survival.

The blow that sent him sprawling to the ground came from nowhere. There was blackness behind his eyes, a dull ringing in his cranium. The pain radiated up through the top of his head and down his neck and shoulders. He felt as if a tree had fallen on him.

From another room, Marcus heard Tommy's voice: "What the fuck, Memo?"

When he opened an eye and saw Memo standing over him with

a gun, he realized he'd been pistol-whipped. His hair felt wet. He touched it with his fingers. Blood.

"Get up and keep walking," Tommy said. Marcus staggered to his feet. He thought he saw Tommy glare at Memo, the kid puffed up from the violence.

"You gonna pop your cherry today," Tommy said.

"Fuckin' A," Memo said.

Marcus lurched forward. His head throbbed. His big toe had started to bleed. He must have cut it when he fell. The pine needles were soft under his bare feet, the morning sun getting hotter. The three of them walked deeper into the woods, Marcus in the lead, the flaps of his bathrobe swaying as he staggered along. After five minutes, they came to a clearing and Tommy told him to lie on the ground.

Marcus looked at him, trying one last time to forge some kind of tenuous human connection. But the big Samoan was serving ice. Marcus had vowed not to beg, and if this was how it was all going to end, there was nothing he could do. He sank to his knees. Instinctively, he grabbed two handfuls of pine needles. What could he do with them? Throw it in their faces? The pine needles were dry in his hands, useless. He did not want his penultimate earthly act to be a spasm of impotent aggression. Marcus lay down now, his face on the forest floor, the pine needles brushing his cheek. He heard Tommy's voice.

"You want to do it, right? Then get up close so it's clean."

Memo would be the shooter. Marcus prepared himself, his final moment of consciousness, the epistemological limit, unification with the universal.

The thunderous boom of the gunshot resonated against the mountains and up to the endless sky.

And Marcus Ripps was dead.

Only he wasn't. Marcus heard a thudding sound and looked over his shoulder to see Memo sprawled on the forest floor. A wet rose bloomed in the gelled hair, and blood watered the dry ground.

243

"I think you gonna miss that audition," Tommy said. Then he removed the gun from Memo's dead hand and jammed it in his own size 54 waistband.

Marcus took in the tableau from his prone position: the Samoan, massive against the looming mountain, the gun, the dead man deep in the craggy wilderness. A hawk soared overhead, looking for a kill. Marcus glanced at Tommy. Had the guy snapped? Was he going to kill the two of them? Or was his captor only interested in exacting brutal revenge on Memo for the deeply ill-advised attempt to cuckold him?

"You all right?" When Marcus replied yes, he was, Tommy told him to get up. Marcus stood and brushed himself off, his ears still ringing from the gunshot. He wanted to celebrate being alive, but the corpse at his feet made that problematic. Memo's eyes were open. A fly skittered along his face. What was the etiquette in this situation? The kid had brutalized him, but it was still unsettling to see him laid out with a hole in his expensive haircut.

Tommy's voice penetrated the reverie into which Marcus had fallen. He was suggesting that they walk back to the road. Marcus looked around uncertainly. The man's entire manner had changed, the threatening countenance gone. This was the guy who had been dandling the family dog in the middle of the night.

"You want a ride home?"

When they were seated in the front seat of the Yukon, Tommy removed the remaining bullets from the gun. Producing a bandanna from the pocket of his jeans, he wiped it clean. He placed the weapon on the seat between them and ordered Marcus to put it in the glove compartment. Marcus did as he was told.

"Why'd you bring me up here?"

"Take care of Memo."

Tommy stuck the key in the ignition. Marcus was still trying to fathom his role in the day's events. But he liked the sound of the engine starting. At least he was alive.

With his nervous system shot, Marcus did not enjoy the ride back. But he managed to retain what Tommy said he would tell Malvina: you got the drop on Memo and flew. I chase you through the woods but you slip away. You not in business tomorrow.

When Tommy turned onto Magdalene Lane he said "One more thing, brah. You get the idea to talk to cops, them your prints on gun."

So that was it. Marcus was the alibi, a clever insurance policy for Tommy in the event someone found the body. Were Marcus to even *consider* telling the police what had happened, this move would serve to keep the impulse in the deep freeze. Why couldn't *he* ever be the one who was thinking three steps ahead?

The truck from the security company was parked in front of the house when Marcus climbed out of the Yukon. The burglar alarm was being installed. Good timing, he thought. Tommy rolled down the window and said "Shalom." Then he was gone.

Marcus found Jan in the kitchen, where she was unloading the new dishwasher.

"Where were you?" Her face was taut. It wasn't like Marcus to just take off. She noticed blood caked in his hair. "What happened to your head?"

"I better ice it."

Jan got out a baggie and stuffed a dozen ice cubes in it. She handed it to Marcus, who sat down and applied it to the nasty lump that had formed. She looked at him as if to say Please tell me this isn't as bad as I think. After determining that Lenore was not within earshot, he reported everything that had happened. The churning anxiety she experienced as she heard the story of his close escape was elbowed aside by immense relief at its outcome. She had listened incredulously at first, but when Marcus finished, tears had formed in her eyes, and now she was hugging him. He rubbed her back, comforting her.

Both of them knew the limit had been reached. Neither of them had the appetite for a war. Smart Tarts was over. They would vacate the Beverly Hills–adjacent apartment. Marcus would inform the work-force. Jan would take the Web site down and remove all traces of the business from the Internet.

Lenore received the news with the same equanimity she had displayed when Jan initially told her about the business.

"It was a swell ride," she said. "I'll miss the ladies."

Chapter 20

The autumn morning on which Nathan Ripps became a bar mitzvah transpired under a blue sky so glorious that Jan's Philadelphia relatives, who were religious people, told Marcus that it must have come from God. The Santa Ana winds were blowing, and the smog that typically encrusted the Valley had vanished with their powerful gusts. The San Gabriel Mountains were clearly visible to the east, the Santa Monica range to the west. It was a day when the San Fernando Valley could be imagined fresh and new. They had engaged a photographer, a young woman wearing a pants suit, her black hair in a thick braid, and she arranged Jan's relatives on the sidewalk in front of the synagogue in various combinations to have their pictures taken.

Jan and Lenore had bought new dresses for the occasion, and Marcus, who traditionally followed Thoreau's dictum to avoid all activities requiring new clothes, had spent nearly eight hundred dollars on a suit. Nathan was thoroughly enjoying himself, beaming at the relatives he rarely saw, relishing their temporary attention on the dappled sidewalk that clear California morning.

Marcus had talked to other fathers whose sons and daughters had gone through this rite, but he was still unprepared for the tightening he felt in his throat when he looked up and beheld Nathan on the *bima* (a word Marcus learned from Rabbi Rachel when he made the mistake, during a pre-bar-mitzvah family meeting, of calling it a stage). The rabbi and the cantor, a young man of Middle Eastern appearance who wore a multihued head covering that looked as if it had been

247

purchased in a Moroccan *souk*, led the congregation in prayer and song, and Marcus saw Nathan as if in a time-lapse photograph. In Marcus's mind, he grew from chubby-legged baby, to electric toddler, to bright-faced kid, and now, as he was passing through the brambles of puberty, into an awkward early adolescence that bore the first seeds of his eventual disappearance from his father's day-to-day life. Marcus glanced over at Jan, who he sensed was experiencing the same inchoate mix of pride, pleasure, and loss that strikes parents in these moments. Upbraiding himself for his rising schmaltz level, he cleared his throat. Marcus had once heard someone say *all gangsters are sentimental*. He briefly wondered if this applied to him. Jan squeezed his hand. He returned the pressure, keeping his eyes straight ahead. He became conscious of a lump in his throat and hoped it would subside before it was his turn to speak.

Nathan read from the Torah, his command of the ancient liturgy sure, his voice clear. Rabbi Rachel beckoned Marcus and Jan when it was time for their speeches. Jan spoke first, facing Nathan across the podium from which the rabbi led the service. She wasn't used to public speaking, particularly the kind that involved personal revelation. At first, she spoke blandly about her love for her son, and how proud she was of him—everything you would expect a mother to say. But then, gathering herself, she said "You might not have been raised in the most religious household, Nathan, but we always tried to teach you to do the right thing. If believing in God helps you to do that, then it's a pretty good idea."

She kissed him on the cheek, and then it was Marcus's turn. He took his notes out of his pocket and unfolded the paper. He glanced down at the single-spaced type, then looked at his son, who smiled back at him. Marcus took a deep breath and launched into a panegyric about Nathan, during which he discoursed on the gift of his essentially sunny nature, his musicianship, his ability at sports, the grace with which he accepted parental prodding where his schoolwork was concerned, his enviable ability as a son and grandson—all the aspects of a young person's life a parent remotely aware of how challenging being thirteen is will appreciate when they bother to pay attention. When Marcus finished, he offered an awkward hug, greatly relieved at having discharged his paternal obligations with regard to this ceremony, and returned to his seat, where he silently thanked the universe for allowing him to get through his speech without weeping. The surfeit of *goodness* he had been witnessing, from Rabbi Rachel, from Nathan, from Jan, and, amazingly to him, from within, all manifested in such a public way before this gathering of family and friends, was making his daily life exceedingly difficult to reconcile at this moment. Watching thin, coltish Nathan adjust the microphone—the boy's shoulders far from strong enough to bear existential weight—Marcus told himself he would be an exemplary citizen for the rest of his days.

"Hello everyone," Nathan began, resonantly. *Resonantly?* Had Rabbi Rachel been giving him public speaking lessons, along with the spiritual insights she had imparted? "I would like to thank you all for being here with me on this special day. In my Torah portion, we find Abraham, Sarah, who is Abraham's wife, and their nephew Lot, going to Egypt because there is famine in their land."

Marcus knew a thing or two about famine. Perhaps not *famine* literally, but he was entirely too familiar with the fear in the heart of one who is unable to provide the necessities of life to those who place their faith in him. He settled into his seat, beaming at his son, so poised and intent. The congregation had been quiet earlier, but now it was dead silent.

Straightening his back, Nathan continued: "Before the three of them arrive in Egypt, Abraham pulls Sarah aside and tells her something that has been bugging him. *As he was about to enter Egypt, he said to his wife Sarah 'I know what a beautiful woman you are. If the Egyptians see you and think* She is his wife, *they will kill me and let you live. Please say that you are my sister, that it may go well with me because of you and that I may remain alive thanks to you.'* Sarah, being the diligent passive wife of the past, agreed to participate in Abraham's survival plan and claimed to be his sister."

Marcus had no recollection of this story from his own meager Bible study. Abraham's choice in this situation was news to him. His engagement with his son's biblical interpretation and delight in the boy's accomplishment were only mitigated by a budding discomfort with the nature of the story Nathan was telling.

"As they entered Egypt, the Egyptians were quick to notice Sarah's radiance. The Torah says *Pharaoh's courtiers saw her and praised her to Pharaoh, and the woman was taken into Pharaoh's palace.* Abraham," Nathan said, now in high dudgeon, "just exchanged Sarah for his life. Not the kind of thing a gentleman would do. However, God did not agree with Abraham's decision to give up Sarah to save his own skin and was angry that Sarah apparently now had two husbands. The Torah tells us *The Lord afflicted Pharaoh and his household with the mighty plagues on account of Sarah, the wife of Abraham.* When Pharaoh finally figured out that Sarah was Abraham's wife, he was furious. As my Torah portion says, *Pharaoh sent for Abraham and said 'What is this you have done to me? Why did you not tell me she was your wife? Why did you say "she is my sister"? So I took her as my wife. Now here is your wife. Take her and be gone!'* " Nathan pounded the podium for emphasis, startling some of the elderly congregants.

"I wonder why God would choose someone as the leader of the Jewish people who could screw things up like this." There were murmurs in the congregation now, an exchanging of glances. No one was expecting a thirteen-year-old bar mitzvah boy—on this day of all days—to lambaste a biblical hero like Abraham with such force and emotion. Marcus, however, was staring straight ahead, seemingly in a trance, and didn't notice when Nathan glanced at him before continuing. "He not only put his wife in a compromising position, but his behavior threatened the lives of Pharaoh and everyone in Pharaoh's household." Here Nathan paused for dramatic effect. He looked out over the congregation and gripped the lectern with both hands. "How could the leader of our people be so imperfect? How could he be, well, so like us? Many of the spiritual leaders and prophets from other religions are seemingly perfect, and yet the first Jew had so many imperfections. Maybe that is what God wanted, to find or create a person so obviously human that people could truly relate to him, so that when Jews think of Abraham, they think of someone like themselves. Some would think the leader of a people should be a model of what to strive for. But maybe God knew trying to be perfect is just not healthy, or maybe God could not find any perfect human beings. Maybe it's just not possible to be perfect."

Marcus nodded at the last observation, thinking *Amen.*

"Rabbi Rachel once told me that until we have children, our first priority is ourselves, our own well-being. Later in Abraham's life, when God asked Abraham to sacrifice his son Isaac, Abraham continued to act selfishly. Some might say it was a noble thing to be willing to sacrifice your own child in the Lord's name, but I just think it was stupid. Why would Abraham risk losing something so important to him for nothing more than a religious belief? Why is religion so important? Isn't how we act what really matters? God tested Abraham and his faith, and many people would say he passed with flying colors. Flying colors? I say, no way. Abraham failed at the most important duty of all, which is take care of those you love.

"I know two people who would have passed that test. My mom and dad." At this, the lump in Marcus's throat grew from the size of a tangerine to that of a grapefruit. "I said to them recently, 'How could you be so selfless with me?' And my dad responded 'Trust me, it's not always easy.' I know it's not easy, but you do it, and I appreciate it more than I could express in words. I love you both . . .'"

Nathan talked for another minute, but Marcus could not hear a word, the sobs were coming so relentlessly. He buried his wet face in his hands there in the front row of Temple B'nai Jesherun, secure in the knowledge that everyone would assume he was convulsed with paternal pride and love for his son.

Which he was.

Up to a point.

What no one else but Jan understood was that Marcus had projected himself into Nathan's reading. Marcus was in Pharaoh's court, and Marcus had to save his skin. That the parallels were not direct made them no less unmistakable, or damning, and he felt his body temperature rising as the inner battle raged and tumbled. Now he was feeling as if his very presence in the sanctuary vitiated his son's accomplishment. If Nathan could so eloquently bring the original patriarch of monotheism to heel, what would he say about his own father? Marcus groaned audibly at the thought, which those around him misinterpreted as a paroxysm of pride. Staring at his shoes, Marcus noticed that the carpeting had become worn and made a mental note to contribute to the temple building fund next week.

At the post-service *kiddush*, held in the social hall of the synagogue, Marcus and Jan accepted congratulations on Nathan's accomplishment. Several people remarked on the iconoclastic nature of his speech, and he took great pride in having raised a boy who, rather than simply regurgitating the religious nostrums he had been fed in Hebrew school, actually seemed philosophically inclined.

Marcus spread whitefish salad on a cracker as he watched Plum and Atlas, who were standing near the dessert table, having what appeared to be a civilized conversation. When he felt a hand on his arm, he looked over and saw Kostya. Wearing a fashionable four-button suit, he was grinning, pleased to have been included in the celebration.

"Li'l Gangsta rocked the mike," Kostya said, handing Marcus an envelope. "For the kid."

Kostya embraced his erstwhile employer, then headed toward the smoked fish. Marcus stepped outside so he could have a moment alone. The sky had taken on a sickly grayish yellow cast. The wind had shifted and now the air had a vaguely toxic smell, worse than smog, more threatening. The powerful Santa Anas were blowing from the north now, whistling through the passes, carrying this foulness with them. His eyes began to water. It was good that Nathan's party wasn't going to be in the Valley.

That evening, sweet, tropical liquids flowed from large plastic martini glasses and down young throats. Boys in groups of fours and fives jumped up and down to neo-punk and hip-hop, too scared to ask girls to dance, untroubled by any homoerotic subtext. Girls who looked far older than thirteen, sloe-eyed and cool in their tight dresses, watched and wished the boys were older and less silly. Two boys were stealing glasses filled with liquor from adults who left them unattended. One girl, whose father owned half of West-wood, wore a T-shirt that said FUCK YOU in a gothic font across her narrow shoulders. Several mothers mentioned this to Jan, who told the girl to please turn the shirt inside out, which she did without incident, although, when Jan walked away, this spawn of privilege and neglect gave her the finger (to the amusement of her snickering confederates). Nathan's male friends bounced off each other like pinballs on the dance floor, rocketing this way and that, spinning, arms akimbo, faces turned upward, whirling round and round in a distant, rapturous echo of eighteenth-century Hasidim. Lenore and her well-toned and exceedingly affable friends from the pole dancing studio enticed the older, more groove-resistant guests onto the dance floor, bumping, grinding, and unleashing the Dionysian propensity that lurks beneath the surface of a bourgeois breast. The white-jacketed bartender was kept busy all night and the intoxicants, copious and of high quality, flowed from bright bottles into glasses, and then veins, leading the ordinarily sedentary from their chairs toward the music, where they found themselves line dancing and didn't for a moment care about how it looked— the sign of a party cranking on all cylinders.

Roon had dispatched regrets via an e-mail BlackBerried from his corporate jet somewhere over the Maldive Islands, *be great to catch up, some other time, congrats!* and had his accountant send a small check for Nathan. Marcus would have liked for Roon to see how he had prospered since leaving his employ, and trusted Takeshi, who was waving his arms overhead in time to the music twenty feet to Marcus's left, to report that the Ripps family was thriving.

Chapter 21

Sunday morning was dark and hazy, the air worse than the day before. Although Marcus drank several margaritas at the party and was exhausted from the revelry, he had remembered to take the customary two aspirins before going to sleep. So the following morning when he swung his legs out of bed and his feet touched the floor, he was able to stand up with no ill effects from the previous night. Because Jan was still feeling the copious amounts of Chardonnay she had imbibed, Marcus thoughtfully brought her a headache remedy and a cup of black coffee while she lay in bed. When he opened the front door to get the Sunday newspaper, he looked out on the street and saw that a fine ash had fallen from the sky and coated every-thing—the lawns, the trees, the streets, the cars. The sky was dense with it. Coughing, Marcus went back inside and turned on the tele-vision. He hadn't watched TV or looked at the paper since Friday, and was not surprised to see that a fire was consuming much of Angeles National Forest. The toxic powder that had fallen on Van Nuys was its detritus.

Nathan and Lenore were still asleep, so Marcus glanced through the newspaper until the young Mexican deliveryman arrived with the platters of lox, bagels, and artfully arranged sliced fruit.

Two hours later, the quiet house was invaded by relatives from out of town who all talked about the polluted air, the layer of ash, and wasn't it wonderful that it hadn't happened yesterday morning? Buoyant sounds of animated chatter flew around the room as everyone discussed Nathan's accomplishment, the local attractions they wanted to visit before returning home, and, for those who were departing today, what time they would have to leave to make their flights. Marcus was telling one of Jan's aunts about the Gene Autry Western Museum when the doorbell rang. Two men in dark suits were standing there. They asked if he was Marcus Ripps. Marcus told them he was, and they identified themselves as police detectives from Valley North. Then they arrested him for pandering and illegal transportation of a dead body.

The holding cell in the Van Nuys precinct house looked like all the holding cells Marcus had seen on cop shows, something he thought about in a conscious effort to keep himself from considering the precise nature of what he was facing. Oscillating between acute shame and sheer terror, he found himself absurdly musing about how the proliferation of police-related entertainment on American television had improved civics, since any casual viewer developed a rudimentary understanding of the criminal justice system.

It was early Sunday afternoon by the time Marcus found himself in the cell, and the other inhabitants were the human flotsam of the previous Saturday night: drunks, brawlers, and an unfortunate burglar who had been stopped for a traffic violation with the contents of someone else's house in the bed of his pickup. Marcus was the only one wearing pressed trousers and a Lacoste shirt, and he was grateful that his cellmates seemed too exhausted to notice that their newest addition appeared to be dressed for a shopping trip to Rodeo Drive. Marcus cursed the fact that he hadn't chosen to wear socks today. He believed his naked ankles broadcast acute vulnerability.

Utter ruination was not something he'd considered when he embarked on his skin-trade sortie. Not really. He knew it was a possibility, but had discarded the thought rather than examine the terrifying ramifications. The luxury of obliviousness was no longer available to him now that he was here in jail trying to repress his olfactory senses, currently being assaulted by an acrid scent he immediately identified as urine. The grizzled man lying near him on the wooden bench filling the fetid air with his snoring had pissed himself. Marcus stood up and walked to the bars at the front of the holding pen, fighting a burgeoning sense of panic.

I don't even know which dead body they're talking about. Is it the one I actually moved or the other one? It could be either. Memo wasn't dead when he went into the forest. I didn't transport him anywhere. He transported me. But no one could possibly know how he got there unless Tommy the Samoan ratted me out. Tommy played with my dog. The man was undergoing a spiritual conversion. It couldn't be him. Then it was Mink who gave me up. Kostya probably lied to me when he said he didn't work her over. He probably kicked the shit out of her and she was too scared to tell me. Goddammit! After I specifically told him not to touch her. Never mind that. It's too late now. How do I keep this from becoming public? If people even hear I've been arrested, I'm a pariah. Nathan! Nathan can't find out. I have to extricate myself from this without him knowing. What if I get convicted? He'll know then. And he'll judge me. I can explain it to him when he's older, the whole big stinking rationalization, but now? He won't buy it. Maybe he'll love me still, I think, but he won't believe me any more and what kind of father can I be with a son who doesn't believe me? Why am I looking out the cell? I should be looking behind me so no one can sneak up. What if I get convicted? How are they going to convict me? They won't be able to. I'll have obstacles, maybe, significant ones like how to make a living, but my family won't have to visit me in prison.

By a stroke of luck, Jan had not been arrested, and Marcus knew that after absorbing the jolt she would immediately hire a lawyer. Unfortunately, he had been informed by the arresting officers there was nothing anyone could do to get him released before his arraignment which, since it was the weekend, would not take place until sometime the following day. His thoughts wandered from his predicament to Julian, who, for all of his crimes, had managed to avoid prison, and then to his grandfather, Mickey Ripps, Dublin tough guy, cock o'

257

the walk. None the worse for three years of hard time, he would have bedeviled law enforcement for years to come had he not been crushed by that errant crate of mayonnaise. But Mickey, he of the rhinoceros hide, was a lot tougher than his younger grandson.

Marcus wasn't surprised by the handcuffs, but he was more than slightly taken aback at being shackled to the row of fellow moral relativists who sat with him in the prison van speeding along the 101 freeway taking them downtown to the Los Angeles County jail, where he would pass the night.

It was late afternoon and Marcus had spent nearly five hours behind bars. In his one phone call with Jan, she had assured him she was doing everything possible, but being that it was Sunday the situation was not going smoothly. He heard the strain in her voice and was thankful she was being spared the indignity he was enduring, at least for the time being. It was difficult for him to picture his wife in jail.

Marcus stared straight ahead as they hurtled down the freeway, listening to several conversations being conducted in Spanish. His linguistic skills had not progressed in the time since he'd been selling cable television subscriptions in East L.A., and the only words he was able to make out were *dinero* and *madre*. Elaborate tattoos crept down the arms and up the necks of the other prisoners, spider webs, hearts, and fantastical beasts, primitive elaborations of their bearers' inner lives. The artwork on some of the exposed flesh was crude enough to suggest prison provenance, which Marcus did not find comforting. Several of the men had pronounced facial scars, the fresher ones purple, the more venerable raised and white, winding roads of violence and depravity, signifiers of lives lived at the end of a blade. He fervently hoped no one would speak to him.

"*Hola, Gringo.*" Marcus looked to his right. A Latino with dyed blond hair and a weight-lifter's body bursting from a stained wife-beater was addressing him. "What did they get you for, tax evasion?" The inmates who understood English convulsed at this, laughing and wheezing. Had their wrists not been cuffed together, they would have pointed at Marcus, further emphasizing his otherness and isolation. In their amusement, these men exuded an ease with their plight not unfamiliar to the riders of commuter trains. Marcus envied their ability to maintain a barrio groove while chained together like a human charm bracelet in a speeding Correctional Services van. "Hey, *pendejo*, are you deaf?" the man with the fake blond hair said, louder this time. Marcus realized, to his chagrin, the guy actually expected a response.

"Pandering," he said, continuing to stare straight ahead.

"What the fuck is that?" He leaned closer now, his breath warm and foul.

Marcus considered lying for a moment. No one in the van had a dictionary, and he knew he could define the word as he pleased. But he sensed that the truth in this context might actually elevate him in their eyes, make them realize that despite his outfit, which had obviously not been selected for intimidation purposes, he was a man of indefinable power, someone with whom to be reckoned. So he said: "I'm a pimp."

At this news, the English speakers erupted into laughter so raucous, it nearly drowned out the sounds of the engine, which was not well maintained and had been making a clanking sound the entire ride. Upon witnessing this burst of jollity, the others leaned in, wondering what they had missed, looking at the dyed blond muscleman for an explanation. Marcus's interlocutor translated for the English-as-a-second-language crew: "*El dijo que es alcahuete!*" instantly causing a second explosion of merriment, and filling the car with braying guffaws that pricked Marcus like a thousand gravity knives. Rapidfire Spanish ensued. It was debated whether or not this could possibly be true and, if it was, would Marcus please arrange introductions once they had been cleared of the crimes they all assured him they had not committed. Marcus knew being an object of their mockery would prevent anything worse from happening to him, and he endured the remainder of the ride certain that no one would want to kill the clown. Cool Breeze, indeed.

Standing in line with his traveling companions, Marcus strategized about how to survive the night. They were being processed for intake, and he wanted to request placement in protective custody. The line moved forward at a brisk pace, most of the prisoners being familiar with the drill. They were issued freshly laundered orange jumpsuits with the words COUNTY JAIL stenciled across the back, and rubber slippers. Marcus had already forfeited his wallet and belt at the previous stop. There were four other men with him in the greasy-walled changing room, and a stone-faced African-American guard with a large sidearm. Slipping into the jail clothes, the material scratchy on his delicate skin, Marcus found that if he concentrated on shutting down and performing the simple task with which he'd been charged, he could move through the moment, connecting it to another, and another, and so get through the remainder of this dreadful day.

Assuming he didn't get killed.

This was something he willed himself not to think about, tamping the terror rising in his breast as he stood in his underwear pulling up the orange pants, regretting the elastic waist, which made him feel like he was dressing for a shuffleboard match at a retirement home.

Marcus was given a brown paper bag with his dinner in it. A short redneck guard with a crew cut escorted him to a large cell on the fourteenth floor. Marcus asked him what the procedure was for requesting protective custody. The guard said that if he wasn't rich, famous, or transgendered, he should forget about that. "Watch yourself," the guard drawled. "If a fight starts, be sure you stay with your own kind." The sense of impending calamity was heightened by the idea that an altercation might break out and Marcus's well-being would depend on the sufferance of some swastika-tattooed white power freak.

He walked along a row of holding pens filled with unlucky souls born so far behind the starting line that all their running couldn't help them avoid the trap door that opened onto a jail cell. The circumstances for Marcus had been different, and he had hastily concluded that his current situation was a supremely earthly retribution for his transgressions. He tried to suppress a mushrooming sense of horror. In an attempt to calm himself, he recalled the deathless words of the dire German: *That which is done out of love takes place beyond good and evil.* They were cold comfort.

The cell door banged shut, and Marcus didn't hear the guard walking away because the tension shooting through his muscles caused him to focus solely on the twenty men he was now with, mostly young, black, or Latino, and hard. The few white guys, unshaven, in various states of disrepair, all looked like this was a step up from where they'd spent the previous evening. As his arrival did not induce an immediate reaction from anyone, Marcus, affecting nonchalance remarkably well, given that he wasn't even certain he could control his bladder, proceeded to an empty space on a metal bench and sat down, pressing his back to the cool cinderblock wall, confident no one could attack him from the rear.

He spent the next fourteen hours in that position, doing breathing exercises, chanting recently learned prayers, remembering old basketball games play by long-ago play, to stay awake, remain alert, anything to keep from losing consciousness in the company of these potentially murderous reprobates. The fear did it, poking and prodding, fighting off any glimmer of the restfulness that might bring dangerous sleep. An hour after he'd arrived there, Marcus ate the bologna sandwich on white bread that was in the sack dinner they'd given him. His stomach gurgled, the hissing and squirting of his intestines as he digested the food a southerly mirror of the silent whirlpool of anxiety spinning through his brain. To give himself something to do, he ate the soft, mealy apple accompanying the sandwich. He had to urinate, but he knew he was going to hold it in.

The middle of the night was the worst. Men more at ease than he (which was everyone else who was there) were able to find positions in which to sleep. Their cacophonous snoring was gravelly in the foul darkness. From his command post on the metal bench, feeling incrementally less threatened each time another man slid into unconsciousness, Marcus began to think about how he had arrived at this juncture. Not in the larger philosophical sense—for that, he knew he had only himself to blame. But whose perfidy had landed him here? He had been sure it was Mink, but now he was less certain. It could have been anyone. And why hadn't Jan and Lenore been arrested? He was thrilled they remained free—their incarceration would have been a catastrophe—but he had no explanation for the mystery. As he hovered on the edge of consciousness, his thoughts drifted to his son's bar mitzvah, the sublimity of the service, the sparkling children at the glowing night party, drinking rainbow-hued cocktails, twirling wildly on the dance floor, ephemeral moments filled with grace and wonder. It was a chapter from a story spun in a gone world.

Jan arrived at the courthouse the following day and posted bail. Marcus squinted when he stepped into the midday light. His whole body ached with exhaustion as he walked down the steps toward the parking lot, holding his wife's hand. He asked if she had found out anything about the charges. She had learned that the dead body was that of Mahmoud Ghorbanifar, Amstel's final assignation. This knowledge simplified things for Marcus, since it narrowed the potential number of enemies he faced. When they pulled out of the parking lot, Marcus told her he didn't want to go straight home.

Jan was driving, since Marcus thought he might fall asleep at the wheel. They were travelling west on the 101 through light traffic. He was staring out the passenger window.

"What did you tell Nathan?"

"I told him the police wanted to ask you some questions, and you had to go on a business trip. I didn't get into any details."

Her presence was reassuring to him, but there was nothing she could have said to make him feel less terrible. It was as if his entire life had burst into jagged shards that could never again be pieced together.

Marcus hadn't been back to the beach at Leo Carrillo State Park since his day trips with Bertrand Russell two summers earlier. Years ago, he and Jan would come here with Nathan and hold his small hands so he could jump over the waves as they rolled to the shore. The beach felt decidedly different now, as they sat on the sand and stared at the ocean. Jan pulled her loose skirt above her knees. The autumn sun was hot and they hadn't put sunscreen on, but Marcus didn't care. The sea air was giving him a second wind. Both of them had taken their shoes off. Jan wriggled her bare feet in the sand.

"Did you ever want to dive into the waves and just keep going?" Marcus asked.

"What, like to Japan?"

"Japan, Thailand . . . anywhere."

"Maybe we should have gone to China."

"It's a little late in the day."

He wished he saw dolphins. Perhaps they might lighten his mood. A line of surfers straddled their boards, waiting for rides. Although Marcus had grown up by the sea, he had never surfed. He wished he could lock into the elemental nature of it now, the sky, the undulating ocean. He wanted to feel its force; its depth and power, to be carried along by unseen currents, tossed, and thrown, powerless, the water pressing down on him in a cold soothing embrace, swimming deeper and deeper into the cool depths, darker and darker until he only had a memory of light, and then no memory at all, and then nothing.

He ran a handful of sand through his fingers. A cool wind blew from offshore. Marcus squinted. His remembered that his sunglasses were in the car, but the few hundred yards were too far to walk. He needed to make some sense of what had happened, try to fit it into a mathematical equation he could work out that would somehow allow him to balance the internal ledger. Marcus had made his money. Debt had released its bony grip from their collective windpipe. He was driving a car he didn't need, but he had made no onerous financial commitments.

263

Marcus stared at the waves, suffused with a gray sadness. It was not the sadness of shame or regret that weighed on him. He had thought about this during his long night in the cell and concluded, no, he was not sorry for what he'd done. He was sorry he'd been caught before he brought the curtain down of his own volition. Although Marcus had worked through the moral implications of his actions long ago, the criminal life caused a certain ongoing strain on his psyche. So along with his sorrow came a feeling of relief. He suspected he would be able to apply the lessons he'd learned in his future endeavors.

Jan dropped Marcus off at the house and went to pick up Nathan at school. The scent of garlic greeted him when he walked in the kitchen door. Lenore was stirring something in a pot on the stove. A stained cookbook was open on the counter in front of her, and next to that a piece of meat was marinating in a mixing bowl. Marcus inhaled deeply.

"I'm making you osso buco for dinner," she said. "You once told me you really like it. I have no idea if it's going to be good."

Marcus was deeply appreciative of Lenore's gesture. He waited for her to mention what had taken place. Instead, she asked him to cut up some lemons and squeeze their contents into a pan for a dessert she was going to bake. He stood silently beside her and removed a lemon from a purple ceramic bowl filled with them. He sliced it in two, then placed the half-sphere in the squeezer and brought the handles together, the tart juice running into the pan. He took another lemon from the bowl and repeated the process. At that moment, standing in his kitchen on this autumn afternoon, he wished he could spend the rest of his life engaged in this simple task.

Later that day, Jan brought Nathan home from a math tutoring session. The house was suffused with the garlicky smell of the cooking osso buco and the scent of lemon cake. Marcus greeted him in the kitchen and tried to act nonchalant, making him a sandwich and

264

watching as he ate it. Ordinarily Nathan would have asked what was cooking, but today he acted as if nothing special was going on.

"Anything happen at school today?"

"Not really."

Had he heard anything? Probably not. And would he have said something if he had? Marcus had no idea. Had Nathan inherited his dissembling gene? That was a troubling thought.

The family ate dinner together that night, and although Marcus complimented Lenore on the food, he could hardly taste it. Later, he and Jan watched the news on Channel 9. After an update on the fire in the Angeles National Forest, the pretty Scottish-Hispanic anchorwoman appeared in front of a graphic that read PIMP DADDY and breathlessly intoned "Van Nuys man Marcus Ripps was arrested for running a call-girl ring yesterday." Jan squeezed his hand and gave him a look that implied she felt sorry for him. Marcus tried not to resent her pity as he sank further into the sofa. When his mug shot appeared behind the news reader, he turned off the television and went upstairs to lie down. After a few minutes, he felt like his nerves were going to cause him to levitate. So he came downstairs to talk to Jan about what to do, now that his situation was public knowledge. He found her in the den, researching criminal lawyers on the Internet.

"Before we do anything else," she said, "you have to tell Nathan."

Marcus agreed and went back upstairs, where he knocked gently on the bedroom door and pushed it open. He saw Nathan seated at his computer, listening to music on headphones as he worked on the lab report for his science fair project. Marcus tapped him on the shoulder, and Nathan removed the headphones.

"You might be hearing something about me at school, Nate, something not so good." Nathan's face remained impassive. "I was arrested, and if we can't get the charges dismissed, there's going to be a trial."

"Why did they arrest you?"

Marcus took a deep breath and launched into a slightly laundered version of the story, one in which the business was a dating service where sometimes people mutually agreed to have sex.

"Are you going to have to go to jail?"

"I don't know." Marcus waited a moment to give his son a chance to absorb this particular reality. "You know I love you, right?"

"So, Dad, are you, like, kind of a pimp?"

"That's what they're saying."

Nathan's face remained neutral. Marcus had no idea what he was thinking, couldn't discern how his young brain was processing this information. Marcus sensed that Nathan was seeing him as if for the first time.

"What's going to happen to me if you go to jail?"

"No one's going to jail, okay?"

Nathan's nervous half-smile did not indicate to Marcus that he was significantly reassured. The silence was pierced by the ringing of the phone.

Jan called out from another room: "Marcus, it's Atlas, for you."

The Winthrop Hall Middle School science fair, one of the major events of the academic year, took place the following evening. Nathan had been diligently working on his project, a scale model of a windmill that actually produced enough power to illuminate a small light, and he expected his parents to attend. Marcus begged off, but Jan did not want Nathan to go alone. She took longer than usual to get ready since this was her first time in public as the wife of an accused felon. She tried on several outfits before she found one she liked—jeans, a fitted white shirt, and a knitted green blazer. Her makeup was applied meticulously and, after taking a last look in the full-length mirror in the bedroom, she was prepared to face her new life.

The science fair filled every inch of the commodious school gymnasium. Student projects were set up in row after row and children and parents perused them with a gravity befitting Nobel Prize judges. Jan was curious if anyone would speak with her as she worked her way along the rows, looking at the children's handiwork. She had been there for fifteen minutes before anyone said hello. An experiment a sixth-grade girl had done about the removal of hair dye had caught her eye, and when she glanced up from the handwritten explanation of the assignment she saw Corinne Vandeveer. Jan smiled at Corinne, who behaved as if she didn't see her, turning away and whispering something to her companion, a fellow Turbo Mom. Jan approached them.

"Hi, Corinne." Corinne smiled tightly, barely offering a greeting. She did not introduce her companion, whose shiny tan, glossy hair, and sparkling diamond earrings combined to create a force field around her head. The woman tried to pretend that Jan was not there. "When's the decoration committee going to meet?"

"It's not."

"What happened?" Jan knew *exactly* what had happened—Corinne had heard about Marcus, and had decided to shun her—but now she just wanted to make her former friend uncomfortable. "I was looking forward to it."

"It's all been taken care of," she said. "Nice seeing you." Corinne and her friend glided away, leaving Jan standing by a project where a seventh-grader had announced his work by creating a board that read DO COMPUTER GAMES MAKE YOU STUPID? The students and their parents swirled around Jan snaking their way through the displays, their voices a dull hum pushing against her consciousness. She felt her internal mercury rise. Her mouth was dry. Jan whirled this way and that, saw the pampered faces, carefree, laughing, the golden few for whom the sun shines, the winds blow, and the clouds part. Who could say that what any of them did to access these halls of privilege was more defensible? She had to concentrate to keep from running out of the gym. Slowly, stately, she walked toward the door. She found a water fountain in the hallway and took a drink. Then she stepped outside to get some air. Jan was distraught at the rank unfairness of her erstwhile friend's behavior. Corinne's husband Dewey Vandeveer, blue-jeaned arbitrage potentate, earned his money in high-level financial manipulation, world economies rising and falling as he and his associates, respectable highwaymen, backed their truck up to the vault and looted its sparkling treasure. But Marcus and Jan were immoral and to be shunned?

After five minutes, she was able to go back into the gym and tell Nathan it was time to leave. He and five of his friends were trading verses from a rap song. There was a moment of protest, but when he saw the way his mother was looking at him, unblinking and serious, he followed her out.

That evening, Marcus tried to focus his mind by reading Aristotle, but the *Nichomachean Ethics* were no match for his imploding sense of stability and order. Everything had spun out of control. He felt as if his very cells were ululating. When he heard Jan's car pull into the driveway, he opened the front door and was waiting there when they arrived.

"How'd it go?"

Nathan walked past Marcus and into the house. Marcus and Jan followed his progress up the stairs.

"Nathan, your father asked you a question."

Marcus watched the boy's retreating form on the stairwell and pondered whether he should order him back down.

"Fine," he said before disappearing into his room.

Marcus looked at Jan, then in the direction Nathan had gone. He was trying to decide whether to follow the boy up the stairs and into his room.

"Corinne Vandeveer completely chilled me."

"What?" Marcus said. He was concentrating on their son, and how to address what was beginning to look like a difficult juncture in their relationship. He didn't expect Jan to introduce a new issue.

"She obviously heard about you and . . ."

"I don't care about Corinne Vandeveer, okay?"

There was no answer the first time Marcus knocked, or the second. When he opened the door, Nathan was seated at his desk with headphones on. Marcus touched him on the back. Nathan glanced at him but didn't say anything.

"I know this is hard for you." Marcus wished he could think of something less lame to say, but he hadn't planned a speech. He could tell Nathan was not in the mood to hear one either. And what could he tell the boy? I did it because of my grandfather? My brother? My faulty judgment? A hypocritical world? A toxic culture? A need to not be crushed, to stake out a place, to make a living? It all sounded absurd and at this moment, as Marcus stood with his hand resting on his son's shoulder, none of it mattered.

"Nate, I love you. That's what's important."

"My friends think you're totally gangsta."

"Really?"

Marcus saw that Nathan was trying to parse this development. The boy couldn't entirely make sense of it. He didn't want to bear down on his son, make him any more uncomfortable than he already was, so he took a moment and tried to relax. It was important he not rush. Marcus looked around the room. Clothes were strewn everywhere, books and papers scattered on the desk, several manga comics lying on the floor near Nathan's open clarinet case. The clarinet itself was on the bed. Marcus picked it up and placed his fingers on the holes, miming playing it in an attempt to lighten the mood. It didn't work. After an interval of silence, Nathan said "Prostitution is a crime."

"First of all, not all laws make sense. I helped some adults, who were consenting, by the way . . . which means all parties agreed . . ."

"I know what consenting means, Dad."

"So I helped consenting adults have sex, okay?" Marcus placed the clarinet back on the bed while he decided just how far to take this exchange. "It's only sex. It's a physical thing, muscles and nerves interacting, and people like it. Many, many people. But because we live in a society with these particular values . . ." This was the tricky part for Marcus, since Nathan had just embraced those values in the most public of ways, and with his father's alleged endorsement. He wasn't exactly sure how to explain religious dogma, insofar as it related to the development of a personal code of ethics to a thirteen-year-old.

"Whatever."

But now he had no choice: "Some of those values are good. Okay, a lot of them. But when it comes to sex . . ."

"They're not?"

"In a perfect world, Nate, you should have sex with someone you love. But, one, it's not a perfect world, and two, there are people who don't love anyone, or can't love anyone, or don't *have* anyone to love and they still want to have sex. They're lonely. Do you understand?"

"Sure." He did not sound convinced.

"People have urges and sometimes they become unbearable. There are other people whose profession it is to provide a safety valve. It's been going on since the dawn of time."

"Pimps and hoes?"

"Yes. At least the hoes . . . the women . . . the ladies . . . Don't call them hoes. It's disrespectful. Look, there are marriages where an ugly rich guy marries a much younger woman, one who's beautiful and in her sexual prime. Some of your classmates at Winthrop Hall, their parents fit into this category. And maybe the wife doesn't really love the husband, but he's rich and she gets to drive a fancy car and live in a big house, and her part of the bargain is she has to have sex with him. So how is that different?"

"Because they're married?"

"Yeah. That makes it okay in the eyes of society, but it's the same principle."

"So Dylan Sussman's mother is a ho?" Nathan said, referring to the alluring mother of a classmate several decades younger than her septuagenarian husband.

"I don't know the woman personally, but listen: Society is accusing me of being a criminal. Now you have a set of moral values, and they're good ones. But here's what morals boil down to for me— treat other people the way you want them to treat you, okay? Everything else is trying to figure out how many angels can prance around on a quark."

"What?"

"It's unknowable, Nate. Treat people well, love your family . . ."

"Do you treat people well?"

"All the time? No. Do I try? Mostly. I didn't say it was easy. Look, I know this is a lot for a thirteen-year-old to deal with, but when you're sitting alone . . ." Marcus looked at Nathan, who was staring away again. "Nate, would you look at me, please?" Nathan acted like he didn't hear. "The Dodgers are in town. Do you want to go to a game?"

"I don't like baseball."

"You played Little League last year."

"It's boring."

"Okay. Maybe you'll change your mind."

Nathan nodded, his face idling in neutral. He still wasn't making eye contact. Then Marcus kissed his warm forehead and retreated. As he sat alone in the living room later that night, *The Last Days of Socrates* unread on his lap, he reflected on what he might have done had his father been in a similar situation. He concluded that his own reaction would probably not have differed much from Nathan's and, so, under the circumstances, decided to consider himself lucky.

Chapter 22

Atlas had wanted to play golf, but Marcus couldn't deal with the idea and suggested having a drink instead. Now they were seated across from each other in a booth in the Paradise Room drinking whiskey. It was just before the dinner rush, and the place was quiet. Techno pop from the eighties played incongruously over the speakers in the red-hued bar. The first thing Atlas wanted to know was why Marcus hadn't told him about the business he was running. When Marcus just raised an eyebrow and ruefully shook his head, Atlas didn't pursue that line of questioning. He agreed he probably would have kept quiet about it too. Marcus was trying to figure out a way to tell him about Plum, but didn't know how to bring it up. They'd been sitting there fifteen minutes when Atlas placed a beer nut in his mouth, chewed, swallowed, and said "I want to be your lawyer."

This was a surprise to Marcus, something he hadn't considered. He had already started looking for an appropriately high-priced attorney to fend off the charges and keep him out of prison. Atlas then told him he'd even do it *pro bono*. Marcus was momentarily knocked off-kilter by the proposal.

"I may be a fuckup in my personal life, but I know how to work a jury. What I did for Cricket Bulger, I can do for you," Atlas said. "I completely messed up with the gambling. No excuses. My fault alone. But I'm clean over six months now. No casinos, no Internet poker, nothing. I'm going to meetings three days a week." Marcus was still trying to figure out a way to introduce the topic of his ex-wife, but Atlas was on a roll. "Your case is going to get some serious publicity. It's a huge incentive for me. It'll be a great comeback story, and I'll keep you out of jail." He paused here and looked into Marcus's eyes. "I need this, and I'll come through for you. I already know how we're going to defend it."

"Oh, yeah? How?"

"I'm gonna make you a folk hero."

"Plum was working for me."

Marcus watched Atlas, awaiting a reaction. He was not pleased with the clumsy way he had imparted the information. The music pulsed insistently through the warm fug of the bar.

"What'd you say?" Atlas wasn't sure if he'd heard Marcus correctly. "Plum, what . . .?"

"She was working for me."

"Doing . . . what was she . . . *what?*"

"As a dominatrix. She worked for the service."

The angle of Atlas's head shifted, and he was now looking at Marcus from the corners of his eyes. "Are you fucking . . . what?"

There was a long silence filled with the sound of tinny synthesizers and a singer whose voice was entirely devoid of emotion. "Oh, man . . ." Atlas said. The magnified bearing of a moment ago was gone and he seemed to visibly deflate. Then, without a word, he picked up his glass, walked to the bar, and reordered. Marcus didn't know what was going to come next. Although their marriage was unsustainable, she *had* been his wife, and Marcus had been at least partially responsible for her new life. Perhaps this news would awaken some submerged chivalrous impulse, causing Atlas to break his glass and grind the jagged edge into Marcus's face. Perhaps the newfound self-control was an act and he would leap across the table, wring Marcus's neck, and leave him dead on the sticky floor of the Paradise Room. Either way, Marcus believed he had to tell his friend.

Atlas was staring at his own reflection in the mirror behind the bar. The bartender, a young guy with the kind of mustache favored by country rock musicians in the seventies, poured another whiskey and slid it to Atlas who immediately took a swig. Then another. Marcus continued to watch as he drained the drink then placed it on the bar and tapped the rim. The mustache gave him a refill. Atlas placed a twenty on the bar and picked up the drink. He slid back into the booth.

"A *dominatrix?*"

"She's a good earner."

"Are you fucking kidding me?"

"I wish. But she wanted to do it, and . . ."

"She finally found something she was suited for."

Marcus was not certain how to read this remark. Was it bitter? Sympathetic? Supportive? Or was it flip; brittle words masking a grievous wound? He felt the need to cushion the blow, stanch the bleeding. Take responsibility. "Atlas, listen, I can . . ."

But before Marcus could launch into his mea culpa, Atlas held up his hand, indicating no further words were necessary. "It's not relevant," he said.

"You forgive me?"

"First of all, there's nothing to forgive. The woman's entitled to make a living, and if she's paying the rent horsewhipping some guy's naked ass, who am I to say you can't do that in America?"

"I'm glad you've got an open mind."

"That's what we want in a jury. Trials are like books and movies. They have narratives that the jurors hook into." A year earlier, Marcus would have been surprised at how quickly Atlas had assimilated this new intelligence and moved on, but now he understood survival techniques on a deeper level. "You're gonna be a world-class defendant. Your job moves to China, you've got a young son, a mother-in-law with health problems, and all you want to do is take care of your family. This is a *redemption* story, man. Life deals you a bad hand and you make the best of it. I'm not going to let the government take you down." Marcus considered this. Certainly, Atlas was motivated.

And he was as close to a friend as Marcus possessed, which had to count for something. He liked that not even the tiniest part of Atlas seemed to judge him. They drank a toast. Atlas predicted: "You're going to be a free man."

When Marcus drove home, he wondered if he had acceded to his friend's entreaties too quickly. He could afford anyone, perhaps he should go on a legal shopping expedition. But that thought was quickly crowded out once more by the mystery of who had unmasked him. Marcus had spent hours trying to unravel this, and as he was pulling into his driveway, it suddenly struck him. Malvina had told him he should have gone to China. As far as he knew, the only people they had in common were women who worked in the business. Marcus had only mentioned it to one person. He was flabbergasted, but not surprised.

No one was home when Marcus returned. As he sorted through the mail, he noticed a package from Dominc Festa, Esq. It was a brown box, eight inches by eight inches, made from corrugated cardboard and wrapped with packing tape. He got a knife from a drawer in the kitchen and sliced it open. There was a note from Festa on top, handwritten, in looping cursive, on a piece of office stationery. It said:

Dear Marcus,

Sorry to hear what you're going through. This has been sitting in a drawer in my desk and I've been meaning to send it to you. When I saw you on TV last night, I realized now was the time. Good luck!
Sincerely, Dominic Festa.

Placing his hand in the box, Marcus removed a small, robin's-egg-blue ceramic urn that contained the ashes of his brother Julian. What, exactly, was he supposed to do with this? The urn was cool to his touch and surprisingly light. Marcus had never held an urn containing human remains before. He would have to scatter them or bury them or do whatever it was you did with ashes, but this was not something he could think about now. In the meantime, where to put them? Not in the kitchen, or the bedroom, certainly. He couldn't put the ashes in the living room where the urn would conjure Julian's malevolent presence whenever Marcus found himself in there. What about the hall closet? Or did that show lack of respect for the dead? He left them on a shelf in the garage office, next to a yellowed copy of *Being and Nothingness*, and tried to forget their existence.

That night Marcus got an e-mail from Atlas informing him the government had only one witness in the case—a former Smart Tart.

Kostya called the next day and suggested that they meet at Pink's that afternoon. He was eating a chili dog when Marcus arrived, watching the traffic with the eyes of a big-cat trainer. They shook hands, and Marcus bought himself a soda. Kostya indicated that they should walk. The two of them headed north past a store selling overpriced antique furniture.

"I know guy, Chechen, came to Hollywood to be stuntman, his shit ain't working out, yo . . ." Kostya looked Marcus directly in the eye. Marcus didn't say anything. "Five thousand dollars, twenty-five hundred up front, the rest when it's done. You want bitch not talk?" Marcus was shocked. Then he wasn't shocked at all. Did Marcus still think he was a toy maker? The right to be appalled at Kostya's offer had been forfeited. Just add water, stir, and the case would go away. That kind of person wound up dead every day. It would be hard to prove a connection. He'd made his bundle, the business was already over. It was tempting. This was his world now. It wasn't as if his prints weren't already on a murder weapon. And when was *that* bell going to ring? "It's fucked up, yo . . . you do 401(ks) and all."

"I need to think about it."

Kostya nodded. Marcus asked him how things were going with Jesus Loves 2 Barbecue. Kostya told him to bring the family over for a meal when it opened. They embraced and parted. Driving over

276

Laurel Canyon back to the Valley, Marcus considered the encroaching shadows, the nether world whose chilly squeeze he'd accepted. He looked at his cell phone and thought about calling Kostya right then, getting it over with. Let loose the Chechen. He would be protecting his family. Why should he go to jail?

It was after midnight, and Marcus and Jan were in the kitchen folding laundry. Neither one could fall asleep. He hadn't discussed his meeting with Kostya, because he wanted to form his own opinion on the course of action he should take, and he hadn't been able to as yet. Marcus rolled a pair of black socks into a ball. Jan was folding one of Nathan's T-shirts.

"If I have to go to jail, do you think you could manage?"

"You're not going to jail."

"But if I did."

"It'd be hard. Not because of money. We have enough to last for a while, but . . . Nate, you know . . ." Jan didn't have to finish the sentence. She placed the T-shirt in the basket on top of a pile that had already been folded.

"What if I told you I found a way to make the case go away?" When she asked him what he meant, he told her what Kostya had suggested. She looked at him as if he'd lost his mind.

"You're not really thinking about it?"

"Obviously I'm *thinking* about it. I don't want to go to jail."

"Marcus, no. Hasn't everything gone wrong enough? If you get involved in something like this . . . I can't . . . I *can't!* Jeez, are you crazy? Neither can you."

He threw the socks into the basket, where they landed next to the T-shirts, and picked up another pair to fold. Marcus was grateful for his wife's simple affirmation, but a moment later found he was wishing there was a way the Chechen stuntman could guarantee his work was untraceable. Suddenly horrified by his thoughts, he went to the cabinet, took out a glass, and poured himself some whiskey. He nervously drained it, then told Jan he was going to try to go back to sleep. Upstairs, he lay down, his mind pinwheeling. The Chechen made him remember Tommy and Memo, the ride north, the long walk through the woods, the gun blast echoing against the dry hills. He'd seen it up close. Not *seen* it exactly: he was lying on the forest floor at the time, his face in the pine needles. But he knew what it looked like when someone was killed and realized he could never indulge that impulse.

Ten minutes later, his gloomy ruminations were interrupted by a soft knock.

"Marcus?" It was Lenore. He told her to come in. The door opened, and she entered holding a joint. Marcus silently regarded her from his recumbent position, not moving. She inhaled and let the smoke run out of her nose. "You want some? It might help you sleep."

"No, thanks." He didn't have the energy or the desire to tell her to put it out.

Lenore wore yellow pajamas with purple vertical stripes that had the effect of making her look like an exceedingly thin commedia dell'arte clown. The dim hall light threw a soft nimbus around her small frame.

"I can't sleep either." She took another hit as Marcus waited for her to continue. "I've been thinking."

"What about?" He didn't really want to talk to anyone right now, but it was better than wrestling with his doom-laden imaginings.

"I want to take one for the team."

Marcus rolled over on his side and propped himself up on an elbow. "Lenore, I have no idea what you're talking about."

"I'm willing to go to the cops and tell them I was the one running the service."

Although he was stunned by her offer, he quickly formulated a response, which was: "Absolutely not."

"Marcus, you can't go to jail." Lenore took another hit, and let the smoke stream from her nostrils. "You have a wife and kid. No one's depending on me. I could do a couple of years, easy."

"No. Forget it."

"You took me in when Shel died, you paid for my medical care . . ."

"Don't appeal to my sentimental side, Lenore, because it's gone. So, look, I appreciate your offer and, yes, I'm touched by it too, but I have to tell you again . . . absolutely no way will I let you do that. No way. Now go back to sleep."

"At least say you'll think about it."

"Give me a hit before you go."

He could tell that her disappointment was not feigned. She handed him the joint, and he inhaled deeply. It had been years since he'd smoked dope, and as it filled his lungs he began to cough. The spasm lasted nearly thirty seconds and so taxed his pulmonary system that he felt exhausted enough to drift into a fitful sleep moments after Lenore said good night.

Chapter 23

On a bright May morning, two years since Marcus had left the toy business, a year and a half since embarking on his second career, and six months after it came to a grinding halt, the man *Channel 9 News* had dubbed "Pimp Daddy" sat at the defense table of the courtroom in Van Nuys Courthouse West, wearing the dark suit he had purchased for his son's bar mitzvah. The apprehension that filled the days leading up to the trial had affected his appetite, and the jacket hung loosely on his frame. Atlas was seated next to him, ready to have at it with the judge, the prosecuting attorney, the media, and anyone who thought they might impede the redemptive story line he intended to construct. Jan sat behind them, unindicted, fearful of an outcome that would send Marcus to state prison for a minimum of three years as mandated by the California penal code. Lenore sat next to her, tortured at having to watch this man, who had always tried to do the right thing by her, being put through the public humiliation that is any criminal trial.

Judge Ruth Wu was a small woman in her sixties. Her gray hair was pulled into a severe bun, and large black glasses perched on her nose. Her robe seemed to be in danger of swallowing her. Leaning forward, elbows on the bench, she called the first witness, Detective Victor Jarvis from the LAPD, a laconic man wearing an in-court-for-the-day suit that rested uneasily on his paunch. He was sworn in.

The assistant district attorney was Maria Mendoza. Sleek-looking, she wore a dark pin-striped suit and black pumps. Marcus watched her, trying to ignore her sexuality. The obvious contempt she had for him perversely rendered her more attractive. He knew there were men who would pay a lot of money for that kind of disdain and up the ante if she wore the right outfit while exhibiting it. Plum had milked that demographic dry. He quickly tried to dismiss the thought as she approached Jarvis.

"Detective Jarvis, who discovered the body of Mahmoud Ghorbanifar in Angeles National Forest?"

"Firefighters who were up there working." His voice was a monotone. He could have been reading from a technical manual.

"And you were the first detective on the scene?"

"I was."

"Why did you suspect the body had been moved?"

"No one goes hiking naked."

"And no one could have taken the victim's clothes?"

"Objection!" Atlas said. "Prejudicial. The deceased in question is not a victim. This isn't a murder trial."

Marcus was pleased that Atlas had interrupted so quickly. He was not going to let anything pass unchallenged. The judge sustained the objection and told Maria Mendoza to continue.

"No one could have taken *Mr. Ghorbanifar's* clothes?"

"The body was found in a remote area. It's unlikely that someone would have found it and then removed the clothing."

"Objection. Speculative!" Atlas said.

"Sustained," the judge said.

"When you brought the body into the lab, what did you learn?"

"There was a pubic hair in his mouth."

"Please tell the court what happened after that."

"We ran it through a DNA database."

"And what did you find?"

"That it belonged to Lenka Robich."

"What did?"

"The pubic hair."

"And what was she doing in the DNA database?"

"She had a shoplifting conviction in London. They take DNA swabs over there, and the information gets fed into the international system."

Given that the physical evidence in question was incontrovertible, Atlas declined to cross-examine the witness. Judge Wu declared a short break. Jan and Lenore went outside, but Marcus wanted to avoid the media. He and Atlas stood next to a window at the end of a long hallway outside the courtroom. Marcus was staring out over the parking structure when Atlas said "I've been thinking about what they're calling you in the media. 'Pimp Daddy.' "

"What about it?" Marcus *hated* the name.

"I think you should trademark it. It's catchy."

"*Catchy?* When this is over, I'm going to want to forget everything about it."

"I'll do it for you. You never know."

Marcus shook his head, bewildered. How could anything positive redound to him from that mark?

Maria Mendoza said "The State calls Lenka Robich."

When Amstel took the stand, she did not look at Marcus. He stared at her, profoundly aware that she twirled his life on a well-manicured finger. Forever the enchantress, she had constructed an entirely new persona for her current role as state's witness. Now she wore a pencil skirt and white silk blouse that made her look like a young corporate executive. In her answers to Maria Mendoza's friendly questions, Amstel detailed how she had come into Marcus's orbit and what had transpired the night of Mr. Ghorbanifar's death. Poised and in control, she drew on her theatrical experience to create a compelling narrative about a sympathetic if carnally inclined immigrant who found herself ensnared in the spider's web. The jury leaned in, awaiting something salacious. It didn't take long.

* * *

Atlas had purchased his well-tailored suit with borrowed money. Now he confidently stood six feet away from Amstel, boring into her. She looked at him as if he was something she was about the scrape off the window of her Escalade.

"Let's be clear for the jury, Ms. Robich. The evening when Mr. Ghorbanifar expired and the night you were arrested—those were two different nights we're talking about, correct?"

"Yes."

"Let's talk about the night you were arrested. How long were you in the hotel room before something happened?"

"Ten minutes."

"And you had already taken off your clothes?"

"Yes."

"How long were you naked before the interruption?"

"A couple of seconds, maybe."

"Then what took place?"

"The police came in."

"How many?"

"I have to guess, I don't know . . . maybe five?"

"What happened then? And by the way, were they all male officers?"

"I think so. I don't know."

"Were you frightened?"

"Yes."

"Did anyone talk to you?"

"They say 'freeze. Don't move. Stay on bed.' "

"What happened next?"

"They go through my bag."

"Where were you at this point?"

"I am still on bed."

"Then what happened?"

"They tell me put my clothes on and collect belongings and we are going to police station."

"After you left the room, I believe you went to the room next door, is that correct?"

"Yes."

"And you were interviewed by a Detective Blaine, B-L-A-I-N-E, of the Los Angeles Police Department."

"Yes."

"And do you remember what was discussed in that interview?"

"I'm sorry. I can't remember anything about interview. I am upset when this happens."

"You don't remember what you said to Detective Blaine?"

"No, I don't."

"Do you remember being taken to Precinct 37 of the Los Angeles Police Department?"

"Yes, I do."

"That you do remember?"

"Yes."

"And you remember you were booked?"

"Yes, I do."

"And you remember when they told you that you were going to be charged with prostitution, you remember that?"

"Yes."

"And what was your response when you heard you were going to be charged with prostitution? How did you feel?"

"Bad."

"You were worried that you could be deported back to Latvia?"

"Yes."

"And you were subsequently informed by someone from the District Attorney's office that if you testified against whoever it was who sent you on the date, that would not occur, is that correct?"

"Yes."

"So after they took you to the Los Angeles Police Department, they booked you and told you that you were being charged. That's when they did a second interview. Do you remember that?"

"Yes."

"And it wasn't Detective Blaine any more. Detective Wolfson took over, is that correct?"

"Yes."

"And it was he who told you that one of your pubic hairs had been found in the mouth of a man whose body had been discovered in the Angeles National Forest."

"Yes."

"And your DNA was in a database because you had a previous criminal conviction?"

"Objection! Not relevant," Maria Mendoza said.

"Overruled," the judge said. Atlas smiled. Marcus was almost enjoying this. His lawyer was trouncing the witness. The judge ordered her to answer the question, but she claimed to have forgotten it.

"Your DNA was in a database," Atlas reminded her, "because you had a previous criminal conviction."

"Yes."

"So once the idea of a dead body was introduced, you became more concerned with what might happen to you?"

"Yes."

"And that is when you exercised your right to a phone call, correct?"

"I think so."

"You *think* so? Yes or no?"

"Yes."

"And who did you call?"

"I don't remember."

"You were arrested, you were allowed one phone call, and you don't remember who you called?" Atlas turned to the jury and rolled his eyes. A few jurors laughed. Marcus could tell they liked his lawyer.

"I was upset."

"After you were charged, after you were in custody, after you were booked, when you were in the station house, and after you made the phone call to the person you can't remember, that's when you said Marcus Ripps was aware of your activities. Do you remember that?"

"Yes."

"Did you receive immunity?"

"I did."

"Who gave you immunity?"

"The Los Angeles Court."

"And the Los Angeles Court is where your own case is being decided, is that correct?"

"Yes."

"And that immunity was granted in exchange for your testimony against my client, is that correct?"

"Yes."

"And what they told you was 'We're going to grant you immunity,' which means basically that you are not going to be prosecuted, correct?"

"Yes."

"But Marcus Ripps didn't send you to that hotel room, did he?" Amstel didn't answer. Atlas glared at her. Marcus shifted in his seat, and the scraping of the chair on the floor was the only sound in the courtroom. "Did he? And remember, Ms. Robich, you're under oath."

"Yes, he did."

Marcus stared at Amstel, but she refused to meet his gaze. For all his experience, he was still surprised that someone could lie so boldly in a court of law. The amorality of perjury disturbed him, something he viewed as a hopeful sign with regard to his own soul.

"You're lying to protect someone else." Atlas paused a moment to let the jury take this in. Amstel eyes shot poison darts at her tormentor. "The reason you're lying, Ms. Robich, is that you fear this other person will harm you if you testify against him or her, but you're not worried about retribution from Mr. Ripps. Isn't that true?"

"No."

"Why don't you tell the court that person's name, Ms. Robich?

The name of whoever it is you're protecting." Now Maria Mendoza objected, telling the judge the defense attorney was badgering the witness. The judge sustained the objection, but Marcus was impressed with Atlas's performance. Amstel was being shredded. He looked at the jury, and several of them were nodding their heads.

Atlas unfolded a sheet of paper and showed to Amstel. She glanced at it.

"Do you recognize this document?"

"Yes."

"Let the record show that this is a contract you signed. Please read the paragraph I've circled to the court."

He handed the paper to Amstel, who looked at the judge before accepting it. The judge nodded to her, and she took the document and began to read. "I, Lenka Robich, agree that Marcus Ripps will be setting appointments by phone for me. We have discussed and agreed he does not expect me to perform any illegal acts for money. If I so decide to perform or participate in anything illegal during the appointments he has set up for me, I am 100 % completely responsible for my own actions."

Marcus noticed Atlas allowed himself a barely discernible smile before he turned to Maria Mendoza and said "Your witness."

Court was adjourned for lunch. Marcus, Jan, Lenore, and Atlas ate at a diner across the street from the courthouse. The conversation had the false jollity that those scared out of their wits will affect when desperately trying to remain composed. While they were waiting for the food to arrive, Marcus's BlackBerry began to vibrate. He checked to see who had e-mailed him: MannishBoy24. Unable to resist, he opened it:

Having a good day, Breeze?:-).

It instantly dawned on Marcus that he had been pinned like a butterfly to the chair at the defense table by the shapely hand of Malvina Biggs. He surmised Amstel had gone to work for her and been apprehended by the police. Rather than be punished by Malvina, Amstel had chosen to sacrifice the man who had provided her with a retirement plan. And there was nothing he could do about it. Marcus silently vowed that it would be the last time he allowed himself to be played by anyone. He thought briefly about Tommy the Samoan, and Memo dead in the mountains, and the gun. Then he pushed the images away.

The District Attorney's office couldn't find anyone else willing to testify against Marcus, so their entire case rested on Amstel's testimony. The newspapers and local television stations had given big play to the story, and several reporters eating at a nearby table stole glances in his direction. Marcus played with his limp chef's salad and tried to ignore them. They liked their stories presented on a silver platter, and right now he felt like a canapé. The fork was trembling in his hand, but he'd already lost ten pounds since being arrested, so he forced himself to take a bite of the food.

Atlas looked at the jury, tilted his head, and grinned. He missed gambling, but this was almost as good, and he bathed in the rush of his own performance. "Ladies and gentlemen of the jury, members of the community, taxpayers," he began, nearly bouncing on the balls of his feet. "One of your own is on trial here today, and his only accuser is a confessed prostitute who is in America with an expired tourist visa. Let me frame this for you in the simplest terms. An illegal alien from the former Soviet Union is accusing my client of pandering and the illegal disposal of a corpse. Let's address the second charge first. It was not the pubic hair of Marcus Ripps that was found in the mouth of Mahmoud Ghorbanifar, it was the pubic hair of the accuser. There is nothing to put Mr. Ripps at the crime scene, no witnesses, no circumstantial evidence, nothing but the word of a woman who lied about her criminal past to get into America *illegally* and makes her living in the sex industry. And let me say, while we're on the subject, that I make no value judgment with regard to Ms.

Robich's line of work. I am not here to condemn her, to cast aspersions on her, to malign her for being a sex worker. That is her choice. What I will malign her for is being a liar. I don't even think Lenka Robich is a bad person. She's *scared*. She's scared the individual who sent her to that hotel—her *pimp*—is going to harm her if she tells the truth, and that is why she's lying in court. Lenka Robich, who is from *Latvia*, whose first language is *Russian*, thinks she can stay in our country while Marcus Ripps, a devoted husband, father, and son-in-law, a respected member of the Los Angeles business community, and a benefactor of multiple charities, goes to prison? I think she is mistaken. I think her logic is flawed and I hope you see through her lie. My client was the production manager for Wazoo Toys, a job he held for nearly fifteen years. The factory he supervised moved to China two years ago and my client chose not to go with it but to stay here, in *America*, where a man has a right to make a living. Marcus Ripps always paid his bills, always looked after his family, so when his mother-in-law, who had been recently widowed, moved in with him, ladies and gentlemen, he didn't blink. No, he welcomed her to his modest home in Van Nuys. Not long after that, his brother, his only sibling, a man he *loved*, died suddenly, leaving him a struggling business. My client took over that business and made it run like clock-work, providing jobs and putting food on his family's table. Some of the businessmen who employed International Friendship Guides may have had sex with women who worked for the service. I don't need to remind you that sex between consenting adults is still not a crime. The accuser put her signature on a document stating in English that if sex occurs, it is not prearranged. The accuser speaks English very well. She knew what she was signing. But she is also an actress in her native country and so is a skilled performer. Don't be fooled by her act. I submit to you that Marcus Ripps is not a criminal, but a model American, someone who cares for others, and not just himself. I ask you, ladies and gentlemen of the jury . . . no, I *beseech* you, to acquit. There is no other choice."

It was an impressive show and Marcus allowed himself a spark of optimism. He smiled at the jurors, but they were all looking at Atlas, who basked in the warm glow of their attention. The judge gave her instructions to the jury, and the courtroom emptied.

Marcus was standing at the urinal in the men's room when he sensed that he was not alone. A moment ago he had been the only one in there, and he hadn't heard the door open. He turned to see Tommy the Samoan standing near the sinks, dressed in a Hawaiian shirt and white drawstring pants two men could have stood in. How did someone this size move around so stealthily?

"You got a raw deal, brah." Marcus zipped his fly and looked toward the door. There was no point dashing for it. He doubted Tommy had come to kill him. Given their current location in the Van Nuys Criminal Courts Building, that would have been exceedingly bad planning. He knew Tommy thought ahead. Still, he had hoped never to see this guy again.

"What do you want?"

"I got rid of the gun."

Marcus was taken aback. This was excellent news, maybe even a harbinger of better days. But he couldn't imagine what had led Tommy to do this—or if he was even telling the truth.

"Why?"

"Got married, Marcus. Check this ring."

Marcus wasn't sure what getting married had to do with destroying evidence, but he didn't need to hear any more. He glanced nervously at the gold band inlaid with onyx and tried to recall if the guy had ever used his proper name before.

"I like it."

"Me and my wife, we moving to the islands, make some babies. L.A. too crazy." Marcus nodded. He didn't disagree. Relocating to the islands sounded like an excellent idea. "You oughtta spank Malvina," Tommy concluded.

Marcus would have loved to pay her back for the agony she had caused, but he understood that revenge without a larger purpose was pointless. He had learned the value of prescience. Crushing Malvina Biggs did not fit with his new, more sophisticated paradigm.

"Tell her she did me a favor."

"I don't talk to that bitch no more." A maintenance worker entered, pushing a bucket and mop. He began to swab the floor. Tommy gently chucked Marcus on the shoulder and vanished as quickly as he had appeared.

Although it was only May, summer heat had already descended on the Valley. A gaggle of media sprouted like mushrooms on the front lawn of 112 Magdalene Lane; but when it became clear that no one was going to make a public statement, they departed. Marcus remained inside with the shades drawn and the air conditioning on. He avoided television and gave his well-thumbed paperback copies of Stoic philosophers Seneca and Aurelius a workout.

As the jury finished their second day, Marcus sat in his kitchen, eating a bowl of strawberry ice cream. Jan was working her way through a bottle of Chardonnay. They had discussed the psychology of the jury ad nauseam and convinced themselves that Marcus would be acquitted. They talked about ideas for new businesses. They chattered to fill the silence. But now the conversation had collapsed under the weight of nerves and emotional exhaustion. Marcus lifted the spoon to his mouth and ate another bite of ice cream, the taste of the cool, silken dairy soothing him.

"I want to scatter my brother's ashes." Marcus had told her about the ashes the day they arrived, but hadn't mentioned them since.

"Now?"

"I feel like going to the beach."

After determining that Nathan knew enough about the Great Depression to pass the test he was studying for, and that Lenore was watching a nature documentary that she had already seen, the Ripps family piled into the minivan. Everyone was quiet as they rode down the 405. Marcus thought about going to Leo Carrillo, still his favorite Los Angeles beach, but that was a strand of sweet memory, the place he and Jan had recently shared an elegiac hour, and he didn't want to forever associate it with the scattering of Julian's ashes. When he did not take the exit that would have brought them to Santa Monica or Malibu, Jan asked him where they were going.

"Cabrillo Beach."

"In San Pedro? I thought Julian hated it there."

"Julian isn't the one making the decision."

Jan nodded. He appreciated the fact that she didn't argue. Cabrillo Beach was where the brothers' parents had taken them as children, where they had fished off the pier, where, when they were older, each of them had gone, separately, to drink with friends, to be with girls, to begin their push against the boundaries that separated them from what lay ahead. Marcus had always been drawn to the dazzling San Pedro coastline, the ocean, the vast sky. He would send Julian off on his own terms.

The sun touched the ocean and the sky radiated salmon, pink, and bloody vermilion. Catalina Island shimmered like an apparition on the misty horizon, its lights flickering like a fading hope. Just to the south, massive cargo ships cruised from Los Angeles Harbor toward the open sea. The lighthouse in Point Fermin Park loomed to the north. A few surfers bobbed in the blue distance, patiently awaiting a wave.

Placing the urn on the sand, Marcus rolled his pants above his knees. Then he reached over, picked it up, and waded into the chilly water. Jan, Nathan, and Lenore watched from the shore.

"I have no idea how to do this," he called over his shoulder. The wind gusted and blew through his hair.

"Should you say something about your brother?" Jan said.

As the remnants of a small wave broke against his legs, Marcus said "Can you tell a dead person to go fuck himself?" Then: "Sorry, Nate. You didn't hear that."

"I know the word, Dad."

"Do you want to say something to God?" This from Lenore.

"I don't think so."

"I think someone should say something," Jan said.

Like an eruption, Nathan shouted toward the darkening sky: "Thanks for the red minibike, Uncle Julian!"

As Marcus turned toward the horizon, the fading shafts of sun, lambent on the dark water, fragmented with the rhythm of the swells and joined together again, pieces of a puzzle, causing Marcus to squint so he could see. Julian hadn't come for Nathan that day, he'd come for Marcus. It was an attempt, however inept and ill-calculated, to reattach the severed cord, to forge something between them, to attempt a scene neither knew how to play. And Marcus, who could not abide this wild card of a sibling, this lifelong and reliable dispenser of emotional pain, had sent him away. Julian's last will and testament, so perverse and unexpected, was the response. But, finally, what *had* his brother meant with his strange legacy? Marcus had periodically returned to this question over the past two years but never satisfactorily answered it. Now, at twilight, knee-deep in the Pacific Ocean and holding all that was left of Julian in an urn, he thought he understood. Julian had challenged him, thrown down a gauntlet. Their grandfather had embraced the world as he found it, capered to its mad music. Their father couldn't keep up, but Julian had inherited Mickey's unbound spirit and resumed the beat. As for Marcus, his brother had placed a shiny object in his hands—a taunt, a joke. Julian never could have imagined that his younger brother would actually assume the mantle. It was preposterous, really. Marcus had always skulked in the shadows, beholden to the whims of others. But now he had proven, finally, that when the dance floor shook and bucked, he knew how to move. Yes, Marcus had been busted, and might be doing time, but he'd survive that, too, and somehow go forth and flourish. So while Julian's bequest was a droll tweak, a slap and a tickle, it was also a seminar where knowledge unspoken passed from the dead to the living.

293

And now Marcus was schooled.

"Dad, what are you waiting for?" Nathan yelled. "It's getting cold!"

Marcus unscrewed the lid. A wave rolled in and he turned to the side as it broke over his thighs, holding the urn at shoulder height to keep its contents dry. He briefly thought of his father and mother, happy they had not lived to witness this. He faced out to sea and turned the urn upside down.

As the last of Julian slid from the container, a gust of wind arrived like an uninvited guest and blew the ashes over Marcus, covering his shoulders and face with soft gray powder. It was in his nose, his mouth, and his eyes and he couldn't see anything, so he only heard the laughter on the shore rising above the sound of the surf. There had been no laughter in his house of late, and the sound, despite the bizarre circumstance that engendered it, was welcome, a familiar comfort in which he blindly luxuriated, if only for a thrilling moment.

Marcus dropped beneath the surface of the water, a farewell, and when he rose from the waves he was cleansed. His eyes were still closed, so at first he could only hear his family applauding, but when he opened them and blinked the briny water out, there they were, waiting for him, smiling as the sun's last rays glimmered in the dying day.

The next afternoon, a phone call from Atlas informed Marcus that a verdict was imminent. They drove to the courthouse and waited in the marbled hallway, not talking. Lenore rubbed Jan's back with her palm, and Jan held Marcus's hand. After only a few minutes, the bailiff, a large black woman with colorfully beaded braids, told them to come into the courtroom.

Marcus watched the jury enter. He could discern nothing on their faces. He'd heard that if the jurors look at the defendant, there will be no conviction. Two of them, an older white man and a Hispanic woman roughly his own age, looked right at him. He felt the perspiration in his palms and wished he'd had the foresight to grab a piece of paper towel from the men's room so he could wipe them dry.

Judge Ruth Wu told Marcus to rise for the verdict. He got to his feet and spread them shoulder distance. Hands clasped behind his back, he smiled at the judge.

The foreman of the jury, a short blonde woman in her thirties wearing a print dress, stood and prepared to read the verdict.

"How do you find the defendant?" asked Judge Wu.

"On the count of transportation of a dead body, we find the defendant . . ." She cleared her throat at this juncture. "Not guilty."

Marcus allowed himself to turn and look at Jan and Lenore. Jan gave an uneasy smile and made a fist which she held in front of her as a gesture of solidarity. Lenore's eyes were shut. She was praying.

"And on the second count?" Judge Wu asked.

"On the second count of pandering, we find the defendant guilty."

Marcus visibly sagged and his knees began to buckle, but he steadied himself and averted an undignified response. He felt a hand on his shoulder. It was Atlas. He did not want to turn around to look at Jan and Lenore. The judge ordered him to report back for sentencing and wished him good luck.

They drove home in silence. Jan stared out the window of the passenger side and Lenore, although she wanted to say comforting things, sensed that it was best to remain quiet.

Marcus had an urge to hit golf balls. He believed the mindless repetition of a golf swing would be relaxing, so after dropping Jan and Lenore at home, he drove to the driving range at Woodley Lakes and purchased a bucket of balls. If anyone recognized him, they didn't say anything. Marcus turned off his cell phone. He was happy to be alone as he teed the balls up, one after another, and, alternating between a wood and an iron, whacked them into the silent distance. After finishing one bucket at what he believed was a leisurely pace, he saw that only forty-five minutes had passed, so he got another. Random thoughts, fears, projections cycled through his mind at such speed that they cancelled each other out. One would arrive like an electrical impulse, flash, and collapse like a black hole, only to be replaced a nanosecond later by the next arrival. But nothing gained purchase. By the time he emptied the third bucket, he noticed he had blisters on both his hands.

Jan was in the kitchen sautéing chicken cutlets in a pan when Marcus got home. He greeted her when he walked in and, instead of saying anything, she embraced him. Marcus could hear clarinet music wafting from somewhere in the house. Nathan's playing was getting better.

"We'll be all right," Jan said.

"Yeah, yeah," Marcus said. "I know."

Nathan was in the den where he had set up his music stand, working his way through a classical piece Marcus did not recognize. He watched through the door for a moment, and when Nathan noticed his father, he stopped and put the clarinet down.

"The Dodgers are playing the Mets this weekend," Marcus said. "I was thinking about getting tickets."

"Okay," Nathan said. Then: "Dad, don't watch me practice."

Marcus was thrilled at the casual brush-off. This was an unexpected victory. By the time he got into the shower two minutes later, the desire to scream had subsided.

Six weeks later, Marcus was sentenced to three years to be served at Chuckawalla Valley State prison, a facility dedicated to the long-term incarceration of medium-risk inmates. He was given one month to get his affairs in order. Atlas, who was devastated by the decision, informed him that the best he could hope for was time off for good behavior.

Marcus spent the days prior to his incarceration reading or watching television and wondering how he could possibly turn his misfortune into something positive. While home one afternoon watching a daytime talk show exploring the topic "Be Mine or Die: Spouses Who Kill," he found himself listening to one of the guests, a portly woman who had just been released from prison where she had served time for running over her unfaithful husband with their RV. To pass the long days, she had projected the stories of her favorite movies on an inner screen. Marcus had never been a big movie fan as an adult, so, while the talk show guest prattled on, he found himself thinking about films he remembered from when he was younger. He recalled comedies, and war movies, and crime stories. He thought about the Italian-American actors who played mobsters on screen. Some of these men came from rough places, and, had fate tipped one way or the other, many of them could have gone into the hard knock life. Instead, each found himself, whether by luck or design, reciting lines in front of a camera, not gangsters at all but a well-remunerated simulacrum of the actual thing. Counterfeit, cartoonish danger would always be a valuable commodity in a world where actual threats were overwhelming. Marcus understood. He had criminal credibility now. Although this struck him as ludicrous, it was undeniable.

Late on a Friday afternoon, when the sun was low in the sky and the temperature cooler, Marcus and Jan headed out on their second walk of the day. They enjoyed the dwindling time they had together, no longer burdened by having to maintain an elaborate illusion. Marcus wore shorts, sandals, and a T-shirt. He'd put some weight back on and appeared healthy. Jan was wearing loose white pants and a white long-sleeved cotton pullover. Marcus thought she looked beautiful, which indicated to him that she had made peace with his impending absence and would get through it without too much *Sturm und Drang*. As they held hands and walked in silence, a large man rode by on a Harley-Davidson Electra Glide Classic. He gunned his engine before disappearing down the street. They barely looked at him.

Marcus said "Isn't it funny how people with enough disposable income to buy a bike like that still like to think of themselves as rebels?"

"That guy's probably a dentist."

"The genius of the company that makes that bike is that they know how to package rebellion and sell it to a guy who works in an office."

"You're a rebel."

"Oh, yeah."

"Marcus, you are." She rubbed his back with her hand.

He put his arm around her, and with mock self-importance, said "Yeah, that's me, I'm a certified, card-carrying criminal kingpin, the genuine article, with street cred, bona fides, and a prison sentence. I'm *Pimp Daddy*. It said so on television. I just wish there was some way to work that."

When they returned to the house, Marcus poured himself a beer and sat in the backyard with Bertrand Russell, who was blissfully unaware that his master would soon no longer be there. It must be glorious to exist in the eternal present, Marcus thought, as he watched the little dog dig a hole. He wished he had faith. He envied those who did, and the blissful afterlife they were promised. In the meantime, this was the dirty world in which he found himself, the moist field on which he played; this realm of animal and mineral, salt, iron, water, dust, light, desire, and darkness. He'd seen it up close, tasted it, felt it in his pores. It was the essence, bountiful and life-giving, and human beings wanted to touch it, wanted to live, to stretch their spines, arch their backs, and, arms spread, face the sun, fingertips reaching upward toward the eternal sky. But they needed to go to school, to work, to make money, to raise families, to bury the dead. He understood. He *knew*. His conversation with Jan had concentrated his mind, and a means of exploiting that knowledge was taking shape.

Marcus drained his beer and went back into the house, where he found Jan talking to Plum on the phone. She looked up when Marcus entered, motioned that he should wait a moment, then said good-bye and hung up.

"Plum wants to have us over for dinner."

"It needs to be soon."

"Tomorrow night all right?"

"Yes, great. Listen, I have this idea . . ."

Plum had left Reseda and was now living in a hillside Craftsman house in Echo Park. Her new home had blond wood floors, and its large windows faced south toward the silvery skyscrapers of downtown Los Angeles. Marcus and Jan were suitably complimentary about the place and conveyed enthusiasm for the architecture and her decorating choices during the obligatory tour they were given upon arrival. It was hard to begrudge Plum the satisfaction she felt at being able to reinvent her life. They dined beneath a trellis at the picnic table in her backyard, surrounded by fragrant bougainvillea and a bursting garden. Plum served a ragout with garlic bread and a salad, and they talked about everything except where Marcus was going to be at this time next week. The food was sumptuous and well prepared, and they drank two bottles of Montepulciano.

Marcus had always perceived Plum to be perpetually if subtly aggrieved, someone who lived under a dark cloud largely of her own making. Clearly, she had found some degree of satisfaction, and it manifested in her easy manner, which was entirely new. Despite his own grim fate, he was happy that one person had gained some ongoing benefit from his choices. By the time they were eating the peach cobbler she had prepared, Marcus was feeling so open-hearted toward Plum that he readily acceded when she asked if they wanted to watch the piece of video art she had been working on.

"It's being screened in a Tokyo gallery," she said. "The opening's next week and I'm flying over."

"That's terrific," Marcus said, trying to mean it.

"I wish we could come," Jan said.

"I owe you guys."

Jan hugged Plum.

Now the three of them were gathered in Plum's home entertainment area in the living room. She had purchased a set of brown leather chairs and a matching sofa, which were set off against a Scandinavian rug. The focus of the furniture arrangement was a large-screen television. Marcus relaxed into the sofa, relishing the supple softness of the leather. He knew this degree of comfort would soon be a memory.

Plum clicked the remote control, and a startling picture filled the screen: herself in full S&M regalia—thigh high, spike-heeled vinyl boots, a leather thong and bustier, the ensemble accented with studded black leather bracelets and a dog collar—and wielding a cat-o'-nine-tails. It took Marcus a moment to realize that she was posing in front of the Federal Courthouse building in downtown Los Angeles, statuesque against a hard blue sky. There she was again in front of the Los Angeles Police Department Headquarters, gazing into the distance, *Washington Crossing the Delaware*, bondage version. And again, her Amazon form in front of City Hall, the sunlight glinting on the silver chains that traversed her weaponized cleavage.

"The piece is about external manifestations of power versus internal ones," the non-video Plum said earnestly, enthralled by her own iconic image. Marcus and Jan nodded. The action then moved to a cavernous Chinese restaurant that was empty, save for Plum, who sat haughtily at a table where two waiters in high heels and women's panties served her.

"I'm commenting on gender roles in a multi-racial context," she said.

"Ah," Marcus said.

After several close-ups of a stiletto heel immersed in a bowl of shark's-fin soup, the action shifted to Plum's dungeon. A naked man was lying on a table, stroking his flaccid penis. After a moment, Plum made her entrance, striding into the room like a Prussian officer. In the tremulous moment before the anticipated violence of the event, it was almost possible to hear the Wagner. The man rolled over to look at her, and Marcus saw his face.

No, it wasn't.

"Hit pause," Marcus said.

"Wait! It's coming to a good part," Plum said. The man was now climbing off the table.

"Hit pause, hit pause."

The man had dropped to his knees.

"Marcus . . ." Jan said.

"Please pause it," Marcus said.

Plum impatiently clicked the remote and the frame froze, but not before the man affixed his lips to the toe of Plum's vinyl boot. Jan looked at Marcus, confused. Then she followed his gaze to the screen.

"Oh, my god," Jan said.

"Do you know who that is?" Marcus asked Plum.

"He told me to call him Samantha."

"Does he know you were taping him?"

"Of course not. But it's only going to be shown in Tokyo. Why are you asking me this? Do you know him?"

"Yes," Marcus said. "Oh, yes."

Roon was flying to Kuala Lumpur that afternoon and was taken aback when Marcus called to ask for a meeting. Marcus sensed that Roon was going to try to avoid him, so he said it was an emergency. Roon relented, but it would have to be quick. Marcus briefly thought about putting on the suit he had worn to Nathan's bar mitzvah, but then realized he did not have to impress his old friend. He was the only one in the elevator of the Century City building wearing khakis and an untucked short-sleeved shirt.

Roon leased President Reagan's old office for conversation value, and the walls were covered with Gipper memorabilia. A Praying President replica of the former chief executive occupied a place of honor on his expansive desk, its MADE IN CHINA label discreetly out of view. The panoramic view of the hills was clear as tequila on this day.

"Pimp Daddy?" Roon said. He was wearing a well-cut blue blazer and crisp gray slacks with cuffs. His white shirt was open at the collar. He leaned back in his desk chair and regarded Marcus.

"It's a brand."

"What, like Nike?"

"I've been trying to come up with an angle, and it struck me, why pay some athlete millions of dollars to merchandise a line of junk with his name on it when you have me?" Roon grinned at the audacity of the notion, but Marcus was unruffled.

"Everyone's got an idea. It's all in the execution."

"I trademarked the name."

Then Marcus pulled out a portfolio he'd placed next to his chair, unzipped it, and spread the contents on Roon's desk.

"Jan did these drawings." They were product designs—artfully rendered eye candy to bewitch a potential investor and float dollars from pockets. Roon leafed through them. "You've still got your factories in China. We make all the stuff over there. China's not the future any more, right? Now it's the present. I have a vision, Roon, a Pimp Daddy empire. It begins with T-shirts, then expands to briefs and boxers, jackets, pajamas, sneakers, men's fragrance, grooming products, wallpaper, wrapping paper, toilet paper, home furnishings, baby products, can you see little Pimp Daddy diapers? Get 'em in the cradle, right? And here's the kicker, we open a chain of Pimp Daddy stores. This could be an international retailing juggernaut—New York, Los Angeles, London, Paris, Tokyo, Shanghai, and I'm willing to give you a taste once you recover the startup money. I think ten percent is fair."

"I don't have a choice, do I?"

"California is a community property state, Roon. Your wife would get half." Marcus smiled. He had him. If he refused, Plum's piece of video art would go direct from the Tokyo gallery to the Los Angeles Family Court. "Things change. You have to adapt. Wear sunscreen."

Roon did not remember having said the same words under far different circumstances several years earlier. He stared at Marcus dully.

302

"There's one more thing."

"There always is."

"I don't want to go to jail."

"No one *wants* to go to jail," Roon said, momentarily buoyed by the vision of his tormentor behind bars. "But it's important that you pay your debt to society."

"You're going to get my sentence commuted."

"I can't interfere with a judge, Marcus. That's a crime. *I'm* not a criminal."

The sanctimony annoyed Marcus, but he cut it with a scythe.

"I don't want you to contact the judge, Roon. I want you to talk to the governor. He's a good friend of yours, isn't he?"

Chapter 24

It turned out that Marcus liked China. He found the country to be a fascinating, fast-evolving amalgamation of East and West, ancient and modern, Taoist and Communist, Buddhist and capitalist. Two months after having his sentence commuted, Marcus sat between Jan and Nathan in the back of a pedal rickshaw being driven through the choking traffic of Guodong, an industrial city four hours from Shanghai. The Pimp Daddy line of goods was going to be manufactured there and, as co-CEOs, they were temporarily needed in-country. Now the three of them were on their way to look at the villa where they would be staying for the next month. Marcus glanced up and saw huge billboards advertising cell phone service, big-screen televisions, a new family resort on the South China Sea. The driver steered out of the traffic and onto a side street. Soon they were ascending a curving road, past tree-shaded homes, light-dappled and radiant in the afternoon sun. This was where the new oligarchs lived.

As they crested the hill, Marcus looked behind him toward the plain below. Factories churning out low-cost goods to be shipped around the globe stretched on for miles and miles beneath a vast sky. Barges bobbed on the waters of the mighty river in the distance. Somewhere below, a massive new road was being built to handle all the trucks that rumbled through, twenty-four hours a day. He hoped to assume his place as an avatar of this up-to-the-minute economy— his products offering moderately priced reflections of the American street in countries around the world. There was a time he would have railed against this development, observed how it represented the weak-ening of this or the vanishing of that. But those days were over and tomorrow beckoned.

Three years later, on an early spring evening, Marcus stands on the deck of his new hilltop home overlooking the San Fernando Valley. Wearing a lightweight wool suit purchased on a recent trip to Paris, he sips a vodka and cranberry juice with a slice of lime prepared for him by the chef. The house, crafted from glass and steel, came on the market just as he and Jan were looking to sell their place in Malibu and move back to town. They like the beach, but there is so much going on with the business, and the constant driving back and forth to the city and to the airport where they lease their jet had become onerous. After nearly two decades on the valley floor, Marcus feels profound relief at being able to gaze upon his former domain from this rarefied perspective. That the deck on which he stands had been Julian's makes it sweeter still. When his brother's house became avail-able, Marcus had hesitated before buying it. He thought Jan might not like the idea, might find it untoward or morbid. But she told him he should live in Julian's house if only to finally vanquish his brother, lay the demon memories to rest. Marcus thought about it and concluded that Julian would have appreciated the twist.

Jan is getting dressed in the master suite, which has an unobstructed view of the Pacific Ocean. Nathan is in his room, filling out a college application. Lenore has married a man she met at the trial, a retiree with a good pension and an impressive collection of hookahs. They live in Orange County, but tonight they are in the living room playing with Bertrand Russell. The family is going out later.

Marcus had proved to be a shrewd strategist, and Pimp Daddy was an instant success. A strategic marketing alliance with a popular hip-hop artist known for beating a murder rap had caused the company to blow up in America. Professional athletes were wearing the line, models were photographed in it, and kids were fighting over the stuff

305

on playgrounds. The company had gone public at the end of the first year and rolled into Europe, South America, and the Far East. Cheap knockoffs were growing like the poppies in the Afghan spring. Marcus had known the brand was indelible when he saw a photograph of a Pimp Daddy T-shirt on a soldier in an African civil war. The picture was subsequently used as part of an advertising campaign, and Marcus donated a million dollars to a fund for war orphans administered by a famous archbishop who was in line for a Nobel Prize. A photograph of the clergyman with his arm around the shoulders of Pimp Daddy's founder was on the cover of the first annual report.

Tonight Marcus is going to attend a dinner in the gilded ballroom of the Beverly Hills Hotel, where he will be honored as Los Angeles Businessman of the Year. He knows these kinds of awards are nonsense, believes they lack real meaning and prey on the insecurities of people successful enough to know better. But perception is important, and this gold plaque will put the seal on his rehabilitation. To further enhance what already promises to be a glittering gala, Marcus has requested that the award be presented by his old friend Roon Primus.

Marcus ruminates about what he will say later that evening when he is at the podium, gazing over a sea of his peers. Maybe he will allude to his humble background and the inspiration of his hardworking father, or regale them with tales of his intrepid, larcenous grandfather. He considers talking about the great minds he was exposed to in his philosophical studies and his years cultivating the common touch in the trenches at the toy factory. He cogitates on what it will feel like to stand in the very ballroom where, a few years earlier, Roon had treated him rudely. He mulls over the story of how he deftly outmaneuvered him and, as a result of his own steady hand and unswerving eye, has now attained heights heretofore unimaginable. Any and all of the numberless struggles and his eventual inspiring triumph are fodder for his after-dinner remarks.

But Marcus knows what people really want to hear.

ACKNOWLEDGMENTS

Thanks to Bill Diamond, Michael Disend, Drew Greenland, Sam Harper, David Kanter, Jeff Rothberg, Leslie Schwartz, Mark Haskell Smith, and John Tomko for generously reading early drafts of this book.

Thanks to my agents, Henry Dunow and Sylvie Rabineau.

Thanks to my editors, Colin Dickerman and Benjamin Adams.

Thanks to my father, Leo Greenland, who remains an inspiration.

And finally, thanks to Susan—my first and best reader—and our children, Allegra and Gabe.

Seth Greenland is the author of *The Bones*. An award-winning playwright, he has also written extensively for film and television. He lives in Los Angeles with his wife and two children.